Thea Harrison is the pen name for author Teddy Harrison. Thea has travelled extensively, having lived in England and explored Europe for several years. Now she resides in Northern California. She wrote her first book, a romance, when she was nineteen and had sixteen romances published under the name Amanda Carpenter.

Visit Thea Harrison online:
www.theaharrison.com
www.facebook.com/TheaHarrison
www.twitter.com/theaharrison

D0532441

By Thea Harrison

Elder Races series:

DRAGON BOUND
STORM'S HEART
SERPENT'S KISS
ORACLE'S MOON
LORD'S FALL
KINKED

Game of Shadows series:

RISING DARKNESS

Kinked

THEA HARRISON

piatkus

PIATKUS

First published in the US in 2013 by The Berkley Publishing Group,
A division of Penguin Group (USA) Inc., New York
First published in Great Britain in 2013 by Piatkus

A CIP catalogue record for this book
is available from the British Library.

ISBN 978-0-7499-5832-9

Printed and bound in Great Britain by Clays Ltd, St Ives plc.

Papers used by Piatkus are from well-managed forests
and other responsible sources.

MIX
Paper from
responsible sources
FSC® C104740

Piatkus
An imprint of
Little, Brown Book Group
100 Victoria Embankment
London EC4Y 0DY

An Hachette UK Company
www.hachette.co.uk

www.piatkus.co.uk

This one is for Amy

*It's all fun and games when
someone loses an eye.*

—ARYAL, HARPY

That's not how the saying goes, dumb ass.

—QUENTIN, IRRITATED

≡ ONE ≡

Aryal floated and spun in the wild dark night.
　　She didn't mind living in New York as some other
Wyr did. The city was edgy and raw in a way that appealed
to her. But this lonesome realm that hung high over the top
of the world—this was her true home. This was where she
came to think, or brood or fling her fury into space.

She flew so high that the air felt almost too thin for even
her powerful lungs. The clouds lay below her, air castles of
shadowed ivory, and the stars above her whirled in their
dance of constellations, their lights telling ancient tales
of places from unimaginable distances. At this altitude,
the stars were so brilliant she almost felt as if she could
leave the shackles of gravity behind forever and fly into
them.

Almost.

There was always that one moment when she reached
the peak of her ability to fly, that one instant of perfection
as she hung weightless in the air, no longer straining to rise
but simply existing in flawless balance.

Then gravity would reign supreme and pull her back
down to earth, but she always carried with her the memory
of how she could touch that one perfect moment.

1

Tonight, she didn't fly for pleasure. She flew to brood in solitude.

She had two hates. One, she held close and nurtured with all of her passion. The other, she had to release.

Her first hate was Quentin Caeravorn.

As soon as she could figure out a way to do it without getting caught, swear to gods, she was going to kill him.

She would prefer to kill him slowly, but bottom line, at this point she would be happy to take any opportunity she could get.

It was bad enough when Quentin's friend and former employee Pia ended up mating—and marrying—Dragos Cuelebre, Lord of the Wyr. Once, Pia had been a thief who had stolen from the most Powerful Wyr the world has ever seen. Now she was his wife and the mother of his son.

Ever since Pia had moved into Cuelebre Tower, the gryphons had gone batshit gaga over her; they all thought she pooped sparkly rainbows or something. Hell, as far as Aryal knew, she actually did poop sparkly rainbows.

The Wyr in general had a more reserved (sane) response to Pia's presence, especially since she continued to refuse to reveal her Wyr form, which Aryal thought was not only a shortsighted decision but also a rather wretched one. How could anybody expect the Wyr to accept or follow her when they didn't even know what the hell she was? The very fact of her existence made Aryal's teeth ache.

Outside of the Wyr demesne, however, Pia's popularity had skyrocketed. Her daily mail had gone from a trickle of letters and cards into an avalanche that required a separate office and its own small staff.

Pia even took Dragos's last name, an old-fashioned move that had Aryal rolling her eyes. Now she was Pia Cuelebre.

Last names . . . they were like word parasites. They attached to people in strange ways, moved across cultural and political lines, traveled the world and reattached to others, certainly at whim and seemingly at random.

Why didn't anybody else see how creepy last names were? They labeled a person as coming from a particular class or geographical area or linked their identity to another person, as if someone's identity had no merit on its own unless it had latched on to another. Aryal refused to pick a last name for herself, as so many of the first immortal Wyr chose to do, nor would she ever take anybody else's.

Pia was her second hate.

Earlier today, Aryal finally, grudgingly, *painfully* conceded she was going to have to let go of her snerk over Pia. That was a bitter pill for her to shove down her own throat. It was sugarcoated by the most lethal weapon in Pia's armory to date: the unbelievable sweetness in her newborn son's face.

After Pia and Dragos had gotten married, they had gone on their honeymoon, where she had given birth unexpectedly. Yesterday, she and Dragos cut short their trip to upstate New York to return to the city. When they had arrived back at the Tower early last evening, everybody had to see, touch, hold and/or coo over the baby.

The other sentinels acted like Dragos had conquered all of Asia overnight, while Dragos radiated a ferocious pride. Almost seven feet tall in his human form, with a massive, muscular body and a brutally handsome face, he would always carry in his demeanor a sharpness like a blade, but Aryal had to admit, she had never seen him look so . . . happy.

As for her, she refused to go anywhere near Pia and the rug rat. She didn't want to have anything to do with them.

Unfortunately, that hadn't lasted long.

Less than twenty-four hours, to be exact.

Earlier today, when she had charged around the hall corner outside of Dragos's offices, she nearly mowed down Pia, who pushed some kind of ambulatory, complicated-looking cart with the sleeping baby tucked inside of it.

Pia looked tired. Her pretty, triangular face was paler than usual, and her ever-present blond ponytail was slightly lopsided with wisps of hair trailing at her temples. One of her new full-time bodyguards was with her. The mouthy woman, Eva. Eva thrust between Pia and Aryal, her bold features and black eyes insolent with hostility. She stood as tall as Aryal, a full six feet in flat boots, dark brown skin rippling over toned muscle.

"You're a menace just walking down the hall," said Eva. "Do you know any speed other than one that might get someone hurt?"

"You and me," Aryal told her on a surge of happiness. "We're gonna go some day."

"Let's make that day today," said Eva. "We can go right down the hall to the training room. With or without weapons. You pick."

"Lower your voices," Pia said irritably. "If you wake up the baby, I'll take you both down."

Eva's expression softened as she looked at the occupant in the cart. Before she could stop herself, Aryal looked too.

And found herself snared irretrievably.

She was astonished at how tiny the baby was. His entire face, in fact most of his head, was smaller than the palm of her hand. He was wrapped tightly in a soft cloth. It looked restrictive and uncomfortable, but she knew absolutely nothing about babies, and he seemed content enough.

Aryal sidled a step closer, her head angled as she stared. Eva made a move as if she would block Aryal, but Pia put a hand on her bodyguard's arm and stopped her.

The sleeping baby carried a roar of Power in his soft, delicate body. Aryal shook her head in wonder. She hadn't sensed any of it before now. How had Pia managed to conceal that much Power when she had been pregnant?

The baby opened his eyes. He looked so alive and innocent, and as peaceful as a miniature Buddha. He had dark violet eyes like his mother's. The color was so deep and pure it seemed to hold all the wildness and mystery of the night sky.

Some vital organ in Aryal's chest constricted. Her hand crept out to him and hovered in midair as, out of the corner of her eye, she saw Pia twitch.

Comprehension clipped her with an uppercut to the chin.

Pia wouldn't trust her anywhere near the baby as long as Aryal held on to any lingering resentment or hostility. She wouldn't teach Aryal how to hold him, and she sure as hell wouldn't ever leave him in Aryal's care. Nobody would, which was hideously unfair because Aryal would cut off her own hands before she would do anything to harm a child, no matter who its parents were.

As she struggled with the realization, the baby worked an arm loose from his straightjacket and stuck his fist in one eye. Surprise and confusion wobbled over his miniscule face. With a Herculean effort he managed to jerk his fist to his mouth. He started to suck on it noisily.

That vital organ in Aryal's chest—that was her heart, and she lost it to him forever.

"Okay," she said, her voice hoarse.

"What exactly is okay, Aryal?" asked Pia.

Aryal looked at her. Some sort of suppressed emotion danced in Pia's gaze. Triumph, maybe, or amusement. Whatever it was, she didn't care.

She said without much hope, "I don't suppose you would at least consider cutting off the cheerleader ponytail."

Pia said gravely, "I will consider it. Not very seriously, but I will."

Aryal met her gaze. She asked straight out, without posturing or bullshit, "May I come visit him?"

Pia studied her for a moment. "Yes, you may."

Aryal looked down at the baby again and a corner of her mouth lifted. "Thank you."

"Don't mention it." The baby started to burble plaintively. Pia said, "I think he's already hungry again. I'd better take him back upstairs."

She pushed the contraption toward the bank of elevators that would take her up to the penthouse at the top of the Tower. Eva followed Pia, walking backward.

"Don't you fret none, chickadee," Eva said in a gentle voice to Aryal. "We still gonna go one day."

Aryal balanced back on one heel and beckoned her with both hands. Bring it, baby.

She laughed when Eva made a face before spinning to follow Pia and the little prince onto the elevator. Then Aryal turned toward Dragos's offices and came to a standstill. She couldn't remember why she had been going to see him in the first place.

Behind her, she could hear the two other women's whispers clearly just before the elevator doors closed. Pia said, "Behold the Power of the peanut. His body mass may be small, but his influence is mighty. The last holdout in the Tower has officially fallen to him."

"If you say so."

Eva sounded skeptical, but Pia had called it. Aryal had fallen in love with that mysterious new person.

Now during her flight, for his sake, Aryal released the last of her resentment into the night.

After all, Pia had only stolen once. While Aryal had been more stubbornly suspicious than anybody, even she had to finally admit that Pia had no real knowledge of Caeravorn's activities, so it wasn't as if Pia had actually ever been a career criminal.

Granted, Pia's theft had been a bad one, but *Dragos* had not only forgiven her, he had mated with her. And Dragos was not known for his forgiving personality.

If a dragon could do it, so could a harpy, right?

Giving up her hate on Pia for the sake of the baby was one thing, and that was hard enough.

Quentin Caeravorn was an entirely different disaster.

Aryal turned her attention back to her first hate, the one she held close to her own breast and nurtured with all of her strength.

Caeravorn *was* a career criminal. He was also a "triple threat," a rare and Powerful mixed-breed creature who was part Wyr, part Elven and part Dark Fae. Aryal didn't have the details of his family history, but one of his parents had to be full Wyr while the other parent was a half-breed, because his Wyr side was strong enough that he could change into his animal form. That gave him all the status and legal rights of a full Wyr in the demesne.

Because he had the legal rights of a full Wyr, and he hadn't been convicted of any crime, he had been eligible to enter the recent Sentinel Games. He had fought his way through to become one of Dragos's seven sentinels, who were the core of Dragos's governing power in the Wyr demesne.

And he had accomplished that, because in spite of al-

most two years of investigation, and several months of concentrated digging before the Games began, Aryal couldn't
pin a single goddamn thing on him.

She knew he was dirty. *She knew it.*

Her leads turned into dead ends and sources dried up.
She would track down somebody only to find out that they
had moved out of the Wyr demesne, or maybe they had died
accidentally (and didn't *that* get investigated thoroughly
too). Or they weren't directly involved in any illegal activity
connected to Caeravorn, they had only heard of things—
hearsay and rumors that dissipated into thin air when she
tried to nail them down into concrete evidence.

Caeravorn was a magician, surrounded by a labyrinth of
smoke and mirrors while he stood at the center of it all,
untouched.

Dirty.

He had gained access to the very heart of the Wyr
demesne, and all because Aryal couldn't get him.

Her mood blackened. While she thought back to the
events that had happened in January, two months ago, she
flew higher and dove just to hear the wind scream in her
ears. The sound matched the scream of outrage in her head.

At the Games she watched every one of Caeravorn's fights,
absorbing every detail. He was killer fast and elegant, and
highly, superbly trained. Normal civilians didn't train to
fight to that extent. Why the fuck didn't anybody else have
a problem with that?

He chose a few times to fight in his Wyr form, a huge
black panther with electric blue eyes that gleamed under
the white-hot lights. In his human form, he kicked ass. As
a panther, he was sinuous, muscular and moved like lightning. He owned every inch of that fight arena and captured
the imagination of almost twenty thousand spectators.

After the Games were over and Dragos had presented his
new sentinels to the Wyr demesne, Caeravorn strolled like
a conquering hero into the great hall at Cuelebre Tower
along with the other seven sentinels. Aside from Quentin,
there were the five who had re-won their places—the harpy
Aryal, the gryphons Bayne, Constantine, and Graydon,

and the gargoyle Grym—along with the other new sentinel, the pegasus Alexander Elysias.

Dragos knew how to throw a hell of a party. It was like a
hundred years of New Year's Eves all rolled into a single
night. There was endless liquor, and loud music from famous
bands, and gourmet food and confetti, and a general stam-
pede at all of them, but especially at the men who were all
buff and reeking of testosterone and victorious swagger.

The night was a triumph for every sentinel—for Aryal
as well, and she had her fair share of propositions too—but
she couldn't let go and enjoy any of them, since the night
had also been her failure.

She held herself aloof, bitterness a hard, heavy knot in the
pit of her stomach while she watched Caeravorn laugh as
someone upended a bottle of champagne over his head. He
was six foot two, with a long, lean body and a cat's quick
grace, spare graceful features, and dark blond hair he had
once worn longer. He had cut it very short for the Games, and
the severe style lay close to the strong, clean lines of his head.

As she stood with her arms crossed, Grym came up to her
side. In his human form, Grym was dark haired with even
features. In his Wyr form, he was nightmarish, with huge
batlike wings, a demonic face and gray skin as hard as stone.

He had his own small share of groupies, as did all of the
sentinels, but Grym actually didn't like to talk much and
that fact tended to put females off, at least after the first
night or two. He was one of the few entities whose com-
panionship Aryal found peaceful, and he had used that fact
more than once to defuse her volatile temper.

She had wished more than once that there was a sexual
spark between them. Unfortunately there wasn't. Years ago,
they'd even experimented, but neither of them had any interest in taking things past first base. They had long since settled
into an unconventional yet entirely comfortable friendship.

Grym stood close enough that their shoulders brushed.
"You didn't get him," he said. "Sometimes it happens. You
gotta let it go."

"No, I don't," she said. She scowled at him.

Grym rubbed the back of his neck. "Aryal, with the kind

of hours you've put into digging into Quentin's life, if you haven't found any hard evidence by now, it's very likely you're not going to."

She shook her head. "Doesn't mean I've got to let it go. Just means I haven't found it *yet*."

He turned to face her, his mouth pursed. "Have you ever considered that he might be innocent?"

She angled out her jaw. "He's not."

"Well, if he isn't, sooner or later he's going to trip up. In the meantime, you earned this night too," Grym told her. "Don't let him ruin it for you."

She made a face as Grym clapped her on the back and disappeared into the crowd, headed for the nearest bar. Caeravorn *was* ruining the night for her. Just the very fact of his presence at the celebration made her stomach tighten. Watching him enjoy himself was about as pleasurable as taking a bath in acid.

He exuded testosterone along with all the rest, an alpha male supremely confident in his own abilities, and why wouldn't he be? He had just clawed his way to the top of the Wyr demesne and earned his place with the best of the best.

Her gaze narrowed. He was a beautiful man, she'd give him that. He owned a popular neighborhood bar named Elfie's, where he tended to wear clothes that were more upscale, but here he dressed simply like the other sentinels in jeans, boots, and a dark blue T-shirt that turned his blue eyes brilliant.

Sex would have always come easily for him. It would come even easier for him tonight. He could have as much sex with as many people as he wanted.

One of his companions was a corporate lawyer for Cuelebre Enterprises, a Wyr lioness who was the antithesis of Aryal in almost every way. Aryal studied the other woman, assessing her as if she were an opponent. Instead of Aryal's six-foot height, the lioness stood at a snuggly five foot six. Males were suckers for females of that size. The other woman had a sinuous, curvaceous torso, while Aryal had an athletic build, her muscles long and lean.

The lioness's limbs were tawny and sun-kissed, her

piquant face cleverly made up to emphasize her tilted eyes and full mouth. She wore four-inch heels, and her waist-long hair tumbled down her back and was lightened with expensive golden highlights.

Aryal had gray eyes and angular features, and the only time she had ever worn makeup was when she had gotten drunk with her friend Niniane, who had somehow managed to coax Aryal into letting her put pink lipstick on her. That experiment had lasted all of five minutes. Aryal wouldn't be caught dead in heels of any height unless they hid a spring-hinged blade, and she barely remembered to brush her thick, black, shoulder-length hair, which was why it so often ended up tangled, especially just after a flight.

The lioness stood on tiptoe and leaned against Caeravorn's arm as she said something in his ear, deliberately brushing her breast against his bicep. Then she sent a warning glance around to the others who stood nearby while she licked at the champagne that dripped off his chin, and Caeravorn grinned and cupped her ass. Clearly if that chick had anything to say about it, she would be his only partner for the night.

Aryal's lip curled. Aw, look. Two Wyr felines going into heat. There wasn't even any suspense to it.

Caeravorn turned to give the female a slow, sexy smile, and his gaze fell on Aryal. His long blue eyes narrowed, and his expression chilled. He said something to the female as he pulled away from her. She gave him a pouting, kittenish smile and made as if to follow him, but as she tracked his trajectory, her gaze fell onto Aryal and she jerked to a halt.

Yeah, that one was irritating, but she wasn't stupid.

Caeravorn shouldered past a few people and approached Aryal, his eyes glinting. He was broad shouldered, lean hipped and long legged, and he had a lithe, almost boneless stride. Aryal's gaze drifted over his hard face and equally hard body. Under the cover of her crossed arms, her talons came out, quiet and slick like well-oiled switchblades. She clicked them together as he prowled close.

So dirty.

He was an outlaw in masquerade. Her gaze fixed on the bulge in his jeans. Was he an outlaw sexually as well?

Kitty Lawyer's antics must have been doing it for him, because as he came toe-to-toe with her, he smelled like healthy male, champagne and arousal. Aryal *hated* the fact that he smelled incredibly delicious.

"You are the most ungracious, obstinate creature I have ever had the misfortune to meet," he said. She cocked her head and contemplated his hard, well-cut mouth. "Give it up, sunshine. You lost."

Genuinely amused, she smiled. She leaned forward until she was in his face, and she whispered, "I know something you don't."

His teeth were even and white as he snapped out, "You fucking wish you did."

"No, I really do know something, Caeravorn. What are you, a hundred and sixty, a hundred and seventy years old?"

He sliced at the air with one hand. "What difference does my age make?"

"You young Wyr are all alike," she said. "Maybe your panther side will dictate a limit to your life span, or maybe your Elven and Dark Fae blood will prolong it, but either way, you don't really understand what it means to be immortal. The past is nearly as limitless as the future."

"Make your point," he growled.

Her voice grew softer, pitched for his ears alone. "I'll give this to you. You've been meticulous, you really have. You've covered your tracks well. But nobody in this world is perfect. That means that you have fucked up somehow, somewhere. That's what I know. I have all the time in the world to find it, *all the time*, and do you know what that means? That means I've already got you. It just hasn't happened yet."

She watched the rage build in his face and body language as she spoke. She might not have gotten him yet, but she got him good enough for now, as she shoved him over the brink and his temper splintered utterly. He lunged for her throat.

"You're not a harpy," he snarled. "You're a fucking pit bull with lockjaw."

Her head fell back, and she laughed as his iron-hard hands circled her neck. Fingers tightening, he cut off her air supply. She hooked an ankle behind his leg and threw her entire body weight at him, knocking him backward.

They crashed to the floor together. People shouted and scattered, while others leaped toward them. All the ruckus seemed to happen somewhere else. Right here it was just her and Caeravorn, in intimate, struggling silence.

As he hit the ground, his hands loosened from her neck. When she landed on top of his muscular length, she twisted to bring up one elbow, hard, underneath his chin. The blow connected and snapped his head back. For one pulsating moment his long, powerful body lay as a supplicant beneath hers, his neck bared as she straddled him.

It was glorious.

Then a freight train slammed into Aryal, knocking her several feet from Caeravorn, who flipped, still snarling, onto his hands and knees. With his head lowered and teeth bared, his gaze fixed on her and he prepared to spring.

Wow, he had really lost it. She must have said something. Out of the corner of her eye, she saw Bayne, Constantine and Alexander pile on top of him, their combined weight knocking him flat again.

Her freight train resolved into Dragos's new First Sentinel, Graydon. Graydon was the largest of all the current sentinels. In his human form he stood almost six foot five, and he carried a good thirty pounds more than the other gryphons.

All of that weight was hard, packed muscle, which currently took up residence on her chest. He pinned her arms to the floor by the wrists. Normally his roughhewn features were set in a mild, good-natured expression, but not at the moment.

Not even bothering to struggle, she looked up at Graydon with her eyebrows raised. "What?"

His dark slate gray eyes were furious. "People have been through hell this month. We've all gone to war, and then we beat the shit out of each other in the Games. Everybody needs a little goddamn R and R, and you can't leave well enough alone for a few fucking hours at a party."

Angling her jaw out, she savored her next words for the rare treasures they were, as she said in perfect, pious honesty, "He started it."

$=$ TWO $=$

Now in March, two months after the party, her own words mocked her. Her triumph at the party had been all-too short lived.

The bitter winds matched her mood. The slicing chill of the wintry air cooled her overheated blood as frustration clawed at her. She let the tumultuous currents buffet and toss her about.

She might have all the time in the world with which to hunt Caeravorn. She just didn't have all the patience in the world. Not when he was a daily fact of her existence. It was one thing to have him constantly in the forefront of her mind as a subject of investigation. Now she never knew when she might run into him at the Tower.

She knew she would run into him whenever Dragos called for a sentinel conference. She started to avoid those whenever she could get away with it, until Dragos stomped on that little maneuver by ordering her to attend every meeting.

Caeravorn was a smooth operator. Everywhere he went, women trotted after him like hypnotized puppies. He was even tempered and charming with everybody—everybody, that is, except Aryal.

They were not just driving each other insane. Collectively they were driving everyone else insane too. Echoes of their feud began to ripple through the other sentinels. Tempers flared until one day even Alexander, who was easily the most mild natured of them all, snapped at both of them. Then Grym and Constantine went at it, verbally ripping into each other like a pair of fighting dogs.

It was certainly no secret that Aryal loved a good fight. Conflict was like mother's milk to her, but this went deeper— it had all the makings of a true schism, and that had to stop.

As she realized that, she thought of something else. Now there was the baby to consider too, because Pia cared for and trusted her friend Caeravorn. She might have had a problem with letting Aryal around her son, but she would have no problem letting *him* have free access . . . and that, to Aryal's eyes, made him even more dangerous than ever.

So as soon as she figured out how to do it, she would kill him.

The decision was a relief. It gave her frustration a viable outlet, and the results would be better for everybody, instead of taking the long course as Dragos had decided on doing. Taking the long course meant giving Caeravorn access to sensitive knowledge and allowing him the chance to do major damage before he could be brought down.

The long flight had finally cleared her mind. She angled her wings to take her out of the wind current and spiraled down to the sprawling city below. A cloudy night covered the city's vast array of lights in a moody cloak. The temperature was barely any warmer closer to the ground. The air felt wet and cold, and icy sleet coated the trees, roads and roof-tops.

She had no intention of changing until she could get inside quickly, since she would feel the cold more in her human form. Instead, she cloaked her presence and flew along the corridors created by the streets and tall buildings, until she came to Elfie's, Caeravorn's bar. At almost four A.M., the bar was closed and the entire ground floor dark.

A sliver of light shone from a window on the top floor, which was the third story in the brick building. She drifted closer, her outspread wings holding her course steady. Caeravorn owned the building and lived in an apartment over the bar. As a sentinel, he now had an apartment at the Tower but he rarely stayed there.

All of the windows on the building were covered with slender, black metal security bars, even the windows on the upper floors. She grinned. Caeravorn didn't trust his safety to the open sky. What a shame.

She flew to the lighted window, grabbed hold of the bars and flapped her wings until she had the tips of the deadly talons on her feet hooked into the side of the building. Her talons were sharp enough to slice through steel. Digging them into the mortar between the bricks was relatively easy.

She tugged experimentally at the bars as she checked out the bolts that fastened them to the wall, but they were anchored solidly in place. All of her weight rested on a half an inch at the tip of her talons, and the bars at the window were coated in a sheet of ice. The perch was uncomfortable and precarious, but she could hold it for now.

The window was cracked open, the curtains not quite pulled closed. Heat and illumination poured out of the gap, and a wordless, tribal music that carried a hypnotic rhythm. It slipped into her bloodstream and pounded at her throat and temples. She peered inside.

The sight slammed her.

Caeravorn and a naked woman were in the room. He wore a pair of midnight blue silk pants that rode low on lean hipbones. His torso was bare. The woman sat on the edge of a bed. She wasn't the lioness. She was a pretty, young-looking brunette, with firm, small breasts and dark, erect nipples.

After one glance at her, Aryal's gaze fastened on Caeravorn. She couldn't look away. His body was simply fantastic. His powerful shoulders and chest were broader than they seemed normally. His height must fool the eye when he was clothed. He looked stern, almost remote, the smooth proud lines of his face closed to scrutiny.

This was not a lovemaking scene, then.

He twisted and reached for something on a nearby dresser, the pale golden skin of his back rippling with muscles.

Compulsively Aryal followed the curved line of his back to his lean buttocks. Her hands were starting to burn from the pain of holding on to the slippery, ice-covered bars, but the warmth of her grip was melting the ice and she ignored it as best she could.

He turned back to the woman, a short piece of leather in his hand. He held the length to the woman's mouth. "Bite it."

Her gaze lifted to his, the woman opened her mouth and accepted the strip of leather. He told her, "Get on the bed. On your knees."

The woman obeyed. That was when Aryal realized the brunette wore silk-lined wrist cuffs with a short length that ran behind her back, along with black stiletto-heeled pumps. The woman climbed onto the bed, facing away from Caeravorn.

Caeravorn yanked down his silk pants. His large, erect penis jutted out over a smooth, tight sac. Aryal couldn't look away as he palmed himself. Her breath grew tight and short, and her entire body felt like it was on fire.

Then she looked up at his closed expression. He looked bored, totally alone.

He told the woman, "Bend over."

The woman did, laying her upper torso on the bed with her knees spread so that her ass pushed up in the air.

Aryal hissed as the pain in her hands grew to be too much. As Caeravorn moved up to position himself behind the brunette, she had to let go finally and let gravity pull her away. As she fell she twisted, wings outspread to buffer her descent. She dug into the air with all of her strength to climb upward into the frigid, cloudy darkness, wild to fly anywhere as long as it was far away.

After Quentin took the woman, he slipped on his silk pants and called a taxi while she cleaned up. Then he paid her and escorted her down the side stairs to the ground floor. It was all perfectly cordial.

KINKED

That was when she made her mistake. She wheedled.

"We had a great time together, didn't we, baby?" she said as she sidled closer.

She probably called everybody baby, Quentin thought. Just like that John Cougar Mellencamp song. It was a lot easier to remember than names. He stepped around her and looked out the glass door for any sign of the taxi. The street was empty of traffic.

The woman came at him again and put her hands on his chest. "When can we see each other again, baby? Let's make it soon. How about the weekend?"

There it was again. Baby. He lifted her hands away. He could have said, *I almost fell asleep but then I came*, but he managed to hold that one back.

Instead, he told her, "I don't know why you worked so hard to pretend you climaxed. We're not boyfriend and girlfriend. We're never going to see each other again."

Her lower lip stuck out. Holy gods, he would rather stick his head in the oven than deal with another sex kitten pouter right now. "I thought you liked the special things I could do for you, baby. Don't you want me to do them for you again?"

Invisible claws ran down a mental chalkboard inside his head. He said, "You didn't do anything special. You did what you were told." For God's sake, he hadn't even spanked her. Hot damn, there was the taxi, creeping carefully down the ice-covered street. He opened the door and a welcome blast of bitter air slapped him in the face. "Good-bye. Don't come back to Elfie's."

Finally offense rippled across her face. "I wouldn't come back here if you paid me to," she hissed.

Yes, she would.

"Yeah, we're done with that too." He had intended to pay for her taxi trip on top of her fee and the generous tip he had already given her, but she irritated him so much, he closed and locked the door firmly as soon as she stepped through it.

"Fuck you, big bad sentinel," the woman shouted.

He braced one hand on the doorpost and angled his head to look out the door. She walked backward to the taxi, giving him the finger with both hands.

17

Hadn't even spanked her. Hell, the handcuffs hadn't been real. They were sex toys, the kind that broke open if someone tugged hard enough. It had been a vanilla version of BDSM—they hadn't even needed to set a safe word. He really had almost fallen asleep.

The *special things* she had done for him.

He hung his head and laughed. It sounded as humorless as he felt.

Those invisible fingers down a chalkboard had left behind a headache, which grew as he climbed the stairs back to his apartment. Elfie's took the entire ground floor of the building. He used the second story for storage for the bar.

His apartment took up the third floor. It was an open-concept design, with a kitchen, dining area and living room all in one huge space, mellow golden oak floors throughout and filled with the clean, spare lines of midcentury modern furniture. Two large, more traditional rooms were set up as bedrooms, each with their own baths.

He had always planned to create a rooftop garden, but an architect had once told him that the entire roof would need to be reinforced first. The project would involve so much upheaval he hadn't yet found the time. Now that he had become a sentinel, he doubted he ever would.

He walked into his bedroom. The album had finished playing and the room was silent. He sat on the end of the king-sized bed and put his aching head in his hands.

Oh, baby.

Aryal's soft, in-your-face words from two months ago swam out of the pain.

Nobody's perfect. That means you have fucked up somehow, somewhere. That's what I know. I have all the time in the world to find it, all the time, and do you know what that means? That means I've already got you.

Those words had a nasty habit of smacking him around ever since she'd uttered them at the sentinels' party. He was being haunted by somebody who wasn't even dead, and he loathed admitting, even in the privacy of his own thoughts, that she was right.

He'd fucked up, all right. He'd fucked up so badly last

spring, he had hurt someone he cared about very much. He had nearly gotten Pia killed.

Last May, when Pia had stolen from Dragos and gone on the run, Caeravorn had maneuvered and manipulated behind the scenes, comfortably anchored in his own self-righteous dislike of the arrogant, mighty Lord of the Wyr.

Dragos had broken treaties and entered the Elven demesne in his pursuit of Pia, and using the 800 number that Quentin had given her, Pia had called the Elves for help. Led by Ferion, the man who had since then become the new Elven High Lord and who was related to Quentin by marriage, a group of Elves had confronted Dragos just outside of Charleston. They shot him with a poisoned, magical arrow that had melted into his bloodstream, limiting his Power and his ability to shapeshift. Then they gave him twelve hours to leave their demesne.

The encounter had happened at Quentin's beach house, so Ferion had called him afterward to let him know what had transpired.

To Quentin, it had seemed like such a simple solution to contact one of Dragos's most Powerful enemies. Perhaps even elegant. He had offered the information to Urien, the Dark Fae King, in return for Urien's promise to let Pia go. Urien would go after Dragos—and maybe Urien could kill the Wyr lord, and maybe he couldn't—but the important thing was, it would give Pia the chance to get away.

In the meantime, Pia had been mating with Dragos. She had gotten pregnant. And by Pia's own account, Urien hadn't let her go at all. Instead, his agents had beaten her, forcing her to escape with Dragos until they confronted Urien and his army on a plain in an Other land, where Dragos had killed everybody but Urien and a few of his winged riders. It turned out that the only thing elegant about Quentin's idea had been in his imagination.

So not only had Quentin nearly gotten Pia killed, but in all likelihood he had almost killed her unborn son. Realizing what he had done—what he had almost caused—had been a watershed moment. It had propelled him on a journey from the man he had been to who he was right now.

Or at least to the man he was trying to become, whoever the hell that was, as he constantly wrestled to tame what lived inside him.

His bedroom was far too hot. It smelled like sex and the woman's perfume, which he hadn't enjoyed to begin with and now seemed sickeningly cloying. Why did women have to stink themselves up with cosmetics and perfumes? Couldn't they appreciate their own faces and bodies the way nature had intended them?

He couldn't stand it a moment longer. He was going to have to air out the place or sleep in the guest room. He strode over to the window, yanked the curtains wide and opened it as far as the pane would go. Then he leaned both hands on the windowsill and stuck his head in the sharp, chill air.

With his first, deep breath, he smelled the harpy's scent.

What. The.

Astonishment held him frozen. He bared his teeth, sucked in another deep breath and scented Aryal quite unmistakably.

FUCK.

Rage surged in on a tidal wave. Incredulously, he shouldered further out the window and stuck his head between the gap in the security bars. He looked down, even though he knew what he would see. Then he twisted around and looked up.

There was no ledge below. There was nothing above but the gutter at the edge of the roof, which wouldn't support the weight of anything larger than a squirrel. For Aryal to leave her scent, she had to have touched *something*. Blood pounded violently through his body as he studied the outside wall more closely.

The city street was well lit at night. Even so, if he hadn't been scouring the wall so thoroughly with his inhumanly sharp sight for any kind of anomaly, he would have missed the sets of shadowed holes gouged into the mortar roughly a yard below the windowsill.

He turned his attention to the security bars on the window. They were covered with a uniform coating of ice—all except for two areas on the bars where there wasn't any ice at all. He put his hands over the areas and gripped the bars. His palms were bigger than the melted spaces, but they were just about the right size for Aryal's hands.

He shoved hard at the bars, and they held, but then he knew they would. When he'd had them installed, he made sure that they were bolted securely. He lifted one damp hand and sniffed it. It smelled, ever so faintly, of Aryal. When the sun rose in a few hours, it would melt the ice completely and wash away every trace of her.

She had been here, very recently, after the sleet storm that had only tapered off about an hour ago.

Had she watched him having sex with the hooker? While he fucked a woman he didn't care about and wasn't interested in, with his eyes closed as his mind wandered and he barely maintained his erection, and he wondered what the hell he was doing with his life?

His chest heaved. He couldn't take in enough air.

She had used her talons to balance at the window. That meant she had been in her Wyr form. As a human woman, she was a constant shock to the system, tall and lean and strong, and completely, rampantly uncompromising. She carried the kind of energy that all ancient, immortal Wyr carried. It shimmered in the air around her, like a jolt of raw electricity. In her Wyr form, she was a gorgeous nightmare, angular features upswept, accentuated, with massive wings colored from gray to black.

How could he have not noticed her presence?

As he thought of Aryal outside in the dark, watching him with those piercing gray eyes of hers, his cock started to stiffen.

Oh, no. He jerked away from that mental image like a scalded cat. *Oh, hell no.* The impulse to violence sparked along all of his synapses, until it became a cascade too powerful to ignore.

Almost two years ago, he had been traveling through his life, complacent with his abilities and his activities, content with the success of both his legitimate and illegitimate businesses, when gradually he became aware that he was under investigation. He did a little digging of his own and discovered who was investigating him.

Aryal had a reputation for being a relentless, inventive investigator, but he hadn't been worried. He knew precisely how he had come to the harpy sentinel's attention—by word of mouth and association. She wasn't going to find anything concrete, because he had always covered his tracks too well. He was talented at doing that.

But then last May happened, he almost got his friend killed and had his change of heart, of sorts. He changed direction in his life and went legit.

Of sorts.

He decided he wanted to have a say in what happened in the Wyr demesne, to invest time and energy into the place where he lived. When the opportunity came available to sign up for the Sentinel Games, he went for it.

If he thought Aryal had been relentless before, it was nothing compared to how she dug into his life after that point. Somehow she was always present. She stopped in at Elfie's a couple of times a week, talked to his employees, issued a warrant for his business books and went over them with a fine-toothed comb, and interviewed his neighbors. He caught hints of her scent several times in the alley behind the bar.

He laughed at her. Ignored her. Pretended to ignore her. Stopped pretending.

Pretended not to lose his temper. Stopped pretending.

Started to push back. Pushed back harder.

Meanwhile, she never, ever stopped.

I have all the time in the world.

All the time.

Had he ever really thought things might change once he became a sentinel? If he had, he couldn't remember it. She had ground that to dust. Of course she had.

Dragos knew exactly how to best use Aryal's talents and personality when he put her in charge of investigations. As the two new sentinels, Quentin and Alexander, worked to settle into their positions, there had been some question of movement of duties among the seven, as they all assessed who might be best for what role—all except for Aryal. She was perfect right where she was. *She was a harpy*, for God's sake.

They say the skies tore the day the harpies screamed into existence.

This time—*THIS TIME*—she had gone too goddamn far.

This time he wasn't going to just throttle her. Swear to gods, this time he was going to kill her.

He showered in painfully hot water and scrubbed all traces of the woman's scent from his body. Then he yanked on fresh clothes, jeans, boots and a T-shirt. Sentinel clothes, the sturdy kind that had some chance of holding up in a fight and were easy to throw away afterward. Because he'd earned the right to go armed in the Tower now, he strapped on weapons too, a knife in a thigh sheath and a Glock in a shoulder holster.

The sheet of ice on the roads forced him to take the drive to the Tower slowly. The sedate trip did nothing to calm his seething temper, which settled into cold, predatory intent. By the time he strode into the Tower, traffic had begun to pick up as dawn lightened the sky and the city awakened.

A study of affluence in every detail, Cuelebre Tower was eighty stories tall. Nobody in their right mind took the stairs. He wasn't in his right mind. He didn't want to have to talk to anybody.

He took the stairs at a steady, relentless pace that did nothing to calm him down either. It did limber up his body, until he felt warm, loose and ready for a confrontation.

Except then he couldn't find her.

One of the first things he had learned about the Tower was where Aryal slept at night, so he went to her apartment and pounded on her door. Nobody answered, and he could hear no sound of movement from within.

He whirled and stalked to the cafeteria. It had just opened to serve breakfast, and people were beginning to trickle in. No harpy. People took note of his rigid face and swift, angry movements and gave him plenty of room. Next stop on his hunt was the massive gym and training area. He circled through, and even went so far as to check the locker rooms.

Goddammit, no.

He was going to have to pause to think about this. He didn't want to. His hands remembered how it felt to latch around her neck, and they wanted to do it again. Flexing his long fingers, he exited the gym—

Just as down the hall, the doors to one of the elevators opened, and Aryal and Grym walked out.

The sight of her was the same shock to the system as it always was, a raw live jolt of electricity that juddered over his nerve endings. Fueled by a surge of adrenaline, his mind leaped to a higher, faster level. This must be what it felt like for humans to jack on amphetamines.

He lunged down the hall toward her, noting every detail about her as he gained speed. As usual, she wore fighting leathers and her thick, black shoulder-length hair was tangled. Even though he knew that meant she had recently been airborne, she looked as rumpled as if she had just gotten out of bed. Her normally pale skin was flush all over with a clear, high color.

She looked as if she was glowing from an internal flame. Even though her face was uncharacteristically drawn with tiredness, she was still more alive than anyone he had ever met, ten times more vibrant than any other woman he had ever seen.

She was . . . glorious.

A stiletto of bitterness lanced him. Gods, if he could ever meet a woman like that whom he didn't loathe as completely as he loathed her, he might lose this whip of restlessness that drove him. He could live the rest of his life and do nothing, be nothing but completely content. It was hideously unfair that he would look at this harpy and realize that about himself.

She saw him coming. Even though his intent was unmistakable, her face lit up, because she was just bent that way. As she turned toward him, she swept one of her arms backward, hard, and knocked Grym in the chest so that he staggered back into the elevator. Then she strode forward to engage.

She didn't even pause to say anything or ask Quentin why. They both knew there were so many reasons.

He leaped at her, and she dove low so that he overshot, but he thrust out one hand and grabbed a magnificent handful of that tangled black hair and yanked her with him.

They tumbled together, growling, arms and limbs entwined. He caught her scent, and she smelled like healthy woman, clean cold air and arousal.

So the rumors about her and Grym must be true. He liked Grym and found the thought of their pairing so offensive that his growling deepened and grew edged.

She flipped him onto his back. Heaving hard, he flipped them over again and covered her straining body with his. As he pinned her long, taut torso, their hips came into alignment. There was rough friction at his groin, along with her wild scent.

It was so goddamn primal.

His cock stiffened again. *Bloody hell.*

Her eyes flashed furiously through her tangled hair. Fire bloomed down the length of his back as she raked him with her talons. Quicker than thought, breathing heavily, he punched her in the face. For one split second he thought she looked surprised and thoughtful. Then she twisted underneath him to knee him in the groin. More fire bloomed in an infernal garden.

He still had one fist clenched in her hair. Snarling, he yanked her head back and struck down, intending to fasten his teeth on her bared throat.

He never connected.

One moment they were locked together in a vicious, intimate embrace. The next moment he was several yards away, sprawled in a tangle against the wall in a complete disconnect with reality. He felt as if he had been kicked by a mountain.

Which in a way, he realized, he had been. His mind caught up with what had happened. Broken ribs protesting, he struggled to roll over onto his hands and knees, and he looked back in the direction of the elevators.

Dragos stood where they had been fighting, the harpy prone at his feet. Grym stood quietly in the open doorway of the elevator that Aryal had knocked him into, hands lax, all of his attention fixed on the Lord of the Wyr.

More details sank in. Dragos was dressed in jeans and a thin silk sweater, and he had one boot planted in the middle of Aryal's back. He looked utterly furious, his roughhewn expression set in lines of brutality.

He also held his sleeping son cradled against his shoulder. Quentin had thought that baby was small before—just six pounds when he had been born, Pia had told him. Held against the tremendous musculature of his father's chest, he looked as tiny as a small child's doll.

Quentin's mind flatlined.

He had thought he didn't hold any illusions about Dragos. He knew that the only thing that could possibly take the dragon down was a dedicated army with inspired leadership and experienced magic users. But if he had ever held a secret daydream of someone besting Dragos in his human form in single, unarmed combat, that daydream had just been shattered forever.

Not only had Dragos just taken down two of the best, nastiest Wyr fighters in the world, he had done it by moving faster than Quentin could comprehend.

And he did it all without ever jostling the baby enough to wake him.

Dragos glared around the hall at the spectators who had been drawn by the violence.

"Go away," he whispered. People vanished. He kicked Aryal over so that she lay on her back, staring up at him. Still speaking so gently that the baby never stirred, he told her, "I have given you more free rein than I have given almost anybody else, and you have just used the last of that up."

The dragon's incandescent gold gaze turned to Quentin. "And you haven't earned any free rein. I am going upstairs to tuck my son into his crib. You will both go to my office right now and wait for me there. You will not speak to anyone else. You will not speak to or fight each other." He glanced at Grym. "If either one of them disobeys me by so much as uttering a single word, shoot them."

Grym drew his gun and said, "Yes, my lord."

≡ THREE ≡

Quentin held his side as he limped down the hall, cataloguing the damage from the fight and that monstrously powerful kick. He guessed he had three broken ribs, maybe more. Whatever the damage was, it was the size of Dragos's boot. His left knee was wrenched badly and he couldn't bend it. The kneecap felt wrong, like it had been dislocated.

He had also done something exceedingly rare for him. When he had landed against the wall, he had been ass over teakettle, completely out of control of his fall. Usually his fast reflexes saved him from that kind of damage, but not this time.

When he added his bruised, throbbing groin and the claw marks on his back to the list, he was actually more hurt now than he had been throughout all of the Sentinel Games, but for a Wyr of his robust health the injuries were minor. He would want to get his ribs wrapped after Dragos yelled at and maybe fired them, but he'd heal just fine.

His gaze slid sideways. Grym walked between him and Aryal, his Glock pointed casually at the floor.

Aryal walked stiffly, her expression grim and mouth tight. One side of her face had already purpled from his punch. As Quentin watched, her gaze slid sideways toward him. The narrow-eyed glance she gave him was filled with pure evil. Then she looked down at Grym's Glock, and her expression turned unhappy.

"You're doing a really good job," Grym told her, his voice mild and encouraging. "I know what you want to ask, so I'll answer right now and save you the temptation. Dragos told me to shoot you if you said a word, so yes, I would do as he ordered. He didn't say where to shoot you though."

Aryal threw up her hands in a silent question.

Grym told her, "I'd probably tag you on your foot."

Her mouth turned down at the corners. She shook her head and pointed to her forearm, while Quentin scratched the back of his head and stared at them. They were discussing in all seriousness which body part Grym was going to shoot?

"Okay, not your foot," Grym amended. "I'd tag your arm. Satisfied? And the point is that you would deserve it. You both would. He really lost it with you. You're lucky he didn't shatter your spines and put you in traction for a month."

Quentin took a deep breath. Both Aryal and Grym turned to him. Aryal looked hopeful while Grym just waited. He let the breath out again silently and Aryal's face fell.

Grym said, "If that was meant as a question—yes, Dragos has put people in traction before."

This was the most Quentin had ever heard Grym talk before. They made their way through the outer offices into Dragos's massive corner office.

Quentin had only been in Dragos's office once before. His lip curled as he looked around.

Compared to the ostentatious luxury throughout the rest of the Tower, the office was almost Spartan. Mostly the room was empty floor space. There was a huge desk and chair, with two more chairs positioned in front of it, a plain mahogany table pushed against one wall, and original multimedia artwork hung on the two interior walls. The two corner walls were floor to ceiling windows, framing one of the most expensive skyline views in the world. French doors led out onto a balcony patio.

Quentin moved to put his back to the one of the interior

walls, crossing his arms and leaning against it for support. He watched as Grym shut the door and Aryal limped over to ease back against Dragos's desk.

Grym registered Quentin's position with a quirk of his black, straight eyebrows then walked over to Aryal. He still hadn't holstered his gun.

The harpy was scowling at the floor, her head bent. Grym flattened one hand on the desk by her hip and leaned on it, angling his head to look into Aryal's face.

Grym said to her in gentle voice, "You make people crazy. You do realize that, don't you?"

Aryal made a face then winced and fingered her swollen bruise.

"Your wildness is actually one of the reasons why so many people love you in spite of the headaches you cause. Why Dragos loves you, even though I know he's never said it. Some Wyr are more tame than others, but we all recognize something of our own wildness in you. Did you know that too?"

Quentin's gaze narrowed, frowning as he listened. Grym talked quietly, the pitch of his voice clearly intended to exclude Quentin. But the other sentinel could also have talked to her telepathically, so he intended for Quentin to witness but not participate.

Aryal looked up at Grym, questions shimmering in her eyes.

Gripped by a compulsion he couldn't control, Quentin cheated. *Don't worry*, he said to her telepathically, *you're still quite rotten and plenty of other people dislike you intensely.*

Renewed fury blazed in her face. She started to push away from the desk, but Grym slammed his hand down on her shoulder and held her in place. Then he glared at Quentin suspiciously and pointed his Glock at him.

Quentin didn't want to laugh. His ribs sent a stabbing pain right through his chest. He couldn't believe Aryal didn't return fire telepathically. Perhaps she didn't trust herself once she got going. He sure as hell didn't trust her. She was crazypants at the best of times, let alone when she got angry.

He also hated the appearance of intimacy that Grym had created, and the obvious deep affection Grym and Aryal had for each other. Not only did it speak of long years of intimacy between them, but it highlighted qualities in Aryal that Quentin didn't want to acknowledge might exist.

He wanted to block out Grym's voice, but he couldn't, as the other sentinel turned back to Aryal. "I have a point to make here. There's a reason why Dragos has given you so much free rein. In a way, you're kindred spirits. Like you, he has his own hellish temper to grapple with and he creates as many problems as he solves. He knows you love him too, and you're committed to the Wyr demesne with every bit of that considerable passion you carry inside of you. So if Dragos says you've used up all the free rein he's given you, Aryal, you'd better listen to him, because he meant every word he said out in the hall. I really think this could be it for you. Be careful how you act when he gets down here. Okay?"

The harpy's angular features sobered as she listened. She nodded.

Grym straightened and turned to face Quentin, his expression growing colder. "Now for you," he said. "Dragos meant every word he said to you too. You haven't earned any free rein. A lot of people like you, and it's probably a lot more than who like Aryal. Most of the sentinels like you. I like you. We also all know that she's been investigating you for a long time. Dragos knows, because *she* hasn't held any secrets back. So what the hell are you doing here, Quentin? Why is she getting under your skin so bad, and what are the rest of us supposed to think when you fly off the handle and continue to attack her?"

All vestige of Quentin's sardonic humor vaporized as Grym's words hit him like individual blows. Maybe they shouldn't have hit him so hard. He had known that some people were suspicious of him just because there had been an investigation. In fact, he had been expecting it. But somehow by what Grym said, or in the way he said it, the other sentinel held up a mirror for him to look in and the reflection was pitilessly uncompromising.

What the hell are you doing here, Quentin?

That was the question. That was the heart of every question.

The office door slammed open. A volcano in the shape of the Lord of the Wyr poured into the room. The walls contracted, and suddenly the office was much smaller than it had been a few moments ago.

Clearly Dragos's self-imposed, ten-minute time-out hadn't improved his mood very much.

Dragos looked at Grym and jerked his head toward the door. Grym didn't say another word. Inclining his head respectfully to Dragos, he holstered his gun, and shot one look at Aryal and another one at Quentin as he walked out, easing the door closed behind him as he went. Aryal straightened from the desk and opened her mouth.

"I have not given you leave to speak," said Dragos before she could start. "You will both remain silent. I don't care what he did." Blazing gold eyes speared Quentin as Dragos said, "I don't care what she did. I. Do. Not. Give a shit."

Anger churned in Quentin on a fast boil, and he almost didn't contain it. He had always bristled at Dragos Cuelebre's particular brand of dominance. The two worst aspects of becoming a sentinel were facing him in this room, and he held himself clenched like a fist, shaking with the desire to spit in their faces and storm out.

What *was* he doing here?

Hands on his hips, the dragon studied him and waited.

Quentin returned Dragos's gaze bitterly and shook his head. No you don't, you arrogant son of a bitch, he thought. You will not drive me away that easily. I've won my way into your Tower by your own rules. If I leave, it will be because I choose to do so for my own reasons, and not because you manipulate me into it.

Something strange flickered across Dragos's face. If Quentin were pressed to describe what he had seen, he would have said that the dragon almost smiled.

Whatever that subtle expression really was, it was gone almost immediately. Dragos strode behind his desk and turned to face them.

Dragos said, "Do you know what I was doing this morning? I was walking Liam so he would fall back asleep and let Pia stay in bed for a little longer. Then I came across you two jokers brawling all over the hall. I should add, brawling in one of the main hallways of the upper floors in the Tower. You had no idea I was there, did you? You were fucking oblivious to everything else outside of your own vendetta. What if I had been someone else babysitting Liam and taking him for a walk—say, Talia, for example?"

Talia Aguilar was a Wyr selkie and the new head of PR for Cuelebre Enterprises. Sleek and delicately rounded, with soulfully large eyes, Talia was gentle to the bone and didn't have a single fighter reflex in her.

Sourness churned in Quentin's stomach. As viciously as they had been fighting, they could easily have plowed into someone like Talia and caused major injury, if not death. A quick glance at Aryal's tight expression told him that she realized it too.

"I'm banishing the two of you from New York," Dragos said.

Quentin moved sharply while shock bolted over Aryal's expression.

Dragos was still speaking in a rapid-fire staccato. It took a few moments for the words to sink in. ". . . and you are going to work your shit out somewhere else way the fuck away from here. I don't want to have anything to do with you until then, and let me tell you, nobody else does either. I'm going to give you an assignment. You have to work together on it, or you both lose your sentinel positions. You cannot return before two weeks are up. You cannot stay away longer than a month. That's your time frame. When you return to New York, you will somehow have made peace with each other, or you both lose your sentinel positions. After the Games, we now have a detailed list of current runners up. It won't be hard if we have to make that transition."

He paused to study Aryal's bone white face and Quentin's rigid posture.

"You have continued to put extra strain on everybody else, right when they could have used a break," he said. "So if you make it back successfully and you manage to hold on to your jobs, you are going to work double time until all the other sentinels have had a vacation. That's how you're going to make this up to them. For today, you're going to pack light. Get your affairs in order. Tend to your wounds. Return here at five o'clock for your assignment. Maybe by then I'll be able to tolerate the sound of your voices. Now, get out of here."

Seething with reaction, Quentin managed to keep his clenched face turned away as he limped toward the door and Aryal followed.

Not less than two weeks. Not more than a month.

Banished.

With the hellion. Maybe he should just hang himself and be done with it, except he would not give the bitch that kind of satisfaction.

I'll win this game, he thought. Just like I've won every other game I've played in my life. Besides, with any luck, the assignment will be dangerous; she'll get herself killed and save everybody a world of hurt.

Then his eyebrows rose.

He cocked his head.

Of course if that happened, it would have to be obvious to everybody that either her death was accidental, or somebody else had killed her.

There might be some merit to pursuing this train of thought.

"Oh, and one more thing," Dragos said.

They jerked to a pause and swiveled to stare at him.

In a blast of heat and Power that knocked them back against the wall, the dragon roared, "DO NOT FIGHT AGAIN TODAY OR YOU BOTH LOSE YOUR SENTINEL POSITIONS."

You know, some days things went wrong in all the right ways.

As soon as she and Caeravorn hit the hall, they shot apart in two different directions. Neither one of them could get away from the other fast enough.

Banishment, with Caeravorn. On some sort of assignment.

With any luck, it would be a really nasty, dangerous assignment.

How horrible. How peeeerrrrfect.

She couldn't wait to find out what terrible fate Dragos had in store for them, because when would she ever get a chance like this again? Caeravorn was going to be a tough bastard to kill, but she was really good at improvising.

She just had to be absolutely sure his death occurred in some way that allowed her to say with perfect honesty that she didn't do it, because when she returned to New York either with his (preferably mangled) corpse or alone, those with truthsense were going to be all over her asking questions.

Ugh, her body ached all over. Dragos had purposely stomped down hard when he planted his boot in the middle of her back, and it hurt to breathe. The side of her face was so swollen she could see her cheek out of the corner of her eye. It wouldn't do to go on assignment already injured, so as soon as she could, she needed to find a healer.

But first, she had something else she needed to do. She went to find Graydon.

He was in the cafeteria, eating breakfast with Sebastian Ortiz, the Wyr wolf who had managed the Games. Ortiz was retired army but still active in civilian work, and he managed security for the parking garage underneath the Tower.

The cafeteria had grown crowded with the breakfast rush. One of the many perks of being a sentinel was an automatic pass to the head of any line, since sentinel business was often urgent and their mealtimes cut short.

Even though she was starving, this time Aryal bypassed the food lines to grab a cup of coffee. When she approached Graydon and Ortiz's table, Ortiz gave her a civil nod, said a quick good-bye to Graydon and rose from the table. Aryal slid into the seat he had vacated.

Graydon sat back in his seat and shoved his half-full plate of food away. He looked at her bruised cheek, the expression on his craggy face cool and shuttered.

She bit her lip then said, "I'm sorry."

He crossed his arms and remained silent. Her stomach clenched and her shoulders sagged. He never used to look at her like that.

"Okay, I'm really sorry," she said softly. She turned her coffee cup in circles. "Did Grym tell you what happened?"

"He told me what he saw," said Graydon, his voice flat. "You guys had met on the roof, and you were going to get some breakfast when Quentin appeared and went after you like the wrath of God. No talking, no escalation. Boom. So you and I both know that's not everything that happened. You did something to set him off. Of course you did."

She didn't bother to dispute it. She didn't actually know what had set Caeravorn off, but she didn't doubt that she had done something. Much as she hated him, she had to concede, he didn't randomly attack people he disliked.

"I am sorry for the extra strain this has been on everybody, and I will fix it. I swear it, Gray. There's going to be a rotation of vacation time, and all the sentinels are going to get a break." She braced herself. "But first Dragos is going to send Caeravorn and me on assignment, and we can't come back to New York until we work shit out between us."

At least one way or another.

Inwardly wincing, she waited for an explosion of swearing or at least some kind of expression of disgust. Nothing happened. Graydon didn't even look surprised.

Her eyebrows rose. "You knew already?"

"I was the one who suggested it," Graydon said. "Dragos called me to talk over ideas when he put the baby down. His ideas involved more broken bones and bloodshed. At least this way, the conflict is going to get resolved one way or another—you will both work it out, or you'll be out. We can't have the sentinels at war with each other, Aryal."

She blew out a gusty sigh. He echoed her thoughts from earlier almost perfectly. "No," she said. "I know."

Finally his cool demeanor warmed. He sat forward and crossed his arms on the table. *I'm glad you told me*, he said telepathically. *Did Dragos just get finished with you?*

She dragged her hands through her hair. *Yeah.*

Graydon smiled at her. *And you came straightaway to find me*.

She lifted a shoulder and nodded.

He put a massive hand on her forearm and squeezed gently. He told her, *You've got to come to peace somehow with the fact that no matter how much you hate each other, you're both sentinels and you have to work together. You have to, Aryal. Nobody wants to lose you.*

She muttered, *That's good to know.*

They just need the vendetta to stop. Make peace with your dead-end investigation. Graydon leaned forward farther to deepen eye contact with her. His eyes were a darker gray than hers, the color of aged pewter, and the expression in his gaze was hard, the set of his mouth ruthless. *Either that or confirm his guilt. I know what Dragos told you. He said to work it out somehow, and he genuinely doesn't care how. He's got enough on his plate trying to figure out how to be a new father. I'm the one who's telling you—you have one more month. Bring home hard evidence and we'll use it together as nails in Quentin's coffin. But one way or another, you need to finish this.*

I know, she said. *I will.*

After that, the rest of her day was almost anticlimactic. The next stop on her agenda was to see a healer who eased the pain in her chest and reduced the stiffness and swelling in her face. Then she went to her office to delegate cases, blast through the most urgent of her emails, and make a half-assed attempt at organizing her desk in case someone needed to find something while she was gone.

As soon as she had accomplished all of that, she went back to her apartment, showered and washed her hair and packed (a fifteen-minute task, as she shoved weapons, credit cards, a few changes of clothes and travel toiletries, several candy bars and her e-reader into a backpack).

Then she ate a sandwich and fell into bed to sleep away the afternoon. She was not about to head out on some kind of assignment to unknown places with Caeravorn when she was exhausted. While she was not averse to taking risks, that just seemed like the height of stupidity.

At 4:55 P.M., dressed in lace-up boots, jeans, a black turtleneck and a leather jacket, and carrying her backpack on one shoulder, she walked into Dragos's offices, which were thrumming with activity. Cuelebre Enterprises never closed at five. She waved at Kristoff, Dragos's senior assistant, who waved back from his cubicle.

Dragos's door was shut. There was no sign of Caeravorn. She waited, not very well, tapping one foot. It was probably too much to hope that Caeravorn had seen the error of his ways and quit.

Unbidden, her mind flashed back to their fight from that morning. His body had been heavy and hard as he pinned her to the floor, his muscles like iron. He was strikingly good-looking even when his lips were pulled back in a snarl.

And when their hips had come into alignment, she had felt his cock stiffen. That beautiful penis of his, unmistakably hard and lying flush against her. She knew just what it looked like.

Her breath shortened, and hunger flashed through her body.

"You just say good-bye to your boyfriend?" Caeravorn said from behind her. His tone was as insolent as ever. "You should have probably taken a little more time with that. I don't sense that you got any real . . . fulfillment."

He could smell her arousal. Her mind whited out. Gods, she wanted to claw at him. She whirled to face him just as Dragos's door opened.

Her gaze clashed with Caeravorn's. His blue eyes were narrowed, catlike on her. He had dressed all in black. Black jeans, black T-shirt, and a worn, black leather bomber jacket; and like her, he carried a backpack.

"Come in," said Dragos.

Somehow, Aryal made herself obey, maneuvering her own body around as though it were a marionette. Every nerve ending on her skin was aware of Caeravorn gliding bonelessly into the room behind her.

Once they were inside, Dragos shut the door.

He turned to face them and said, without preamble, "I'm going to send you to Numenlaur."

═ FOUR ═

Numenlaur.

The name resonated in Quentin's marrow. His emotions roared as he heard Dragos say it, a single outcry of the soul.

Numenlaur was the first and oldest Elven land, the fabled birthing place from which all others had come. The Other land had been closed off from the rest of the world for millennia.

Once upon a time, he would have been filled with curiosity and wonder at the chance to see Numenlaur, and he would have given anything to go. Now he still felt the echoes of that same compulsion, only it was underscored with dread and grief, for Numenlaur had become a wasteland, emptied of the Elves who had once lived there.

As if from a distance, he heard Aryal ask, "Why do you want us to go?"

Dragos's expression shuttered as he looked from the harpy to Quentin. He assessed them both, his golden gaze moody and calculating. He said, "Ever since the battle at Lirithriel Wood, Pia has been keeping in close contact with her friends in the Elven demesne. They remain completely overwhelmed with what happened."

38

Quentin had no idea what his own expression might reveal. He turned abruptly, putting his back to the other two as he struggled to get in control of his feelings.

"Overwhelmed" was a massive understatement. Two months after the battle in Lirithriel Wood, the Elven demesne in South Carolina remained devastated. One of the ancient Guardians of Numenlaur, Amras Gaeleval, had apparently gone mad and enslaved all the Numenlaurians in a Powerful enthrallment, driving them to attack the Elven demesne just outside of Charleston.

Gaeleval had tricked his way into Lirithriel then tried to enthrall the Elves there as well. He did not manage to capture everybody, but he drove those Elves he did enthrall to attack their own people. Friends cut down friends, and families were decimated. Gaeleval had set fire to Lirithriel Wood, killing its spirit in an attempt to drive the High Lord Calondir and those Elves he had not managed to capture over the crossover passageway to their Other land, where they would have faced extinction at the hands of Gaeleval's army had not Dragos, Pia and the Wyr become involved.

For the first time in decades, Dragos himself had called the Wyr to war. In a confrontation in the Elven Other land, Dragos killed Gaeleval and broke the enthrallment. In the process, Calondir, the High Lord of the Elven demesne in Charleston, had also been killed. So had at least a third of the Numenlaurians.

Of those who had survived, a significant number were still catatonic. Others failed to recover. They were lethargic, distant and without appetite, and many were physically malnourished and ill from a multitude of problems that had occurred through long neglect and lack of proper shelter.

The surviving Lirithriel Elves that Gaeleval had captured ended up faring better overall than the Numenlaurians. They had been enthralled for only a short time, and they were physically healthier and more robust. Even so, many struggled to reconnect with life. A few, unable to cope with losing so many friends and family, had committed suicide.

Quentin had lost friends and family members too. The

High Lord Calondir himself had been his uncle by marriage. The Elder tribunal had deployed a Peacekeeping presence to Lirithriel, setting up a small city of Quonset huts as field hospitals, and aid continued to pour into the Elven demesne. The Elves faced a long, hard road to survival.

Dragos had continued speaking. "As far as I know, Numenlaur continues to be abandoned. It has occurred to me that others may also have realized this, and may be interested in what they can find there. I want you two to go and assess the situation."

Quentin swiped at his face with the back of one fist as he glared out the window. He had to clear his throat before he could speak. He said, his voice low and savage, "If this is some kind of order to loot in disguise, I won't participate."

In the glass of the windowpane, he watched Dragos's blurred reflection turn to him. After a moment, Dragos said in a measured tone that spoke of self-control, "If I felt the desire to loot for Elven treasures, I would not send others to do it. I would go myself. What I want you to do is prevent others from looting. Check the land. Secure anything you might find dangerous. If anyone has trespassed, kick them out. From my understanding, Numenlaur has only one crossover passageway that leads to central Europe. Secure the entrance if necessary. If you haven't killed each other by then, report back to me."

Of all the assignments Dragos could have picked, this was actually one that Quentin wanted to do. Marginally calmer, he asked, "Have you contacted Ferion about this?"

"I haven't bothered to," Dragos said. A hint of bite had entered his voice. "Numenlaur does not belong to Ferion. Besides, he's in over his head as it is."

Quentin couldn't disagree. His cousin Ferion was a good man and would eventually make a fine High Lord, but too much had happened, and the losses and destruction were catastrophic.

After a moment of silence, Dragos asked, "Any questions?"

Quentin turned to face the others but kept silent. Aryal wore a scowl, but she said nothing either, only shook her head.

Dragos said, "Kris has your plane tickets. You're departing out of JFK, and your flight leaves soon. You'd better be on it." He paused. "Close the door on your way out."

Quentin's gaze clashed with Aryal's. Her stormy gray eyes promised him anything but peace. So be it. He gave that promise right back to her in a thin-lipped smile.

It might be harder to engineer a fatal accident in what had become a virtual ghost land, but it could still be done.

And he was an expert at covering his own tracks.

Let the war games begin.

Dragos's assistant Kris was waiting outside his office, plane tickets in hand. The young dark-haired male handed one envelope to Aryal and the other to Quentin. Aryal yanked out the contents of her envelope and scanned the pages. Her eyes rounded. "You booked *coach*?"

Kris shrugged. "Only seats available to Prague at short notice. Dragos said to book the first flight out, and that's what you got. Meanwhile the corporate jet stays parked in the hanger. You guys must really be in the doghouse." He looked at them sidelong. "Erm, just so you know, I'm supposed to verify that you both get on that flight. There's a car waiting downstairs for you."

"Oh hell, no." Aryal's shoulders twitched as she gave Quentin one last glare. "Nobody said we had to ride to the airport together. I'll meet you there."

Quentin watched her leave then looked back at Kris, who had settled at his computer again. "You ever take a vacation?" he asked the other male.

Kris shrugged, eyes on his screen. "This is my vacation."

Quentin shook his head. Guess there was all kinds of crazy. He checked the contents of his envelope. Aside from documents he would need when he reached the Czech Republic, there was a printout of an electronic plane ticket. He noted the time of the flight and sighed. No wonder there was a car waiting downstairs. He had been so busy that day, sorting first through his sentinel duties and then seeing a healer and arranging matters at Elfie's, that he hadn't

41

yet had time to stop at the penthouse to see Pia and the baby. He'd hoped to talk to her before they left, but now he couldn't.

He gave Kris a nod and left, taking the elevator down to the lobby. As he went, he called Pia's cell. It rolled over to voicemail without ringing, which meant her phone was turned off. Was that coincidence, or intentional?

After the automated prompt, he said, "I'm sure you know by now what happened this morning. I wanted to see you and Liam before I left, but now I can't. Listen, Pia, I— I'm sorry." Sorry for everything. Sorrier than you can know. He bit the words back, guilt sitting like a ten-pound weight in his chest. "I just wanted you to know, it's never going to happen again. That's a promise."

After he disconnected, he tried Ferion's number, but that phone call rolled over to voicemail right away too, as the new, overburdened High Lord never answered his cell phone anymore.

Instead of leaving a voice message this time, Quentin hung up then texted Ferion, his fingers moving quickly over the small screen. Going to Prague this pm. Will call when I get there.

For a moment he hesitated, teetering on the edge of adding more. But Numenlaur was too painful and charged a subject to put into a text message. He hit send, clicked off his iPhone, shoved it into his pocket and when the elevator doors opened, he strode through the crowded lobby to the main steps outside.

The day had started out bitter and was ending gray and bleak, but the bite of the cold wind felt good on his skin.

A black Cadillac Escalade idled at the curb. Winding through the heavy crowd of rush hour pedestrians on the sidewalk, he opened the passenger door. Vivaldi's *The Four Seasons* poured out of the interior. He looked inside.

Alexander Elysias lounged in the driver's seat, his long body relaxed. As a pegasus, he had the distinction of being the only herbivore among the seven sentinels, all the rest being predators of some sort. The difference played out in his personality as well. He was easily the most even tempered and patient of them all.

Predator Wyr tended to be dismissive of herbivores, an unfortunate tendency that did not play out among the sentinels. All of them had watched Alex's fighting in the Games arena. Not only had they seen Alex's proficiency for combat for themselves, but they had also come to realize that his easygoing demeanor went hand in glove with a strong, steady personality, keen intelligence and a kind of innate dignity that tended to settle the most abrasive and volatile of them.

The expression on Alex's handsome, dark mahogany face was pensive. It vanished into a welcoming smile as soon as he saw Quentin. The tension that had been knotted between Quentin's shoulders eased as he returned the smile with a lopsided one of his own and slid into the passenger seat.

Going through the Sentinel Games together had been a bonding experience of sorts. Out of all the people who lived and worked in the Tower, Quentin had just two friends. One of them was Pia, and the other one was Alex.

"Hey there," he said. "You're the first thing that has gone right this whole gods' cursed day."

Alex said, "I can imagine. So far I've heard about fifty different versions of what happened this morning." He craned his neck, looking beyond Quentin to the crowded sidewalk. "Where's Aryal?"

"She decided to make her own way to the airport." Quentin slammed the door, settled his pack between his feet, buckled his seat belt and slumped back. "No doubt she's flying."

"If it was any warmer out, I'd offer to shapeshift and fly you out too," said Alex. "It can be a good way to beat rush hour traffic, but in this weather you'd freeze your balls off."

A grin hooked the corner of Quentin's mouth up. "Your concern for my balls is touching. Really."

Alex laughed as he shifted gear and pulled away from the curb. "I just didn't want you screaming like a girl in my ear the whole way." He shot a glance at Quentin. His eyes were dark, intelligent and calm. "Want to talk about it?"

Quentin sighed and rubbed the back of his head, then admitted the truth. "Dragos banished us, and we deserved it. We're supposed to work our shit out someplace else. He's sending us to Numenlaur."

Any vestige of humor in Alex's face vanished. "Numenlaur. Man, that's gonna be a hard trip."

"Tell me about it." He heard himself saying, "Still, I'm . . . glad he thought to send someone there to check on things."

"Careful, buddy," Alex said. "You might be getting close to admitting that Dragos isn't as bad as you thought he was."

"I wouldn't go that far," he said immediately.

A smile crept back over Alex's dark features. "Of course you wouldn't."

Quentin glowered at the lanes of bumper-to-bumper traffic. "I'm never going to like him. That's all there is to it. He's arrogant, demanding, he has an evil temper, and I'm pretty sure he invented the word 'conniving.'"

"Go on, tell me how you really feel," Alex said. "Don't hold back."

Quentin refused to smile. "As far as I'm concerned, he does only two things right. He makes Pia happy, and he loves Liam. Okay, maybe three things. I used to think the feudal system in the Wyr hierarchy was bullshit, but—it works."

The other man drove quickly and competently, weaving through the slower vehicles. "And don't forget, you were also glad he mustered the Wyr to go to Lirithriel."

"Yeah, but I question his motives," Quentin growled. "He may have done the right thing, but not for the right reasons."

"There's no way you can possibly know that," Alex countered. "I'm more of a behaviorist. Dragos did the right thing. Period. That's what counts. You can have all the right reasons in the world. They don't mean shit, my friend, if what you do causes harm."

Alex didn't know anything about Quentin's involvement in last year's events. The other sentinel had spoken in his typical easygoing manner, but still his words punched Quentin in the gut. "There is that," he said bleakly.

Despite rush hour, they made good time getting to JFK. Still, if Quentin had been a normal passenger, he would have been in trouble trying to make the flight. Because of his sentinel status, he would be able to expedite his trip through the security lines.

Alex pulled to a stop at the passenger drop-off curb and clapped him on the shoulder. "Have a safe trip, and as much as she makes you crazy, don't kill each other. You're both sentinels for a reason, you know, and we need you."

Quentin grasped the other man's shoulder briefly. "You and I have only known each other for a couple of months, but I already owe you many drinks for the times you've talked me down."

Alex raised his eyebrows with that trademark smile of his that already charmed so many females and was fast becoming famous in the Wyr demesne. "Good thing you own a bar, huh?"

He laughed. "I guess it is. Catch you later."

A flight attendant closed the door as he boarded the plane. Another one lit up when she saw him. She purred, "Let me show you to your seat."

Oh please God, not another sex kitten. There was a time when he would have taken advantage of that purred invitation in her voice, but there were winsome, flirtatious sex kittens everywhere he looked, and they all had so many emotional needs.

"That's all right, thanks," he told her. "You're busy."

Her face fell as he turned away, but it was for the best. He had no interest and he didn't have anything to give her. As he looked for his seat, he kept an eye out for Aryal. The flight from JFK to Prague was nine hours long. With any luck, they would be in opposite parts of the plane.

But his damnable luck had been running against him all day. He scented Aryal before he caught sight of her. She slouched in her window seat, chewing gum while she flipped through a magazine. She wore the evidence of her flight. Her hair was tangled as usual, and that high color burned again underneath her normally pale skin, glowing like a flame lit from within. Her feminine scent bore a clean, sharp freshness, like she had captured a slice of the wild March wind and brought it with her.

The seat beside her was empty.

It was his seat.

Of course it was.

He looked around at the large, packed plane. It was filled with mostly human passengers, although he caught sight of one or two of the Elder Races dotted throughout the cabin. No other visible Wyr. There wasn't another empty seat anywhere in sight.

Of course there wasn't.

He looked down at the person who occupied the aisle seat. A young teenage boy, maybe thirteen years old, sat hunched over an electronic game.

"Hi," Quentin said to him.

The boy grunted but didn't look up.

"I'll give you a hundred dollars if I can have the aisle seat," Quentin said.

That brought the boy's head up. As he opened his mouth, a woman from across the aisle snapped, "You'll do no such thing. Robert, ignore that man. Never take money from strangers."

"But mom," the kid said as he blinked up at Quentin. "It's a hundred dollars and it's just an aisle seat."

"Get over here! Change places with me." Quentin rubbed the bridge of his nose, watching as the boy got up. Resignedly, he shoved his pack into an overhead compartment, slipped out of his jacket and stuffed it underneath the seat in front of his, then he slid into the middle seat, buckled himself in and crossed his arms.

He was over six feet tall. Aryal was just a few inches shorter than he was. Together they were packed in like sardines, their arms, hips and thighs touching. Her heat and energy washed over him, sharp like vodka straight from the freezer but hot like mulled whiskey.

"Before you say a word to me, shut up," she muttered out of the side of her mouth. "If I have to look at you, I'm going to punch you."

God, yes. Adrenaline flooded his system. He was ready and itching for the fight, but there was nowhere to take it. If they started to brawl here, they might blow out the side of the plane and take everyone else aboard down with them.

On his right side, the mother of the teenage boy heaved herself into the aisle seat and glared at him. He said, "It was just a hundred dollars, and just the aisle seat."

"Don't talk to my boy again," Mom told him.

Jesus. He let his head fall back against the seat with a *thunk*. He had to fly nine fucking hours like this. It was a goddamn pressure cooker.

Something was bound to explode. If something didn't let up soon, he thought it might be him.

The flight attendants did their show-and-tell while the plane taxied into position and accelerated down the runway, lifting into the air with a mechanical roar. Cranky Mom on his right played Sudoku with a pencil. On his left, Aryal finished flipping through her magazine and dropped it onto her lap. He glanced sideways at it. Somehow she had found the time to buy a copy of *Rolling Stone*.

Aryal mimicked his position, crossing her arms and tucking her elbows tight against her side, while she leaned as far away from him as she could get, hunching against the interior wall of the plane and glowering out the window.

The relief at the inches of space she managed to put between their torsos was marginal compared to the upsurge of irritation Quentin felt. She had no fucking tact. None whatsoever. Her body language screamed that she would do almost anything to get away from him—anything except deplane.

Besides, she could lean sideways all she liked, but the seats were so goddamn miniscule, their thighs still touched. He looked down at the length of her legs alongside his. Her bone structure and musculature were slimmer than his, undeniably feminine while also strong and athletic.

He had watched her bouts at the Games. Hell, of course he had. Like most of the contestants, he DVRed the bouts so that he could go through them again, analyzing each fighter's strengths and weakness. He had pored over Aryal's fights time and time again. It was only smart to study his enemy in an effort to discover any weakness.

During the Games, the contestants had their own box. Once they had gotten far enough through the rounds that the contestants' numbers were limited, the new contenders mingled with the five sentinels, exchanging sharp, assessing glances and friendly smiles. When he wasn't competing, Quentin had lived in that box.

Aryal fought with power and confidence. When she struck, she was fast as a snake, and the one time she chose to change into her Wyr form, she rioted across the sands of the arena like a joyous minitornado.

The sight was so magnificent, Quentin was on his feet before he realized it, along with the rest of the stadium. She laughed as she fought, her face vivid and wild, talons out and flashing in the white-hot lights, and everything about her *aligned*.

She never once lost command of the placement of those huge, gray-to-black wings, and once when her opponent, a massive, thousand-plus-pound polar bear, lunged to strike at her, she leaped into an aerial cartwheel that carried her soaring over his head. As she had flown over him, she reached down in an almost leisurely movement, the talon of one finger extended, and raked a thin, teasing cut along his muscled back.

It was a blatantly gratuitous maneuver, but it was so precisely executed, and the smile on her face was filled with such feral gaiety, Quentin found himself shouting along with all the others. In that moment all thoughts of resentment were temporarily suspended for sheer love of the artistry she displayed with such abandon. She owned that fight from beginning to end.

When she put her opponent on the ground for the last time, Grym, who had been leaning against the box railing beside Quentin, straightened and threw a fist pump into the air, roaring, *"MY GIRL!"*

The sentinel's ferocious glee had broken Quentin out of the moment. Remembering it now, he scowled, shifting position carefully in his tiny space in an effort to get more comfortable. He sensed Aryal's body tense. When he looked at her, he saw that her gaze had cut sideways. She watched him out of the corner of her eye as he tried to get comfortable.

Unbidden and unwanted, Alex's words echoed in his thoughts. *You're both sentinels for a reason, you know, and we need you.*

Damn that pegasus.

Quentin was born a killer. He had the instincts of a predator. Despite that, he had never killed indiscriminately. His impulse to throttle Aryal was one thing, but the quiet intention to murder her was an entirely different thing. It was too far off even his screwed-up moral compass.

You can have all the right reasons in the world. They don't mean shit, my friend, if what you do causes harm.

He shifted again as his admittedly dysfunctional conscience nagged him. He had thought he had the right reasons last year, and then he'd ended up causing so much harm. This time, hell, he didn't even have any right reasons. She just drove him crazy.

So quietly that only he could hear her, she hissed out of the corner of her mouth, "Stop moving."

In a quick, neat move, he took the magazine from her lap before she had a chance to react. Her whole body twitched as she made an aborted move as if she would snatch it back before she could stop herself. He flipped through the pages without really looking at them while she glared at him. On his other side, Mom tucked away her Sudoku book, slipped a circular foam airplane pillow out of a canvas bag and anchored it around her neck, then settled back in her seat for a snooze.

He was saturated with Aryal's scent, drowning in her presence, and there wasn't any escape for eight and a half more hours. Thank God her flight had washed away that irritating hint of arousal. Honestly, he couldn't figure out what she and Grym saw in each other. They didn't match in the slightest.

"It's going to be a long month for you, isn't it?" he muttered.

The look on her face turned heartfelt. "Gods, yes."

Everything about her goaded him. Unable to stop himself, he said, "I just can't figure you and Grym out. You're so mismatched. Other than you, he seems so sane."

For a moment an amused smile hovered on her lips. "That's because you're an idiot."

He stared at her mouth. The anger that had been simmering all day had to come out somehow. He switched to telepathy. *So what did you see earlier this morning when you spied on me at my bedroom window?*

Her eyebrows shot up, her amusement vaporizing. *That's what set you off this morning, isn't it?*

He turned to look at her full on, his expression burning. *What did you see?*

Something complicated flashed across her angular, upswept features. Funny, he wouldn't have tagged her as complex. Then there it was again, a hint of arousal in her scent. It was invasive, filling his lungs as he involuntarily took a deep breath. Unwanted. Delicious. A muscle in her narrow jaw flexed, and she looked furious.

Comprehension dawned. He laughed, low and angrily. He said, *It's not you and Grym at all, is it? You into chicks?*

Once he'd said it, he couldn't strip the image from his imagination. Aryal, bending over another woman, perhaps a petite one like the brunette hooker, one of her long, lean hands palming a breast while they kissed.

Fury at his own unruly imagination battled with his body's reaction. His unruly cock began to stiffen.

Aryal's gaze flashed. She said very softly between her teeth, "I've had a few chicks in my time. They're tasty little morsels, like soft, pink hors d'oeuvres. You got a problem with that, asshole?"

FUCK. The shock of her words bolted through him, and

a new image blazed in his mind. Aryal, crouched between a woman's thighs, her dark head nestled at the woman's pelvis.

His stirring cock turned into a raging hard-on. His entire body stiffened, rebelling against it, as his own scent filled the air. The ridiculousness of it didn't escape him. There they sat, hazardously trapped and betraying themselves by reeking of their own cravings, while the passengers around them napped, oblivious to it all.

Then that internal whip that constantly drove him pushed him to whisper, "You and me. We're going to have this out when we get to Prague."

Aryal gave him a slow, dangerous smile. "You know we will."

≡ FIVE ≡

A ryal couldn't sleep but she pretended to, hunched in her corner again as far away from Quentin as she could get, eyes closed and face turned to the shuttered window.

She was deeply disturbed by their exchange.

Oh, not the verbal part. The *pheromone* part.

What exactly had caused Quentin's electric blue eyes to dilate, and his own arousal to scent the air? Was it the idea of a little girl-on-girl action? If so, he was in the company of millions of other males across the planet.

But something about his own reaction made his whole body tighten in protest. He didn't like whatever had turned him on, and Aryal didn't think he was the kind of guy to be bothered by the thought of two women making love.

Had it been her own traitorous response to remembering his admittedly fantastic body? Yeah, that might have pissed him off. It kinda pissed her off. And there was nowhere to go to get away from each other, except to the lavatory.

After their exchange, Quentin eased out of his seat and disappeared.

At first she thought that was where he had gone. Maybe he had decided to give himself a hand, so to speak, and ease off some of that tension. She pictured him in the tiny cubicle,

52

looking at himself in the lavatory mirror, his jeans unzipped while he palmed his erect penis just as he had earlier that morning in his bedroom. Her whole body clenched tight.

Goddammit.

But her mind didn't stop there. Oh no. She had to put herself in the scene too.

Standing right behind him, unzipping his jeans. Reaching in the opening to pull out his cock. His skin would be hot silk over that hard, engorged muscle, the broad tip damp.

There was no denying that he was a beautiful, beautiful man.

Where would his hands be while she was doing all this to him? What was he doing?

She thought of the handcuffs on the brunette, and the leather strip he had given the woman to bite. He would want to take control. He was that kind of guy. Huh-uh, this was her fantasy. She took control. So his hands were pulled overhead, and he was handcuffed to a railing.

He was furious with her, because he was always furious with her, and she couldn't really imagine him any other way. And his penis was stiff as a board.

She could do anything she wanted to him.

She massaged that heavy, thick work of art in her hands, watching him in the mirror over his shoulder as his long, rippling abdominal muscles tightened. If he tasted anywhere near as good as he looked, she could feast on him for days.

Her breath shortened, and her hands fisted. Part of her was horrified at what she was imagining.

Oh, not the sex fantasy part. The *Quentin* part.

She jerked her thoughts away from the image and cast about to focus on something else, anything else. Something excruciatingly boring. She thought of the paperwork piled up on her desk. She was already behind, and spending two weeks to a month away was only going to make it worse. Nobody was going to write those reports for her. It would all be waiting for her when she got back.

She wondered if there was anyone she could coax, coerce

or blackmail into doing them while she was gone. Off the top of her head, she couldn't think of anyone. With her and Quentin out of the picture, none of the sentinels back in New York would have the time, nor, after this morning's little stunt, would any of them have the inclination to help her out. Those reports were her karma.

Her sharp hearing picked up muted laughter from the nearby galley. A couple of the people laughing were feminine, and one was unmistakably Quentin. He wasn't doing anything interesting in the lavatory. He was flirting with the flight attendants.

The last of her lingering arousal soured into irritation. She twitched a shoulder, more annoyed with herself than with anything else. The longer he flirted with them, the longer he stayed away. They could have him.

Eventually Quentin came back and eased into his seat. Aryal kept her eyes closed. She sensed that he was looking at her. The touch of his gaze was almost physical, and the skin along her cheek tingled.

He shifted, a slight creak of leather boots and the brush of denim. She *knew* without looking that he was bending closer. She could feel the heat of his body, and her muscles tightened, twitching with the desire to smash her fist into his face.

Back off. *Back off.*

He whispered, "I know you're not sleeping."

The warm, moist breath from his words licked along her cheek in an invisible caress. It was intimate and sensual. It felt good.

Her body was a gun, and the desire for violence vibrated like a finger on the trigger. Just one good punch. One well-placed punch with the full weight of her body behind it would do a lot of damage to that sexy, treacherous face of his.

But it wouldn't be just one good punch. It would be a match to dry kindling, and there were too many innocent, vulnerable people surrounding them in quarters that were much too tight. She was going to have to wait.

She held still, not breathing. He hesitated then eased back into his seat. Then the hours scrolled by slowly, flowing over the plane's wings into the past, and they didn't speak again for the rest of the interminable flight.

Eight o'clock in the morning in Prague was as bleak as New York had been, the temperatures hovering just above freezing. The skies were overcast, gray streaked with pale light, and as the plane dropped in altitude and prepared to land, Aryal could see a light snow sprinkled on terra-cotta-colored rooftops and in fields surrounded by dense hedges and stone walls.

Disembarking was an excruciating process. They were on a Boeing 757 and Aryal guessed the plane had carried over two hundred and fifty passengers. When it came Quentin's turn, he slipped into the aisle and gestured for her to precede him.

Even though they were still surrounded by other people, she couldn't bring herself to put her back to him. "That's all right," she said. "You go ahead. I'll be off in a minute."

Watching her with a narrowed gaze, he inclined his head and moved forward when the line allowed. She waited until he was ten people ahead of her then slipped into line too.

They kept their distance from each other as they went through customs. Entering the Czech Republic was a longer, more involved process than leaving the States had been. Along with their passports, they had to provide documentation of their sentinel status, declare their weapons and purpose, submit their packs to a thorough check, and then wait for the Czech customs officers to make phone calls and independently verify their presence.

Aryal's temper was shredded by the time they were finished. She was tired, bitchy and starving, and her right fist was still stuffed full of that one good punch that she had not yet thrown. That fist kept asking her, *When? When?* She didn't know, other than that it needed to be outside of the airport, and preferably out of Prague itself.

If she were on vacation, she would have enjoyed playing tourist, touring Prague Castle and Old Town and drinking Czech beer, but Prague was just a leg on their journey. The crossover passageway to Numenlaur was located a couple of hours' drive away from the city, deep in the heart of the dense Bohemian Forest.

On her own, Aryal would shapeshift and fly the distance, but she didn't have the capacity to carry someone as large and heavy as Quentin for any kind of distance. Hands on her hips, she studied her enemy. He looked as tired and as irritable as she felt.

She said abruptly, "We need a hot meal, and we need to rent a car. We should pack some supplies in case we run into any issues with hunting for food, and right now I can hardly stand to look at you."

Quentin's lean features wore a sour look as he contemplated her. "Go rent a car and get something to eat," he said. "I'll get supplies. I know a good camping store, and there are Tesco grocery stores dotted throughout Prague. We're both predators, so I know you need a lot of protein too. Meet me in two hours southwest of here, at the junction of highways E48 and E50. We'll need to take E50 for the first half of the journey to the Forest."

She cocked her head. "You've been here before."

"I've toured Europe," he said, his tone short.

"Fine," she said, relieved he had come up with a solution that meant she could get a break from him. After all, working in partnership didn't mean they had to be joined at the hip. "Two hours."

He pointed at her. "Then we talk."

Oh yay. Her fist was ready for that conversation. She gave him a tight smile, flipped him off and strode away. After a quick look around the airport, she bought some Czech koruny, the local currency, as the Republic hadn't yet converted to the euro. Then she located the car rental companies and rented a Peugeot 207 Affaire from Europcar, which was supposed to be a van, but by American standards was just a hatchback. While at the rental counter she bought a map, and after consulting it, she drove through the narrow European streets until she had found the highway junction Quentin mentioned.

She stayed on local streets and cruised around, studying the area. A heavily industrial section lay spread out near the highway junction with what looked like warehouses, many of which were boarded up and had the appearance of long neglect. The gray day and half-melted snow didn't help matters. The whole scene looked dismal and bleak, and utterly deserted.

Deep in thought, she went on the hunt for some hot food. By then the local time was almost eleven o'clock. She found an old, crooked pub with dark, worn wooden tables and benches. The pub had just opened for the day's business, and she ordered a huge meal of a double helping of pork, potatoes and bread dumplings, and cooked cabbage, and she washed it all down with a beer from a local brewery. As both a predator and a large avian Wyr, she needed a lot of calories and she ate like a trucker. The hot food steadied her and sharpened her thinking.

Afterward she ordered three donutlike pastries called *koláče*, much to the fascination of her taciturn server. When she was finally through with eating, she ordered a second beer and nursed it between her hands, staring out a dirt-streaked window as she contemplated the upcoming "talk" with Quentin.

How in hell was she supposed to get along with him? She had no idea. If they tried to clear the air, they might just kill each other after all. If she sucked it all down and tried to pretend—well, she was horrible at pretending and hiding how she felt. She might as well go back to clearing the air again.

That led to killing, which she actually didn't have a problem with, except that *she* wasn't supposed to kill Quentin. She was supposed to find some outside agent in the guise of an act of God that was supposed to kill Quentin. Pushing her beer to one side, she thunked her head on the table. Argh, Dragos! How did this whole thing get so complicated?

Actually, she might feel bad about her whole plan except that she knew Quentin was a career criminal, a dangerous man who could not be trusted. Getting rid of him really would be the right thing for everybody.

A soft voice sounded at her elbow. "Miss, eat too much? Maybe need some plop plop, fizz fizz?"

She lifted her head and squinted at her well-meaning server, a middle-aged woman with a kind, apple-dumpling-soft face. "I'm fine, just exasperated."

"Oh, sorry," the woman said, looking apologetic. "No understand hisaxpillated."

As most ancient Wyr did, Aryal knew a variety of different languages, but she didn't know Czech. She pointed at her empty plates. "Good lunch."

The woman smiled and nodded. "Good!"

After Aryal paid for her meal, she thumbed on her iPhone. The cost of mobile roaming from Europe was astronomical, as much as two euros per minute or more, but it wasn't worth buying local phones in case someone from New York needed to get in touch with them. Besides, very soon, they would be headed into an area where cell phones wouldn't work.

She found Quentin's number and texted him the location of the pub. Then she settled back, watched out the streaked window and waited.

Ten minutes later a taxi pulled up to the pub. Quentin slid out of the backseat, his long, lithe body moving with his signature boneless grace. Not even the gryphons moved like he did, their heavy, muscular lion's bodies intermingled with the body of an eagle's. Quentin was sleek and sinuous, a racy Ferrari surrounded by bulky SUVs.

The harsh, gray daylight emphasized his strong bones and hard, closed expression. His cheekbones were two sharp arcs slicing across his face. His short, dark golden hair and bright blue eyes stood out against the colorless surroundings.

Aryal's heart pounded. She slid out of her seat and strode outside.

Quentin's frowning gaze connected with hers with a clash she felt all the way to her bones. She jerked her head at the rental, and he gave her a curt nod. The taxi driver had parked and stepped out to open the trunk of his car. Aryal unlocked the hatch of the Peugeot and stood back as the two men loaded supplies into the trunk.

Just as he had promised, Quentin had known exactly

where to shop, because not only had he bought food, but he had bought basic camping supplies as well. Packages containing two small dome tents, tarps and sleeping bags, and other gear went into the backseat. She thought she saw the tip of a liquor bottle in one of the bags. He had been fast and thorough.

After Quentin paid the driver, who left, he turned back to Aryal and held out his hand. "I know the route we need to take," he said. "I'll drive."

There it was again, his love of control.

"You can't," Aryal told him in a pious tone. "You're not on the rental policy. I drive."

Like she gave a fuck about the terms of the policy, but she did get a lot of satisfaction out of denying Quentin something. Yeah, she was just that petty.

His face tightened but he didn't bother to say anything. Instead, he pivoted and stalked to the car to slide into the passenger seat. She jingled the car keys in satisfaction and climbed in too.

Oh gods, the car was almost as bad as the plane had been. The small, enclosed space trapped the heat from their bodies together. Quentin's male scent washed over her, tantalizing, even addicting. Her traitorous body reacted to it even as her uncertain temper teetered at the edge of some kind of cliff and fell off.

She jammed the car into gear and gunned the engine. They shot down the street.

Quentin muttered a curse as he braced himself against the dashboard and yanked on his seat belt. "You're a goddamn menace."

"I know," she said almost happily as she headed for the warehouse area. Her fist tingled in anticipation.

They passed the entrance for the highway. Quentin twisted to stare at her. He said slowly, "You missed the turn."

She didn't bother to reply. Instead she pressed down on the gas pedal. They rocketed into the deserted area that she had found earlier. She could sense that Quentin's long, powerful body had gone combat tense. He was waiting for her to pull the car to a stop, his fast catlike reflexes poised to respond.

So she punched him before she stopped the car.

Her right fist shot out and caught him square in the jaw. The blow snapped his head to one side and slammed him against his door. Aryal stomped on the brake hard. The car slid to one side, tires squealing on the wet, slick pavement. She jammed the gear into park, shoved open her own door and rolled out before the car ever stopped skidding.

As quickly as she moved, Quentin was just as fast if not faster. As the car shrieked to a stop, he poured over the roof and leaped at her, his whole body moving with fluid power and his face, released from civilized constraints, transformed by fury.

Aryal feinted and danced out of his reach, as he made a grab for her. He missed, just barely, and the tips of his fingers slid lightly down her face and collarbone like a lover's caress. Her skin tingled from the contact, warm in the frigid wet air. Should she change and take to the air? Not yet. It felt too satisfying to get down and dirty with him here on the ground. *So dirty.*

She spun, bent at the waist and kicked backward. Her legs were powerful weapons, built for springing high into the air so that she could take flight from the ground. If she had made a solid connection on any part of his body, bones would have snapped.

Instead she only managed to kick air. Iron hands latched onto her ankle. Quentin heaved, and then she was airborne after all. He swung her like a bat at a baseball game, spinning backward. Wind whistled in her ears.

When he let her go, she flew into the corrugated metal of a closed warehouse door. The hollow boom echoed off the surrounding buildings as she slammed into the ground. A starburst of pain bloomed where she made contact with the wet concrete. If the maneuver had happened to almost anyone else, at the very least it would have knocked the breath out of them, but her rib cage and lungs were as powerful as her legs.

She coughed and rolled, pushing hard, hard, because *gods* he was fast. His boot caught her in the ribs before she could gain her feet. He kicked her so hard it lifted her into the air, and she slammed back into the metal door again.

She hit the ground a second time, only this time she landed on her hands and knees, and all her talons flicked out, switchblade fast. This was finally getting interesting.

She couldn't kid herself. He let her get to her feet. He stood poised on the balls of his feet in a boxer's stance, fists ready. She straightened slowly, watching his eyes. They were hard and flat, showing nothing of his intention.

He threw a high jab, aimed at her face.

She didn't try to block it or hit back. Instead she slid sideways as she grabbed his wrist, twisted at the waist and yanked. He had thrown his body weight forward in the punch, and she used that extension to propel him around so that he struck the corrugated metal door. He was tensing to gather himself for a spring even as his back hit, but she could have told him not to waste his effort.

It was too late. She had him.

Even as he impacted, she slammed his wrist into the door, all five of her talons splayed. They were strong enough to pierce metal, and that's what they did. She drove them through the door until she literally pinned his wrist, using her own hand as a handcuff. As he instinctively brought up his other hand to strike at her, she grabbed that wrist and drove her talons into the door, tightening the fingers of both hands. Her fingers were not as hard as her talons, and the torn metal cut into her flesh.

It was worth it.

Sharp incredulity twisted Quentin's face as he realized what had happened. He shouted in rage point-blank into her face as he tried to heave her away from him. It strained her grip through the metal of the door. He was immensely strong, and he might have been able to manage it in almost any other position, but with his arms splayed and her body pressed against him, he couldn't get enough leverage.

Her voice hoarse, she said, "That never would have worked if you had been any of the older sentinels. They would have known better than to try to trap me against this kind of door. It's one of those things you learn. If you live long enough."

He snarled wordlessly, his long, powerful body straining against hers, and it was every bit as glorious as when she sprawled on top of him at the sentinel party. Every bit, and more. He arched his back, pushing hard against the door so that fresh pain bloomed in her rigid hands, and he tried to knee her.

She wasn't as vulnerable down there as a male was, and again, he couldn't quite get enough purchase to knock her off of him. With an agile twist of her hips, she opened her legs and straddled his long, hard thigh as he shoved upward. He connected with her sex, not hard enough to bruise but enough to almost lift her off her feet.

She gave an almost soundless grunt and clamped her legs together on his thigh. He bared his teeth and shoved upward again. Even through the barrier of their clothes, the friction felt good. She didn't need anybody else to tell her how twisted that was. But he was all there, too close and personal, his muscles bunching and flexing underneath hers. The sound he made was raw and animalistic, and he was all trapped, all hers.

They were both breathing heavily. She let her eyes drift half closed as she looked at the strong line of his tanned throat and imagined licking it while his head was tilted back in supplication. Sexual heat flashed through her, stronger than ever before. Instinctively she tightened her legs on his thigh. It increased the friction, and a jolt of intense sensation pierced her body so that she sucked air.

Quentin was staring at her, his face savage. A hard length grew against the jutting bone of her hip. She froze as the delicious, addicting smell of his arousal wrapped around her, as warm as a silken blanket and as inevitable as a python's tightening coils.

Realization clunked her over the head. She had a feeling it had been trying to get her attention for a while now.

He was fighting the same unwelcome attraction for her as she was for him.

She laughed. Talk about twisted. There they were together,

tied up in their own little knot. She whispered, "You know, we ought to just have some hate sex already, and get it out of our system."

If she had thought his eyes were brilliant before, now they turned incandescent.

The erection pressing against her hip grew harder and longer. The air between them was so charged, they could light up the city for blocks around. It tingled across her nerve endings, raised the tiny hairs at the back of her neck.

Nobody had ever accused Aryal of having an excess of sanity. She deliberately pressed her hips against the hard length of his cock, causing friction for the both of them. They both hissed.

Quentin bent his head close to hers, his teeth bared. Even though she had him trapped, he was still very dangerous. She watched him warily. She knew he had some kind of magical training, and she held herself tensed for some kind of offensive spell.

But he didn't reach for any magic tricks. Instead he growled, "You may have me pinned at the moment, but you're trapped too. You can't do anything with your hands locked like that."

She twitched a shoulder. She could feel the blood pounding in his body. "I promise you, it's worth it."

He was breathing deeply, his gaze focused with laser intensity on her mouth. "I smell your blood."

"That's been worth it too," she whispered. Her hands were going numb. At this rate, she was going to have to work at getting them unclenched again.

He roared, "*WHAT IS IT GOING TO TAKE TO GET YOU TO BACK THE FUCK OFF!*"

Stray floating strands from her tangled hair blasted back from her face. She let her head fall back, carefully arched away from him so he could not strike at her throat with his teeth, and she laughed again. "I dunno, maybe a confession?"

"A confession." His gaze ran compulsively down the line of her throat as if he couldn't help himself, but his voice was flat, disbelieving. Then something seemed to snap inside of him. He snarled, "You want a confession? Fine. I broke the law. I broke it more than once. I broke it lots. I liked breaking the law. Are you fucking satisfied now?"

He caught her with her mouth hanging open, and every word he spoke was the truth. She shut her mouth with a snap. "Goddamn it, I *knew* it," she said softly. "What do you do, run a smuggling operation?"

"I don't run a smuggling operation. I *did*. In the past. I shut it down last year. You won't find any evidence, because there isn't any. I'm that good. Everything that happened is locked inside my head. Shipping manifests. Dates, times. I never put any of it on paper. I worked with a double-blind system. Nobody knew the other parties involved. Most of them didn't know they were smuggling."

She picked apart every word he said with her truthsense dialed high. Her eyes narrowed, she asked suspiciously, "Why did you stop?"

His chest heaved as he gave an explosive sigh. "Something bad happened. I tried to do something. I wanted to help out a friend and had good intentions, but I almost got a couple of people killed. After that, I pulled the plug on everything except the bar."

"So that's it—that's everything? That's all you did?" Everything except the *something* he had tried to do, at any rate. She asked hopefully, "No espionage?"

He snorted. "No."

She made a face. "No murder for hire? No spying?"

"Sorry to disappoint you," he snapped. "I made damn good money. That's it."

Good gods, he was telling the truth. She tried to disbelieve it anyway, but couldn't muster any conviction. It was . . . disappointing. She pressed, "What did you smuggle? Drugs? Human trafficking? Guns?"

He glared at her in exasperation. "Don't be so goddamn dramatic. Of course I didn't. I smuggled in liquor for the bar, gold and diamonds, some artwork. High-dollar stuff. I might have dabbled in some magic items from time to time."

She scowled. At the most he had cost the Wyr demesne

some tariff money, and a whole lot of her time. "If that's all you did, why the fuck didn't you just say so earlier?"

He sneered. "You've got to be kidding me."

She studied him, her mouth twisted with frustration. After all this time, that was it. He lost his temper bad enough to spit out the truth, and she didn't give a shit about any of it after all. She said, watching him closely, "You really gave it all up. You don't break the law in any way, anymore."

"No." Everything in his hard voice and face radiated the truth. "Not since before I decided to try out for the Games and committed to becoming a sentinel."

"Bah," she said in disgust. "How pathetic."

All that obsession, all that work. For what?

She forced her stiff fingers to open and wiggled them out of the holes her talons had torn into the door. Letting go of his wrists as she backed away, she shook out her aching hands and inspected the cuts on her fingers. They stung, but they weren't too bad. They would heal soon enough.

Quentin pushed away from the metal door immediately and didn't stop moving until he was several yards away. All the time he stared at her with narrowed eyes. "That's it," he said. "That's your whole reaction—'how pathetic'?"

She gestured impatiently. "I don't care about any of that shit."

Hands on his hips, he angled his head, the perfect image of a man who had been pushed too far. In a very quiet tone of voice, he said, "You. Don't. Care."

Was it something she said? She curled a nostril at him. "No, I don't."

He detonated.

≡ SIX ≡

Quentin's wrath took him outside of his body until he felt as if he hovered in the open area, an invisible spirit looking down at the two figures from above.

He roared, "What the fuck do you mean you don't care? What have the last two hellish years been for, IF YOU DON'T FUCKING CARE?"

Aryal stared at him as if he were a lunatic. "Well, I didn't know what you'd done, did I? You're a dangerous man. You proved that when you became a sentinel. I knew you did something, but I didn't know you did just *that*." She threw out her hands as she spoke, making a throwaway gesture. "I can't believe I wasted all that investigation time on a petty thief."

He was airborne before she had finished speaking the last words. In one giant leap, he was on her, his hands fastened around her throat again. The flying tackle knocked her flat on her back on a snowy patch of pavement. He sprawled on top of her, instinctively shifting so that he trapped her with the weight of his body.

He had never felt this way before, about anything or anyone. Someone was growling. Belatedly he realized that someone was him. He pounded her head on the pavement. "All. That. Time. All. That. Time."

He was vaguely aware that she had grabbed him by the throat too, the tips of her talons poised at his jugular. He should probably care about that.

She said in a choked voice, "In retrospect, we should have talked about this while I still had you pinned."

"You would make a pacifistic saint homicidal," he panted.

She burst out laughing.

He was strangling her. And she *laughed*.

Incredulity wormed its way into his rage-soaked brain. He stared down at her.

Her angular face was suffused with color, those stormy gray eyes dancing. Her black hair spread out in a sulfurous fan, gleaming dark against the white snow. She didn't care that his tightening fingers cut off her air supply any more than he cared that her hand was poised to tear out his throat.

His gaze focused on her mouth. She had a kind of strong femininity that was completely unlike the bright artifice and colors that so many modern women employed. No makeup, no jewelry, no fancy stuff done to her hair, and no floaty, flouncy clothes. Nothing about her looks took after conventional beauty, but her mouth was exquisitely formed, the bold lines of her lips softened by generous, curving flesh.

We all recognize something of our own wildness in you. Who had said that? Grym. Her lover.

"You and Grym can't be mates," he growled. "Someone would have said something if you were." She would have been much more stressed at the thought of a month's banishment from New York. Mates did not thrive well without each other.

If anything, she laughed harder. "You're still an idiot."

He had to do something to shut her up, or he really was going to kill her. The pure, hot flame of his fury shifted. The extreme emotion had torn him wide open, and a maelstrom of sexual aggression screamed in. The muscles in his body felt paper-thin, barely able to contain the emotion.

Shifting his hands to fist them in the thick, silken hair at the back of her head, he lunged down to conquer her reckless, anarchistic mouth.

He felt the surprise jolt through her body as his lips locked over hers. She lay flat underneath him *where she belonged*, and he didn't coax, tease or entice as he would have with any other woman. He took. Breathing heavily, he forced her mouth open and plunged deep inside with his hardened tongue. His body, his mind, were all on fire. Dimly, a small part of him, the cool intellectual part that wasn't wholly driven by his internal whip, grew a little thoughtful about his lack of control.

Aryal growled, a husky wild note that shuddered over his skin and went straight for his cock, and she kissed him back savagely. They ate at each other as if they were still fighting.

Their surroundings could hardly be any worse. It was chill, damp, and they were sprawled on the hard pavement and out in the open. Anyone could come along and see them at any time.

None of it mattered. Images ran through his mind like molten lava. He wanted to flip her over, get her in a headlock and hold her there, strip down her jeans and take her in the ass.

Hard and rough, baby. No holds barred, no ritualized courtesy and no safe word, just pure animal rut. He wanted to dominate the shit out of her and make her scream while she lost everything to her own climax.

She shifted the hand from his throat to grip the back of his head.

He knocked her hand away and snarled against her lips, "Don't touch me."

Her eyes flashed. She bit his lip hard, and he reared his head back. A thin, warm trickle tickled his skin. She'd drawn blood.

"What's the matter with me touching you?" she asked. Her gaze turned challenging. "Do you like it too much?"

She was too accurate. She saw too much.

She was a demon, Lucy Ricardo on crack.

"Hate sex," he said. He didn't recognize the sound of his own voice.

Get it out of his system. Exorcise her from his mind and body.

Fuck yeah.

"You want it," she said.

He became aware of what they were doing. She had wrapped those long legs of hers around his waist so that their pelvises aligned through the layers of their clothing. She had wrapped her Power around him too, and it felt hot and keen like a slicing, summer wind. They were rocking together in a pagan rhythm that echoed the coursing in his blood. He had palmed one of her breasts, gripping the slight, high mound through her sweater.

His eyes narrowed. "You want it too."

Her expression mocked him. "Don't let it go to your head. Just your penis."

He almost laughed, but the verbal sparring had brought his thinking back online and he remembered his rage instead. He thrust away from her with a muttered curse. Her legs loosened from around his waist, and he rolled to his feet.

Aryal stood too, shaking off the snow from her back and stamping her boots. He watched as she walked over to a clean patch of snow and scooped a little into her hands. She gritted her teeth as she washed the blood from her fingers. The cuts were already closed, but they looked angry and red, and she moved her hands like they pained her.

Served her right. Driving her talons *through* a metal door? He shook his head and strangled the impulse to be impressed, as he swiped at his knees, knocking snow off too. Some had melted, and his jeans had two wet patches that felt cold and clammy. She would have wet patches all down her back.

Then he anchored his hands on his hips. Instead of murdering her, he had determined to actually try to have things out with her once and for all, but by gods, she didn't make anything easy.

"I'm back to my original question," he growled.

"Are you?" The glance she gave him was full of indifference. "That's probably not very pleasant."

"What the fuck? Seriously, just answer me. *You owe me that*. For so long you have been riding my ass every which way you could. When I finally say screw it and tell you what you've been angling to hear all this time, the only response you've got is to say, 'meh, don't care.' All of this is after making so much racket about me being a career criminal. Believe me, I'm used to you being crazy, but that has a disconnect that makes no sense even for you."

"Not at all," she said. She finished cleaning her hands, shook off the snow and turned to face him, mirroring his stance. The thing was, when he looked into her eyes, the whack-job harpy appeared to be quite lucid. At the moment she looked amused again. "You being a criminal—that was important, because that was how I was going to trap you. I don't actually care that you broke the law, Quentin. I don't actually care much about the law, period."

He raised his eyebrows skeptically. "You have a funny way of showing it."

She twitched her shoulders, as if shaking off an irritating fly. "What I care about is whether or not you have endangered the Wyr demesne. Smuggling some high-dollar luxury items? So we didn't get some tax revenue we should have gotten. Big fucking deal. If you go after Dragos—if you do anything to actively try to hurt any of the people I care about—that's when I will come after you, and I won't stop until I hurt you bad, or you end up dead, or maybe even both of those things. That's my bottom line. It's really quite simple."

He spun away from her sharply to stare out over the abandoned area without really seeing it, his explosive rage easing back down to a simmer. One way or another, it always came back to Dragos. She would hate to know what he had done last year, and he had no intention of telling her.

"Why Dragos?" he murmured, almost to himself. "He and the Wyr demesne are two different things. Dragos could die and the demesne would go on." He looked over his shoulder at her. "I'm speaking theoretically."

"Some form of the demesne would go on," she said. She shook her head. "It wouldn't be the same. And it wouldn't be as strong. I will never forget what Dragos did when he united the Wyr. No one else could have done it. I'm well aware that you don't like him, but whatever else you may say, no one else can do the job he does. He's got the strength, the ambition and ruthlessness, and he's got the financial acumen. Forcefulness and prosperity. That's a hell of a combination. Hell, you were there this morning too. We're two of the best Wyr fighters in the world, and he stomped our asses."

That he had.

Somehow they had managed to move away from the craziness, the violence and the sex, and they were almost having a rational conversation. Quentin wasn't sure what to make of it, except he was a long way from trusting it, or her. He rubbed his aching jaw where she had punched him and laughed under his breath.

He had to give it to her, she'd made some moves he hadn't seen coming. He wasn't about to underestimate her again. He tilted his head as he turned back to her, and he gave her a catlike smile. "Listen to us," he said. "If someone didn't know any better, they might think we were almost close to making a truce."

An evil gleam crept into her narrowed gaze. "A truce?" she said. "Just because we smacked each other around, did a little bump and grind and exchanged more than three words at a time? Fuck, no."

That internal whip that drove him?

Sometimes it felt good.

He purred, "There we go."

She still refused to let him drive, even though he knew she didn't care about the rental policy. There was nothing more infuriating than someone who was being pedantic about something you know they don't give a damn about.

She drove back to the highway entrance, and in a matter of moments they were moving southwest toward the Bohemian Forest. He made a mistake once. He didn't make it twice. He wasn't about to ride shotgun without a seat belt on while she was in the driver's seat.

Prague and the immediate surrounding area were densely urban, but once they traveled beyond a certain point they were surrounded by scenes of almost desolate beauty, the countryside washed of all its colors in the wintry day. It was as if a giant, unseen hand had taken all the smog from the industrialized area and smeared it over the landscape.

Quentin knew better. He had traveled through the Czech Republic in finer weather and remembered the blue skies, green fields and richly hued lakes.

They traveled in silence for a while. Neither one of them reached to turn on the radio. The heat from their earlier passion lingered, like half-seen coals in a banked fireplace. Images of what happened kept flashing in his mind's eye. The way she had tricked him and pinned him against the metal door, her lean body pressed against his. The way he had slammed her into the ground and held her, hands around her throat.

His hand on her breast. Her thighs clamped on his. Her body undulating underneath him.

It disturbed him, but not because they were so violent.

Because he wanted to do it again.

He felt like something dark at his core, something that he had kept leashed all his life, had broken loose and was running renegade. He, who took control whenever he could, didn't feel in control of himself at all. He shifted restlessly in his seat. When he glanced at her Aryal was frowning, lost deep in thought.

She broke the silence first. "Dragos had said that to the best of his knowledge, Numenlaur had only one crossover passageway, the one that led here to Earth that was barred so long ago. But the Numenlaurian army was in the Lir-ithriel Elves' Other land when we confronted them, so is there really only one crossover passageway from Numenlaur or does it connect to that Other land as well?"

When the Earth had been formed, time and space had buckled, creating Other lands that were connected to Earth and sometimes to each other by dimensional crossover passageways. They were magic-rich places where combustible technologies didn't work, and where time ran differently than it did on what Quentin liked to think of as the mainland.

Sometimes the Other lands were immense, as was the Dark Fae land of Adriyel, and they had several crossover passageways to other places. Sometimes the Other lands were mere pockets of space that led nowhere.

Quentin's eyes still felt dry from the sleepless night and the long flight. He rubbed them as he said, "Dragos is right. Numenlaur does only have one passageway."

She sent him a frowning glance. "You know this for sure, how?"

"I talked to Ferion when I went to get supplies," he told her. As she turned her head to look at him fully, he added irritably, "Don't get pissy about it, and keep your eyes on the road. I wasn't selling state secrets. Dragos never said anything about keeping our assignment under wraps."

She looked like he had stuffed a slice of lemon in her mouth, but after a moment she grumbled, "Fair enough. I wasn't aware that you had a personal connection to the new High Lord."

"It's not a close connection," he said. "We're family by marriage."

"It's close enough that you were able to get him on the phone," she pointed out.

He pressed his thumb and forefinger against his closed eyelids until he saw red stars. "When I was younger, we spent some time together, took vacations and went hunting, that sort of thing. Now that he's become the High Lord, I think getting him on the phone is going to become harder and harder to do over time."

She mulled that over. "I've heard that Ferion was the late High Lord Calondir's son, but is he Beluviel's son too? It takes two to make a baby, and the woman has the more significant role in the process by far, but at some point Beluviel always disappears from the conversation."

"Ferion is not Beluviel's son," he said. "He was born a long time ago. I don't know the whole story, other than

Beluviel and Calondir hadn't always gotten along. They had been living separate lives when Ferion was born. Later, they came back together when the Elven demesne was formed in what became the United States, and they stayed a strong partnership ever since, at least in a public and political sense. I can't speak to the reality in their private lives."

Aryal pursed her lips. "Since Beluviel was Calondir's consort, why didn't she become the High Lady, or whatever she would have been called?"

He shrugged. "Like I said, I'm not on the inside of that family circle, but from what I've heard, Beluviel didn't want to become Lady of the Lirithriel Elves."

"Pity," she said. "I don't have anything against Ferion, but I've always liked Beluviel." She glanced at him. "So what did he say when you talked to him?"

"Dragos was right, Ferion's overextended. He has thought of Numenlaur but has not had a chance to do anything more than send a small party of Elves to guard the passageway. He also sent some trackers over Lirithriel's Other land to trace the path of the Numenlaurian army back to its source."

"Why?"

"He wanted to make sure that Gaeleval hadn't abandoned any enthralled Elves who might have been too sick or injured to keep up with the rest of the army."

Aryal winced. "Do you know if they found anybody?"

"Nobody alive," he said grimly.

She swore quietly.

Quentin took a deep breath. "Anyway, Numenlaur isn't the only crossover passageway in the Bohemian Forest. There's one that leads to the Lirithriel Other land too."

Aryal frowned. "I guess I'm not surprised. There may be even more than those two passageways. The Bohemian Forest is a very old and witchy place. Not sentient like Lirithriel Wood was before it burned, just witchy."

Quentin understood what she meant. The Bohemian Forest, called *Šumava* by the Czechs, was actually a low mountain range that extended from the Czech Republic to Austria and Germany, and the area held one of the oldest forests in the world.

Quentin had spent some time hiking there when he was younger. At first he had gone to look where the fabled Numenlaurian passageway was rumored to have stood, but the magic used in barring the passageway hid it from outside eyes and he was never certain he had found where it was supposed to have been located.

He told her, "Well, Gaeleval took advantage of the proximity of the two passageways. He marched his army out of Numenlaur, through the forest, and then into the Lirithriel Other land through the second passageway. Nobody here on Earth knew a thing."

"If Ferion's got Elven guards on the Numenlaurian passageway, then our assignment is little more than in name only," Aryal said. She blew out a sigh. "Well, the main part the assignment isn't. More than half the reason Dragos sent us here was to get rid of us."

Quentin angled out his jaw. He couldn't deny it. He looked sideways at the same moment Aryal did. He was immensely surprised when they both burst out laughing at the same time.

It felt strange, almost good, like they shared a moment of camaraderie. His laughter faded and he scowled at the thought. "We may not be doing any of this for Ferion, but he's glad we're going to check on the passageway. He asked me to give him an update when we get back. There's no cell phone reception in the forest, and he hasn't heard anything from the guards since they went in."

Her eyebrows rose. "How long ago was that?"

"He didn't say exactly, but from the gist of the conversation, I think it had to have been at least three weeks ago." Quentin tried to straighten his legs as much as he could. His muscles were protesting sitting for so long in such confined spaces.

"And he hasn't heard from them since?" She shook her head. "Sloppy. They should have sent someone out with an update by now."

He sighed. "Yes, an update would have been good, but you don't know that it was sloppy. They might have found some need to cross over to Numenlaur. If that happened, then you've got to factor in time slippage from the Other land. Ferion didn't sound too worried. He'll just be glad to hear how things are going."

After that they fell silent again, as if talking with some kind of civility had been enough of a strain that they couldn't sustain it any longer. Just over an hour into the journey, a bit south of Plzeň, they switched highways to continue in a more southern direction that would take them to the northern edge of the Forest. After passing through another urban cluster, they passed quickly into countryside again.

The Forest was growing in popularity as a vacation destination, and it had several camping grounds along with ski resorts. They would be able to drive in a fair distance before they would have to park and hike.

Still, Aryal had to slow the Peugeot as the roads grew narrow and winding. The amount of traffic dropped to almost nonexistent. Even though the low surrounding mountains were streaked with patches of white, probably both ski resorts and campgrounds were all but deserted. The weather was too warm for satisfactory snow cover for skiing, but too cold and damp for all but the hardiest of campers.

Aryal spoke, disrupting the long silence. "If I was on my own, I would have taken to the air by now, and I would scout for the passageways by feeling for land magic."

Quentin rubbed his face. "It might still be useful if you did that when we got closer." He looked at her over his hand. "I just realized you're old enough to remember the time before Numenlaur closed itself off from the world."

It was sometimes easy to forget how much older the other sentinels were than Quentin, including Alex, who had made passing references before to ancient Grecian wars as if he had lived through them—and no doubt he had. Wyr tended to live very much in the present, more so than almost all the other Elder Races. Quentin had thought before that it must have something to do with their animal natures.

"Sure, I'm old enough," she said. "But the world is a very big place, and I had no interest in what Elves were up to. I've never been near the passageways here."

He almost asked her what she had been interested in, all

that long ago, before he remembered he could hardly stand to hear the sound of her voice and caught himself.

Instead, he said, "Ferion confirmed that the Numenlaur passageway is very near where the stories say it is. That means I've been through that area before. We'll have to park at one of the camping sites and hike in."

"All right." She paused. "I suppose we've passed the point where we might be able to stop at a farmhouse and rent rooms."

Quentin rubbed his face. "Yes. We've got two options for tonight. There's a turnoff soon for a ski resort. It might be open, if you want to try there. Or we can rough it."

Amusement flashed over her face, keen and bright like a blade. "I like roughing it."

Pow, the banked sexuality that smoldered between them came roaring back to the surface. It filled the interior of the car. He listened to the tiny sound of her breathing, the subtle friction of air as she shifted in her seat.

She was squirming.

He knew exactly what he would have done if they hadn't been in a moving vehicle. He would have advanced on her, pushed her back against some kind of surface. He would have taken her chin, tilted her head back and bitten her throat.

He just didn't know whether he would have done it before or after he kissed her.

"*Hate sex,*" he hissed.

Her eyes flashed to him. She looked furious, or agonized.

He ran his hands through his short hair and stretched, deliberately arching his back. Her hands clenched on the steering wheel so that the knuckles showed white.

He laughed, low and soft. She started it. By damn, it was good to know he got under the harpy's skin just as much as she got under his.

She was good at shock value, he would give her that. The things that fell out of her mouth were sometimes as raw as the punch she had thrown at him earlier.

Maybe the idea was growing in its appeal now that it had been with him for a few hours. If he wouldn't let himself kill her, he could at least screw her until they were both senseless.

Then maybe he would get rid of whatever poison she had injected into his system.

His hands fisted as he remembered the feel of that taut, tight body of hers pinning him against the warehouse door. Nobody had ever pinned him, aroused him, and then laughed in his face before. He owed her for that. Hard and raw.

Her life was one eternal rampage. Maybe it was time someone turned the tables on her and went after her with the same kind of relentlessness with which she went after the entire world.

And maybe it was past time that someone took that harpy down a peg or two, and showed her who was boss.

⇒ SEVEN ⇐

By the time Aryal finally parked the car in a gravel parking lot at a deserted campsite, it was late afternoon and clouds obscured the nearby mountain peaks. Tantalizing hints of land magic had begun to tickle at her senses for the last half hour or so of the drive. She longed to take flight and hunt for the elusive feeling, soar over the mountain range and kick her feet in the thick clouds.

The day had warmed enough to melt the patchy snow at the lower altitudes, but sunset came early in March in the Czech Republic, and the temperature was already falling again. When she opened the car door, the damp chill air was like a cold, wet washcloth slapping her in the face. The fresh air smelled wonderful, and it felt good and bracing, but it wasn't enough to cool the heat pouring through her body.

Grateful to be out of the confinement of the car at last, she stretched her aching back. Instantly an image of Quentin stretching in the car flashed in her mind. He looked like a great, lazy cat as he did it, his blue eyes vivid in his tanned face. He smelled like virility and feline Wyr. The scent got up her nose and made her crazy. Her Wyr side wanted to claw at him. Hell, her human side wanted to claw at him too.

Gods, this had turned into a long trip already, and they were only on the first day. And she had lost her only comfort, the conviction that everybody would be better off if she just committed a quiet, itsy-bitsy little murder.

Aryal flew by her instincts, and every instinct had screamed for so long that Quentin was a dangerous man. And he *was* dangerous. Not many creatures could get her down on the ground with their hands around her throat.

Had she let that skew her perspective? Is that why she had pursued him so relentlessly? After all, a dangerous man would make an exceedingly dangerous criminal.

But he had been telling the truth earlier, and so had she— she really didn't care about the smuggling he had done. If she pushed it and continued to squander her time digging into his past, maybe she could get enough evidence to kick him out of his sentinel position, but what would it cost her?

He was already well liked, and he was Pia's special *friend*. And Aryal had taken sober note of not only Dragos's words, but of Grym's as well, along with the cold assessing way that Graydon had looked at her when she had gone to talk to him in the cafeteria. She had already used up all of her considerable free rein with not only Dragos, but with almost everybody else too. She was riding high on everyone's annoyance radar and low on tolerance. Nobody's first impulse was going to be to give her any slack.

So she spent the drive doing something she rarely did, which was considering the possible consequences of her actions. The exercise hurt her brain and offended her nature. But the bottom line was, all that effort and upheaval would be to pin him for crimes that she didn't give a shit about anyway. Gah, if only he had been a spy, or involved in some super secret assassination plot against Dragos or somebody else she loved!

At least she didn't have to give up her hate on him. She just had to give up the whole "hunting for an act of God to squash him like a bug so she could innocently present his crushed and lifeless body to Dragos" plan.

She had to admit, that did make life a lot simpler.

And besides, giving up on the plan was one thing. She could still hurt him a whole lot if he gave her any reason to. She cheered at the thought.

They were going to have to leave the car, maybe for some time, so she had parked in an unobtrusive spot underneath some trees for whatever shelter that might offer from the elements. As she looked around, she noted that the camp-site had permanent metal grills for cooking. Probably small animals had built nests in half of them. She preferred set-ting up her own fire ring.

It was early to stop for the day, but there was also no reason to wreck themselves. This land was beautiful, but it would not be friendly terrain in mid-March, and it was not like they could push hard, finish their assignment and go home early. And Dragos had already said they couldn't show up again in New York before two weeks were up.

They'd already had a sleepless night and a transconti-nental flight, and Aryal had eaten only one full meal since yesterday. Granted it was a big meal, but her body was tell-ing her that it was ready for another one.

Quentin had exited the car too. He studied the scene with one arm resting on the car roof. Lifting his head, he scented the breeze. He said, "There are wolves in these mountains."

Sentinel or no, a large enough pack of any kind of pred-ator could bring one of them down, but the wolves weren't really a threat to either her or Quentin. Any wolves would sense that they were the more dangerous predators and normally give them a wide berth. A wild pack would have to have an overriding reason to attack them.

She could also take to the air and leave behind any con-frontation, and if Quentin couldn't outrun them, he could go to high ground, maybe climb a tree, and wait them out. The weather wasn't bitter enough to turn any wild pack desperate enough to tree him for days until *he* became des-perate enough to take them on.

But wolves could become a nuisance, especially when they cooked food, so they would still need to stay wary. She said briskly, "We should set up camp."

He tilted his head from side to side, stretching his neck muscles. "All right. I did the bulk of the work this morning, so I'm going to take off and see if I can hunt down some fresh game for supper. You can set up camp."

"Hey!" she exclaimed. Hunting was the fun chore.

He didn't stay to argue with her. Instead he shapeshifted into a massive black panther and after one expressive glance at her, he glided away. She made a face, looked around at the deepening dusk and set to work.

She was tempted to erect just one tent and claim it, but if he came back with fresh meat, she wanted some, so she set up a proper camp with a tarp strung between two trees in case of rain or snow, and the two dome tents set on more tarps on opposite sides of a ringed campfire. Modern materials made camping a breeze. The dome tents were light, portable, and erected within five minutes.

Not only had Quentin bought sleeping bags, but he also had picked up thin insulating pads that would protect them from the bitter chill of the ground. They weren't as comfortable as air mattresses, but they weren't as heavy and bulky either. Everything he had bought was top of the line and lightweight for serious, long-distance hiking.

The most time-intensive thing was gathering wood for a campfire. She worked on that quickly, and after she had gathered deadwood from the immediate area, she jogged around the larger campsite to see if anybody had left wood behind from the previous season.

She was in luck and found a couple of armloads. She hauled them back to camp, started the fire, and opened the bottle of twenty-six-year-old scotch she had found in one of the bags in the car. As she took her first pull from the bottle, the black panther slipped out of the gathering darkness, two winter hares in his mouth.

Reflected light from the new flames flickered in the panther's strange, brilliant blue eyes and gleamed along his glossy black pelt. He was an oddity in that his Wyr form was so black, yet in his human form, his hair was a dark blond. It was probably a product of his mixed-race heritage. As he padded toward her, his heavy, graceful muscles flowed underneath his skin, causing the light to ripple along his long, powerful body.

The skin at the back of her nape prickled. This was why she was so convinced he was dangerous. If she dove at him as a harpy, he had the speed, power and size to snatch her out of the air.

She refused to let her reaction show, so she sniffed, took another swig from the bottle and told the panther, "You're the one who wanted to hunt. You'd better not be bringing those to me to clean. The fire's going to be ready in a few minutes. Hop to it." The panther stared at the bottle of scotch then up at her with an unblinking gaze. She shooed him with one hand. "Go on, you stinky cat."

The panther let the hares fall to the ground, then he shape-shifted into a crouching man who was every bit as dangerous as the animal. He said pointedly, "That is not your scotch."

Up until that very moment, she'd had every expectation of sharing the bottle with him. After all, sharing resources was what camping mates did, but his attitude spun her in a sharp one-eighty.

"Of course it is. I found it, didn't I?" She took another long swig, capped the bottle and tucked it securely under one arm. Then she pointed out, "I set up your tent. I didn't have to."

He glanced around at the camp she had made. "That was not worth a twenty-six-year-old bottle of scotch," he said. Still, he scooped up the hares and strode off, returning very soon with the carcasses skinned and cleaned.

By then the flames were burning steadily. She had already constructed a roasting spit from forked branches, with a third branch set across the fire. In no time, they had the hares set on the spit.

The wind had turned bitter as the last of the light fled, but the campfire threw off light and heat, and the liquor was a smooth fire that slid like golden lava down her throat. Aryal knew Wyr urbanites who would shudder at having to spend the night out in weather conditions like this, but they had been tamed so much by civilization, they had grown soft and dependent on modern conveniences.

She didn't understand those Wyr. They had lost part of their souls, or bartered them away for their flat screens and hot tubs, electricity and refrigeration, and deadbolts that kept out other things but most importantly locked them in.

She *loved* the night.

After their supper had been set to cook, Quentin straightened from his crouch, turned and glowered at her. "Hand it over."

He looked moody and pissed. But then he always looked moody and pissed around her. It always startled her whenever he smiled at anyone else. First, that he was capable of smiling at all, and second, that he looked so damn good when he did it.

Why did she feel the compulsion to constantly rile him? Honestly, she wasn't contrary *all* of the time, just usually around people who made her crazy. She shook her head. "Finders keepers. Possession's nine-tenths of the law. And besides, I don't want to."

"I hate you," said Quentin, "so goddamn passionately."

She shook her head and tsked. "You young Wyr feel everything too much—"

This time he didn't launch at her. Instead he advanced on her slowly, his eyes full of intent. She smiled as she uncapped the scotch and held it up to her mouth.

He snatched at it, hooked his fingers around the bottom of the bottle and kept her from drinking. She pulled and he pulled, and amber liquid sloshed out of the top.

"I'm curious," said Quentin. "Is every harpy like you?"

She braced herself and tugged harder on the bottle. She couldn't budge it from his grasp. More liquid sloshed out. "We're pretty rare," she said cheerfully. "I'm considered one of the more sociable ones. Most harpies don't tolerate living in society well. They get around too many people, and they get all whacked-out and slashy."

"Sociable." He barked out a laugh and advanced more, until the bottle was sandwiched between their torsos. He gripped the bottle neck, his hands sandwiching hers.

She tilted her head and assessed him. Hell if she was going to retreat just because he decided to get all aggressive and push into her personal space. Heat came off him in waves. It felt more delicious than the heat from the fire.

She said softly, "What are you doing, Quentin?"

"Honestly," he said, just as softly. "What does Grym see in you anyway?"

She exploded. "How many times are you going to bring that up? *We're not lovers!* Grym and I are friends. Here's a newsflash for you. I. Do. Have. Friends. Maybe that concept is a little difficult for you to grasp."

He put a hand over her mouth.

It brought his scent up close and personal under her nose. His palm felt hard and callused against her lips. She almost licked it to find out if his skin was salty.

She said telepathically, *That's got to be one of the more stupid gestures I've ever seen.*

He growled, "But it looks so pretty."

She remembered the woman who had been with him, soft and feminine, handcuffed and obedient. What would it be like to give control over to him? To feel his powerful body moving over hers, in hers, while he did anything he liked to her? Anything at all.

In her case, he'd probably take the opportunity to throttle her again.

What would it be like if he gave control over to her? Her skin prickled, a hot shivering sensation.

She jerked her mouth away from his hand and heard herself saying, "I was going to kill you."

Well, she hadn't exactly planned on admitting that. She watched his lean face warily as he laughed, a low wicked chuckle that vibrated through the bottle between them.

His gaze had turned reckless. "I was going to kill you too."

Her eyebrows rose. "You might have tried."

Actually he might have succeeded, just as she might have. There had never been a time when sentinel had fought against sentinel. Each of them had highly individualized talents. Even the gryphons' talents differed from each other. But they were all comparable in terms of strength, agility and cunning.

He tugged again at the bottle and this time, losing interest in the tug of war, she let go. He took a long pull. She watched the long muscles of his throat work as he drank. When he finished, he said, "I still might try."

Her smile turned mocking. Was this their version of détente? He wouldn't be talking about it, if he really meant to try. Neither one of them would. They wouldn't give away that much of their intentions. She told him, "Now you're just flirting."

Fat from the cooking meat dripped onto the fire and it hissed. One corner of his sexy mouth hooked up as, moving at a leisurely pace, he turned away from her.

She nearly grabbed him by the jacket and yanked him around to face her again, but she controlled the predatory impulse and watched as he squatted to turn the hares on the spit. He splashed both hares with the liquor. It caused the flames to flare up, searing the meat.

She liked the sight of him on his knees. She would like it better if his head were tilted back in supplication. The alpha male, subjugated to her.

She didn't know why the impulse to change into her Wyr form took her over. She just did it, and walked up behind him. Even though she was silent, his back tensed. He was aware of her every move.

She reached out to trace the shell of his ear with a talon. "You like to dominate pretty, soft girls," she whispered. "The hors d'oeuvres. It feeds something macho inside, doesn't it? Makes you feel like a big, strong man." He turned his head to stare up at her, the firelight gilding his hair. She stroked very lightly at the sensitive whorls inside his ear and smiled as she watched the shudder that shook through his body. "You play such pretty games. A strip of leather, toy handcuffs. None of it is real. You would never dare to really give up control yourself, would you? You don't have it in you."

He glanced at her wings and down her body. His face blazed with something hotter than the fire. Deliberately he straightened to his feet and looked at her. He said, "You have no idea what I would do, or what I would dare."

Her wings flared out. With a forefinger, she pressed the

razor-sharp tip of her talon against the curve of his lower lip. Pressed very gently, until a single ruby drop of blood welled.

He never moved or turned away. All his bones stood out, the shadows accentuated with the force of whatever it was he felt.

The harpy leaned forward and licked the drop of blood away. His blood tasted rich and heavy, and his lips tasted like whiskey.

She smiled, barely containing the hectic urge to hurtle into space. "I dare you to give up control to me," she said.

"That's twice you've drawn my blood," he said between his teeth. "I owe you something for that."

She had no way of knowing what he was feeling, only that it was something powerful enough to cause him to breathe heavily, as if he had been running for a very long time. He licked his own lip, touching his tongue where hers had already gone.

And he smelled like sex again, hot and sultry, and more intoxicating than any liquor. She hissed, *"I dare you to give it up."*

His eyes flared as he took her by the chin. His claws had come out. "I'll take that dare," he growled. "Just as soon as you give up control to me."

Her laughter pealed out over the clearing. She yanked her chin out of his hold. Then she gave in to the desire to leap into the night. She winged away from the clearing without looking back.

No one controlled the harpy.

No one.

Quentin ate both hares, because, screw it. If Aryal chose not to stick around, she forfeited any supper he had caught and cooked.

Then he sat with his head in his hands. Every now and then he fed logs into the fire and took pulls off the bottle of scotch. A fitful wind gusted through the trees overhead. They didn't get any rain or snow, but the weather in the

Bohemian Forest at this time of year was unpredictable at best, and that situation could turn in a matter of minutes.

Him, give up control. To Aryal.

It was the most self-destructive, cockamamie idea he'd ever heard.

Yet as he faced the harpy, his reaction to her had been more uncontrolled than ever.

He had never before been so close to her when she was in her Wyr form. The sight of her took his breath away. She was still recognizable as Aryal, but her features had become more upswept and pronounced. Her piercing eyes would be able to pick out prey from miles, and good gods, those wings. They spread out behind her in a huge fan. Short, dark gray feathers covered the tops of the wings, close to the powerful humerus bones that held them aloft. They darkened down the wing to the long primary feathers that were pure black.

Like her face, the racy, slim bone structure and musculature of her nude body was accentuated. Her slight high breasts were tipped with small nipples, and from the waist downward, her hips and long legs were covered in small gray feathers that looked like they might be soft. He wondered what she would do if he ran a hand down her thigh.

If only she wasn't so goddamn magnificent.

She looked alien and completely wild, and then she had leaped into the air, defying gravity. That was when he got it, when he really understood what Grym had meant, because he didn't just grasp it with his head. He felt it with his gut.

She didn't fit the concept of what a modern female should be like, and that made her even more annoying to a modern, entitled male such as he. She didn't defer to his opinion or mask her own spiky personality to fit the concept of any modern behavior, because she wasn't modern. She was truly one of the most ancient and wildest of creatures.

The fact was, she had probably already curbed herself in some way to fit in at the Tower as much as she did. For the most part, she kept her slashes down to verbal jabs and her predatory instincts focused on her investigations. The rest of her was just plain ornery.

He chuckled without much amusement. He couldn't even say that he had just grown obsessed with her, because he had already been obsessed with her for some time. Now that his obsession had turned sexual, he couldn't seem to turn it off. Or maybe it had been sexual all along, and he had only just come to realize it.

She had been right. He had never given up sexual control to anybody else. What would it be like to give it up to her, that pure, wild creature? It was never going to happen, so he would never know.

The nape of his neck prickled, and instinct made him tilt back his head and look at the cloudy night sky. There a gorgeous nightmare spiraled, wings outspread to their fullest as she cocked her head and looked down at him.

How long had she been up there, circling overhead and watching him?

His body clenched. The panther in him wanted to leap at her and drag her down to earth. The man wanted to cover her with his body, and make her give all of that purity and wildness over to him.

She came down and landed a short way away from the trees, snapped her wings back, and shapeshifted into her human form. Then she strode into the camp. She must have flown high, because her black hair sparkled with wetness.

She seemed centered somehow, revitalized. Flying for her must be what taking to his panther form and running in the woods did for him. That was when he had an epiphany.

She had a whip that drove her, just as he did.

She squatted in front of the fire without saying anything. They sat in silence for some time. Oddly enough, it was almost companionable.

Quentin looked at the scotch. The liquid was significantly low in the bottle. What the hell. He offered it to her, and after a moment's hesitation, she took it.

"When you spied on me in my bedroom," he said, "you liked it."

She cocked her head at that, considering it for a moment before she shrugged. She drank a mouthful of scotch and passed the bottle back to him. "I loved your cock. The woman and the toys annoyed me."

He burst out laughing, and a smile hovered at the corners of her mouth. "I'll confess," he said. "The woman and the toys annoyed me too."

Aryal looked at him sideways. "Then why do it?"

He took a deep breath and straightened his back. It was a good question.

Why did he do it?

He could have said several things, and any one of them might have been true. He did it because he wasn't quite the loner he wanted to be. Because he had a high sex drive, and he was looking for something. Whatever it was, he hadn't found it yet.

Because the games weren't right, but they were on the road to something, to a place where he needed to be. Because the games gave him a structure, a way to hold himself back so that he didn't damage someone who was more vulnerable than he.

He drank then said, "It's complicated."

"No, it's not," she said. "You're bent, like me." He looked at her closely. She was not angling to get him angry. She was simply speaking the truth as she saw it.

"What are you talking about?"

"You can dress it up in those designer clothes you wear at the bar, and turn on the charm, but strip off all the clothes and the charm, and what lives underneath is raw and dark." Her voice was flat and quiet. "You're never going to really find yourself the way you've been going. You're always going to feel restless and dissatisfied, until you realize that the games you've been playing don't feed the animal that lives inside of you."

"You're full of bullshit," he snapped. Her words bit him to the bone. He tried to push them away by scoffing at her, while the part of him that had torn loose and was running renegade ran harder than ever.

"Am I?" She stood and stretched with abandonment, as

free and wild in her human skin as she was in her Wyr form. She looked down at him, and there was a strange expression in her gaze, something he'd never seen in her before. "There isn't anything wrong with the darkness, you know," she said, almost kindly. "It's just as beautiful as anything else."

He stared as she walked over to one of the tents, unzipped the flap and crawled inside. A muscle in his jaw twitched. He rubbed at his cheek to make it stop then finished off the scotch. There was no reason in the world not to.

Then, because there was no one to fight with, he crawled inside his own tent. He took off his boots, but kept the rest of his clothes on as he climbed into the sleeping bag. Within minutes, his own body heat had warmed up the bag and he was comfortable enough, at least physically.

Mentally was another matter. He stared at the shadowed ceiling of his tent until the fire outside died down. Then he closed his eyes and pretended to sleep while silence roared in his head.

Where it was so dark.

⹀ EIGHT ⹀

Morning brought sunshine and warmer temperatures. Quentin had his tent broken down, tarps folded and the last embers of the campfire stamped out by the time Aryal climbed out of hers. She stood staring down at the empty fire ring, her face blurred from sleep. He contemplated the sight sourly. While he had been staring at the ceiling of his tent, she had been sleeping like a baby.

She said, "I was going to make coffee."

"Too bad," he snapped. "We need to get moving."

"So that's how today is going to be, is it?" She made an exasperated I-give-up gesture, glared at him and took down her tent.

While he waited for her to finish, he opened up two cans of sausage and beans and ate the food cold. Soon after, Aryal did the same, grimacing as she swallowed her breakfast. They each packed what they could carry, the lightweight camping gear tied below their backpacks.

"Let's go," he said as soon as Aryal shouldered her pack and tightened the straps.

She gave him a dirty look. "I'm not going to hike all day with you when you're in this kind of mood."

She was talking about a mood. He rolled his eyes and

put his hands on his hips. "You're going to try to fly with that on your back?"

When Wyr shapeshifted, some magic inherent to the shift itself transformed whatever they wore along with them. The speculation was that it had something to do with how Wyr defined their own personal space, but the shapeshift didn't work for special loads like the backpack.

She shrugged. "I can carry it. We're headed southwest, right?"

"Yes," he said, his tone short. He knew he was being an ass, but he couldn't seem to stop himself. "See the ridge at the top of those foothills? Follow that as it curves along the range. The passageway to Numenlaur will be close to where that ridge ends."

"Right." She didn't bother with more conversation. She shapeshifted, her wings flaring into existence on either side of the pack straps.

"Aryal," he said.

She paused to look at him, one sleek, black eyebrow arched.

"Don't go so far as to land at the passageway without me. The Elves that Ferion sent to the guard the passageway are stressed and isolated. They've lost friends and family, and they haven't had any news for weeks about how things are going in Lirithriel. Wait for me to get there before you do anything." He paused, gritted his teeth and added, "Please."

"Understood." She turned away from him and launched.

Quentin watched her gain altitude. She was in her element in the air, everything about her flight graceful and full of power. He couldn't believe she had actually chosen to leave rather than argue with him. It seemed unlike her.

He rubbed his face, struggling with contradictory emotions. As abraded as he felt this morning, her presence could only be like salt in a wound. But he was still annoyed with her for being able to leave so effortlessly. He wanted to pick a fight with her. She had said some pretty goddamn presumptuous things last night, and he took exception.

The silence was pretty peaceful though.

If he had been human, the hike to the passageway would take a couple of days, and much longer if a snowstorm blew in. He couldn't get there as fast as Aryal could by flying, but he could still make the journey quicker than humans could.

He took off jogging at an easy, ground-eating pace. Within a half an hour, he was so hot, he had to stop and strip off his jacket and sweater. He folded them up and used them as padding for the backpack, which he slipped back on. Once he was certain the shoulder straps wouldn't chafe his skin, he resumed jogging.

The clouds that day were little more than filmy swathes of white, like transparent silk across the ice blue sky. The late winter sun was bright, pale gold on the muted greens and browns of the forest. The deciduous trees were leafless, allowing for him to see further in dense areas, but the evergreens were thick and vibrant.

He could pick up speed with more surety of his footing in the rolling meadows, but the uneven paths through the forest were slick with melted snow and damp moss. There he could only manage the steady, careful jog. Then he reached a point where the paths didn't go, and he had to strike out on his own.

Throughout the morning, he brooded. Contrary to what Aryal had said the night before, he wasn't anything like her. She had assumed that he wasn't facing some kind of internal truth about himself, and that wasn't the case.

He didn't think that the darkness that lived at his core was wrong, or evil. He didn't try to deny or hide from what was inside of him.

He tried to protect everybody else from it.

He knew what kind of strength he had, and he knew that he had dangerous attributes. So had his father, who had seen him trained from an early age, both in magical and martial arts. His father's goal had been to avoid him becoming a loose cannon, with too much ability and not enough skill. Quentin had kept up with the training when he reached adulthood because the push and strain appealed to his aggressive nature.

The result was that he could kill with a single blow. Breaking a couple of bones was even easier, especially if his sex partner were a human.

But if Aryal wasn't on target with what she had said, why did he still feel so restless and dissatisfied?

At midday he reached the ridge. He followed along the edge until he came to a lake, where he decided to stop. He had burned off his breakfast and then some a long while ago. He drank his fill from the bone-numbing cold water. The lake was such a deep blue, it looked like a huge sapphire rested in the depths underneath the surface.

Then, instead of taking the time to set up a fire ring and cook, he opted to do what he had done that morning, which was open up a couple of cans of food and eat the contents cold. It wasn't appetizing, but it was fuel. He was looking forward to a hot meal that night, though.

He sat on the large trunk of a fallen tree as he ate. His body gradually cooled, but the light breeze still felt good on his sweaty skin. The temp was probably in the midforties, but he didn't plan on stopping long enough to cool down to the point where he would want to shrug on his sweater again.

A shadow fell over him. He looked up. Aryal coasted on a thermal overhead. She wheeled and came in for a landing, then shapeshifted and walked over to him. Her color was high, and she looked more vital than anything else on the landscape, an intense concentration of energy and physicality.

She had found somewhere to stash her pack, because she was no longer carrying it. Her gaze fell to his bare chest and lingered. He turned away and snapped at the last of his food, swallowing it down without really chewing.

Aryal sat beside him, drew up her legs and wrapped her arms around her knees. "You're making good time," she said. "There's a hunter's cabin that I think you can reach by nightfall, if you push."

A hunter's cabin would be shelter in the form of at least four walls and a ceiling, and probably a fireplace too. Hunters' cabins were rarely large, luxurious places. They would be lucky if there was more than one room. It meant sharing a confined space with her again. He heaved a sigh that was halfway to a growl. "We'll see."

She tilted the toes of her boots up and looked at them. "I found a passageway."

Irritable at his meal that had been filling yet not satisfying, and in the mood for something sweet, he had begun to dig in his pack for an energy bar. He frowned at her. "You found *a* passageway?"

She grimaced and lifted a shoulder. "It seems to be in the right location, but I didn't land like you asked, and I don't know that it's the Numenlaur passageway." She looked at him sidelong. "Thing of it is, I didn't see any Elves nearby, so I'm not sure."

He considered that as he tore the wrapper off his bar and took a bite. "Did you catch sight of a camp?"

She shook her head. "Nothing. It couldn't be the second passageway, could it? The one that leads to the Lirithriel Other land?"

He chewed thoughtfully. He wouldn't have thought she would have flown that far off course, but just in case, he asked, "Can you sketch where you found it?"

She slipped off the tree trunk, found a stick and started drawing in the mud at the edge of the lake. "I followed your directions. Here's the ridge. It curves around the edge of this outlying mountain that sort of sticks out from the rest of the range like a stubby thumb."

He lifted his eyebrows. She certainly had a unique perspective from the air. He said, "Okay."

"The ridge ends here, in a deep big ravine." She slashed at the mud. "It's actually bigger than a ravine, more like a canyon. That's where the passageway is."

"That sounds right," he said. "Remember, I've never seen the passageway myself, but that's pretty much what Ferion described. The other passageway is a good fifteen to twenty miles farther on south from there."

She looked up at him. "So where are the Elven guards?"

"Elves are very good at blending into their environment," he said as he finished the bar. He rinsed out the empty cans, crushed them underneath the heel of one boot and tucked the metal back into his pack.

Aryal stood tapping her foot. "I know that." She scowled. "Okay, so maybe I didn't actually set both feet on soil, but I flew down really low, right over the tops of the trees and sometimes in between them. I don't think the guards are there, Quentin."

He gave her a long look. He didn't waste time calling her on her legalistic thinking, just focused on her story instead. He also didn't bother asking her if she had seen any signs of an old campsite. When the Elves broke camp, they removed all traces of their visit on the land. If they had been there and departed, they wouldn't have left any signs for someone to find.

"So either I found the wrong passageway . . ." she said.

He glanced again at the map drawn in the mud. "You didn't."

"Or for some reason the Elves felt the need to cross over into Numenlaur," she finished.

"I guess they might have," he said. "I wonder what could have caused them to cross over, and if they did, why didn't they leave someone on guard at this end, like they had been ordered?" His shoulders were not happy about his picking up his pack again. He paused before he slipped it back on. "There's a third possibility. Maybe they never arrived."

"Whatever the possibilities, they lead to just two questions," she said. "Where are the Elves now, and why aren't they where they are supposed to be?" She focused on him. "Stop that. Take your pack off."

He asked suspiciously, "Why?"

"I'll take it." She held out her hand. "You'll make better time without it. If you can change, you'll definitely reach the cabin by tonight. The passageway is just a couple of hours' hike beyond that point. We can be there by midmorning."

He paused as he thought about that, studying her face. If he handed over his pack, Aryal would have all of the supplies along with the car keys.

Even if she decided to do something pissy, like take off with everything, the theft wouldn't hurt him, only inconvenience him. He knew his survival skills were more than good enough to handle the terrain, and he would keep his weapons on him.

He had hesitated a moment too long. Her eyes narrowed in either disgust or impatience. She said, "Don't be stupid. I thought we were at least past that point."

"Fine," he said. "Hold on a moment."

Along with handguns and knives, they had both brought short swords, the kind that could be stowed along the length of the inside of their packs. Legally, they could have brought long swords, but those tended to be more trouble than they were worth on long airplane flights.

He was already wearing the knife. He opened up his pack and drew out the sword and the gun, then handed the pack over to her.

She slid it on with a near-soundless grunt, and adjusted the weight.

"Where's the cabin?" he asked.

She gave him directions, shapeshifted and visibly braced herself. She had gone much farther than he had already, and yes, she had a pair of wings that allowed her to cover more distance quickly, but she had also scouted the surrounding terrain with what sounded like a great deal of care. He didn't think it was easy for a large avian Wyr to coast so low to the ground that she could fly between trees. She had to be tired.

The word he wanted to say stuck in his throat a little. "Thanks."

She made a face. "I just want to get to the passageway as fast as we can, so forget it."

"Already done." He stood back and watched her launch.

Man, she might get under his skin like the most irritating splinter ever experienced, but he had to admit one thing. She was truly something to see when she took flight.

He shapeshifted too, and the panther raced after the harpy, following the direction of her trajectory.

. . .

Aryal landed at the hunter's cabin with a sense of relief, and as soon as she could, she shrugged out of Quentin's backpack. As a harpy she could fly for days if needed, but that was if she stayed in her natural state and she didn't try to carry any extra load. With weapons, some canned and dehydrated food, clothing and the camping supplies, both hers and Quentin's packs had been significant weights to haul around in the air.

The cabin was nestled in a hollow of land and surrounded by trees that would provide some protection from the most severe weather. It was a rough building, not much more than a single room, with a fieldstone fireplace and wood-framed bunk beds, but there was already plenty of firewood stored in a lean-to. There was also a clear running stream for fresh water, and a cleaning station for fresh game or fish.

She tossed Quentin's pack into a corner, built a fire in the hearth, and as the warmth began to fill the space, she shook her sleeping bag out on the bottom bunk and threw herself on it with a sigh. She guessed it was early evening, around five thirty. Back in New York, it would be approaching midnight. Here, darkness was beginning to spill into the corners of the land, covering the secretive pockets where shy creatures hid. Tonight was going to be cold. It might even snow.

She closed her eyes and drifted. All her drifting thoughts swirled back to Quentin.

Coming upon him shirtless as he ate lunch had been a shock. Maybe it wouldn't have been if it were high summer. She hadn't expected the sight of his broad, bare shoulders in the winter landscape, and she had coasted for a few minutes just so that she could stare.

Last night, his face had turned to stone when she spoke the truth as she saw it, and this morning his temper had been so foul, she couldn't fly away fast enough. She wasn't sure what she had said that had struck him so hard, but she figured if they really weren't going to kill each other, the best thing that could happen for the both of them was to get a little space from each other and regroup.

Taking the day to be by herself and surrounded by nature, not by concrete and asphalt, had worked wonders on her own temperament, and when she had talked to him at midday it had seemed to help him as well. He'd been calmer, if not exactly cheerful.

And half-naked.

Win-win.

She stretched, her shoulder muscles aching pleasantly, and toed off her boots. Then she sat up, stripped off her clothes and shapeshifted into the harpy again. Once she had changed, she went outside to splash off in the stream. The harpy loved it, but the biting cold water carried melted snow off the mountains and it was much too frigid for her to enjoy in her human form. The cabin didn't have running water, nor was there any way to heat up large quantities of water, so this was the closest she was going to get to a bath tonight.

After she finished, she went back in the warm cabin and shapeshifted into her human form. She pulled on fresh underwear, then dressed in the same clothes she had on earlier, enjoying the peace and quiet of having the cabin to herself while she tried to make up her mind about whether or not she would try to seduce Quentin.

Hate sex still sounded awfully good. Biting him while they rolled around on the floor and screwed each other like crazed monkeys . . . She could take that gorgeous penis of his into her body, lock her legs around him, pump his rocket engine and not let go until they both shot to the moon. Mmmm. Yeah.

But they had already almost gone beyond that point into some other strange place. It was still an angry place that mingled sex and violence together, as they dared each other to do things they would never consider doing.

Except.

It would be truly magnificent to get him, *Quentin Caeravorn*, on his knees, to harness that sexy man and own him for a little while. He was no submissive, and that would make it even sweeter. The thought of it was almost enough to get her to agree to the dare. A time where he submitted, and gave up control to her, and in return she would give the same to him.

The problem was, neither one of them were submissive types. They were both dominant personalities.

Hell, Aryal didn't even fit very well into a normal BDSM definition. She had explored clubs for a short time, intrigued, but the bottom line was, the lifestyle was much too intricate and stylized for her. She had neither the interest nor the patience to learn all the codes of conduct. She wondered if Quentin had.

Giving up total control to someone else either called for a radical kind of trust and immense self-control, or it called for a certain kind of suicidal craziness.

She didn't trust Quentin, and she was certain he didn't trust her.

That only left the other option. She threw herself on the bottom bunk again, stretched her arms over her head and laughed.

The cabin door opened. Quentin walked in, bringing the scents of the forest in along with him. Fresh cold air gusted through the room.

He looked around the cabin and took everything in with one quick, assessing glance. Only then did he look at her, eyes narrowed. He shut the door behind him.

Inane words ghosted through her head.

There you are, so you made it. About time you showed up. Feel like taking off your shirt again?

She asked, "What are you going to fix us for supper?"

He glowered at her, so apparently his mood had returned to normal. "I fixed supper last night, and you didn't stay around to eat any of it."

"That was then." She yawned. "This is now."

"You could have fixed something for supper yourself by now," he pointed out.

"No, I couldn't. I did a lot today, and I only just got clean." She put her arms behind her head, watching him under lowered eyelids as he hefted his pack from the corner where she had tossed it and set it on the cabin's only table. "The bathroom's all yours."

His head lifted, and he looked around the cabin again, then at her with his eyebrows raised. She smiled and pointed to the door, and he laughed.

The sound was even more shocking than the sight of his bare chest had been earlier.

Listen to us, she thought. I crack a joke, he laughs. We are actually being halfway civil to each other.

The concept was so strange, she felt as though they were screwing around with some kind of law of physics.

After he dug through the pack, he set containers of food on the table. They both had a few cans of beef stew left, along with some energy bars, and a few dehydrated meals that Aryal would rather be near death's door before she would touch. After contemplating the selection, he shook his head. "Screw it. This is good enough for now. I'll hunt tomorrow."

She grunted and pushed off the bunk. "I'll heat up a few cans of stew."

She took two cans from him, and two from her pack. While he disappeared outside, she opened up the cans and set them close to the fire. He came back shortly afterward, with his hair damp and his tanned skin ruddy from washing. He watched her stir the stew and, using the sleeve of her sweater, rotate the cans so that they heated from all sides.

The silence grew weighted. More words occurred to her, things she imagined another female might say.

About last night, I hope I didn't hurt your feelings. If I did, I'm sorry. Are you okay?

But the thing was, she wasn't sorry for what she had said. She had spoken the truth as she saw it. And she didn't think she had any power to hurt Quentin's feelings. For that to happen, he would have to hold her in some regard so that her opinion mattered to him. At the most, she had irritated and infuriated him.

As far as asking if he was okay . . . She glanced sideways at his unrevealing expression. The strong bones of his face were accentuated in the firelight. The tiny mark she had made on his lower lip had long since healed. He looked as he so often did, self-contained and remote, a citadel with a door of hammered gold guarded by an intricate, magical lock.

What would it take to unlock that door? Some kind of incantation written in a language she didn't know.

She felt the same impulse to needle him that she always did when she saw that expression. For once she held it back. Instead she carried the hot cans over to the table, two at a time.

"Thanks," he muttered.

She ate her own stew thoughtfully without replying. A second thanks in one day. He might be okay, but he was still acting a little off. If she took herself out of the equation, what was left?

She asked, "Do you know any of the Elves that Ferion sent to guard the passageway?"

"Yes, I do." He scraped the last of the stew out of one can. "There are four of them, including a young Elf named Linwe, who is Ferion's niece on his mother's side."

The Elven community was a tight-knit one, made even more so by the recent tragedy. She knew how she would feel if any of her friends were missing. She rubbed her face and said, "You know, we don't have to spend the night here. If you want we can push on until we get to the passageway."

He lifted his head from his food to look at her. "Push on."

"Yes." She widened her eyes at his look of surprise. "You're worried about them, aren't you?"

"I'm concerned about them, yes," he said. He pushed away the empty cans. "But whatever has happened, we need to remember they don't know that we're coming. They can't have any idea that we would wonder about their absence on this end of the passageway. And none of them would casually disobey orders, especially on an assignment such as this. Either you made a mistake and they really are camped at the passageway entrance—"

"I didn't make a mistake."

He didn't attempt to argue with her. "Or they must have a compelling reason for not being there. No doubt we're going to find them on the other side."

"Okay," she said. "It makes sense. But we can push on if we need to."

A crooked smile hooked up one corner of his mouth. "Did you just offer to do something nice?"

Nice. She shrugged away the word and sniffed. "Not only do I have friends, I know what it's like to worry about them, and want to do something to help them if I can."

He sat back in his chair, stretching his legs toward the fire. "You're friends with Niniane Lorelle, aren't you? Didn't you go to Adriyel to help her when she was on her way to her coronation?"

"Yes, I did, along with Rune."

He regarded her curiously. "What was it like?"

"The trip? Got to camp, investigate a murder, catch some people involved in treason, and go to a lot of parties. It was fun." She yawned. "All except for the bit where Niniane was kidnapped and Tiago almost died."

Amusement crept into his voice. "As fascinating as your account of the trip is, I didn't mean that. What was Adriyel like as a land?"

"Beautiful." She studied him underneath her lashes. "You weren't yet born when Urien closed the border, were you?"

"That's right. It was before my time. My father is half–Dark Fae and half-Elven, but he was raised by his Elven mother and didn't maintain close ties with the Dark Fae branch of our family tree. Now he lives in Palm Beach."

So his mother was the Wyr. Aryal was fascinated with the concept of having parents. She thought if she'd had parents, they would have driven her crazy. Or she, them. "And your mom?"

He shook his head. "She died a long time ago."

"Have you tried to get in touch with your Dark Fae family since Niniane opened the borders?"

A grim smile pulled at his mouth. "They're dead too.

That side of the family bet on the wrong horse and got hanged for it."

"Get out." She sat up straight. "Were they involved in the conspiracy that killed Niniane's family?"

He shrugged. "Apparently so. Remember, I'd never met any of them. They were just names to me. My father was pissed when he found out—not at the Queen, but at our family for having gotten involved in murdering the royal family."

"Interesting," she murmured. He hadn't shaved that day, and pale gold dusted his jaw. His beard was a lighter shade than the smooth, sleek cap of hair on his head. Occasionally as he tilted his head, the firelight caught him just right and tiny sparks of light flared on his skin. It was . . . distracting. She wanted to lick his jaw, to find out if his beard was soft or rough, and bite at those tiny glints of light. She told him, "All right, yes."

It was almost too subtle to see, but she had been watching him closely and could tell that his body had tensed. He turned and looked at her, his gaze full of barriers and secrets. "All right, yes—what?"

"I'll take your dare," she said, and her smile was just this side of a slow slide into suicide. "If you take mine."

≈ NINE ≈

That surprised him. She could see it in the quick dilation of his vivid eyes. Then he burst out laughing. The sound was darker, harsher than his earlier laugh had been. "I don't believe you."

"You should." Leisurely, she stood, and he did too, springing upward with a catlike quickness that had her wondering if he had ever been truly relaxed that evening, or if his appearance had been disingenuous.

Disingenuous. She liked that word to describe him. It fit. On the surface, he was smooth charm with everybody else at the Tower, cloaking the blade that she knew lived inside him.

Genuinely curious, she asked, "How did you and Kitty Lawyer get along?"

"Who?" He looked blank.

"The chick you were with the night of the sentinel party. Wyr lioness, lawyer. Painted nails, high heels and possessive." Kitty Lawyer had licked his chin too. Aryal's smile soured. She'd forgotten that until just now.

He made a slicing gesture. "Not the topic at hand, sunshine. The topic *you* brought up, I might add. Unless you're just throwing things out there at random to see if you can get a rise out of me."

Mmmm. A rise. That sounded like fun. She turned away from temptation and forced herself to concentrate on what they were talking about. "I meant what I said."

"Now you're fucking around with me. You know you couldn't do it." He came around the table at her.

His predatory instinct had kicked in. Ooh, she should probably flutter around and act all flustered. Instead her eyes widened. "Not any more than you could?"

He circled her, as if assessing her physical attributes. "We've been down this road already."

"Have we?" He had reached her back, where he paused, standing in utter silence. He was trying to rattle her. It wasn't working. She stood still, arms crossed, in an appearance of relaxation while inside, adrenaline kicked in. Okay, maybe it was working a little. "I propose a different turn down that road. But of course, if you're not interested, we can stop talking about it right now and hit the sack."

He was interested. She could sense it pouring off him. He circled around to face her again, appearing casual again, except she knew better. The pulse at the base of his jaw pounded. He drawled, "I'm listening."

She took a deep breath. "We hold an experiment and set a time limit. We get fifteen minutes each of total control over the other person. You think you could handle that?"

Once she had thought of the idea, she couldn't stop. Surely fifteen minutes was doable. She could do almost anything for that long, including holding her breath. It would totally be worth it to own fifteen minutes of his ass.

Quentin looked suspicious. After he thought for a moment, he said, "Fine. On one condition. Your time comes first."

"You wish." She snorted. "We'll do a coin toss."

"No coin toss. You brought it up. They're your terms. You go first." His smile had turned catlike in anticipation. "Besides, you've bloodied me twice. You owe me."

"I don't owe you anything. You pounded my head on the pavement and throttled me. Twice."

"You pinned me against a metal door with your fucking talons, for God's sake." He moved so close, he was in her face. They stood toe-to-toe, looking in each other's eyes. "You punched me."

"You punched me first," she pointed out. It had been a hell of a strike too, much faster than she had expected. She had admired that—and made a point to never forget it.

"Are we going to keep going like this forever, or are you going to strike the bargain you offered?" He gave her a hard smile that glittered in the firelight, put a finger under her chin and tilted her face just so. Then his mouth came to hover over hers, their skin barely touching. He whispered, *"Give it up, Aryal."*

Her breath came short and fast, and he had to know it, because the only way he could be closer to her was if he were French-kissing her. He started to laugh again, only this time it sounded angry. He really did think she had just been fucking with him.

She said, "Deal."

He froze.

It was her turn to laugh. She always loved the feeling of cutting loose, no matter where she found it. Jumping off a cliff, starting a chase, losing all the doubts and questions and analyses. She was the original Nike girl. Just doing it.

She might not trust him, but she trusted her own judgment. He wouldn't kill her. There was no way he could do it in this kind of setting and hope to sell it as an accident to Dragos back home, and besides, he had been telling the truth about that earlier. Just like her, he'd had the impulse and given it up.

If he hurt her really badly, he was going to have to cut her loose at some point, and then it was his turn.

And if he tried to renege on his part of the bargain, well.

Hell hath no fury like a harpy who's been fucked over.

"Fifteen minutes," she told him. "Set your iPhone's clock when you're ready to start. We wouldn't want to lose track of such a short amount of time."

Inside, her heart was leaping about like a jackrabbit. If she could have pounced on it to make it stop, she would have. How badly was she going to hate this? She needed to keep her eye on the prize—her time with him, or a real sense of righteousness as she kicked his ass.

Angling his head, looking the very picture of incredulity, he backed up, dug in his pack until he found his iPhone, turned it on and programmed it. His thumb hovering over the screen, he glanced up. Anticipation had sharpened his lean features until he looked even more predatory than ever. "Last chance to back out."

Surprised that he even offered, she snorted, the sound derisive. "It's just fifteen minutes. You're not that scary. Do it."

He pressed the iPhone. Held it up and showed it to her. Fifteen minutes were counting down on the screen. Carefully he set it on the table.

Then he sprang at her, and even though she had been expecting him to do something, somehow she hadn't been ready for his incredible speed. He pushed her back until she hit the wall. Already they were both breathing heavily, as if they had been fighting for a very long time.

He pressed his long, hard body against hers and took her chin in one hand, and with the other hand, he held a stiffened finger under her nose.

"Shut up," he said. "Don't say a word out loud or telepathically. We're going to have fifteen minutes of silence from you. I know that's going to break your head, and the thought of that makes my day, so just fucking do it. Don't touch me, and did I say, shut up?"

Laughter exploded out her nose. She opened her mouth.

He glared at her. "One word, sunshine, and you forfeit your fifteen."

Ouch. She had words, so many of them, crashing into each other like a freeway pileup. She made a frustrated noise and panted a little with the effort to hold them back.

He stroked her hair. Her gaze slid up and sideways to track the movement of his hand. His expression was sharp, electric. He looked fascinated with whatever he saw in her expression. "Can you do it?"

She widened her gaze and shrugged. She honestly didn't know. Of all the things she had been braced for, she hadn't expected this. As an adversary, he was diabolical. As a potential sex partner, the diabolic part grew exponentially.

He chuckled, and the husky sound was full of triumph and intent. Then he bent his head and kissed her.

Really, really kissed her. Deep and full out, his tongue invading her mouth, his lips hardened and hungry as he pressed against her body. Kissing and kissing her.

Her hands came up.

He said in warning, telepathically, *Huh-uh.*

They hovered in midair. Clenched into fists.

Meanwhile the pileup of words continued on the freeway in her head. The wreck was tremendous and ugly, and the force of holding all those words back while keeping her hands off of him, while he continued to leisurely, thoroughly, sensually explore her mouth, caused her whole body to shake.

He never said she couldn't kiss him back. She did so, aggressively, while she growled low in her throat, and his hot, accelerated breathing gusted over her cheek. His hips pinned hers, and the long, hard length of his stiff cock pressed against her belly.

She had the impulse to grab hold of his hips and yank him harder against her—and caught herself just in time before her hands connected. Damn it! *Why didn't he just tie her up and make this easy?*

He sensed her struggle, of course, and laughed wickedly against her lips. The hoarse sound vibrated against her chest. He put his hands at her waist, slipped them under her sweater and the thin cotton undershirt she wore underneath, and slid them up the length of her narrow torso until he reached her high, slight breasts.

She never wore a bra. She hated them and didn't need one. His hands collided with bare, sensitive skin, and they both sucked in air. She threw out her arms, and her fists slammed into the wall.

Quentin. Caeravorn. Is. Touching. Me.

She liked having her breasts fondled. She wasn't any stranger to it. It was still the *Quentin* part of the whole equation that bent her head.

He dragged both of her tops up and stared down at her

naked torso as he rubbed callused thumbs over the dusky, erect flesh of her nipples. Sensation jolted through her, jagged bolts of lightning strikes that hit at her moistening sex.

Desperate for something to grasp so that she could keep her hands off of him, her talons flicked out. She dug them into the walls and held on. His expression was clenched, the tanned skin darkened. He muttered something under his breath. Her mind was too hazed to figure out exactly what he had said. It had sounded very like a curse.

Then, still flicking one nipple with the nail of his thumb, he bent his head further, pulled the other nipple into his mouth, and bit her.

Pain joined the lightning bolts of pleasure, each sensation heightening the other to an almost unbearable pitch. She had always liked the mixture of pain and pleasure, like the raw fire of brandy coupled with the smooth sweetness of chocolate. She cried out wordlessly, arching her back to offer her breasts to him, and hooked one leg around his waist to pull him tighter against her, rubbing the center of her aching flesh against his erection. Heat from their bodies wrapped them in a velvet inferno.

Do it. Bite me again. She nearly strangled on her own tongue. Son of a bitch.

After the bite, he suckled strongly, each pull as devastating as a blow. She cried out again, the sound sharp with the unbearable ache building in her body.

The only sounds in the cabin were sexual ones that created a mélange of urgency. The abrasion of cloth, rasp of breath, the sounds that he made, the sounds that she made.

Until a foreign noise thrust into the mix. An insistent beeping.

Fractured thoughts and impulses climbed over the wreckage in her head, and tried to make themselves coherent. What the hell . . . somebody hit whatever that is . . . make the noise stop. . . .

Realization hit.

It was the alarm on Quentin's iPhone.

His head lifted. They looked at each other. His eyes were glazed, hands still clenched on her rib cage.

What to do.

She wanted, needed him to continue. She almost grabbed him to kiss him again. In fact, she was surprised she didn't. The only thing that stopped her, the one thing that was more compelling than the hunger rampaging through her body, was a single thought.

She yanked her talons out of the wall and retracted them, and smacked his shoulders with the palms of her hands, hard enough to make him stagger back a few steps. With a smile that blazed across her face, she said, *"My turn."*

Quentin was on fire.

His body was ablaze, his mind hazed with smoke. This small slice of power that Aryal had given him was the headiest thing he had ever experienced. It ravaged his senses like napalm, clinging to everything and transforming the landscape inside of him. She, who was normally so uncontainable, was under his control.

He looked into her uncommon face, twisted with agonized desire. The tendons in her arms stood out as she dug her talons into the wall and struggled to do as she was told. She had arched her torso away from the wall in an unconscious offering to him. It caused her abdomen to hollow out underneath the graceful arc of her rib cage. Above that, the curve of her slender breasts flared. The small nipple he had bitten and sucked had turned red as a ripe cherry.

Everything about her was racy, streamlined and built for speed.

Greed swallowed him whole. He gripped her with both hands, fingers imprinting on the canvas of her flesh, and thought, *you are mine right now.*

BEEP BEEP BEEP BEEP BEEP BEEP BEEP.

What? He shook his passion-fogged head.

Her head came up, dark eyes wild with some internal storm. Something hit him, knocking him back a few steps. A half second later, he realized it had been her.

"My turn."

No. NO. He wasn't ready to stop, to give her up.

"I need more time," he said. He didn't recognize the sound of his own voice.

"That's another bargain." She yanked down her tops and gestured with a shaking hand at the noisy iPhone. "Do something about that or I will."

Dear Christ. He stalked over to the table and jabbed at the phone, and it stopped the incessant noise. Then he leaned both hands on the tabletop and struggled to get control of his breathing. The scent of her arousal was an aphrodisiac so strong he felt kicked in the teeth.

"I'll set it for the next fifteen minutes." He began to punch it in.

She moved up behind him, curving her long body along the line of his as she laid her cheek against the back of his neck. "What if I wait?" she said against his skin.

He froze, not quite believing what he heard. "You wouldn't," he growled. She couldn't wait. She didn't have it in her. Hell, he didn't have it in him to wait either.

She put her arms around him and ran her hands down his chest. He looked down, compulsively, watching her hands travel down his body. His cock was on fire along with the rest of him, and it jerked as her hands came closer to it.

"Have you ever been taken from behind?" she whispered.

He tilted his head back, astonished at his own crazed reaction to everything she did or said. He said roughly, "Men aren't my thing."

The pressure from her hands grew lighter as they reached his jeans. She passed them over the aching bulge at his crotch in a teasing caress. "Have you ever been taken by a woman wearing a strap-on? Using a dildo? Fucked from behind until you explode all over her hands? I doubt it. You're probably too dominant, aren't you?"

The images she created seared his mind, and his own reaction astonished him. He would never consider such a thing, never give himself over to someone else like that.

Except.

He thought of Aryal moving behind him, moving *inside* of him as she cupped his penis in both hands. The concept was so startling and strange, he nearly came right there in his pants.

It wasn't as though he had never heard of a strap-on before. It was the thought of Aryal using one. On him. Everything she did was so goddamn sexy, it was breaking every rule he thought he had in his head.

He hissed, "Am I setting the alarm or not?"

Her hands flexed. He listened to her hard breathing, feeling it against his back. She wanted it bad. He could feel it in the rigidity of her body, smell it on the rich scent rising off her skin.

The bizarre thing was, he was starting to want it bad too.

Even though it wasn't like him, and he never gave up control. There was something about her impetuous leaping into situations that was seriously screwing with whatever scraps of sanity he might have otherwise had.

She said, "Set it."

He punched the button and stared at the screen as fifteen minutes began to scroll by.

He wore a belt with his jeans so that he could attach his knife sheath and the holster of his gun to it. He watched her hands go to the belt and unbuckle it. She yanked it out of his belt loops. "Take off your sweater."

He straightened, yanked off his sweater and threw it aside. The air felt good on his overheated skin.

"Turn around," she said.

He turned to face her, his longtime enemy and unexpected partner on this exploration that was rapidly becoming more intimate than any other exchange he'd had before.

Her expression was stripped of everything else except the same kind of hunger that was driving in his blood. He looked at the belt she still held, then up again at her face. She met his gaze. "Lie back on the table."

He warred with his instincts that wanted to snatch at the belt, wrap it around her neck and haul her close for another one of those kisses that were so hot they seared him somewhere deep inside, in a place that was invisible to anyone else.

But she had struggled with her part of the bargain too,

and met it, and part of what he had enjoyed about her was witnessing that struggle, and how she had overcome it.

Her gaze was sharp and steady. If he reneged on this, there would be no second chance with her, no opportunity to explore more of that which he had just gotten the merest taste.

He moved the iPhone to a chair, sat at the edge of the table and lay back. His torso covered the length of the table, from his head to his ass, while his legs spilled down to the floor. She took his legs and nudged him sideways until he lay with his head in one corner, the opposite corner ending between his thighs and causing them to fall slightly apart.

"I'm going to make this easier on you than what you did with me," she told him. Her voice sounded shredded. "Hands over your head."

His gaze went back to the belt. That's why she still had it. It wouldn't be easy, but a leather strap, no matter how sturdy, couldn't hold him if he felt endangered or enraged enough to snap it. Still, he had to fight to control his instincts enough to put his arms over his head. He did it, watching her face closely.

She strode around the table and slipped a loop of the belt over his hands and fastened it to the leg of the table. Then, moving rapidly, she came back around, unbuttoned his jeans and yanked them down his legs. Just like that, within a matter of a few moments he was naked and spread out like a feast before her gaze.

His contradictory instincts grew more chaotic, and his body clenched. He hated the sense of vulnerability. He was not supposed to be the one on the table. He was supposed to be the one standing where she stood.

She stared at him with a wide, fixed gaze, her eyes dilated so that they were almost totally black. He felt it as a physical touch, as she lingered on the bulging muscles of his arms, down the angle of his chest as it narrowed to his long abdomen, to his erection where it lay heavy and thick on his stomach.

She yanked his legs wide apart, and a growl erupted from his throat. Before he could stop himself, he wrenched at the leather strap that pinned his arms. The strap held, and he managed to stop before he broke it. Pushing between his legs to hold them apart with her hips, she held up a forefinger where a single talon had emerged.

"I like blooding you," she told him in a gentle voice. She ran the talon along the inside crease where his leg met his groin. An instant later, a line of fire flared where she had given him a shallow cut.

Goddammit, she had marked him.

The growling that came out of him then was feverish and wild. He sounded like he could savage her to death. He almost felt like he could. "What the fuck, Aryal."

"A little memento for you," she whispered. "It'll heal fast, but until it does, every time you move or shift your position, you'll think of this moment."

He would get her for this. He would—

She came down between his legs, resting her weight on one elbow braced on the table, lifted up his stiff cock and swallowed him whole.

Everything in his head splintered so thoroughly that there weren't even fragments left. There was no pretty foreplay, licking or teasing, or looking up at him seductively. She just opened her throat and took him all the way in. Then she pulled back and suckled at the broad, thick, sensitive head. After a few moments, she plunged her head down again.

Her eyes closed as she concentrated on him, and her mouth and throat were so hot and wet and tight, and *confident*. She had known what she wanted from the moment the timer had been set, and she had gotten it, gotten him, with a minimum of effort and without any wasted words.

She fucked him with her mouth, a tight pistoning. He fucked her with his cock, shoving up and up, while the fire from the cut joined the fire in his blood. He hooked his legs around her back, holding her in place. She palmed his tight sac while she worked him, squeezing and molding the round, sensitive flesh. Then she put her hand down her own body.

It took a moment for him to understand what she was doing. She was working herself while she suckled at him.

Gods, his explosion was building, and it felt like it was a long time in coming. Years, definitely. Maybe his whole life.

BEEP BEEP BEEP BEEP BEEP BEEP BEEP.

They both froze. She pulled her head up from his penis to stare at him.

There it was in her face, that wild juncture from which anything might happen, anything at all. She was a nexus point, pulling all possibilities together into herself.

He roared, *"IF YOU STOP I WILL MURDER YOU!"*

Laughter broke out over her face, along with fresh heat.

While the electronic alarm jangled in the air, she bent and took him in her mouth again, squeezing on his distended flesh, and she didn't stop until the fire poured out of him in convulsive spurts of lava.

She swallowed all of his semen with such evident relish, it caused him to spasm further. He emptied everything into her until he had nothing left to spill, no internal whip or twist, and he felt completely hollowed out and clean.

He had nothing left inside of him when she finally let him go. She looked drunk, a little dazed. She didn't untie him. She straightened and turned away, then abruptly disappeared from sight as she sat on the floor. A moment later, his iPhone sailed across the air and stopped shrilling when it hit the wall. He wanted to laugh, to take her by the hair and shake her, then kiss her.

Instead he lifted his legs and pulled with his arms, curling over himself until he somersaulted over his head and off the table. He worked quickly to loosen the belt from his wrists.

When he did, he stopped and stared down at his arms. The belt had marked his wrists when he had yanked at it, leaving reddened welts. He rubbed the area. It wouldn't last, nor would the thin, bright line of fire at the juncture of his legs.

The last half hour had been the longest half hour of his life, and the shortest.

He hated that it was over.

⟹ TEN ⟸

Neither one talked much after their "experiment." Quentin dressed quickly, then they moved around with care, giving each other plenty of space as they set the cabin to rights before going to bed. He went outside to relieve himself and rinse out the food cans before crushing them. Then he toured the immediate area around the cabin but found nothing to concern him.

Mostly he enjoyed being out of the heat and closeness of the cabin. It was going to snow sometime that night. He could smell it in the chill, wet air. When he finished his patrol of the area, he stood staring up at the shadowed mountains swathed in clouds. He still felt clean, emptied out. It was remarkably, disturbingly peaceful.

As he moved about, the shallow cut at the juncture of his leg was a constant, irritating pain, even though it had already closed over. Every time he moved, he felt it. The sensation kept her words in the forefront of his mind.

Every time you move or shift your position, you'll think of this moment.

Him, naked and splayed on the table. Her, standing between his spread legs.

His cock was the most disturbed part of him. It stiffened again into a hard, insistent ache.

He didn't want to obsess about what had happened, so he wouldn't. He was just surprised at how hot Aryal was, that's all. She wasn't his type, in about any way that you could imagine. He felt like he was a sexual tourist, trying out a few things that were aberrant to his nature. Soon the vacation would be over, and they would go back to their real lives.

Until that happened, he was here and now, squarely in the middle of tourist season, hard again with hunger and already plotting the details that he would offer for their next bargain. If he wasn't concerned about the guards who were supposed to be on watch at the passageway, he would have walked back inside and offered her new terms immediately. But he was concerned, and they didn't have time to hole up at the cabin for a day or two and play.

Afterward, though. Dragos had given them a time limit of a month, and a lot could happen in that span of time.

When he went back inside, she had already moved her sleeping bag to the top bunk and climbed into it, turned to face the wall. In the dying light of the fire, he stood and looked at her sprawled figure. Here was another way she was atypical. They'd had sex, but there was no cuddling, no soft words, no clinginess or seeking reassurances afterward. Hell, she was probably already asleep.

He grinned, climbed into the lower bunk and fell asleep almost immediately too.

The next morning they ate a quick breakfast and headed out early. Snow had fallen, a good three inches. The snowfall wasn't enough to do much more than slow them down slightly, as the ground was slick and wet, but it was pretty. The evergreens and the bare branches of deciduous trees were painted in white.

This time Aryal didn't take to the air. She chose instead to hike with him, and he didn't question her decision. She had finger combed her hair into some semblance of order, and her expression was distant and thoughtful. He wondered what she was thinking.

At first he was loath to break the silence and simply enjoyed the beautiful surroundings and the animal movement of his body as they hiked. Then the fact that she didn't say anything started to irk him.

About an hour into the hike, the final irritation from the cut faded as it finished healing. Aside from his broken iPhone, there was nothing left as evidence of what they had done.

And his internal whip came back, always driving, driving him.

Since she had scouted out the area yesterday, Aryal had taken the lead in the hike. He quickened his pace to catch up with her and took hold of her arm. She stopped and turned to face him, her head angled in inquiry.

Not that long ago, she would have swung around fighting if he had dared to touch her.

He moved to stand right in front of her, just to get as close as he could to the heat from her body. It licked along the surface of his skin.

Her expression was closed, revealing nothing. A single black strand of hair blew across her eyes, and she raised a hand to brush it back. The angle of her slim wrist and those long, dexterous fingers pulled at the whip inside of him.

"Half an hour," he said.

Her sleek eyebrow rose slowly, and the expression in her eyes turned assessing.

She was surprised? He didn't buy it. "Oh come on," he said. "You can't tell me you haven't been thinking the same thing."

"That's a double negative," she told him.

Even though he knew she did it on purpose to needle him, it still drove him crazy when she turned pious. If there was anyone who had *no room at all* to pull off that attitude, it was she.

He put a hand at the back of her neck, a deliberately possessive hold, and pulled her even closer to him. He did it to needle her back, but she allowed it. Look at how far they had come in such a short time.

Not far enough. They had so much farther to go, the end of the road lost in a tantalizing, mysterious distance.

"Admit it, sunshine," he growled. "You want another bargain too."

She yawned a little and scratched at her ear.

Wasn't *anything* straightforward with her? The reason why it didn't matter that he knew she was trying to rile him? Because it was working.

His gaze focused on her fabulous mouth. The image of her sucking on him flared in his mind, as searing as a flash fire. Those lips, closed over the thick rigidity of his cock, her throat working to take him in.

His entire body pulsed with urgency. He pulled her the last of the way toward him and fastened his mouth over hers, succumbing to the urge to ravish and take.

She met him halfway, and they ate at each other. She gripped his hips, and he ground his heavy erection against her as he circled her neck with one hand. She felt as if she had a fever, she was so hot. As he lifted his head to look down at her, a violent tremor shook through her body.

He could not keep his lips off of her. He ran them along her cheek, amazed at how soft her skin felt, and sucked the tender lobe of her ear into his mouth. He told her telepathically, *I want to put a collar on you.*

A leather collar, with a buckle. It would show darkly against her light skin. And her hands chained behind her back. She wouldn't be able to shapeshift in that position. Her wings would have no room to materialize. All that wildness, that fierce freedom, claimed and owned by him.

Mine. Mine.

Her answer was a telepathic snarl. *Dream on, mother-fucker.*

Where's your spirit of negotiation, sunshine? He hadn't even gotten the chance to feel her wetness last night. The lack disturbed him greatly. He pulled the hand from her throat and ran it down the front of her body to cup her between her legs.

She hissed and arched her hips, rubbing against his palm. She said, *I don't even know what you would have to give up in order to make that happen. Maybe your soul for all eternity.*

He laughed, the sound rough in the early morning air.

I wasn't joking, she told him. Her telepathic voice had turned uneven.

Of all the things they should be doing, this was not on the list. His hand slid upward to the fastening of her jeans. He didn't know why she had chosen to wear jeans on the trip instead of her usual fighting leathers, but he didn't pause to ask.

She growled at him in warning, but he was beginning to read her nuances and could tell it didn't have much heart.

He unbuttoned the jeans, unzipped the fly, then whispered in her ear, "Take off your backpack."

She shook her head jerkily. Both of them were panting as though they had been racing a long time. "We should keep going."

Going and going and going, hurtling forward down that dark, unknown road.

But that wasn't what she had meant. "We won't stop long. Take it off." He licked the shell of her ear. She tasted like every addictive drug ever named. "Consider this a little something to sweeten the pot on our next deal."

"We haven't made a deal." But her hands moved. She unbuckled the strap at her waist, and shrugged out of her backpack. It fell to the snowy ground.

He pressed his mouth to her pulse. It beat a rapid tempo at the side of her throat. She felt it too, this hectic, crazy rush.

Then he straightened, spun her around and pulled her back against him. He moved so fast that she cried out, and reached over her head. She tried to get a hold on him by gripping him at the back of the neck too, but he jerked his head to one side. She grabbed the collar of his jacket instead and held on so tightly the tendons in her wrist stood out.

He pulled her hips back so that his cock was nestled between the cheeks of her ass. Then he pushed her hair to one side and bit her at the nape of the neck. They both stood frozen like that for a long moment.

He took one hand and slid it from her hip to the open fastening of her jeans. And inside. Underneath her underpants into a tangle of her damp, warm hair.

Do you know what I imagined the first time I consciously thought of you in a sexual way? he asked telepathically. He held her in place with an arm clamped around her ribs, and his teeth at her neck.

Her ragged breathing sawed at the chill air. "What?"

I thought of taking you in the ass too. Pinning you and taking you. Clearly we have been thinking along the same vein.

"It's a dominant thing," she whispered.

It's a sexy thing. He probed deeper, wiggling into the tight space, and his fingers plunged into silken, wet flesh. Holy gods. They both groaned.

He stroked her, a slick slide along a small, stiff nubbin of flesh, while he bit her hard. She shuddered and cried out a second time.

Now her lean, strong body was arched back against him. He put his head on her shoulder, stroking her with a hard, steady rhythm. "My cut healed," he said into her neck. "I hated it when you marked me. I was so pissed at you I almost kicked you in the face. Now, it's strange. All I can do is think about how it's gone. Half an hour each, sunshine. You can't be done. Admit you want it too. Agree to it. *Do it.*"

"Yes, goddammit!"

He stroked her hard, and she clamped both hands over his to hold him in place as she sobbed for breath. He felt the quivering of her soft, private flesh, the rhythmic arching of her pelvis as she pushed against his fingers.

There was his climax, the one he should have claimed from her last night.

It wasn't enough. He needed to climax again, himself. He wanted and needed to be buried inside of her when she came.

But it was enough for now.

When she was finished, her fingers loosened. He pulled his hand out and let her go. She staggered but caught herself before she could fall. He strode away without looking back.

As he walked, he licked his fingers.

They tasted like her; warm, wet and wild.

. . .

Quentin was a bastard, but she already knew that. Honestly, it was part of why she was beginning to like him in spite of herself.

Her thigh muscles were shaking so that she could barely stand upright. She watched as he walked away. Was he licking his fingers? Even though she had just climaxed, the thought made her pulse.

She had come into existence at the beginning of the world. Maybe she hadn't been one of the most analytical of creatures for a while—like most of the truly ancient Wyr, the original harpies had lived as instinctively as animals, and had learned language and culture some time much later—but she did remember that bright, new beginning.

And the point was that she was old. She'd had sex in every imaginable position and variation. She was experienced, and she knew what she liked. A lot. And being dominated was not part of that mix.

So why did she find that bastard's moves and his dirty talk so sexy?

He had really wanted that half hour bargain. She smiled. She wanted it herself. She was looking forward to that date. A half an hour of owning him, tasting him, teasing him and making him come. The thought made her dizzy.

But for now, they had other things they needed to concentrate on. She zipped up her jeans, grabbed her backpack and hurried after him. When she was close enough, she threw her pack so that it hit him in the back.

He whirled around. "What the hell?"

"That was for walking away," she said. "I carried yours yesterday. You carry mine."

His eyes narrowed. "Why?"

"I'm going to scout around. We're getting close."

He bent to pick up the pack. "Fine, but don't go too far, and don't engage if you see the guards, okay?"

"Yes, I already know that," she said impatiently. "I'll be back in a few."

124

She shifted, crouched and—what was he smiling about? Was he smiling at her? Nah, that couldn't be right. He scowled at her, he didn't smile. After a blinking pause, she sprang into the air.

Rolling foothills hugged the ridge they followed, and the landscape looked different with the light covering of snow. She navigated by the landmarks that she had marked mentally the day before, and wasn't fooled by a little dusting of snow.

Since they were close to the passageway, she didn't bother to climb too high in altitude. She studied the landscape carefully, her sharp gaze noting minute details.

One thing about a snowfall was that it made tracking footsteps and finding recently used trails paint-by-numbers easy.

There were no footsteps anywhere, no trails. No subtle hint of wood smoke in the sharp, clear air. No flash of movement from anything but the occasional glimpse of spooked wildlife that sensed the nearness of a dangerous predator and bolted to hide.

Convinced, she wheeled around and headed back to Quentin. From a distance, his Elven heritage seemed pronounced in the leggy, graceful build of his body. It was only as she grew closer that the anomalies of his mixed heritage, such as his broader shoulders and more muscled torso, became clear.

He was keeping an eye out for her and paused as she descended. She landed in front of him, and when she saw the question in his eyes, she shook her head. "They're not there," she told him levelly. "I'm sure of it."

He took a deep breath and rubbed his face as he thought. He hadn't taken the time to shave that morning, and the light golden bristles were more pronounced on his lean cheeks and jaw. They had felt soft and tickling at the back of her neck. A shiver ran down her spine as she remembered, along with another pulse of arousal.

He met her gaze. The blue of his eyes was startlingly sharp against the wintery background. "I have a favor to ask of you," he said abruptly. "It just occurred to me that they might have had some reason to travel to the other passageway. I can't think what could have happened to make them do that, but I think we should know before we actually cross over to Numenlaur and try to look for them. Will you fly out there and scout for them while I take a look around here?"

She nodded. "Makes sense. If we're thorough now, we won't have to double back on ourselves later. See you soon."

She launched again and this time she did climb high. The day was warming up, and the rising temperatures were melting the snow, which covered the vista in a haze that sparkled slightly where the sunshine hit it directly. The scene was stunning, and one part of her gloried in the landscape that was unbroken by any signs of habitation.

However, most of her attention was focused on the hunt. She flew hard, due south, and after a couple of miles' distance, the magic of the first passageway stopped overwhelming her senses so that she began to feel the first faint tickle from the second one.

Adjusting her direction accordingly, she flew straight for it, studying the land below as she went. Sure, Elves blended with their surrounding and walked lightly on the land, yadda yadda yadda, and if they were really trying to hide, she might find the hunt more challenging. But as Quentin had already pointed out, this party didn't know they were coming and had no reason to hide anyway.

At least, no reason that she could figure out.

Her normal flight speed was almost twice that of an eagle's. She could fly up to a hundred miles an hour when she really pushed it, and this time she pushed it. She reached the second passageway in short order and passed around it several times, moving in circles of increasing size with each pass.

Where were those pesky Elves?

Nowhere that she could see.

Finally she shook her head and shot north, flying hard.

Quentin was easy to locate. He wasn't trying to hide either. He had stashed the packs somewhere, changed into the black panther and loped along the edges of a very large meadow that lay a quarter of a mile or so in front of the Numenlaur passageway. He poured over the land, sleek and rippling with fluid muscles moving under the shining black coat. She plummeted to wheel around his head.

The panther glanced up at her. Quentin said in her head, *Find anything?*

She answered aloud. "No."

The panther changed direction and headed back toward the Numenlaur passageway. *I've covered all quarters of the surrounding area. The land carries no scent of them.*

She wasn't surprised. They hadn't been in the area recently, and the melting snow would have washed away any scent that might have lingered.

When he stopped and changed near a large pine, she landed and changed too. She watched as he ducked under the pine's low-hanging branches. He emerged a moment later with his jacket and the packs. He handed her pack to her, and she shrugged it on, while he shouldered his as well.

His face was hard, the planes and angles set, but she thought she was beginning to read him pretty well, and she knew his worry had spiked.

"Did you see anything up close that seemed unusual in any way?" she asked.

"No. No signs of any damage, no dissipating magic, nothing." His voice was flat. "Did you?"

"Everything looked normal."

"Okay," he said. "Ready?"

She nodded. They had already discussed it all. There was nothing left to say.

Together they turned and walked to the passageway.

The Elven passageway in Lirithriel Wood, in South Carolina, had been intricately carved from end to end. This passageway looked entirely natural, the entrance to the canyon just another part of the landscape. But the land magic that poured off of it told a different tale. It was a very strong passageway and the only entrance that led into a fabled land.

She wasn't glad that the Elves were missing, but she had to admit, she was thrilled that they gave her and Quentin a reason to make this crossover.

Quietly, side by side, they started the journey into Numenlaur.

≡ ELEVEN ≡

As they walked the rocky, uneven passageway, she craned her neck, trying to look everywhere at once. She saw out of the corner of her eye that Quentin did the same thing.

The canyon walls that rose high on either side of them obstructed their vision of any surrounding landscape, but halfway through the passage, the snow disappeared, along with the pale wintery sky that had canopied the Bohemian Forest. The temperature grew much hotter, so much so that they had to pause to shrug out of their jackets and sweaters before they continued. The overhead sky turned a brilliant, deep blue crowned with the intense yellow gold of a summer sun.

The scents came next, wafting down the canyon corridor on a breeze, tantalizing and rich with the promise of abundant growth, and spiced with the perfume of strange flowers. Among the old tales of Numenlaur that Aryal had heard were stories of fruits that were so delicate and flavorful they could bring tears to one's eyes.

In those stories, Numenlaur was a rich, fertile land with olive and eucalyptus trees, a land that other ancients described as flowing with milk and honey, a paradise lost that held palaces, groves and temples more ancient than those found in Egypt and Greece. One, called the Temple of the Gods, supposedly housed statues of the seven Elder Races' gods that stood several stories high, interspersed with heavy, massive pillars of white marble.

All in all, the place was going to have a pretty tough time living up to the hype.

They reached an area where the canyon floor was bottlenecked. The passage was so narrow they had to walk single file. She gestured for Quentin to go through first. He hadn't revealed much reaction about their journey in, except for a quick flash of something that looked like real hunger before he managed to shutter his expression. He ought to be the first one to see what was a very important part of his cultural heritage.

Cultural heritage—it was another concept that fascinated her.

They passed around a curve. The passageway opened up, and so did the view.

The canyon ended in profuse greenery. She moved to walk at Quentin's side. He nudged her and pointed, and that was when she looked at the canyon walls. Two massive, ancient pillars were carved into the bedrock on either side of the canyon's opening. They rose four or five stories in height.

"They face inward," said Quentin. "They were not meant for anyone on Earth. They were meant for the Numenlaurians."

Not placed in an entryway, created to impress the newcomer, but at the exit.

She said, "It used to be important for them to travel out to the rest of the world. It must have cost them a great deal to close the passageway."

"When I hiked through this area about thirty years ago, I couldn't sense that anything was here. It was as if the passageway never existed. Somehow they cloaked it. I don't know of any spell that could have done that, but whatever they did would have taken tremendous Power. If Amras Gaeleval was the guardian, did he maintain the cloaking so that people couldn't enter? Or did he guard the way so that people couldn't leave? Maybe he did both."

Unease trickled down her spine. "That's a creepy thought."

The look on his face was cynical. "I've got a talent for them."

They walked out of the passageway, into what was either a hot summer morning or evening. Sunshine slanted at an angle through the nearby trees. She studied the bushes and the long tough grass around the canyon's entrance. The foliage was too rich for a desert climate, and none of it bore signs of any moisture from morning dew. It was evening, then.

Quentin squatted and ran his hand lightly over the grass as he studied the ground. "If the four Elves passed through here, they did it some time ago. There aren't any footprints, and there's no scent."

She put her hands on her hips as she looked around. "What did Gaeleval do, live like a wild man in the trees? There isn't anything here except for the pillars carved into the cliffs. Which makes sense since this place wouldn't have been a priority for any Numenlaurian for . . . however long of a time has passed in here."

In Other lands, the lands did not necessarily correspond with the geography that surrounded the passageways that led to them. The sun shone with a different light, and time moved at a different pace. The phenomenon was called time slippage.

Millennia had passed on Earth since Numenlaur closed itself off from the rest of the world. That did not mean that the same amount of time had passed in Numenlaur, although since the event had happened so long ago, the passing of time here had to have been significant in some way.

The length of time was certainly significant enough to leave the entrance to the canyon looking natural and over-grown. If there had been a road or a path through here once, it had disappeared long ago.

She spun backward in a circle, giving the area a second,

closer look, and because she was who she was, that meant she looked up.

Set into the cliff beside one pillar, there appeared to be a long ledge. From the ground it was difficult to tell for sure, but the line looked too even to be a natural break in the granite. She tapped Quentin on the shoulder and when he straightened to his full height, she pointed to the ledge. "There. And I think that line that cuts to the left might be a narrow path. See how it goes down gradually?"

"Okay," he said. He glanced at her. "I don't suppose you can lift my weight into the air."

She tapped her foot as she tried to decide how to answer him. Just how sort-of friendly and kind-of cooperative was she feeling toward him today? She was not one of those females who got all gushy just because she had a little fun and a guy gave her a climax. Especially if that guy was someone she had been determined to murder not that long ago.

Finally she admitted the truth. "If we were just going from here to there, I might be able to manage it. Want to give it a try, or do you want to follow the cliff along the ground to see if you can find where that path meets the ground?"

If he annoyed her on the way up, she could always drop him. The thought made her feel better about herself.

"You don't need to strain yourself for something this unimportant. I'll see you at the top." He loped away, his head angled to study the cliff as he went.

She shapeshifted and flew up to the ledge. Once she had landed, she shifted back and looked around with satisfaction. The ledge was much larger than she would have guessed from below. It was wide and spacious, and cut into the cliff itself where there was a finished facade with a door and shuttered windows. The line she had noticed was indeed a narrow path that led up the side of the cliff.

She shrugged out of her pack, let it fall to the floor and tossed her jacket and sweater on top of it. She was tempted to go into the dwelling without waiting for Quentin to catch up, but as she turned her gaze to the view that was visible over the treetops, she lost the impulse and stared.

The landscape rolled out in a downward slope from the passageway area, and a large lake or a sea sparkled a silvery blue in the distance. The edge of land curved around to a promontory where a long, white-pillared building dominated the scene.

The building's proportions were perfect. It was a monument of graceful simplicity. She shaded her eyes with one hand. Her avian eyesight was especially suited for long distances, and she clearly saw the outline of tall figures in between the pillars.

Other buildings of marble and limestone dotted the coastline, tall beautiful structures of classic design, not quite Greek or Roman—these had been built much earlier—but somehow they were evocative of both.

Along the visible part of the shore, slender piers held graceful Elven ships of ancient design. The sight of ships like these had all but disappeared from Earth itself, where the Elves, along with everybody else, had adopted ships with modern technology and design. On the horizon of the silvery blue water was a dark blue silhouette of land. She squinted, trying to discern details, but she couldn't tell if the land was an island or another promontory. It was possible they were in the bowl of a very large bay.

Quentin came up the narrow path with sure-footed, confident grace, and he joined her to look out at the view. If he hadn't come to stand right beside her, she would have missed his quick, quiet intake of breath.

"Yeah," she said. "It's stunning. When the Elves break away from hiding everything in the landscape, they really break away in style."

After a long moment, he turned to glance at the face of the cliff. He gestured to the door. "You didn't peek inside?"

"I got distracted by that." She waved in the direction of the temple.

"Yeah, that's a hell of a distraction." He gave the view another long look. "I could look at it all day."

She turned away and walked over to the door. It had an

ornate metal handle. She held her hand over the handle, checking for magic. There was none. She tried it, and the door opened easily.

A waft of cooler air from the interior brushed her face. It smelled stale and vaguely exotic, like some kind of Elven spice. Curiosity was goading her forward, but she forced herself to be pragmatic. "Nobody's been in here for a long time."

Quentin approached and stood at her shoulder to breathe deeply. After a moment he said, "There's a whisper of old Power, but it's very faint, like dissipating magic, and it doesn't feel active in any way. Exploring here can wait. We should move on toward the coast."

She had known he'd had some kind of magical training in his past, and wasn't surprised that what he said confirmed it. Mixed-race creatures who were "triple threats" were relatively rare and tended to have high concentrations of Power.

She said slowly, "I want very badly to take to the air and fly over the land just out of sheer curiosity, but I don't think I should quite yet."

He gave her a quick glance. "What's your thinking?"

"If the Elves abandoned their post and came in here, they had a compelling reason to do so. That compelling reason might not be very . . . friendly. We don't necessarily want to broadcast our presence right away."

"Can you cloak yourself?"

"Yes, from most creatures." She held his gaze with hers. "Could you sense me?"

"Probably," he admitted. "But I'm pretty sensitive to magic."

She shook her head. "We don't know what happened. But they didn't leave anybody at their post."

He said slowly, "Which means that, if they came here, they were dealing with something that took all of their combined strength and concentration."

She lifted a shoulder. "I just think until we know something, we'd better be wary."

"Good point." He turned away from the open doorway

and looked across the scenery again. "Let's see how far we can get before the sun sets."

It needed to be said. She told him quietly, "You know they might be dead, right? I mean, there's no recent sign of them anywhere that we expected them to be."

His jaw and body tightened. He didn't look at her. "Anything's possible. Including that."

After a moment, she sighed. "Well, hopefully we'll discover a much less catastrophic explanation for what's happened. Ready?"

He nodded. She took a few moments to repack her things, and he did the same. Guns and ammo went into the special side pocket created just to carry them. Combustible technologies didn't work in Other lands, and guns were worse than useless. They were downright dangerous.

They strapped on short swords at the hip, stuffed sweaters inside the packs, and tied jackets to the outside. As soon as they were ready, she followed him down the path that wound down to the lower surface some distance away.

Nearby, a path led into the trees. The ground looked like it had been well trodden, but fronds of leafy, delicate greenery had grown over it. After considering it, they looked at each other.

Quentin shook his head. Following it was too obvious.

She agreed. She nodded.

They stepped into the forest about twenty yards away from the path and moved quietly through the underbrush. For a long time they remained surrounded by a silence that was heavy with the lingering heat of the day.

The sunlight faded as full night approached, deepening the shadows on the forest floor. Her sharp hearing caught the furtive sounds of rustling in the distance, but nothing moved anywhere near them. The wild creatures that lived here sensed their presence.

I want to hunt, she said in Quentin's head.

He hesitated. *Fresh meat sounds good.*

He didn't need to explain his hesitation. Lighting a fire to cook a meal would broadcast their presence more loudly than using the overgrown path would. She could eat raw meat, but she had lost her taste for it many generations ago. It was one of the things she had lost to civilization.

She sighed. *Maybe tomorrow.*

Definitely tomorrow, he said. *Either that or we need to harvest more food supplies from any living quarters we find. We've eaten almost everything we brought with us.*

How they acquired food might very well be dictated by what they found. It made sense for them to go quickly and quietly into Numenlaur as an initial approach, but if they didn't find anything unusual, there would be no reason to remain quiet. Then they could hunt, cook and harvest food supplies in any way they liked.

Okay.

After that they didn't speak for some time. They kept moving until she could see glimpses of the moon through the branches of the trees. While the temperature cooled with full night, the constant breeze that sighed in the trees overhead rarely reached the forest floor, where the air remained close and warm.

They came to a stream where the streambed itself was much wider than the modest flow of water that currently ran down the middle. The abundant foliage spoke of plenty of rainfall, so the land wasn't under a drought. The stream probably carried the snow runoff from higher ground during the spring, then shrank in size during the summer months.

It created a widened area, much like a clearing. To their left, the path that they had been following led to a long stone bridge that spanned the entire streambed.

When they stepped out from underneath the trees, the air felt much cooler. They both moved to drink their fill of the delicious, pure liquid, scooping it in handfuls. When Aryal had finished, she dumped a handful of water at the back of her neck. The cold trickle of water on her sweaty skin was both a shock and a relief. She wiped her mouth and sat back on her heels to look up at the night sky.

The stars were so sharp, clear and bright, they looked as though she might be able to pluck them from the sky if she flew as high as she could. The moon was massive, appearing three times larger than what could be seen from Earth, and it was partially obscured by the top of the trees.

"We might as well take a break," Quentin muttered.

"Works for me." Aryal moved to the edge of the forest where she found a dry, grassy place. She threw down her things and sprawled beside them, loosening the sword buckled at her hip.

Quentin padded over to join her, setting his pack alongside hers. She noticed all over again how he moved silently, despite his size. He levered himself down to the ground beside her with his usual cat's grace. He hardly ever lost his footing, and when he did, he recovered himself quicker than almost anyone else she knew.

His body and his face might be in deep shadow, but she knew better than ever just what he looked like. Not only what he looked like, but how the most private part of him tasted.

The image of him, tied and spread out in front of her like a feast, flashed through her mind, and she reacted physically, hunger flaring again in a sharp, urgent pulse. Gods, he had been perfect in every detail, golden tanned skin, lean-muscled body, and an aura of danger that was to her as intoxicating as catnip. He really hadn't liked it when she tied him down. She could tell by the muscle that bunched in his jaw. But he had submitted, and that had been an epic moment.

And when she had taken that gorgeous, succulent penis of his into her mouth, he'd hissed between his teeth, a quick, inward drawn breath. It made his long abdominal muscles tighten into a rippling cascade that bunched and flexed underneath his golden skin.

She took in deep, even breaths. She didn't need to be able to see him to know that his long body had tightened. She could sense it, like the crackle of electricity in the air. He rolled onto his side, propped his head in one hand, and growled very softly, "We're going to enact that bargain soon."

Part of her catalogued just how romantic the scene was. Starry night, oversized full moon, and that long, arched stone bridge stretched out as a backdrop for the dark silhouette of one of the sexiest men she had ever seen.

She didn't have a romantic bone in her body, and she was not affected by any of it. Well, not much. Sure, maybe the sky. She was always a sucker for a beautiful sky, especially when she could fly up into it. And the scene was pretty enough. Certainly the man was sexy, especially when she had him hogtied to a table.

None of that led to romance.

She scowled and told him, "Our bargain is null and void at the moment. No electricity, no clocks, no way to time a half hour. And I'm not trusting you without some kind of an independent timekeeping device."

He laughed under his breath. The deep sound was witchy and wicked. It wound its way into her mind, like the brush of a black cat along her bare skin, and it enticed her to do things she would never otherwise consider doing, like twisting to mirror him, drawing him close and kissing him.

She almost did it, but then she pulled back at the last moment.

"We can amend the bargain. I'll bet we could find an hourglass in some kitchen when we raid for supplies."

"I had no idea you were so interested in me," she mocked.

"My interest in you is purely pornographic." He reached out to trace her mouth with a finger. "Your tongue is very talented when you stop using it to talk."

Laughter threatened to shake through her. She stifled it. She didn't want him to think she found him amusing, and he sure as hell wasn't charming. "Remind me to tell you that you say the nicest things—when you start saying them. Maybe that's what I can use my half hour for, to compel you to compliment me."

His teeth flashed in a shadowed gleam of a smile. "You think I couldn't compliment you without being compelled?"

"I don't care about the compliments," she told him. "I just want to watch you struggle."

He slipped his forefinger between her lips and penetrated deeply into her mouth. Not only did she allow it, she sucked him. His breathing deepened.

"You'll have to find some other way to do that, then," he whispered. "I've hated you, and you've pissed me off more than anybody else I've ever met. You're also one of the best fighters I've ever seen. I watched you every time you were in the Arena during the Games. And I was too mad to admit it at the time, but what you did back in Prague, when you pinned me against the metal door, was crazy awesome. And of course then there's your mouth. Your wet, warm, extremely dexterous, tight mouth." He pulled his finger out slowly until just the tip rested between her lips. Then he pushed it back in, fucking her in an almost leisurely way. "See how much better things are when you shut up?"

She had known hate sex with him would be hella good. It was even better in this . . . place they had come to, this not-quite-hate-but-something-else place. *If you find an hourglass, I'll consider it. But next time I go first.*

"What if I don't want you to go first?" he murmured, sliding his finger along her tongue in a slow, intimate stroke. "What if I want to bargain for something else?"

Behind the silhouette of his head, something moved on the bridge.

It was a quick black streak of—something.

She rolled to her feet and drew her sword in the same motion. In one lightning-fast, fluid motion, Quentin sprang upright and whipped out his sword too. He spun to put his back to hers, and only then asked telepathically, *What is it?*

Whatever else she might think or feel about him, his instincts as a fighting partner were dead-on accurate. She approved. She said, *I saw something move on the bridge.*
What?

She could feel him at her back through the thin material of her T-shirt. His body heat radiated against her skin, and the back of his shoulders brushed hers. She said, *I don't know.*

They watched and listened. Nothing moved except for leaves in the wind. The only noises she heard were normal night sounds. She scented the air and smelled nothing out of the ordinary, and, because she was who she was, she looked up. There was nothing in the sky that didn't belong there.

All the while, Quentin stayed at her back, hot as a burning ember and steady as the earth underneath her feet. She had the time and the space to think, *all of that coiled danger at my back, and for once it's on my side.*

It felt strange, good and even exhilarating.

He didn't relax, but after a few moments, he asked, *You're sure.*

Yes, I'm sure I saw something, she told him. *No, I don't know what it was. It was a streak of something black. It didn't look like it was connected to anything, and it moved independently of everything else. It was almost like—*

She looked up at the night sky again. The entire scene radiated normality. She didn't trust it. She stared at the bridge, and studied both ends where it disappeared into the darkness under the trees. It was empty.

Quentin spoke out loud. "It was almost like what?"

"It was almost like a shadow, except there wasn't anything physical attached to it," she said. "Or it wasn't attached to anything else."

She grabbed her pack by a strap and strode for the bridge. Leaving behind any belongings was a rookie's mistake. Quentin followed and they leaped onto the bridge. Throwing their things together, they moved to opposite ends of the bridge.

Aryal stopped just before stepping off of the bridge and going under the tree line. She still held her sword. She bent and sniffed at the stone, running her fingers lightly over it. It was dry and still held a lingering warmth from the heat of the day. There was no scent of any creature that passed by recently, just the faint odor of dirt, recent rain and mildew.

She straightened and retreated to the packs without putting her back to the dark, shadowed forest, and she didn't stop until she came to Quentin.

Full moonlight fell on them. It was almost as clear and bright as daylight. It emphasized the strong slash of cheekbones on his face, and that lean, stubborn jaw. He sheathed his sword and stood with his hands on his hips. "No magical residue," he said, still speaking quietly.

She sheathed her sword too and told him, "If you say anything about disbelieving me, I'm probably going to punch you again."

"Wouldn't dream of it," he said. "Remember, I saw how you reacted. You're one of the oldest creatures I've ever met. You're also one of the most combative, and yet you're still alive. I give your instincts and reactions full credit for that, because my gods, the total number of people and creatures who must have tried to kill you over the years must be mind boggling."

She narrowed her eyes and tilted her head. "I think I'm going to take that as a compliment too."

A quick grin flared and died on his face. "You would. So, what we have is something very dark and quick that moves independently, and leaves no footprints, no scent, and no magical trace behind."

"That sounds right."

He walked over to their packs and handed hers to her. "That sound like anything you've ever run into before?"

She shrugged her pack on. "Nope."

"So what we really have is an anomaly."

"That's about the size of it, although it's only an anomaly to us," she pointed out. "It might be a perfectly natural part of the environment here."

After donning his own pack, he belted it at the waist. His head bent, he said, "I don't like anomalies."

"I don't either." She looked at the shadowed forest ahead of them. "In my experience, there's almost always an explanation. And it's hardly ever a good one."

≡ TWELVE ≡

Quentin rubbed his face. It felt like his life was full of too many goddamn anomalies. So many of them centered on the sexy, frenzy-inducing female who stood beside him.

His modern mind kept snagging on the concept of her identity. Part of him kept insisting she was masculine, but then he would look at her, really look at her, and realize that she *was* feminine in a way he had never known before—strong, confident, and completely devoid of the mannerisms and characteristics that popular culture defined as femininity.

She wasn't ruled by fear of defying conventions. As far as he could determine, she wasn't ruled by fear in any form, and all her emotions were painted in primary colors. At times it seemed primitive, even exasperating, but it was always colorful and exhilarating.

When she loved someone, she would do so completely and passionately, no reservations or qualifications, or the kind of emotional blackmail that said "I will love you if you will only do this, or be that."

What would it be like to be loved with that kind of . . . purity?

He looked at her and experienced a sense of freedom, a previously unnamed, unidentified emotion. Something inside of him had cut loose, the wild, dangerous part of him he usually kept under such strict control. It felt like it ran unfettered.

Usually the only time he felt this way was when he had turned into the panther and took to an uninhabited area so that he could roam without concern of running into humans or other creatures. Where that wild part of him was going and what it would do when it got there, he didn't know.

He forced himself away from useless reverie and concentrated on the tasks at hand.

"All right," he said. "I think we should keep moving. We don't have any shelter here, and we do have a lot of shadowy places where any number of anomalies can hide."

"Agreed," she said. "We should keep going until we find shelter, break out of the forest, or until morning comes."

Without any further discussion, he headed off the bridge and away from the path, into the forest. Rather to his surprise, she allowed him to take the lead without argument. They moved quietly through the underbrush. Even though they hadn't been attacked, all of his senses remained on high alert. He didn't like the number of unanswered questions they had accumulated.

He guessed that the coastal scene they had seen earlier was as much as twenty to twenty-five miles away from the cliff house. Moving carefully through the dark as they were, they wouldn't reach that before morning. He was starting to get tired, which meant Aryal had to be getting tired too. Instinct drove him now, and he didn't think it would be a good thing to go into the city without getting some rest first.

He said as much to Aryal telepathically.

Makes sense, she said simply.

He waited but she didn't say anything more. It was another one of those anomalies that he had begun to accumulate. They weren't arguing nearly as much as they should have been. Since she could pull an argument out of thin air, that probably meant she was plotting something, but his whack-job radar wasn't going off, so he doubted his own conclusion.

It was interesting to experience her as an asset, as opposed to a drain or an outright danger. He could acknowledge that her skill set made her useful in her sentinel position in investigations, but that was an intellectual observation. Now he was actually experiencing what it was like to work with her as a partner, and she was every bit as good as he would have expected any of the other sentinels to be—fast, sharp, relevant and logical.

He liked what he saw of Aryal as a working partner. He respected it, respected her. That was another anomaly.

Of course so far they hadn't really had to interact much with other people. And they did pretty much kick the shit out of each other already. He grinned.

Time became a formless thing that passed uncounted in the shadows. He sank into his animal awareness, feeling the muscles of his body work while he noted the details of his surroundings. It wouldn't do to relax and slip into carelessness. He watched the more intense shadows, looking for anything that seemed especially dark and that moved differently than any of the leafy fronds or tree limbs that swayed in the breeze.

When he finally came up to another tree line, the change was so abrupt it surprised him. He stopped before breaking out of the underbrush, and Aryal brushed his back before she stopped too.

They had come upon a meadow with long, coarse grasses that looked tall enough to come up to their chests. That meadow could disguise a lot. He glanced at the sky that was beginning to lighten in one direction. Okay, he was calling that direction east. Dawn was not that far away. It was still too dark to see much beyond what was close in front of them, but he guessed that, as long as they had hiked, they had reached the other side of the forest and were now probably a few miles away from the coast.

"I don't think we're going to get any better place to stop before we reach the coast," he said. "And I don't want to get there without having had some rest first."

"We should camp here," she said. "And take watches. That way we'll both get some sleep."

"Works for me."

Aryal lost a coin toss, which meant Quentin could rest first. He ate a protein bar quickly to stave off the worst of any hunger pains. It didn't have enough calories to satisfy him, especially after the expenditure of energy over the last two days, but it would be enough to let him take a nap.

He stretched out underneath a tree to catch any shade it might give after the sun came up, and he used his pack as a pillow. Aryal stood nearby, leaning back against another tree with her arms crossed and one booted heel hiked up on the trunk. She didn't face either the meadow or the forest, but positioned herself at an angle so that she could look easily in either direction.

She looked comfortable, capable, and alert enough to stand guard all day.

He watched her surreptitiously from under lowered eyelids as she tore open a protein bar and took a bite. She had tied her hair back with a piece of leather, but a few fine strands fell forward on the clean line of her forehead. The T-shirt she had worn underneath her sweater was a plain white cotton tank top. It hugged the long slim line of her torso, highlighting her high, slight breasts and the twin peaks of her nipples.

His body clenched with hunger. He thought of how her breasts felt in his hands, the softness giving way under his touch, how her nipple tasted in his mouth.

Unbidden, what she had said yesterday played through his mind again.

If you do anything to actively try to hurt any of the people I care about—that's when I will come after you, and I won't stop until I hurt you bad, or you end up dead, or maybe even both those things. That's my bottom line.

It really was quite simple.

From everything he had heard, harpies rarely gave anybody a second chance at anything. If you got on their shit list, you usually stayed there forever. She really might not care about his smuggling past, but he also realized what a huge concession she had made when she let go of her investigation. There wouldn't be any more chances after that.

If she ever found out what he had done to Dragos and Pia last year, he had no doubt what would happen. It would be open war again, and this time the hostilities between them wouldn't stop until one of them was dead.

That was the thought that finally leashed the unfettered, wild part of him.

He turned his head away from her. Only then was he able to get some sleep.

She woke him after a couple of hours, and without a word they exchanged positions. Dawn had broken, bringing humid warmth. He felt sweaty and dirty, and he wished they were near running water again.

Aryal curled on her side and threw part of her jacket over her face. After that she didn't move. Quentin rummaged in his pack for the last of his food. He had one more can of beef stew, which he would be heartily glad to see the last of, and three protein bars left. He ate all of it except a final protein bar. He wanted to eat that too, but instead he tucked it away. The promise of new, different food was close, but it wasn't with them yet.

The sun rose higher and so did the heat. The area was quiet except for the occasional drone of insects and trill of birdsong. No unexplained shadows, no anomalies, at least not any within sight.

He hadn't had the chance to think much about the four missing Elves—too much had been going on, and Aryal had consumed most of his attention—but now he did so with a sense of foreboding. He didn't know two of the names that Ferion had given him: Cemalla and Aralorn, the one female, the other male.

He did know the other two Elves, Linwe and Caerreth. Linwe was a firecracker, a young Elf who had recently dyed the tips of her spiky brown hair blue. She had laughing brown eyes and a propensity to teasing—or at least she had before the tragedy at Lirithriel Wood.

Quentin was quite fond of her. They were not related, either by blood or by marriage, but he still considered her part of his larger family group. Caerreth was a shy young male, bookish and remarkably insensitive to his surroundings. Quentin had met him before on his visits to Lirithriel.

All four of them, Ferion had told him, were younger and less experienced. They were the ones who Ferion could spare. Quentin shook his head. The longer time passed without any explanation for their absence, the higher his concern spiked. He was antsy to get to the coast and start investigating, to see if they could find any sign of the Elves there.

He judged the time by the sun's position in the sky. When he estimated a couple of hours had passed, he said to Aryal, "Time to wake up, sunshine."

Her sleep-roughened voice sounded from underneath the jacket. "You need to stop calling me that. I don't know anyone less filled with sunshine than me."

"I like the irony," he told her.

She rolled to a sitting position, her hair all over the place. She raked it back with both hands and groped for the leather tie that had come loose in her sleep.

"Why don't you cut your hair short if it annoys you?" he asked curiously. He stifled the odd, foolish twinge of regret at his own words. Her hair was another thing about her that was simply beautiful, the long black strands thick, luxurious and gleaming, but more often than not she seemed impatient with it.

It had been wonderful to sink his hands into that soft black mass, to imprison her by clenching a fist into it, and pull her head back and kiss her. He pushed the thought away. Like an irritating gnat, it refused to be swatted and hovered at the back of his consciousness.

"Getting a haircut takes time," she said. She dragged her pack open and wolfed down breakfast. He noted, with a little amusement, that she didn't tuck any of the protein bars aside for later but kept eating until the last of her food was gone. Then she looked around with a disgruntled expression. "First item of business is we've got to secure more food one way or another."

"The coast should be just four or five miles away now," he said. "We're bound to start seeing some dwellings soon. At the very least, we should be able to find some wayfarer bread."

Outside of Elven communities, their wayfarer bread was a rare, prized commodity, but within Elven communities, it was a staple of almost every home. Vegetarian, delicate and flavored with honey, the bread was famous for its delicious flavor, healing properties and long shelf life.

However, Aryal didn't seem impressed. She made a face. "I suppose it's calories and will do in a pinch," she said.

"I don't know why I keep finding this hard to believe, but you actually are contrary in just about every conceivable way," Quentin told her. When she rose to her feet, indicating she was done with her meal, he scooped up his backpack and shouldered it. "Everybody loves those wafers. Everybody except you."

She flipped him off, the action casual, even companionable, as she strapped on her pack and grumbled, "I have a sweet tooth. They're not bad. But I need a lot of calories, and I'm getting really hungry for fresh protein."

He ran his gaze down her lean, racy frame. She flew with power and speed, and that took a lot of energy. He was feeling the need for fresh protein too. "We'll get some today, one way or another." He turned his attention to trekking through the meadow. "I'm not inclined to fight my way through that long grass. I think we should give up the stealthy approach and take the path. We're leaving a scent trail anyway, and if your anomaly from last night was sentient, something has already become aware of our presence."

"The direct approach." She shrugged. "That works for me." They moved along the tree line until they found the path. It was wider as it cut through the meadow grass, as if this portion had seen more traffic. Aryal said, "Let's get somewhere, already."

She sounded impatient, as if her self-imposed grounding was starting to wear on her, and she took off down the path at a jog. Quentin grinned as he followed her down the corridor created by the long grass. The sun beat down on their heads, and the wind caused the grass to ripple in long silvery green waves much like the surface of an ocean.

They could see farther ahead of them now that it was daylight, to a distant patch of white-capped water. He caught glimpses of that blue land or island, and he wondered what was over there.

After jogging for a couple of miles, they reached a slight incline. As they ran upward, they left the grassy meadowland behind, and when they reached the top, the coast lay spread out in front of them, closer than ever.

The path cut a zigzag down a long steep hill. A few houses with terraced gardens populated the hillside. A cluster of more buildings dotted the area at the bottom, where a dirt road angled toward the city by the sea. Every line of the city in silhouette, every building, was gracious and elegant. The sight pulled at something inside of him.

For the first time since clearing the forest, he turned to look behind them. The cliffs that held the passageway rose higher to a mountain range that covered the horizon.

"What happened to their horses?" he said suddenly. "Gaeleval enthralled the Numenlaurians. They crossed to the other passageway in the Bohemian Forest. Then they made their way across that Other land to the entrance to Lirithriel Wood, and they were all on foot. There wasn't a single horse anywhere in that army, and Elves love their horses. So where were they? Where *are* they?"

Aryal gave him a quick look, and her face shadowed. She said nothing.

Abruptly he turned away, rubbed the back of his neck and looked at the ground, while a hard, hurting knot ached in his chest. She didn't have to say anything. He knew the answer as well as she did.

The enthralled Elves had been zombielike, devoid of will and intention. They had been in wretched condition, poorly dressed and often without shoes. They hadn't had

148

the capacity to look after themselves, let alone look after any other living creature. If any of their horses had been put to pasture when the Elves had been enthralled, the horses could have had a good chance of survival. If they had been stabled, they would have starved to death.

The city they looked down upon was more beautiful than many of the great cities on Earth, and it was worse than lifeless in the aftermath of a holocaust.

He shut down his feelings and turned professional. "Pia told me that she talked to Gaeleval in a dream the night before Dragos killed him."

"Did she?" Aryal sounded thoughtful. "Did she say what they said to each other?"

He looked over the idyllic coastal scene without really seeing it. "Did you know he wielded something called a God Machine? That was how he enthralled so many Elves and did the kind of damage that he did. It amplified his Power."

"I know." She sounded cautious, as if the God Machine might be some kind of taboo subject, but Quentin had heard some of the old Elven stories and had already known of the *Deus Machinae*.

"In her dream, Pia asked Gaeleval how he had gotten the Machine," he said. "Camthalion, the Numenlaurian lord, had held his Machine for a very long time, ever since Numenlaur closed itself off from the rest of the world. Apparently it drove him mad. He summoned Gaeleval to the palace, where Gaeleval claimed he found everyone dead. Palace attendants, Camthalion's children and their mother. They had been kneeling in the throne room, and their throats had been slit. Camthalion had poured oil over his head and set himself on fire."

"That's pretty fucking crazy," she said softly.

He gave her a sharp look. "Maybe it happened the way Gaeleval said it did, and maybe it didn't. Maybe Gaeleval was the one who killed them. Whatever the real story is, I think there's going to be some ugly shit down there."

She took a deep breath. "I understand." They both fell silent. After a moment, she tapped his shoulder. "Hey," she said. "Come on. My mouth is burning up, it's so dry. We need to find water. Let's get down to those houses and see if there's anything to eat and drink."

He nodded and turned back around.

The path was steep enough that it made jogging a bad idea, so they descended at a slower pace. The first house they came to was a surprise. It was set into the hill, and they didn't see it until the path turned and took them right by it. The front of the house faced the sea and was painted white, and flower beds were planted in front of it.

The door stood open.

Quentin had his sword in his hand before he was fully conscious of drawing it. Aryal drew hers more slowly. She whispered, "It might have been open all this time."

"It also might not have," he said.

They were going to harvest what they needed from the homes they found, but they were also going to take only what they needed and treat the property with respect. The thought that someone else might have come and looted through the belongings of a Numenlaurian victim caused anger to torch along the corners of his mind.

He strode for the door and pushed it open with one flattened hand, while his sharp gaze noted every detail and he expanded his magic sense. There had been no recent Power expenditure.

The interior of the house was shadowed and cool. He walked inside while Aryal threw open shutters, letting in more light. The furniture looked minimalist and comfortable, and a fireplace with a simple hearth had half-burned logs. He wanted to check to see if the logs were cool, but first he needed to make sure the rooms were clear.

He found a body lying in the doorway of a bedroom. It was an Elven male, lying face down, long hair spilled about his head and shoulders. He had been dead for some time.

Quentin did not know that because of any state of decay, as he would with any human or mortal body. Some alchemy of their race caused Elves to look as natural in death as they had in life for years. When they finally began to decay, or so he had heard, they smelled sweet, like crushed flowers.

He could tell the male had been dead for some time because the body had been partially eaten. Wildlife had gotten into the house. The lower half of one leg was missing entirely.

He carefully eased the body over, and several insects scuttled away. The male wore soft, loose clothing, such as what one might wear to bed, if one wore pajamas. He had been stabbed several times, and there were defense wounds on his arms.

Quentin looked beyond the body into the bedroom. The bedcovers had been thrown back on the bed. The Elf had been disturbed while he was resting.

Aryal had moved to join him. She stood staring down at the body for a long moment. Then she stepped over it and walked into the deeply shadowed bedroom. "There's evidence of a partner," she said. "Feminine clothes, jewelry, et cetera. I've looked through the other rooms. There aren't any other bodies."

He took a blanket off of the bed and covered the body carefully, then stood, slamming the door on his emotions again. "In Lirithriel when Gaeleval enthralled the Elves, he did it at night, when most of them were asleep. Not everyone was asleep though, and the ones who had been enthralled attacked the others. It looks like the same thing could have happened here."

In the middle of the bedroom, she turned to consider him. "This is going to be a grim homecoming for any Numenlaurian Elves who recover enough to make it back."

"I know." He wiped his forehead with the back of one arm. "We should check to see if there's any food that might still be useable."

"Right."

Aryal moved past him and he followed her. The dwelling was a simple one, and the kitchen was recessed back into the hill. He heard the sound of trickling water as he stepped into the room, which was in almost total darkness until Aryal struck a match. The tiny yellow flame threw enough illumination for her to locate a lamp set on a table. She lit it and stepped back. A cooking hearth was inset into one wall. The chimney would have to go through the soil of the hill itself to provide some kind of outlet for the smoke. Against another wall, an underground spring provided ample running water, which trickled out of a fountain.

Even though Numenlaur had been cut off from the outside world for so long, the house seemed thoroughly modern in concept as it used natural elements as assets. It would be warm and easy to heat in the winter, and stay cool in the summer.

While he admired the design of the house, Aryal moved around the kitchen. She walked into a deep recess that must be some kind of pantry. Then she walked out again.

"The cupboard shelves are bare," she said. "Somebody's been here before us."

The blunt words sent a jolt of adrenaline through him. "You're sure it isn't wildlife."

He hadn't quite phrased it as a question, but she answered as if he had. "There's been some wildlife in there. It's messy and stuff has been knocked to the floor and spilled. But there's no wayfarer bread, or anything preserved in jars that might be portable."

Wayfarer bread was stored wrapped in leaves that were a natural repellant. The leaves masked the smell of the bread, and they tasted bad to animals and insects. "All right," he said. "We had an instinct to be wary. Now we know for sure."

She shrugged and walked over to the fountain to drink deeply and wash off. When she was through, he moved in to do the same. The clear, pure water was delicious and immensely refreshing.

Aryal said, "It could have been the missing Elves."

"Could have," he said. He ducked his head to wet his hair. The cold on the back of his neck was a shock to the system and sharply bracing. "But I don't believe it. I don't know two of the Elves, and I've only met the third so I can't speak for them, but I find it hard to imagine that Linwe could have walked by the body and just left it alone. I think she would have covered him, like I did. She certainly would have shut the door to keep out any more scavengers."

"So it was somebody else." She leaned back against the table, one foot kicked over the other. "Maybe the reason why the Elves are missing? Maybe they came in after whoever crossed over." She shook her head. "Wait a minute, does that make sense? If the Elves had found evidence of someone who came into Numenlaur, why didn't we?"

"This all could have happened weeks ago," he reminded her. "The evidence could have been washed away by the elements by now."

She pushed away from the table. "Whatever the answers are, we're not going to learn any more here. Let's go."

He blew out the lamp, and as they left the silent house, he shut the door firmly behind them. At least if the dead Elf had any surviving friends or family, they would have something to bury when they returned home.

They continued down the hill and stopped at a few more houses on the way. The next home didn't have any dead bodies. It also didn't have any food. The third home was also empty of bodies, but this time they found a few loaves of wayfarer bread. They broke open the wafers and ate them immediately.

It wasn't enough food, but Quentin felt a pickup in his energy immediately. As he wiped his mouth with the back of one hand, he said, "Whoever was scavenging got their needs met after looking into only a few pantries, and they hit the same houses we did, on the route from the passageway, so we're looking for a small party. One, maybe two people."

Aryal thought about it and nodded. "That's how I would call it. Let's hit one or two more houses and see if we can get some supplies, then move into the city."

The next house they came upon was large, clearly the home of someone prosperous, and it had a stable and a large pasture. Quentin paused on the path to the door, staring out over the land. He couldn't see the whole pasture.

Aryal paused too and looked in the direction of his gaze. She scowled but said, "Check out the pasture if you want. I can search for food."

"Okay." He handed her his backpack and walked over to

the pasture. Putting one hand on the top wooden rail, he vaulted over the fence. He jogged into the field until he could see around a copse of trees to the other end. If there had been any horses in the pasture, they had leaped the fence a while ago, and he wouldn't bother checking in the stable. He spun around and jogged back.

As he approached the section of fence nearest to the house, Aryal exploded out the front door. Already primed for possible trouble, his heart kicked. He stared as she ran several yards, stopped, and turned in a circle with one hand pressed to her flat stomach, the other over her eyes. The part of her face that was visible was clearly distressed. *Was she injured?*

His sword was in his hand before he realized it. He raced to the fence and leaped over without touching it. She bent at the waist, and he put on a burst of speed. As he reached her, she was making a soft noise, as if she sobbed for breath.

As if she—*Aryal*—sobbed.

His world bled with wrongness. He put a hand on her back, and she flinched. She hadn't realized he had approached? He glared at the open door of the house. She had set their backpacks together just outside.

He asked harshly, "Are you hurt?"

She shook her head and straightened. Her expression was clenched, her eyes filled with horror.

What the fuck?

"What happened?" he asked more quietly. Even though she had indicated she wasn't hurt, his gaze ran down her body anyway, instinctively checking for harm. The way she had clutched at her stomach, it was as though she had been stabbed.

She swallowed, and her mouth twisted. "Horses weren't the only creatures that the enthralled Elves failed to look after, Quentin."

═ THIRTEEN ═

Aryal could see that Quentin hadn't yet pieced together what she meant. He looked sharp, fierce, still ready for battle, his sword gripped in one hand while he rubbed her back with the other. She didn't think he was aware that he was doing it.

He started for the house, and she grabbed his arm. She told him, "It serves no purpose for you to go in there."

He glared at her, jerked out of her hold and strode for the house.

She put a hand over her eyes with a sigh. Some people always had to take the hard road. Then, because she knew what was waiting for him in that still, silent house, she followed at a slower pace.

He moved from room to room, his movements angry and aggressive. Then he came to the doorway of one room and stopped with a jerk as if someone had punched him.

Fresh tears flooded her eyes. Gods, she hated crying. She walked up behind him and this time she was the one to put a hand on his rigid back.

It was a beautiful room, clearly the jewel of the entire house. Loving care had gone into every detail, from the bright treasures of tapestries that hung on the walls, to the handmade toys, the books, and the three gold and jeweled animals that sat on a shelf.

The most precious jewel of all lay in the beautifully carved cradle, his tiny body dressed in soft, embroidered silk. His skin glowed, bright ivory and peach. From his delicate, rosebud mouth to his miniscule, pointed ears, he was perfect in every way. Like all dead Elves, he looked as if he had fallen asleep moments ago.

Quentin's jaw worked.

She said, her voice hoarse, "The door was shut. Not the door to the house—that was unlatched. This door. I think that's why he's still so perfect. None of the wildlife could get in here."

He turned his head and looked at her. His eyes were reddened. "All of them? All of the babies are dead."

Her mouth worked again, and two tears spilled over. Damn it. "Any child that was too young to enthrall must have been left behind, which means any child too young to fend for itself."

She had seen horrible things in her life, but this was one of the most appalling and heartbreaking. Children were rare to the Elder Races, as if nature compensated for their long life spans, and they came most rarely to the Elves. Sometimes Elves longed for children for thousands of years, and they greeted the birth of each one with joy.

The death of any single baby or child, of any species, was a terrible tragedy. The death of all the Elven babies and young children in Numenlaur was simply unspeakable.

His chest moved, a quick, involuntary movement. He whispered, "I thought before they were crippled from everything that has happened to them. This will have cut out their heart. No wonder so many are committing suicide."

When she had opened the door, she had been totally unprepared for what was inside, and the sight had slammed her so hard she had tried to run away from the pain. Now, she did the opposite. She walked into that beautiful room and sat on the stool beside the cradle to gaze at the baby's face. Her face tickled. She wiped at it, and found that her cheeks were wet.

"I don't know how to walk away from him," she said. She picked up one of the gold animals, a frog with emerald eyes, and turned it over and over in her hands. It was small and heavy, and something in her mind told her that it meant something significant, but she couldn't figure out what it was. "It feels wrong to leave him lying here unprotected. What if something manages to get in? And we can't bury him. That would be stealing even more from his parents, if either one of them survived. They can't come back to just find their baby gone." Her voice broke. "Goddammit."

As he had done when they had talked about the Elven horses, Quentin spun to turn his back on the room, but this time he turned around again as if he couldn't help himself. He walked toward her, every line of his body speaking of reluctance.

She wiped at her eyes again. "It's not that I haven't seen bad shit before. Battlefields with thousands of dead, and thousands more injured and dying." She barked out a dark-sounding laugh. "My gods, have I seen bad shit. I just haven't seen this kind of bad shit before."

He knelt beside her and looked at the occupant in the cradle. Quentin's face was still clenched as he fought with his emotions. In a barely audible voice, he said, "I want Amras Gaeleval alive again so I can hurt him. A lot."

She put a hand on his shoulder, gripping him tightly. His muscles were rigid. "Now you sound like me."

He glanced at her, pain pooling in his eyes. Then in a gesture that seemed as natural as breathing, he took hold of her hand and leaned his forehead against it.

Had she really reached out to him, and had he really accepted it?

Wonders never ceased.

She looked at his bowed head and slumped, broad shoulders. This wasn't fun pain. This was the bad kind of pain, and nothing about it was like brandy and chocolate. This was more like taking a knife to the gut and then watching yourself bleed out.

Something welled deep inside. She supposed it was compassion. Or maybe empathy. Whatever it was, it moved her to set the frog on the floor and reach out with her free hand to stroke Quentin's soft, dark gold hair.

He looked at her over their clasped hands, a raw, direct look. When she met his gaze it was with a shock of connection that shifted something important inside.

Then he squeezed her fingers and let her go. "I can seal the door," he said. "If there's anyone with magic sense in the area, that'll pretty much tell them we're here."

"If it leaves him protected, so be it," she said. "Besides, I know we chose to be wary but I'm no good at pussyfooting around."

A ghost of a smile played over his firm, well-cut lips. "I'm glad you saw fit to tell me, because otherwise I never would have known."

It didn't feel right to punch him in that room, so instead she shoved him lightly, enough to rock him but not enough to knock him over. She rose to her feet. "Do what you've got to do. How long will it take?"

"Five minutes." He picked up the gold frog and set it carefully back into place with the other two figurines, then stood too.

They were quite lovely, exquisitely shaped and detailed, down to the folds in the frog's eyes. If the set were kept together, on Earth it would fetch a fortune, especially with today's gold prices.

She paused and cocked her head. "So we have one or maybe two people who came into Numenlaur," she said softly. "And they are not here to loot for treasure."

Quentin swiveled to face her, his gaze keen. "Because the figurines are still here."

"Along with the jewelry in the first few houses we went through," she told him. "I didn't look at them closely, but I remember seeing some serious sparkle."

"Which begs the question," he said. "Why did they come here?"

"Come on." She slapped him on the shoulder. "Do your thing so we can get out of here. It's time we hit the city."

He nodded, and she left him to go through the pantry supplies. They had hit pay dirt with this house. There were several wafers of wayfarer bread, along with cured meat, jerky, nuts, and dried fruit. She took everything they could carry and, chewing on a strip of jerky, she knelt outside to tuck the new supplies in their packs while the Power from Quentin's spell built in a slow flare that snapped and disappeared, like a rubber band settling into place.

Her head lifted, and she looked around, assessing the surrounding landscape that seemed so quiet, as if she and Quentin truly were the only ones around.

Maybe one of the Elves in the missing party was a magic user and could sense what Quentin had just done. If they were still alive. Or maybe they had just attracted the attention of the trespassers, and maybe those trespassers weren't friendly.

If so, bring 'em on. After discovering the tragedy in the house, shedding tears and suffering through pangs of empathy, she was in the mood for a little gratuitous violence.

They walked the rest of the way to the coast, both eating jerky. The sun beat down on their heads from a cloudless sky as the afternoon turned sweltering. Then a breeze picked up, blowing off the water and bringing a welcome respite from the heat.

Aryal didn't want to look at Quentin, and she was glad he didn't seem to be in the mood to talk. She didn't have to glance at him to know how he walked, moving his long, muscled body with that smooth, boneless grace of his that ate away the miles like a sleek Porsche purring down a road. She could do with not seeing him at all for a couple of months, but for the moment that option wasn't in the cards.

Her fingers kept remembering the silken glide of his short hair as she stroked him, the feeling of his forehead pressed to the back of her hand as he gripped her. The way he had come running when she had burst out of the house, his expression sharp with concern. His hand, rubbing her back. The raw emotion in his face as he stared at the tiny occupant of that exquisitely carved cradle.

She was in real trouble, all right.

She was in imminent danger of believing Quentin Caeravorn might actually be a decent man after all. Or at least part of him was, the essential part, the part that could be counted on to do the right thing when push came to shove.

Hrmph. She would rather be caught dead before she admitted that to anyone back in New York. It would completely trash whatever reputation she had. With everybody. She was quite sure right now that some of them didn't expect both her and Quentin to return in one piece.

And well, as far as that went, it was early days yet.

The curving road followed along the coast just on the other side of barrier dunes. She couldn't contain her curiosity and had to jog over the dunes to taste the water, which was salty. From the shore, she could see a few more details of the blue land in the distance. It looked like an island. A dun-colored line at the water hinted at sand, and a glimpse of green trees on a sharply rising slope rose from the water. Through the trees on the slope, she could see some kind of building.

She made a promise to herself to fly over the next day to explore it, or at least take enough time to make a quick pass over it from the air. She had kept herself grounded for too long, and she was beginning to feel it as a jittering in her bones.

As they reached the shore, the temple on top of the promontory became larger and clearer as well. The figures, along with the pillars that interspersed them, were easily fifty feet tall and dominated the landscape. There were three statues along the side of the temple that faced them, and from the shoreline she could see the profile of the figure facing out over the water. It was male. Was that the god Taliesin, and would the other half of the figure be female? The pattern would make sense if there were three statues on the other side of the temple. One statue for each of the seven Elder Races gods.

Quentin had joined her at the edge of the shore.

"The water is salty," she said to him. She nodded at the temple. "Have you heard any stories about whether or not the palace is part of that temple?"

"No," he told her. "But making a guess right now, I'd say not. I think that's the palace." He pointed, and she followed the line of his arm to the long building that hugged the top of the hill where the promontory reached the mainland.

Built of limestone, with four marble pillars at the front, the building glowed golden and white against the green foliage and blue skyline. An immensely long staircase was cut into the hill and lined with stone.

She sucked a tooth and made a small grimace. "Yeah, that looks palacey all right."

He grinned. The lines of it creased his lean face. "Come on. No time to lollygag and play in the water."

She followed him over the barrier dunes, watching as his powerful body and long legs made short work of the slippery sand. Some contrary impulse made her say, "You know, just because we've sexed it up a couple of times and shared a bad moment over—back there—doesn't mean I like you very much."

He turned to face her, blew out a huge breath and rolled his eyes. "Whew, that saves me from having to ask you to back the fuck off. For a while there on the walk, you were getting a little clingy."

Internal pressure built. She tried to swallow it down. Then their eyes met, and they both burst out laughing.

It felt a lot like the camaraderie she had built up over the years with the other sentinels, not quite the same, but it felt good. He looked great, tanned and blue eyed and bathed in sunshine. He was the very picture of the kind of man who'd had the world laid at his feet by every female he had ever met.

He could have anyone he wanted, anytime he wanted. He was sexy, alpha, secure in himself, and the world adored him for it. He was only messing around with her because there wasn't anybody around, and if they wanted to go back to their jobs, they were stuck with each other's company for at least the next week and a half.

Hell, it was the only reason why she was messing around with him too, wasn't it? She might have found him . . . okay, sexually intriguing . . . back in New York, but she would *never* have acted on anything, especially when she had been so suspicious of him.

Her own feelings confused her. She hated when they did that, almost as much as she hated to cry. Complex, confusing feelings felt like she had a crowd of strangers in her head, and they were all shouting for attention in some foreign language she didn't understand.

She cut her laughter off abruptly and scowled at him. That only made him laugh harder, and of course *that* made her feel prone to violence.

Which made her feel better.

Gods, she was a fucking mess, sometimes.

She waved a hand in the air and stomped off. The last five minutes had become meaninglessly complicated. For good measure, she flipped up her middle finger and was rewarded with a guffaw. Oh, screw it all, anyway.

But as much as she didn't know what to call it, and try as she might to deny it, something had happened back in that beautiful, terrible nursery. Something indefinable but important had shifted between them. She just wished she knew what it was.

Then they reached the center of the city, and she put it all behind her.

By modern standards on Earth, it wasn't very big. The entire area was easily reached by walking. Many of the large buildings looked like spacious homes, while the rest appeared to be perhaps government buildings, and some looked like shops. Given the size of the Numenlaurian army that Aryal had seen, that would mean many of the Elves must have lived scattered across the land.

The only way Gaeleval could have ensnared them all— or at least the majority of them—was either by patiently combing the countryside, or by casting the enthrallment at some point when the Elves would have gathered here en masse, either for a holiday or some ceremony. Given the location of the bodies they had discovered, Gaeleval must have walked the length of Numenlaur, harvesting people across the land like wildflowers.

They quartered the streets and walked down all of them systematically, looking up at the buildings and inspecting blind alleys. Even though this area was the most developed they had seen since they'd crossed over, there was a symmetry to how the buildings aligned with the countryside, and how the streets and paths followed the natural curvature in the land. Houses nestled into groves of trees, and flower gardens flourished everywhere, overgrown now with weeds.

Skeletons lay strewn in the streets. Scavenging wildlife had made short work of the bodies left out in the open. At one point, Quentin bent to gently pry a sword from a skeleton's grip. It was a long, lethal piece of loveliness. An Elven-made sword, she knew, was a true joy to wield, slender yet strong, perfectly balanced, and with an edge so sharp it could slice a single hair.

She watched as he wiped it off carefully and inspected the length. Then he swung it back and forth, spun around and lunged with it, testing its mettle. He looked like he was floating as he moved, a Fred Astaire of death. His prowess with fighting had been quite clear at the Sentinel Games, but the Games were unarmed combat and this was something else entirely. With a few skillful moves, he showed just what an accomplished swordsman he was, and he was mesmerizing to watch.

She dragged her gaze away from him and walked over to the skeleton. It still gripped the empty sheath. The Elf must have barely gotten the sword unsheathed before dying. She wiggled the sheath out of the bony fingers and inspected it. It was simple and elegant, the artistry wholly in the sheer beauty of how well it was made.

She wiped it off and handed it to him. "You should take it. The sword looks like it was made for your hand."

He hesitated, then sheathed the sword and buckled it at his trim hips. "We should get one for you too," he said. "And I want a longbow if we can find one."

Not many people could wield an Elven longbow, which

was six feet long and a powerful long-distance weapon. She stood as she admitted, "I wouldn't mind a longer sword."

"Keep on the lookout," he told her. In contrast to his hoarse reaction in the nursery earlier, his voice was even, analytical. He'd clearly found a way to box his emotions. "Their owners can't use them anymore."

It didn't take very long to find another sword for her. After they had cleaned it off, they continued inspecting the city. The day had begun to slide away from them, the sun starting its journey to the horizon. Shadows lengthened on the cobblestone streets.

The complete stillness in combination with the well-maintained streets and buildings was creepy, like some kind of Elder Races version of *The Walking Dead*. When they weren't talking to each other, the only sounds she heard were their footsteps, the occasional cry of seabirds and the sound of the waves hitting the nearby shore. It was a completely different experience than exploring an area filled with ruins. Ruins graciously gave one a sense of the passing of time, blurring disaster and tragedy into a distant thing.

This—this gave her a sense that someone was going to walk around the corner at any moment, but they didn't. Or that someone was watching them from the windows of nearby buildings. Which they weren't.

Were they?

She walked in a large circle, studying shuttered windows, corners of buildings, hiding places in the shrubbery. And saw nothing.

Still, the nape of her neck prickled, as a sixth sense insisted that someone, or something, was watching them.

Quentin noticed her behavior, and his attitude sharpened. She liked that he didn't nag her with pointless and distracting questions, but that he simply adapted his behavior to match hers. They were learning how to respond to each other like a fighting unit.

"I want to go up to the palace," she said. She wanted to go to high ground and study the scene. If someone—or something—was in the city with them, sooner or later they would give themselves away.

He said, "Let's go."

They had followed a small side street that led to several houses set against the backdrop of a hillside. The hill was terraced and beautifully landscaped with a profusion of flowering trees and bushes that perfumed the air. Many of the flowers were strange to her, which made the scene seem even more otherworldly.

To reach the palace, they had to turn back to the main street. As she turned, something black flashed at the corner of her eye.

Something too black for the rest of the lengthening evening shadows. Something that moved independently of any breeze.

She spun toward it, staring. And saw nothing. She looked up at the sky and at the rooftops of buildings. Nothing moved from above. Easing her newfound sword out of its sheath, she strode over to where she had seen the shadow, at the corner of a waist-high, fieldstone wall that bordered one of the houses.

She looked both ways, along the wall. There was no quick-moving black streak. No scent. Everything about the scene appeared just as it should, except now she wasn't buying it.

Quentin said, "I'm starting to feel like I'm color-blind or tone-deaf." He sounded amused, yet when she glanced at him, she saw that his body was taut and his eyes never stopped moving. He had drawn his sword too, and while the point was casually lowered, he had clearly stepped up to high alert. He asked telepathically, *What did you see?*

Same thing as last night, she said. She stood on the balls of her feet, ready to move fast if needed. She tilted her chin back and forth, stretching her neck, and shook her arms to loosen the tension that had built up in her shoulder muscles.

Quentin strode toward the open archway in the stone fence.

Thirty feet beyond him, something black streaked between two buildings. He whirled toward it before Aryal had a chance to call out. He said, "I saw that one. But I don't know what I saw."

"I don't either," she said, walking rapidly to the area between the two buildings. The cobblestones were worn, the ground uneven. It was the opening to an alley that ran parallel to the main road, and it led to another side street. "I don't think it's physical. There's no scent. There aren't any tracks."

He joined her, looking down the alley. "If it isn't physical, what is it?" he asked quietly. "Some kind of ghost or spirit?"

"Your guess is as good as mine."

The cobblestones were pebbled with the different colors of stone, and the warm brown-gold of the buildings was deepening with the growing shadows. Sunshine still shone directly on the other side street at the opposite end of the alley, topped with the white and blue of a cloud-dotted sky.

A black streak ran across the mouth of the alley, left to right.

Aryal and Quentin raced toward it. They plunged onto the street, looking in the direction it had gone. It had vanished from the sun-drenched scene.

She wiped her hot forehead as she turned to look at the surrounding area. This little street led to a park with stone benches and shade trees surrounding a shallow reflective pool. She glanced at Quentin, who was scratching the back of his head. He was scowling and he looked as frustrated as she felt. Then she looked back at the alley they had just exited.

Two black shapes were in the alley, moving toward them.

She smacked Quentin's arm with the back of her hand. He jerked around.

The shapes were long and waist high, and they moved like shadows, except they were unattached to any corporeal body. Her mind kept insisting it could make sense of their shapes if she stared long enough at them. She caught a glimpse of legs, a narrow muzzle.

"Now I can sense them," Quentin said. "Faintly, anyway."

"They look like some kind of animal," she said. The shadows crept closer, black in the darkening alley. She cocked her head. "Are they stalking us?"

"It does look that way." Quentin narrowed his eyes. "I wonder what they can do if they catch us."

Movement flickered at the corner of her eye. She looked down the street, in the direction of the park. More shadows approached them, pouring across the ground with intent. Recognition struck. She said, "They look like wolves. Very big wolves. Some of the Wyr wolves can get that big."

"Aryal," Quentin said.

When she looked at him, he pointed in the opposite direction. Even more shadows crept closer. There were twelve shadows altogether, and they were acting in coordination with one another, moving just like they would if they were a real pack. And now they had her and Quentin surrounded.

She turned and put her back to Quentin's so that they both faced outward. "We don't know that they can do anything," she pointed out. "Weird shit sometimes happens in the magic of Other lands. They really might be animal ghosts."

"Let's try to break through their circle and get to the main street," he said.

She didn't bother to argue with that idea, mostly because she was curious to see what the shadows would do.

Together they turned and sprinted toward the shadow wolves that stood between them and the main street.

The wolves attacked.

⸻ FOURTEEN ⸻

Three wolves rushed Quentin. He braced himself as one leaped for him, and he slashed at it with the sword. His blade passed through the shadow as if it were empty air. Black teeth flashed, and his forearm caught fire as slashes appeared on his skin.

He shouted, "They can bite!"

He shrugged out of his pack and let it fall to the ground. Aryal was cursing. Pressure clamped his left ankle and denim tore. One of the shadows had latched onto his boot. He tried to shake it off, but there was no physical body to dislodge. Narrowly he managed to dodge another two shadows that jumped at him. Goddammit, there were too many of them and they had no bodies for him to hit.

Aryal's Power surged.

He managed to glance over at the harpy. She had torn off her backpack too and dropped her sword. Two shadows had fastened onto her, one on her arm and the other on her thigh, and the upsurge in her Power blasted them backward. Both wounds were bleeding profusely, and she looked furious. She shouted, "Ever fight a Djinn before? Like that."

At first her words made no sense to him. These couldn't be *Djinn*? He had never actually had occasion to fight a

Djinn, although he had met a few in the past. They were creatures of air and fire, beings of pure spirit, and their Power was unmistakable. These felt nothing like Djinn, but . . .

Aryal whirled and threw out her arm in a roundhouse punch at one of the shadow wolves that lunged at her, her Power concentrated in her arm. Her fist passed through the shadow, but she seemed to knock it off its course. It fell to the ground and crouched low.

Then Quentin understood. These might not be Djinn, but they still appeared to be spirits that could affect the physical world. Power used as an offensive weapon could affect them. He flung out his hand, whispering a repel spell, and it knocked one of his shadow attackers back.

But while it did so, three others leaped at him. He ducked one, repelled another and the third bit deeply into his bicep. It hurt like a son of a bitch. He could feel blood flowing out of the wound.

Fire flared in his right thigh just over the knee. Beyond the shadow that had bitten him, another paced. The ones he had knocked back were gathering too. There were too many of them. He and Aryal were in real trouble—or at least he was. Aryal could take wing and fly out of the fight.

He gathered his Power for the strongest repel spell he could throw. If he could only knock them all back, he might be able to sprint fast enough to get away.

Out of the corner of his eye, he saw that Aryal had shapeshifted into the harpy. Her Power surged again as she kicked two of the shadows back. She shouted, "Get your ass over here if you want a lift. Let's shoot for the top of a building and regroup."

He didn't have time to smile. He blew out the hardest gust of Power he could and knocked back the ones that were closest to him, but there were too many shadow wolves between him and Aryal.

He heard her say, "Never mind, I'll get you."

She crouched to spring, just as a new shadow wolf poured out of the alley behind her. It was bigger than all of the others, and moved with more power and speed. As it leaped, Quentin shouted a sharp warning.

He was too late. Huge black teeth fastened high on the carpal joint of one of her wings. Bone snapped, the sound sickeningly audible. Aryal gave a high, wild shriek of anguish and rage. She tried to whirl, to shake the shadow off of her, but it held on. Blood fountained as it ripped through her flesh. Two more shadows attacked, one tearing at her heel and the other ripping through her thigh muscle. She staggered and collapsed.

Quentin roared and lunged, flinging a repel spell at the shadow wolf that was still latched onto her wing. It tumbled away, even as she rolled over onto her hands and knees. Head lowered, she tried to get to her feet, while her savaged wing lay in an awkward sprawl. She couldn't get her injured leg to support her weight.

Shadow wolves poured into the space between them before he could reach her, too many for him to knock away. Fiery pain exploded in one of his calves as a wolf sank its teeth into him. He twisted to fling a repel spell at it.

By the time he had turned around, shadow wolves had torn Aryal's other wing, and the largest one held her pinned with its teeth at the back of her neck.

A woman wearing jeans and a tank top walked out of the alley. She was human, of average height, rounded at breasts and hips, and she looked to be perhaps in her late thirties, with dark hair and eyes, and a Slavic face with high cheekbones.

She also carried more Power than Quentin had ever felt before in a human, and more than most of any of the magic users he had met of the other Elder Races.

She gestured with one hand. All the shadow wolves halted their attack, except the largest one that kept his hold on Aryal's neck.

The woman said in accented English, "Now is a good time for you to surrender."

They were outnumbered, and he knew he was outclassed magically, but Quentin still gathered up his Power. He couldn't throw a repel spell at the shadow wolf that held Aryal pinned, or its teeth might very well snap her neck. He could sure as fuck throw something offensive at the woman though.

The woman looked at him. "If you cast another spell at me or my wolves, you will kill your partner. Release your Power."

And there it was, everything he had once thought that he wanted to achieve.

All it would take is one more spell, and Aryal would die by someone else's hands.

A hot, furious feeling shook through him.

No. *NO.*

He released his Power. "Tell your creature to let her go."

"Not yet. I have to make a decision first." The woman crossed her arms and sighed heavily. "I know who she is. And I can guess who you are. You have presented me with a pretty problem. I do not have anything against the Wyr from America—yet."

"I know who you are too," Aryal whispered hoarsely. Her hair hung down over her face, and she had dug her talons into the cracks between the cobblestones. "Galya Andreyev. Only I thought you never left Russia."

The woman frowned and said, "It is really unfortunate that you have recognized me. Now you have increased my problem, and that is not at all pretty."

The woman made a throwing motion with her hand, and flung out a dark web filled with stars. Instinct took over and Quentin lunged sideways, attempting desperately to avoid it. But as fast as he was, he couldn't move fast enough, because the web wasn't any more physical than the shadow wolves had been. It settled over his head to cover him completely. He tried to throw off the spell, but it sank underneath his skin before he could cast a counter-measure.

He thought he caught a glimpse of a night sky as he tumbled headlong into darkness.

Something dripped.

The sound was making him crazy. He needed to get up to turn off the faucet. He rolled over on the remarkably hard, cold bed, and woke up.

He was alone, and he lay on the floor of a prison cell. No weapons, no backpack.

The cell was dry and very plain, just the ceiling and floor, three stone walls, and a fourth wall made of metal bars that radiated some kind of dull-feeling magic. In one corner of the cell, a shallow hollow in the floor with a hole constituted a primitive latrine. Faint light spilled in from somewhere, throwing deep shadows, but his feline sight did very well in deep shadows and even in full darkness. Instinct told him he had not been unconscious for very long. He thought that the light could be the last of the day's sunshine.

He looked outside of his cell. He could see two cells across from him. One was empty, and the other one held a long, still length with gray-to-black wings spilled over the floor. Aryal. There was red too, a great deal of it, and he could smell the coppery tint of both her blood and his.

Water still dripped somewhere nearby, and there were voices.

"That was a harpy," an Elven male said. "And I don't know what the man was, but he wasn't human."

"That was Quentin," a light, female Elven voice said. Relief flooded Quentin as he recognized Linwe's voice. "At least I think it was. He's part Elf. And if that was Quentin, I bet the harpy was the sentinel Aryal. She looked bad."

"I wonder when they'll wake up," said a third Elf, another male. That was Caerreth, the bookish male.

"I'm awake," Quentin said hoarsely. He rolled onto his stomach with difficulty and sat up. "Linwe?"

"Yes, it's me," said Linwe. "Oh thank the gods. I mean, not that you're here locked up too, but that you're you and awake. It's good to hear your voice. Are you all right?"

He inspected himself. The worst wounds were the bites on his biceps and his thigh, and as he probed at them, he discovered they hadn't yet closed. He frowned. Given his Wyr abilities, they should have closed over by now. "I think so," he said. "I've got a few wounds, but they aren't too bad. You?"

"I'm okay—there's three of us, and we're okay. We're really hungry though."

"There were four in your party," he said. He eased off his T-shirt and tore it into strips. Then he used the strips to bind his wounded thigh tightly and, with considerable more clumsiness, the bite on his upper arm. "What happened to the fourth?"

There was a small silence. Then Linwe said bleakly, "She didn't make it."

Linwe said "she," which meant it would have been Cemalla. Damn. He closed his eyes. He was getting tired of hearing about Elves dying. He said, "I'm sorry. How long have you been here—and do you know where here is?"

One of the male Elves answered him. "We're in the prison underneath the palace in Numenlaur. We've been here for almost two weeks."

Elves could survive a long time without food and almost as long without water, but if they hadn't had any liquid or nourishment in all that time, they had to be feeling poorly. He asked, "How long has it been since you've eaten or drank anything?"

"The witch who imprisoned us has been bringing us wayfarer bread and water every three days," Linwe said. "But the last time was three days ago, and she didn't leave any food or water when she brought you and the harpy in. We're wondering if that means she's decided to stop feeding us."

"I met the witch," he growled.

"Of course you did." She sounded dispirited and listless. "I'm not thinking very clearly."

"Don't worry about it, Linwe. If I were you, I wouldn't be thinking clearly either."

Getting food and water every few days was barely sustainable. The thought of them imprisoned for almost two weeks, getting hungrier and thirstier as they listened to that water drip, infuriated him.

He pushed himself to his feet and walked over to the bars. He wasn't familiar with the exact spell that had been smelted into the metal, but it would be something to contain dangerous prisoners with a possible proficiency in magic. Every Elder Races prison had something of the same, some sort of way to dampen a prisoner's magic.

He tried touching the metal, and whatever magic it held stayed inert, so he grasped two bars and looked at the crumpled figure across the way. Aryal hadn't moved yet, although if she had been hit with the same spell as he had, she should be awake by now.

"Hey," he said quietly to her. The sight of her ruined wings made him feel slightly crazed. He remembered the sound of her bone snapping. "Time to wake up, sunshine."

She didn't move or give any sign that she heard him. His throat tightened. She might be unconscious. The witch wouldn't have locked her up if she had been dead.

Or at least she wouldn't have been dead at the time she was locked up. If his wounds were still open, so were hers. She had been quietly bleeding all this time. Was the dampening magic on the bars interfering with their Wyr abilities to heal?

"Say something, Aryal," he said.

Goddamn it. Come on.

She said in quiet, broken voice, "I'm not healing."

After that, she didn't speak again for a long time.

"I'm not healing either," he told her.

She didn't respond.

He started to pace. It made the wound in his thigh ache worse than before, but he ignored it. From down the hall, Linwe said, "That's how Cemalla died. She got injured pretty badly when the witch's wolf shadows attacked us. Her wounds wouldn't clot. She bled out a couple of days after we were brought here."

Caerreth, the bookish Elf, said, "I could have saved her if my magic had been working."

"You're a healer?" Quentin asked.

"I'm not very advanced yet," he said. "But none of us sustained any injuries that would have required complicated healing spells or surgeries."

Quentin was no healer, but he thought Aryal's wings might call for some complicated healing or surgeries. He resisted the urge to smash his fist into the wall, as any possible damage he might do to his fist might not heal. He muttered, "We need to get the hell away from these damn bars."

Caerreth said somewhat pedantically, "Yes, we do, but in regards to healing, we've had a long time to think about things, and we don't think that the dampening spell in the bars down here had anything to do with Cemalla bleeding out. After all, healing is a natural physical process, not a magical one. We think it has something to do with the wolf shadows themselves."

The younger Elf made a good point. It sounded like they had used their imprisonment to try to think things through.

"Have you seen anything like them before?" Quentin asked.

"No, so we don't know anything for sure." Caerreth sounded like Linwe did, very tired. "All we have is supposition. Have you seen anything like them before?"

"No. Do you think their bites are poison?" Quentin didn't feel poisoned. He just felt in pain. He stalked back and forth, pacing laps.

"The wounds haven't acted as though they were poisoned," said Caerreth. "I think it has more to do with the nature of the creatures themselves."

"I thought they were spirits, or ghosts," Quentin said. He completed another lap and spun. How much blood had Aryal lost? Was she close to bleeding out?

"If they are," Caerreth said, "and they can still affect the physical world, what if the wounds they inflict are spiritual in nature?"

Quentin thought about that as he prowled every inch of his cage. Spiritual, the way that Caerreth meant it, didn't mean feelings or emotions, or some kind of religious experience. Instead it meant of the soul, or the incorporeal, as opposed to the physical. Magic had the same distinction, as it was spiritual in nature—incorporeal—but still had the Power to impact the physical world.

"If you're right," he said, "then magical healing might work."

"Which we can't do in here," said Caerreth. He sounded as dispirited and listless as Linwe had.

Quentin wasn't dispirited or listless. He burned with rage and determination.

He said, "That's all the more reason why we have to get out of here. But then we already knew that."

With that, he turned all the considerable force of his attention onto one thing: escape.

To test the dampening spell in the prison bars, he ran through a series of practice spells that were akin to a musician playing scales. The dampening spell activated, and he could feel it acting in counterpart to his. It was more sophisticated than anything he had encountered before. He cast a stronger spell and felt the dampener adjust to the shift, an equal weight of null to his magic.

The one dampening spell that he knew was more simple and oppressive, pressing the null as a dead weight throughout the air of the prison or cage, so that the magic user could not even summon Power to cast a spell in the first place.

That kind of dampener needed to be recast periodically because it expended Power all of the time. The spell on these bars would have been much more difficult to cast, but it would last much longer, perhaps indefinitely, only becoming active when needed and providing only enough Power necessary to block each surge of Power.

He studied the construction of his cell. He was not surprised to find that it was as well constructed as the dampening spell had been. Perhaps he could dig furrows between the stones if he had a sharp implement and years of time to do it. But even then, he didn't think he would achieve much more than a couple of deep holes in the thick walls.

Now to try his ace in the hole. Holding his breath, he attempted the minimal shapeshift that would bring out his panther's retractable claws.

He had heard a lot of argument over the years about whether the Wyr's ability to shapeshift should be classified as magic or as a natural attribute. The real answer was that it was both, but it was also a kind of magic that was fundamentally different from other magic structures. Sometimes spells that were cast in counter to other magics didn't affect the Wyr's shapeshift ability at all.

Sometimes . . . luck did swing his way.

The claws on his right hand appeared, more slowly than

176

he could flick them into existence outside of the cell, but they were there. He concentrated on his left hand, and five more retractable claws materialized. He stretched the fingers on both hands out and looked at them in satisfaction.

It was like nature just wanted him to have all these lock picks readily at hand, so to speak, and available. And Quentin had explored all kinds of training for his natural talents.

He walked over to the bars and set to work, arms through the bars and wrists bent so that he could get at the lock from inside the cell.

Sometimes magical locks required the matching magical key to unlock them. He hoped that wasn't the case for these cells. After all, the dampening spell and the excellent construction of the cells were barriers enough if the prisoner were stripped of any possible tools. He held his breath and prayed that the builders of the prison were as logical about the construction of the lock as they had been about everything else, as he used the two curved claws of his forefingers to probe for the hidden tumblers inside the lock. When he felt the slight resistance that indicated he had engaged them, he twisted carefully.

The lock clicked open. He pushed open the door to his cell and walked out.

The prison block was a simple one. It appeared to be U-shaped, with an iron-reinforced oak door at the bottom of the U. The Elves were held in cells just around the corner from the door, on the other leg from where he and Aryal were held. They were talking, their voices slow and tired, and didn't appear to notice the slight sound his cell door made as it swung open. He caught a glimpse of still bodies in some of the other cells neighboring his and Aryal's, but he turned his attention away from the sight. There was nothing he could do for any of them.

Listening warily for any sounds outside the cell block, he moved quickly over to Aryal's cell, picked the lock and eased the door open. He rushed to her prone figure and kneeled at her head.

She lay on her stomach and showed no reaction to his sudden presence. He stroked her black hair to one side and felt for a pulse. Relief blew through him as he found one. It was thready and too rapid, but it was there.

"Hey, sunshine," he said softly. "You in there? Feel free to get snarky and cuss me out anytime now."

She didn't say anything. Maybe she was unconscious.

Gods, she was a wreck. He was appalled at the state she was in. Those magnificent wings of hers were sprawled awkwardly on either side of her body, torn and broken. That last shadow wolf had known exactly what to do when it attacked her. It had very clearly intended to ground her, and that was what it had achieved.

If she hadn't hesitated to take off, she might have gotten clean away. She had waited for him, and when he couldn't get to her, she had said she would come for him.

A burning knot sank into his chest, like the same emotion that gripped him in the tragic nursery, only this time it was even hotter, more painful. Avian Wyr typically did not survive well if they lost the ability to fly.

This couldn't cripple her. That was all there was to it.

First, though, he had to make sure it didn't kill her.

Carefully he moved her. He didn't try to turn her onto her stomach, because that would shift her wings too much. Instead he lifted her up until he could hold her, putting her head on his shoulder. She lay against his torso in a dead weight.

He tilted his head sideways and looked into the harpy's wild face. Her eyes were half-open. Did that mean she was still conscious?

"I'm going to give this to you straight up, sunshine," he whispered into her ear. "You look like hell. Our wounds aren't closing over. We need to get out of this cell block and away from the dampening spell in here. Then maybe we can see about getting some magical healing. But to do that, you either need to be ambulatory or you need to be portable, and right now you're neither."

He looked down at her again. Was that a flicker in her half-closed eyes?

"You have to shapeshift," he told her. "That might slow down your bleeding some, since—since so many of your wounds are on your wings. And if you can't walk, at least I'll be able to carry you."

"My wings are bad," she whispered.

The burning in his chest grew more intense. He steeled himself against it. "Yeah," he said. "Your wings are bad. You'll probably need surgery. Maybe even a couple of surgeries. The sooner we finish here and get home, the sooner we can get to that and you can take to the air again. But you've got to move first."

There was no self-pity on that feral, beautiful face. There was no emotion at all. "The thing is, Quentin," she said in a perfectly rational-sounding voice, "I don't know that I can do that."

If she was too injured to shapeshift, if she had lost too much blood, she might really be dying.

"No," he said. He shook his head. "No. I do not accept that."

"Gods forbid something might happen that you don't accept," she said dryly. Her eyes closed.

"Stop it!" He shook her, not caring if it hurt or not. Hell, if it hurt, it might be just the jolt she needed. Her eyes flared open again, and she glared at him. Anger was good. It was awesome. He smiled at her. "I'm going to pinch you until you shapeshift."

One corner of her mouth twitched. "You really are a bastard, aren't you?"

"You say that like it's news. Or even a bad thing." He found a place under her arm where she wasn't injured, and he pinched her hard.

A spark lit her dull gaze. "Ouch."

"Come on, sunshine," he growled. "I'm not leaving without you, and I haven't got all day. And if I have to drag you by the foot, you're going to be a hell of a lot more uncomfortable than you are right now. Shift!"

Her breathing quickened, and her face twisted. He could feel the struggle in her body as she strained. His heart started to pound as he waited. A low, shaking moan came from her lips.

He shouted in her face, *"COME ON!"*

She bared her teeth and screamed back at him, an infuriated harpy's shriek. And her wings slowly disappeared from sight. The alien quality of her features smoothed into the more human-looking Aryal. Her features were too pale and damp with sweat, and the area around her eyes was hollow with dark shadows.

Relief made him almost giddy. Who the hell could have ever guessed that he would come to care about what happened to this prickly pain in the ass he held in his arms? "There you are," he said. He hugged her. "Good job."

She glared at him and pinched him back, hard. "You suck."

He barked out a short laugh, hugged her tighter and pressed a kiss to her temple for good measure. One of her arms crept around his waist, and she held him back.

A cautious-sounding Linwe said, "Is everything okay over there?"

"Everything's okay," Quentin said firmly. He looked into Aryal's bitter gaze, and though he answered Linwe, he spoke directly to Aryal. "Or it will be."

It had to be okay. He wouldn't let it be anything else.

≡ FIFTEEN ≡

If Aryal thought about the damage that had been done to her wings, panic set in, so she tried not to think about it.

That wasn't going so well.

She'd had a lot of time for what-ifs in her life, and if she couldn't fly, she didn't know that she could live. Flight was sewn into her nature. It marked the shape of her body. It went deeper than her sense of her own identity, into her state of being.

After she shapeshifted back into her human form, for all intents and purposes her wings appeared to be gone. But that wasn't true. They were still there, still a part of her, and she could still feel the pain from the broken bones and the bite wounds.

She could still remember the agonizing grip of the shadow wolf as it crushed the critical carpal joint, and she knew at that point that the wolf might have already killed her, and everything else that happened after that point would be just her waiting to die.

The shapeshifting had been so hard, afterward she shook like a drug addict going through withdrawal. Quentin gripped her tightly. He sat back on his heels as he held her, and at first she couldn't even lift her head off of his shoulder.

Belatedly she realized she was resting against his bare, warm skin. She focused on the steady, strong heartbeat against her cheek. Concentrating on something outside of herself helped to stave off the panic.

He rested his cheek against her temple, and the light dusting of whiskers along his jaw felt good. She didn't often like men's beards, as sometimes the bristles felt prickly, but Quentin's beard was as silken as the rest of his hair. In contrast, his wide, tanned chest had very little hair on it, just a light dusting of gold.

A sluggish curiosity stirred. Her voice sounded rusty as she said, "Your shirt's gone."

"I used it to bandage my leg and arm." His arms eased. "Speaking of which, we need to bind your wounds. You've already lost too much blood."

She pulled away and helped him to tear strips of her tank top off at the waist, which he used to wrap her visible wounds tightly. It wouldn't stop the bleeding, but it would slow it down. As she watched him tie the ends of the cotton on her thigh, she asked, "How did you pick the lock?"

He smirked at her. "I have talented claws."

Despite his lighthearted rejoinder, his gaze was sharp and assessing as he looked down her bloody figure. She looked down at herself too. They had left enough of her tank top so that it covered her breasts, and her jeans were torn and grimy with blood and dirt.

"You are one post-apocalyptic babe," he said. "If only you had a padded bra to make you a C-cup."

"Keep up with the wisecracks, why don't you?" she told him. "I've started a tally. Help me to my feet."

He put an arm around her waist and lifted her up. She held herself stiffly, unable to do anything to ease the pain of unseen wounds. When he let her go, he did so carefully.

At his unspoken question, she jerked her head to the open cell door and said, "Go on, help the others. I'll manage."

She was going to try to walk down that hall, and she

didn't want him to see her struggle. He hesitated and his eyes narrowed, but when she waved a hand irritably at him, he turned and walked out of the cell.

She limped slowly down the hall. Her thigh held up under her weight, just barely, but her entire back felt like it was on fire. Even taking a deep breath hurt.

The Elves greeted Quentin with sharp exclamations that were quickly hushed. She left him to his reunion. There was a barred window at one end of the short hallway that held the door to the cell block. She limped over to it.

The window wasn't big enough for a grown person to fit through, and it was the only source of fresh air for the whole block. When she looked out, the window opened over the water, so the prison area had to be carved into the cliff itself.

A gust of air blew in, hitting her in the face. It felt cool and damp. She put a hand to the sill to lean on it as she sucked in fresh air and looked out. The island was just visible, and she felt the constriction ease somewhat in her chest. The light was fading fast from the day, and the water was a deeply shadowed blue. Soon the daylight would be completely gone.

She focused on the island. She had meant to fly over there, at least briefly.

Razor teeth fastening on her wing. Her carpal joint crushed. Muscles torn.

Dread flooded her limbs, and she breathed shallowly through a wave of nausea. She had to find some sort of short-term goal, or the panic was going to drive her crazy.

Galya Andreyev might not have anything against the Wyr from America, but now Aryal sure as hell had something against the Russian bitch.

"I owe you one," she whispered. "And I always pay my debts."

Aryal owed the witch a bad one. Focusing on payback was a good enough goal for now.

Behind her, the others were talking. "Aryal and I need healing, and we need to leave the cell block as fast as we can," Quentin said. "But we need to do it smart. Do you know if the witch sets any of her shadow wolves to guard outside this block?"

"No," Linwe said. "We haven't seen them since she locked us up."

"The witch didn't need them when she came in here," said one of the Elven males. "We were already captured. Besides, if they're magic, they couldn't come in anyway."

"Interesting point," said Quentin, with that tone of voice he used whenever something had particularly caught his attention. "Do you think they are a creation of hers from some kind of spell?"

Aryal answered him. She said over her shoulder, "I think they may be spelled or magical in some way, but they are not the product of a spell—at least not wholly. I think they are individual entities."

"Why?"

"Their behavior was too sophisticated for one person to orchestrate. They exhibited pack behavior and lured us to where they wanted us to be before they attacked. And the twelve wolves kept us occupied so that the thirteenth—the alpha—could take me by surprise." She forced a swallow down her dry throat. "It was quite efficiently executed."

A short silence greeted her words. Then Quentin said, "That makes a lot of sense."

"I'll tell you something else that makes sense," Aryal said. "That first shadow wolf I saw on the bridge back in the forest—I think that was a sentry. When we crossed over into Numenlaur, it must have tracked us for a while and then ran on ahead to alert the others. At least that's what it looks like."

"They did something very similar to us," said one of the Elven males. "We found the witch's trail leading into Numenlaur. There was plenty of snow cover on the ground, and her trail was unmistakable. Our orders were to stop anyone from looting, so we crossed over to track her down. We didn't bother to leave anyone on guard—after all, it was just one set of footprints, and we thought we would be back over to the Bohemian Forest quickly."

"Did you go into any of the houses?" Quentin asked, his

tone neutral. Aryal wondered if he asked because of the dead baby they had found. If these young people hadn't yet realized that all the babies in Numenlaur were dead, she certainly didn't want to be the one to tell them.

Sounding embarrassed, Linwe said, "No, but we think the witch did. Her trail seemed to lead inside a few of the first houses, but it also continued down the path. We were moving fast to try to catch her and cross back over as soon as we could. We screwed up. We all wanted to get a glimpse of Numenlaur. That's why nobody stayed behind. Then the shadow wolves trapped us, and the witch threw some kind of sleep spell, and the next thing we knew, we woke up here."

"So the shadow wolves are pack, they're intelligent, and they communicate with each other," said Quentin. "And they act independently from the witch. Actually they sound a lot like Wyr wolves."

"And they're affected by magic," said Aryal. "Don't forget that. Power affects them, and it looks like the nullifying spell in here might too."

Her thigh throbbed, the invisible fire all along her back was getting worse, and she was growing light-headed from standing so long. Just as she started to turn away from the window, she saw a flicker of light on the island. She paused and stood on her strong leg, gripping the bars with both hands, her eyes narrowed. She hadn't imagined that, had she?

No, she hadn't. There it was again, a flicker of light, like a torch or a lantern. In the distance it looked small like the winking of a firefly.

She asked, "Does anybody know what's over on that island?"

There was a pause as everybody adjusted to the apparent change in conversation, and footsteps sounded behind her. She glanced over her shoulder. Quentin, a wan-looking Linwe and two Elven males walked toward her. Compared to the shock of seeing a shirtless Quentin moving toward her, his tanned chest wide over those lean hips and long legs, the Elves looked willowy and somehow unfinished.

Quentin was scowling. He said, "Are you trying to bleed out? What are you doing standing up?"

She told him, "I'm watching a light on the island. Some-one's over there."

She swayed. He strode forward to put an arm around her. She twitched a shoulder angrily but she didn't push him away. Instead she took the help he offered and leaned on him. He stared out the window too.

"I think the university is over there," said Linwe from behind them.

Aryal's eyebrows rose. When Quentin glanced at her with a silent question in his eyes, she shrugged. She hadn't even known there was a university.

Linwe was continuing. "When we first woke after the witch locked us up, she asked us a lot of questions. She's not just looting for treasure. She's looking for something spe-cific. She didn't say what, but from the things she said, I think it's either an item of Power, or maybe it's a spell. The university here has a library that's famous among the Elves, kind of like the lost Alexandrian library in ancient Egypt."

Aryal met Quentin's gaze again. "She must want that item or spell very badly," she said. "Because I've never heard of her leaving Russia before, and she's willing to risk making an enemy out of Dragos."

"That's if Dragos catches her," he pointed out, the deep shadows on his face accentuating his sardonic expression. "To catch her, he would have to know what happened here in the first place, and for that, there would need to be wit-nesses. She was not best pleased with you when you called her by name, sunshine."

"And she doesn't seem to be the kind of person to lose track of details or make forgetful mistakes," Linwe added in a small voice. "I don't think she just forgot to feed us today. I think she chose not to. We were always expend-able, and when you guys showed up I think she decided to, well, expend us."

Quentin was still staring at Aryal, the weight of his intent gaze palpable even in the near dark. "You called her by name," he said. "Galya something. You know who she is."

"Andreyev," Aryal said. "Galya Andreyev, from the Russian Steppe. Don't let her looks fool you. I forget how old she is, but for a human she's very old. Unnaturally so, like over three hundred years, and she didn't turn into a Vampyre to achieve that. She did it by some other means. And no, I don't know how."

"How do you know of her if she never leaves Russia—or never did until now?" Quentin asked.

"Dragos knows her," she told him. "Or at least he knows of her. He claims that Galya Andreyev is one of the most Powerful witches in the world. You remember when Urien had Pia blackmailed into using a finding charm? Dragos said at the time that he knew of only three people who could have made that charm—Urien, Rune's mate Carling, and Galya Andreyev."

Quentin swore. "I knew as soon as I looked at her that I was outgunned on the magic front."

She started to say more, but lost her train of thought as the world grayed around her, and Quentin's arm tightened until he had her hauled tightly against his lean body. "We have to get out of here now," he said.

"What about the shadow wolves?" one of the Elven males asked. One of these days, Aryal was going to figure which of them was which. Right now, she didn't give a rat's ass as she could barely hold on to her own name.

"If they're out there, we'll just have to deal with it," Quentin said harshly. "Those wolves were able to do the kind of damage they did to us because they caught us by surprise. I'll bet they did the same with you. But Power affects them, and I've had a chance now to think about what that means. I've got a few offensive spells that I think will be effective." He said to Linwe, "Your job is to help Aryal. Caerreth, as soon as we're beyond the influence of the cell block, you work on healing her. Aralorn, you and I are the guards. As soon as we feel we're beyond the dampening magic, we stop and keep it at our backs. There's a boundary somewhere. It's in our best interest to use it. If the witch comes, we slide back over the line. It doesn't matter how Powerful she is. It's going to nullify her magic too. Got it?"

Aryal couldn't focus her eyes properly, but everybody must have nodded, because Quentin passed her gently over to Linwe. The Elf was smaller than she was by several inches, and she slipped easily under one of Aryal's arms, putting an arm around her waist.

"You lean on me," Linwe said softly.

"I don't think I've got a choice," Aryal said.

One of the Elven males came up on her other side. "I'm Caerreth," he said. "You can lean on me too."

While she couldn't see his features very well in the deepening darkness, she would know him again by his scent. He was much taller than Linwe, so she slipped an arm around his waist. "Thanks," she muttered.

"Don't mention it," Caerreth said. "You and Quentin came after us when you found that we were missing. If it weren't for you, we would still be locked up. Helping is the least we can do."

Quentin had glided away to go to the cell block door. As he worked to pick the lock, Aryal and her helpers followed more slowly.

"The dampening spell is on this door too," Quentin said, his voice quiet.

Aryal caught the small, distinct sound of the lock clicking open.

What a useful trait, having your own lock picks on the ends of your fingers. She envied him those. Her talons were too thick, and they were too hard to file into a thinner shape. And she was fairly certain she was a sharper thinker than this usually, but she had lost too much blood and was so light-headed, she was surprised she was still conscious, let alone still stringing thoughts together in a semicoherent fashion.

Someone nudged her, and she came alert with a start. She'd lost a few moments. The cell block door was open. Quentin and Aralorn slipped out, disappearing into even darker shadows.

Quentin appeared again almost immediately. He said, "There's a stairway. The dampening spell appears to wear off by the time you reach the top. We'll stop there. Come on."

Caerreth and Linwe had to carry most of Aryal's weight up the stairs. She couldn't hold back a groan as their lifting strained her back. Ahead of them on the stairs, she saw the silhouette of Quentin's head as he turned to look down at her. But he said nothing, and after a few minutes they had reached the top where Aralorn stood, waiting tensely.

They were in a hallway that stretched in either direction. It was shadowed, cool and quiet, and for the moment free of shadow wolves. That was all Aryal had a chance to see before Linwe and Caerreth eased her down onto the floor.

"She has to be on her stomach," Quentin told them.

As they eased her over on the flagstone floor, she helped them as much as she was able. Normally so strong, her own weakness filled her with rage.

Someone knelt beside her head. It was Quentin. He put a steady hand at the back of her neck. His hand was warm and bracing. She closed her eyes against how good it felt. He told her softly, "You have to change again. Do it quietly this time, hear?"

She nodded, bracing herself, and reached for the shape-shift.

Usually shapeshifting came so easily, like second nature. This one was brutally hard, taxing her meager resources, and, oh gods, it hurt. She swallowed down a scream and strained. The shift felt chainsaw rough and barely within her reach, but finally with a pained grunt she managed to change over to the harpy.

Her broken wings spilled over onto the floor.

There was a silence, where the only sound was her shallow panting. Quentin stroked the back of her head.

Caerreth whispered, "She needs a hospital."

"Well, she's not getting one," Quentin snarled. He sounded savage. "So pull up your big-boy pants and fix her."

"I need light for this."

The younger Elf barely got half the words out of his mouth before a small ball of light snapped into existence. Aryal managed to look over one shoulder. The light hovered just beside her head, and the magic from it felt like Quentin's Power signature. She coughed out a thready laugh.

"Okay," said Caerreth. He sounded a little scared. "Thanks."

Then the Elf set to work, and Aryal sagged from relief as the first cool wave of magic washed over her, blocking the pain. He worked deftly on the various wounds all over her body but hesitated when he reached her wings.

"Um, Aryal," he said softly. "I can set the broken bones and help them to fuse, but I can't repair this crushed joint, and if I throw a general healing spell on your wings, it's going to heal wrong. You won't be able to bend or flex it."

Razor teeth fastening . . . crushed. Torn.

She shook all over. Yeah, you've killed me, bitch.

She couldn't bear to look at her wings again and rested her cheek on the cold floor as she whispered, "Do it."

Then Quentin appeared in her line of sight. His face was upside down. She blinked rapidly, trying to clear her sight.

He had lain down on the floor too, on his stomach, his head turned toward her. His bare wide shoulders looked especially naked against the flagstone floor. He was dirty and haggard, the lines of his face set, but his gaze was the bluest she had ever seen.

Blue like the sky, steady and clear and filled with infinity.

"You should be on watch," she whispered.

"Aralorn's on the lookout," he said. His voice was as steady as his eyes. "And I have fast reflexes. Besides, if the shadow wolves were here, they would have shown up by now. I think they're with the witch."

Caerreth muttered instructions to Linwe, who braced her at the shoulders, and she felt strong tugging on her wings as Caerreth set the bones.

Aryal's face worked, and she clawed at the floor. She wanted to strike at the Elves, to knock them away from what they were doing to her.

Quentin grabbed her hand, gripping it hard. "We already knew you were going to have to have surgery," he said. "This isn't news."

"Leave me alone," she hissed.

"Like you left me alone these last two years?" His expression was relentless, and his grip tightened to the point of pain. "Like you left me when the wolves attacked? I don't think so, sunshine."

Caerreth threw the healing spell. She felt it sink into her, fusing torn flesh and broken bones together. Fusing the joint. Halfway through, she twisted her fingers around and clenched Quentin's hand.

Dead, dead . . .

She realized she was whispering it. ". . . dead. Bitch, you are so dead."

"That's right," Quentin said, his voice pitched low. "We're going to take her down. She's a dead woman. She could have asked for whatever the fuck it is that she's looking for. She could have borrowed it. She didn't have to lock them up. She didn't have to do this to you. She made choices."

The healing spell faded. Caerreth was done, at least with her. "All right, Quentin," Caerreth said. He sounded shaky. "Now it's your turn."

Somehow Aryal pulled out another shapeshift. It helped that her wounds had been closed. They still hurt, along with her wings, but she could tell that the healing had taken root, dispelling whatever had caused the wounds to remain open in the first place.

She forced herself up onto her hands and knees. Linwe ran forward, putting an arm around her to help her get to her feet. Aryal looked down at the ground. Quentin had rolled onto his back and sat up. Caerreth was already working on him.

Aryal looked up at Aralorn, then at Linwe. She could barely stand upright, and the Elves weren't looking any better. And Caerreth was doing all that healing while he was just as depleted as the others.

She said in a rusty-sounding voice, "We all need food, water and real rest. There's got to be plenty of food supplies in the palace kitchens. And the safest place to rest is down in the prison cells."

Quentin lifted his head. Aralorn turned to look at her.

She twitched a shoulder. "Think about it. Bitch tries to come into the cell block, the wolves can't join her and she can't use magic. I only hope that happens, because that means we've got her. And I really need to get her."

"Aryal's right," Quentin said. "The most dangerous thing will be hunting for the palace kitchens to get food and water. I'll do that."

Linwe said, "I'll go with you."

"You sure?" Quentin asked. He rolled to his feet as Caerreth finished with him.

Linwe said, "I'm the only one who wasn't injured. And I can run fast."

"Okay."

They watched as Caerreth worked on healing the wounds that Aralorn had. By that point the healer wasn't looking good. When he finished, Caerreth said, "I'm tapped."

The young Elf was looking down at himself. That was when Aryal realized he was bandaged too, with defensive wounds on both his forearms. Quentin walked over to him and gripped his arms. "When it comes to healing spells, I'm a one-trick pony," Quentin said. "Are these wounds simple enough for that?"

Caerreth nodded, and Quentin spelled his arms. Afterward, he looked at Aryal. "You might as well go down below. Linwe and I will join you as soon as we can."

She nodded dully. "See you soon."

Her heart and head were pounding, and her mouth was dry. She had pushed past her limit some time ago. She didn't wait to see Quentin and Linwe slip down the hall. Instead, she eased down the stairs to the cell block, bracing herself with one hand against the wall.

Aralorn and Caerreth followed. "It goes against all of my instincts to walk back in there," Aralorn muttered. "If something happens to Quentin, and the witch traps us in there, we're caught again and as good as dead."

"I know," Caerreth said tiredly. "But we might take more damage if we stayed at the top of the stairs and got caught there. I think we've just got to trust Quentin and Linwe to take care of themselves and get back to us with supplies."

While Aryal heard them, she didn't care. All she cared about was going horizontal again as quickly as she could. When they entered the cell block again, she went into Quentin's cell because hers was too bloody.

A formless noise filled her ears, like that of the ocean. It was odd, because she could have sworn the ocean was on the outside of the cell block window. She made her knees unlock one at a time, and forgot to catch herself, so she fell in a sprawl to the ground.

That was the last thing she knew for a long, dark while.

≈ SIXTEEN ≈

Stalking through the dark, silent halls of the palace's underbelly was like a video game gone bad. Any moment now Quentin felt like they were going to run into a water trap populated with piranhas, while logs swung to and fro overhead and shadow wolves jumped out of nooks to attack them.

He rubbed his face and forcibly banished the image from his mind. He wasn't quite as bad off as any of the others, but he needed to get some rest, and soon.

He said to Linwe, "Be sure to memorize the way back in case you need to run it by yourself."

"Aw, damn it," she said miserably. "I'm not going to need to."

He was terrible at dates, birthdays and such, but he thought Linwe had to be around thirty or so, which was quite young for an Elven adult. Making any kind of direct age-to-adulthood correlation to shorter-lived races, such as humankind, didn't compute, for she had already lived as a responsible adult for several years, yet she still retained the liveliness of youth.

He remembered her as a little girl, with her wide, naughty grin and eyes sparking with some kind of mischief. She

194

had been adorable and adored, and had pretty much run wild in Lirithriel Wood for the first fifteen years of her life. He hadn't visited the Wood often, but he remembered once she had run up to him with a laugh that was bigger than she was. She must have been all of five years old. When she had reached him, he'd picked her up and swung her high, setting her on his shoulder.

An echo of the burning pain came back in his chest. He couldn't let anything happen to her. Not her too, on top of all the massive losses the Elves had already suffered. He grabbed her by the arm, hauled her close and hugged her fiercely. After her first twitch of surprise, her arms came around his waist, and she hugged him back so hard her slight body shook with the strain.

He bent his head and said in her ear, "You will run if I tell you to. Do you hear me, young lady?"

"Quentin, that's not my job . . ." she said.

"*Linwe*." He injected all the command he could into his voice. "You don't have the magical aptitude for this kind of fight. And you. Will. Run."

"Fine!"

He pressed a kiss to her forehead. He knew he was being overbearing and patronizing, and he didn't give a shit. They all had to react to stress in their own way. This way was his.

He let her go, and they moved on.

After climbing a few staircases and another fifteen minutes or so of searching, they found the kitchens, which were as large as Quentin had expected. Linwe ran to the water pump over a large basin, and pumped out enough water to immerse her head in. While she drank and splashed water on herself, he located the pantries. He checked to make sure he wasn't near any windows, then he spelled a small ball of light and began collecting supplies.

The pantry held massive amounts of anything he could have hoped to find: wayfarer bread, nuts, dried fruits, jerky, cured meats and dried fish, wheels of cheese, apples, honey, jars of jellies and jams, olives, pickled vegetables and pickled eel, along with potatoes and other tubers, spices, oil and huge sacks of grains.

One pantry held barrels of wine, barley beer, and bottles of liquor, along with wineskins. Given the size of the palace, there were probably other storerooms full of both wine and the foods that were suitable for long storage, but the contents of these pantries alone would be enough to feed the four of them for a few months.

Not that they would need to be here for that long. He gave a quick thought for how differently time might be passing on Earth, then dismissed it. That was a reality to face at another time. It bore no relevance to their immediate situation.

He opened one wineskin, tilted it up and poured wine into his open mouth, then corked it again. It was criminal to waste Elven wine in almost any kind of circumstance except this one. He handed the wineskin over to Linwe along with five more. "Empty those and fill them with water, while I pack some food."

She took the skins and headed back to the water pump. He started throwing a selection of everything into four large canvas bags. Theoretically what he packed should be enough to feed them all for a week, except that he wasn't sure how much food the Elves would need to eat to replenish their strength. He knew for sure that he and Aryal would eat a significant amount of food, especially protein. He tucked some apple brandy into the sack he intended to keep for himself.

The food and water were essentials, but he really wanted a few weapons and he wouldn't turn down a blanket or two. He was also starting to twitch about how long he and Linwe had been gone from the others, so he banished the light, waited a few moments for his eyesight to adjust, and then scoured the kitchen for knives and linen tablecloths.

The tablecloths he found were long and heavily embroidered, which added to their thickness. They would make weird but effective blankets. After that, he stacked all of his finds on a table and waited for Linwe to join him.

She finished filling the last wineskin, slipped over to him and appeared to study the supplies he had gathered. "I shoulda set a limit on your credit card," she said, with a ghost of her normal good cheer.

He ruffled her hair. "I know this loads us down, but it does cover all the basics."

"I'm not complaining," she told him. "It's all I can do to keep from eating everything in one of those canvas bags right now."

He dug into one of the bags and handed her an apple. While she took quick bites, they gathered up all the supplies and headed back down to the cell block. Determined to catch the first hint of any of the shadow wolves' presence, he kept his awareness hyperextended, but they had a quiet, uneventful trip.

As soon as they pulled open the cell block door, Linwe called softly, "It's us. We're back."

Aralorn and Caerreth met them at the door. Quentin kept a skin of water, the canvas sack with the largest amount of meat and the apple brandy, two of the tablecloths and most of the knives, and let the others sort out the rest. He took a few moments to pick the lock shut on the cell block door, and he told the others, "Set watches."

Then he went in search of Aryal.

He found her in the cell he had been locked in, curled into a tight ball, and the coil of tension that had been wound so tightly in his gut eased. Still, as depleted as she was, she could be dangerous if she was startled out of a sound sleep.

To warn her of his presence, he said, "Hi honey, I'm home."

She didn't move, but he knew somewhere inside of her, her animal form had heard him. He walked over to her, sat down and set the knives within easy reach. Then he told her, "I'm going to put a hand on your shoulder now. Don't bite me."

He curled a hand along the point of her shoulder. He could tell she was chilled, because tiny goose bumps were raised along her skin. He shook her gently and told her, "I have water, apple brandy and meat. Which do you want?"

She uncurled slowly, moving as though her whole body ached. She mumbled, "Brandy."

"Okay, but you can only have half of it." He was not quite lying, just withholding information. He had a second bottle in the sack. He uncorked the first bottle and set it into her groping hand.

Then he placed one of the folded tablecloths in her lap, and he pulled out the different kinds of food, setting it out in front of them. He chose a hunk of cured meat and tore into it caveman-style, washing down the dry bites with swallows of water. Exhaustion pulled at his bones. With one part of his attention, he noticed how Aryal drank the brandy but didn't reach for any of the food.

Various reactions occurred to him. He considered each one and set them aside.

Finally he said, "You want to hunt the bitch, you've got to eat properly and get more rest, because, sunshine, you can barely sit up straight. I'm not going to take you with me or have you as a fighting partner if you're going to be a liability."

The silence in the cell was sour. Then she reached forward to slap her hand down randomly on a pile of food. "Oh gods, you brought more wayfarer bread."

"All you got is bitching and whining?" he said irritably. "That's not all I brought. Most of it is meat."

He sensed her leaning further, feeling over the offerings. She picked up a jar and shook it. "What's this?"

"Pickled eel," he told her. "If you don't like it, I'll eat it."

She said, her voice slow and tired, "Pickled eel and apple brandy. Huh."

For some reason that made him laugh. "Put that way, it sounds pretty awful." He paused, then reached for the bottle. She put up a token resistance but let him take it. He drank, and the light, fiery liquor sliding down his throat was one of the few good things that had happened that whole, gods-cursed day.

In the other hall, the Elves talked quietly together. Already they sounded more animated. Hope and carbohydrates were a powerful combination.

When the hollowed-out feeling in his gut had eased, he said quietly, "After we eat and get some sleep, I want to send the others back. They aren't equipped to hunt the witch. They can cross back over to the Bohemian Forest and stand

guard as per their original orders, and maybe send someone out to update Ferion and Dragos."

Aryal was silent for a while. She said, "If Galya reaches
the passageway, you're setting them up for a bad confrontation."

"They don't have to engage. They can let her go, and she
can be tracked down to wherever she lives in Russia." Tired
of the dryness of the cured meat, he set it aside and reached
for a wheel of cheese and a small jar of olives, set with a
honeycomb wax seal. "Besides," he said, "we're not going
to let her reach the passageway."

He sliced off a piece of cheese and handed it to her, then
sliced off some for himself and broke open the jar of olives.
As she chewed, Aryal said, "I want one of these bars."

He didn't understand that. He hadn't brought any food
that came in bars. "What?"

The indirect moonlight from the single window was so
faint, for many races the cell would be in total darkness,
but his eyes were especially suited to the night. He saw her
gesture to the cell door that stood wide open. "These bars.
I want one of them with the dampening spell still on it so I
can stab her with it."

His eyebrows rose as he considered that. "That's actually
an awesome idea," he said. "Unfortunately, the cells are so
well constructed that I don't think it's feasible. We'd need a
blacksmith, and by the time the smith separated one of the
bars, probably the dampening spell would be broken."

"A girl can dream, you know," she said. She had sounded
bad before, and now she sounded utterly exhausted. "Give
me that bottle again."

He passed it over to her. "So, who do you love?"

She drank from the bottle and wiped her mouth.
"Excuse me?"

"Name somebody you love."

"Why?" She sounded baffled.

Impulse was driving him, and he didn't want to try to
explain it. "Just because," he said. "You're friends with
Niniane. Do you love her?"

"Ye-es." Now she sounded cautious.

"Suppose Niniane was in trouble, and it was bad." She nudged his arm with the bottle and, surprised she offered, he took it and drank. "Suppose," he said, "someone Powerful that you didn't know had threatened her."

"Are you telling me that you know some plot against Niniane?" she asked suspiciously. "And you're only just now bringing it up?"

"No! I'm creating a hypothetical scenario."

"I'm back to 'why' again." She wrapped the tablecloth around her shoulders and lay down. "But go on."

He felt filthy and the cat in him was offended, but there was nothing to be done about it for the moment. He put the folded tablecloth he'd kept for himself on the floor to use as padding for his naked back. Then he lay down on it beside Aryal and stared at the ceiling.

"Suppose," he whispered, "you tried to help your friend by trapping the person who threatened her. And suppose your plan backfired, and you ended up hurting both of them. What would you do?"

She coughed out a chuckle. "Feel bad. Is this about what happened when you decided to mend the error of your ways and gave up smuggling?"

The stone floor made a wretched bed. The only way he could be more uncomfortable was if he were still bleeding. He said, "Yep."

Aside from the quiet sounds of the Elves settling to sleep, silence pressed down on them. Aryal whispered, "What did you do, Quentin?"

He closed his eyes. "When Dragos went after Pia last year, and the Elves shot him with the poisoned arrow, did you know that Pia had been staying at my house at Folly Beach?" She didn't say anything. She didn't even appear to be breathing. He continued, "I traded the information to Urien in exchange for his promise to let Pia go. Urien didn't keep his end of the bargain."

After a moment, she said, "Why the fuck did you tell me that now, when I'm so tired I can hardly breathe?"

Aside from exasperation, she also sounded genuinely mystified. He muttered, "I figured that would be a good thing. Less opportunity for you to go ballistic before you had a chance to think."

More time passed. She whispered, "You manipulative bastard. Why did you tell me at all? You didn't have to. Nobody is bothering to ask questions about that anymore. You got away with it."

"Nobody else knew about it. That doesn't mean I got away with anything." He rested a forearm over his eyes.

She turned onto her side until she was facing him. "It's been eating away at you all this time."

"Kinda," he muttered.

She smacked him on the shoulder with the back of her hand, and he jumped. "What the hell, Quentin?" she said between her teeth. "Did I not just get done telling you the other day that I would go after your ass if you did anything to hurt anyone I cared about? Did you really make the very best decision you could have made after hearing someone say something like that to you?"

He couldn't help himself and started to smile. "What are you going to do about it?"

She smacked him again. "I don't know. I can't believe you made me mad at you after being so—so nice to me today. What is wrong with you?"

"There's the sixty-four-thousand-dollar question. I mean that literally. You figure out what's wrong with me, and I'll pay you sixty-four thousand dollars." He rolled onto his side to face her. She jerked her tablecloth closer around her shoulders, muttering under her breath. He stroked her hair, and she froze. Somehow the darkness made it easier for him to admit, "It sickens me to think I hurt Pia the way I did, and I still don't like Dragos, but I'm growing to respect him. I'm sorry I did it."

She reached up to pull his hand away from her hair, and then she didn't let go of it. "You still haven't said why you told me."

"Beats the hell out of me," he said, in a tone of confession.

She lifted up her head. She accused, "You're lying."

"Am I?"

"And that was prevarication." She sounded more betrayed at that than when he had told her what he'd done.

"Was it?"

"You suck!" She pinched him hard in the bicep. "Give me a straight answer, or I swear somehow I'll find the energy to kick your ass right now."

"Ouch!" He knocked her hand away and leaned forward so that they were nose to nose. "Maybe," he whispered, "working with you is starting to feel like a partnership, and maybe I'm shocked at how good that feels. I mean *you*, for God's sake, are the last person on the planet I would have ever expected to feel that way about. Six days ago we were trying to kill each other in the Tower."

"Gods, has it only been six days?" she muttered. "It feels like forever."

He decided to ignore that. "So maybe I told you the truth because I don't trust how this feels. And maybe I told you the truth because that's what real partners do—at least that's what I've heard they do anyway. Maybe real partners know how to say to each other, 'yeah, you fucked up and now it's okay to move on,' and maybe I would like to hear somebody say that to me just once, sometime in my life. So now it's up to you, sunshine. Polish your vendetta if that's what you really want. Just keep in mind, you need me to take down that witch. Let me know what comes after that."

As aggressive sounding as the words were, saying them still left him feeling raw and wide open. Man, he had a gods-given talent for self-destruction. He rolled away, putting his back to her, and rubbed his chest where that burning pain had settled.

Aryal said, sounding exceedingly aggrieved, "You're like some kind of high-maintenance girlfriend. I have one of the worst days of my life. Hell, I might be crippled. *I might never fly again.* That's beyond my worst nightmare. I don't know if I can live with it, and yet somehow tonight has become all about you. What about what I need?"

"What do you need?" he whispered.

She said tiredly, "I could use a hug. And you're the only person around who can give me one. So put out, will you?"

It shocked him immensely, that she would be so open and frank enough to say it. It shocked him even further to discover he could really use a hug too.

He rolled back and reached for her, and she came into his arms, hugging him back. "I'm sorry about the bad timing," he whispered. "It seemed like a good idea at the time."

"Shut up," she said. "I'm so mad at you I can hardly think straight."

"Of course you are." He sighed. Even their conversations were twisted. "You're not crippled. You're just not healed yet."

Her chest convulsed silently. He never would have known if he hadn't been holding her. "The joint is crushed. I felt it."

"You're going to fly again." He pushed all the conviction he had into the words. "You *will*, Aryal. Healers can do miraculous things with joint repair these days. If all else fails, there's joint replacement. You're going to fly again. I swear it."

He knew he might not be right, but she didn't need that kind of honesty right now. She needed optimism and belief, and he put everything he had into giving it to her.

Her chest convulsed again. He kissed her temple. She didn't cry easily and wouldn't let go. It felt like it was wrenched out of her, and she fought it every step of the way. "It's okay," he said. "It's going to be okay."

Funny how while he was comforting her, for some reason, the burning pain in his chest had eased.

"I can't believe what a drama queen you are," she told him.

"*Me*?" He was genuinely astonished.

"You made a mistake. Sure, it was a bad mistake, but nobody died except the bad guys. What are you going to do, cry 'mea culpa' and beat your chest for the next ten years? Everybody's over what happened but you. I am not saying this because you wanted somebody to. I'm saying it because it's true. Move the fuck on already."

Her words were rough, but they were sincere. He went from burning to lightness. It might have gone to his head a bit, because he rolled her over onto her back, and he came up over her to kiss her.

She made a muffled noise against his lips. She sounded incredibly grumpy. Then she kissed him back.

They were both filthy, blood streaked, and the cold floor was making him nuts. None of it mattered. This wasn't about sexual passion. Or maybe it was, but it was about something else too, something that was more important.

That made him suspicious. He didn't know what to call that important, unknown thing, but whatever it was, it felt necessary and right. He teased her lips and she licked at him. Then he deepened the kiss until their tongues met and caressed. She tasted of apple brandy, heady and light.

The sensation went to his head. He eased over her more fully, pressing one leg between hers. The friction of denim cloth from their jeans was a quiet sound interspersed with the sound of their deepening breath. She ran her hands up his back, her touch on the expanse of naked skin sending a shudder through him.

He couldn't believe he hadn't been inside of her yet. He needed to know her response to that most basic and primitive joining. Her long lean body was a match for his. It felt amazing to stretch out along her and revel in her feminine strength, like it unlocked a previously unacknowledged part of him.

Somewhere inside of him, that wild, dangerous part that he kept so tightly leashed broke loose and started running unfettered again. He had just enough presence of mind to wonder where the hell it was going, and why it needed to get there so urgently.

Neither one of them was capable of consummating a goddamn thing, yet still they kissed and kissed. He ran his fingers up her torso, underneath her ruined T-shirt to stroke at the graceful swell of one breast. He played with her soft, distended nipple as she cupped the back of his head, holding him down to her mouth.

Finally he pulled away enough to kiss the corner of her lips, and he leaned his forehead against hers. She stroked his hair, and it felt like a miracle.

He sighed. "Okay, when you're not making me batshit crazy, I guess maybe I like you after all. But if you tell anybody that, I'm going to have to throttle you again."

A soft explosion came out of her nose. She said, "An hour."

"What's an hour?" He fingered a strand of her soft hair.

"I want to renegotiate our bargain, to be consummated at some future date when neither one has had the shit kicked out of us." A thread of humor laced her words. "Unless that happens for purely recreational purposes, of course."

He paused to listen inwardly to his own reaction. The loudest part was relief and respect. After admitting to how devastated she was, she had not only mustered humor and genuine emotion, but now she had taken the first step to making plans beyond taking revenge on the witch.

Underneath all of those reactions though, ran a bloodred pulse of hunger, coursing in a subterranean river through his arteries and filling him with greed.

An hour was an eyeblink, a mere moment in time. He had squandered more time than that when deciding where he wanted to go for dinner on a boring day. An hour was woefully inadequate considering all the things he wanted to do to her, and with her.

Considering all the things that she would do to him. Somehow he had gone from enduring that thought to wondering.

And wanting.

He said, "No hour. A night, from dusk to dawn. You get one, and I get one. No stopwatches, no alarms going off, no hourglasses." The wild part of him ran harder, and his voice deepened. "No rules."

A shudder ran through her, and the feel of it thrilled him. "You would do that, give up total control for that long."

"I totally would do that, if you would." He put his mouth over hers to feel her warm, moist breath. "Do you dare?"

She started to laugh almost silently. The uneven puffs of air against his lips were like bubbles of champagne. He breathed them down and felt them enter his bloodstream, coursing with his greed. She told him, "You know asking a harpy if she dares to do something is like waving a red flag in front of a bull."

"I had hoped," he admitted.

Even as he said the last word, she spoke over him. "Yes."

Triumph roared through him, and with it came an epiphany.

This thing with Aryal wasn't aberrant. Those things in his nature that she showed him weren't aberrant. They were a part of him that he didn't know existed until Aryal brought a light to shine on them. This wasn't sexual tourism. It was sexual discovery.

He barely heard over his internal realization what she said next. "You know other people—any other people—would think we were crazy."

He understood exactly what she meant. Hell, they didn't even do BDSM in any straightforward fashion, and they certainly didn't follow the norm or any of the suggested guidelines. He didn't think there were any subculture groups who would approve of the rampant disregard either he or Aryal gave for safety checks.

He didn't want a safe word, and she didn't ask for one. They were both dominant, and he knew for a fact he wouldn't be a switch—someone who switched the dominant role with the submissive role—for anybody else but her. And he was almost certain she wouldn't either.

She quieted that internal whip that drove him because she became the whip, her soul as sharp as a knife.

He could cut himself on her, wrap her in his arms and be her buffer. Heal her from herself, bruise himself on her.

Let her heal him. Let her be his buffer.

They were so unapologetic, so *kinked*.

He said, "We're perfect."

⹀ SEVENTEEN ⹀

After he spoke, they fell silent, as if they had gone more than far enough for one conversation. There were implications everywhere in what had just happened, and Aryal didn't want to consider any of them, nor did she want to decipher any of the unfamiliar emotions that rioted inside of her. That crowd of strangers, yelling in an incomprehensible language, was back in her head.

Except one of those strangers was perfectly understandable, as it held up a giant spongy finger that pointed to a placard that said, "Total fucking win-win."

She considered sinking back into despair, because at least she understood that emotion, and it hovered around the edges of all the others, ready to bring down the weakest in the herd.

But she was no longer as shaky and hollowed out as she had been before the nap, the food and the cuddle, and she couldn't manage to give in to it.

Sometimes being too stubborn for her own good turned out to be the best thing for her.

So she broke things down into words of one syllable, since that was apparently what she could handle at the moment.

Fuck it then. Kill the bitch, have some great sex, go home.

She counted backward. Yep, all one-syllable words. That'd do.

While she deconstructed her life, Quentin eased off of her and stretched out on his back again.

Somehow, something had shifted when she hadn't been paying attention, and the part of him that was feline no longer bothered her. She simply enjoyed his animal grace.

He tucked one hand behind his head with a sigh. "Are you going to come over here or not?"

She decided that it sounded like a great idea, so she edged close to settle against him, putting her head on his bare shoulder. Fitting herself against his body felt incredible, her leg hooked up over his. She shook out her tablecloth/blanket over both of them and draped her arm across his chest. He put his arm around her and pressed a kiss to her forehead. He seemed to be more demonstrably affectionate than she was. It took her outside of her comfort zone, but she . . . liked it.

Sleep stalked her, but she fought it off enough to mumble, "I bet you act romantic with every female you've ever dated."

His response was a long time in coming, more of a grunt than a real word. "Yup."

Not that they were dating, but . . . "You talk like shit to me."

He grunted again. "Can't tell you what a relief that is."

Tucked in between pockets of decency and a conscience, he was still a bastard.

One corner of her mouth lifted in a smile. She let sleep take her.

The pale light of predawn woke her.
Razor teeth. Crushed.

Adrenaline flooded her system, bringing with it a wash of nervous energy. Her body ached all over. Caerreth had closed her wounds and started them on the right path, but they were still healing. She needed more rest. She needed real rest and recuperation, but she couldn't relax enough to let sleep claim her again.

She eased her head off of Quentin's shoulder and looked at him. He was sound asleep, his lean jaw covered with more pale gold beard. His face wore the marks that the last couple of days had put on him. Even asleep, it made him look edgier and more dangerous than he did back in New York, and she had thought he'd looked dangerous then.

Then, he'd looked like a sleek, well-fed predator cruising through a crowd of unsuspecting pussycats. Now he looked more like what he really was, a man who would do anything he had to in order to survive.

A man who tried to be good in spite of himself, but who was really bad enough that she wanted him at her back in a tough fight.

She hadn't told him that she liked him too, when he wasn't driving her batshit crazy. It wasn't any of his business how she felt about him.

But in the predawn silence, in the privacy of her own mind, she admitted a truth. Maybe she more than liked him.

The crowd in her head woke up and tried to riot again. She rolled her eyes and eased away from Quentin, trying not to disturb him. He had not been as injured as she had, but he needed more rest too, and he didn't stir as she sat up.

She tucked the tablecloth around his torso, crawled over to the food they'd left strewn over the floor and ate a weird but filling breakfast. Actually, pickled eel and apple brandy weren't so bad together. Then she went into "her" cell, where the blood on the floor had dried, used the crude latrine in the corner and splashed her hands off with water from the wineskin. A proper wash and clean clothes were high on her list of needs that day.

Second only to finding weapons and Elven armor.

When she went to peek out of the window, Linwe was keeping watch by the cell block door. She nodded to the young Elf and looked outside. The sky was cloudless, the wide expanse of water calm. It was going to be another scorcher of a day.

She went around to the other side of the cell block, gesturing to Linwe to follow her. The other woman did, her fine-boned face sparking with curiosity. "Let's wake the other two," Aryal said to her quietly. "We need to make some plans and act on them."

"Okay," said Linwe.

Together they shook Aralorn and Caerreth awake. The males sat up readily enough, wiping at their tired faces. Despite the short night, they all looked miles better than they had before.

Aryal sat back on her heels, testing her thigh wound. It held. The other three were watching her expectantly. She said, "Here's the plan. You guys are leaving as fast as you can."

"Wait, what?" Linwe said. The two males looked confused.

Aryal told them, "You need to take enough food to get you through a two-day run, harvest water on the go, and leave Numenlaur. On the other side, one of you needs to hike out of the forest to update Ferion, and make sure that Ferion updates Dragos. The other two will stand watch. Don't let anybody into Numenlaur. If the witch and her wolves are the first ones out, the news about us won't be good. If that happens, don't do anything. Hide and let her pass. But neither Quentin nor I are planning on letting that happen." She looked at the three sober faces. "Who has magical aptitude aside from Caerreth?"

"We all have some," said Linwe. "Caerreth has the most aptitude, but Aralorn has more offensive Power. I know some basics like how to spell a light, but my strengths are more physical."

"She's killer with a bow and arrow," Aralorn said with a small smile. "A little like Hawkeye in the Avengers."

Dear gods, he was talking about comic superheroes. They were so young.

Aryal rubbed her tired, gritty eyes. "Okay," she said. "If I were Galya, I would have sent one of the shadow wolves back to the passageway to stand guard, so we have to expect that. I doubt it will try to follow you back over the

passageway, because if there is one there, I think its purpose is to bring back word of someone crossing over. Plus
it might not be able to travel that far away from Galya. There's
something that connects her and the wolves, and that connection might be a magical one. If it is there, it might not
attack you. Then again, it might, so you need to be prepared. If you don't know how to throw a simple repel spell
yet, Quentin will teach you when he wakes up. You're
going to have learn it fast, because I want you out of here
by midmorning."

All three of them argued. They had heart, she'd give
them that.

Aralorn said, "But you need us."

She leaned her elbows on her knees and gave him a level
look. "No, we don't," she said. She'd never been one to
mince words, and now was not the time to start just to save
this young man's pride. "We need each other, we don't
need you. *You* need to leave so that you don't become col-
lateral damage. Two communities of Elves have lost
enough. Your people need you, and you can't forget it."

Something happened then, a shift of their eyes, a change
in the air. Even though she hadn't heard anything, she looked
over her shoulder.

Quentin stood behind her, arms crossed, leaning one
bare shoulder against the frame of the cell door, and she
was struck all over again by the differences between him
and the others. He looked mature, muscled and mean, and
his steady gaze met hers.

She didn't know the words to describe his expression.
All she knew was that his regard was so intent, it caused
her to flush hot all over. He nodded to her. Then he looked
beyond her to the other three.

"Who needs a magic lesson?" he asked.

Caerreth raised his hand. Aralorn said, "I know the
spell."

Linwe said, "To be honest, I won't learn it fast enough.
I'll be of more use helping with something else."

"Okay, Caerreth," said Quentin. "It's you and me,
buddy. Let's go into my office."

He led the younger Elf away to the other side of the cell block. Aryal called after him, "Unlock the door as you go, will you?"

He raised a hand in acknowledgement just before he disappeared. She turned to the other two. She squinted at Linwe. "Weren't you wearing battle armor back in January? Where is it now?"

Linwe looked at the floor. "Back home."

"Ah," said Aryal. As Linwe's skin darkened, she said with a twisted smile, "I usually wear fighting leathers, but you know what? Leather tends to get squeaky in the cold so on this trip I decided to wear jeans instead. Who knew. Can you make the two-day run in full Elven armor?"

Both Linwe and Aralorn looked very sharp and alert.

Linwe said, "I can." Aralorn nodded.

"Then here's what I think," said Aryal. "I think if Elven armor is magic resistant, then it's very possible it'll do a damn good job of protecting against those shadow wolf bites. We need to find a barracks and an armory, where we can get five sets of armor and weapons. You know that's gotta be close by the palace. I'll tell you what else I think. You remember that three-day feeding pattern you were talking about, Linwe?"

"Yes."

"Yesterday was the day she was supposed to feed you and she didn't, right?"

"That's right."

"I think Galya's been traveling back every three days from the island to feed you. Bringing us down on the same trip yesterday was killing two birds with one stone." Aryal rubbed the back of her neck. "And I think Quentin was right—she didn't make the choice to stop feeding you until we showed up, and I recognized her. Anyway, the point is, if her search is focused on the island, I think she's still over there now. And except for any sentry that she's probably sent to the passageway, I think the shadow wolves are with her, or they would have attacked you and Quentin last night when you went to get food." She paused to consider her own logic. "So I think it's still a risk to go hunting for the barracks, but it's a calculated one, and the odds are in our favor. Are you game to go with me?"

"Hell, yes," Aralorn said. Linwe hopped to her feet in answer.

Aryal smiled. Galya Andreyev must want something pretty fucking badly, if she was willing to be responsible for six people's deaths in order to get it. And if she was willing to kill that many people, what she wanted was something she wasn't supposed to have.

It felt good to take steps toward stopping her.

She stood too. "Let's go."

She walked around to the other side of the block where Quentin was teaching Caerreth the steps to throwing the repel spell. Caerreth wouldn't be able to practice it until he left the cell block, but at least he would know how to do it.

"You need to practice this every time you stop to eat and rest," Quentin was telling him. "If the shadow wolf attacks, it's going to be wicked fast. You won't have time to dither."

The young healer looked even more scared than he had last night. Aryal said to him, "Imagine it's like an arterial wound. You have to act fast before your patient bleeds out. This is the same thing, only you might become the bleeder."

Caerreth paled. "I guess I see your point."

Quentin said to her, "You're not helping, sunshine."

She gave him a wide-eyed look. "Was it something I said?" She watched with furtive pleasure as he bit back a smile. She told him, "I'm taking two of the kids, and we're going to the mall, honey. You know, looking for weapons, armor, that kind of thing. We'll be as quick as we can."

"Drive safe," he said, his gaze going sharp.

She gave him a limpid glance. "Oh, you know me. I can never parallel park the minivan right."

He burst out laughing. "Now that is a nightmarish image."

She smirked and walked out.

He called out after her, "Be fast. Don't make me come after you."

Linwe and Aralorn waited for her at the cell block door. Aralorn looked a little leery of the banter, but Linwe's eyes were dancing.

When Aryal reached them, she said loudly, "What can I say. When your dad hit middle age, he turned into a worrywart." More quietly, she said, "Let's go."

Finding the barracks was as much an exercise in logic as anything. They had to work their way upward, and for the first part of the journey, Linwe took the lead until they reached the kitchens, which were on the ground floor and not dug into the cliff itself.

The kitchens were located on the side of the palace that faced inland, away from the Temple of the Gods and the sea, and they had plenty of windows to allow for fresh air and natural light.

Dawn had long since broken, and the cloudless morning had turned bright. The heat was beginning to build up. The Elves were going to have a challenging run on their hands, wearing the armor. Aryal walked through the large kitchen area, looking out windows as she considered the placement of the nearby buildings.

She said, pointing, "There. That long, low building. That's the barracks. There'll be an armory of special shit somewhere here in the palace, stuff that Camthalion himself and any of his heirs would have worn, but I don't want to waste time hunting for it. I'd rather go for the plain battle armor."

"How do you know that's it?" Linwe asked as Aralorn joined them at the window.

She shrugged. "I don't for sure, but logic tells me it is. The building is plain. Also, look at its position. It almost completely blocks the way from the mainland, except for that road. It is an effective barrier, which is great protection. You would want soldiers in that building, in case of attack."

Linwe smiled at her. "I'm kinda girl crushing on you right now."

Aryal gave her a wry smile. Once not that long ago, she would have taken the opening Linwe gave her and started a flirtation, but now she couldn't summon the interest. "You're awfully cute too. Let's go."

She took the lead as they headed out the door at a jog.

The building was around two hundred feet away, which they crossed within a few minutes. When they found a door and entered, they discovered that Aryal had guessed right. Rows of bunks filled a large open area. Attached to one side of the building was an armory with suits of armor and a wide variety of weapons: longbows and arrows, short swords, long swords, maces, battleaxes, spears, throwing stars and knives. Despite her desire to hurry, Aryal had to pause a moment to stare at the treasure with covetous glee.

In one special cabinet, they found shelves of Elven healing potion. Each bottle shone against her mind's eye like stars.

They moved fast and collected everything they needed, enough armor for all of them, a basic complement of weapons, and supplies of the precious healing potion. As tempted as she was by some of the weaponry, Aryal focused on getting long swords for herself and Quentin, along with longbows and arrows. The shadow wolves wouldn't be overcome with physical weapons, and she doubted that Galya would either. The real treasures were the armor and the healing potion.

Linwe and Aralorn had buckled on armor right away, which was an intelligent choice—it gave them immediate protection and made everything else easier to carry. After she saw what they had done, Aryal did the same.

As she finished buckling the chest plate into place, Linwe came to join her. Linwe said telepathically, *I'm really happy about you and Quentin.*

What?

Aryal's head came up. Her internal crowd of new emotions started to riot again. She stared at Linwe. *What do you mean?*

The younger woman's friendly smile faltered. *You and Quentin. You're together, aren't you? I mean, you spent last night together, and the way you look at each other . . . and he follows you with his eyes with an expression I've never seen before. I just thought . . . I mean, it seemed obvious. . . .*

Aryal ran her fingers through her hair and tried to massage

some kind of rational thought into her tired brain. *He follows me with his eyes?*

Linwe grimaced, looking embarrassed. *I got it wrong, didn't I?*

I don't know, she admitted. And there was that giant spongy finger again, pointing to the placard. Total fucking win-win. She tried to give Linwe a smile, but it felt like it came out all twisted and wrong. *It's early days yet. We're still feeling our way.*

We're perfect, he had said. And when he said it, everything inside of her pulsed in recognition of the rightness of it.

I don't know, she said again.

For a moment she faltered. As her sense of purpose flatlined, she felt lost, even confused, and fear rose up to slash at her with black, razor-sharp teeth. Nothing felt familiar, not her physical surroundings and not the landscape within, and her future wasn't looking very survivable. She had no business considering whether or not she was "together" with anybody. She closed her eyes as despair attacked.

"Here," Linwe said gently, brushing her lax fingers aside. "Let me finish buckling that for you."

As Aryal let the younger woman work the fastenings, she looked out the barracks door that they had propped open. The door faced the palace, and beyond that, the sparkling sea. At the height of the promontory, the island was more visible than ever.

A sailboat cruised the water, leaving a silvery trail in the water behind it as it approached the mainland.

Aryal's hand shot out. She gripped Linwe's shoulder with such force the younger woman looked up at her wide-eyed. "Which of you is the fastest runner?" she asked.

Linwe and Aralorn answered at the same time. Aralorn had been sorting out armor for Caerreth. He looked up as he said, "She is."

"Me," said Linwe. "Why?"

Aryal hauled her around and pointed to the boat. Linwe sucked in a breath, but before she could say anything,

Aryal shoved her toward the door. "Get Caerreth out here now. Move!"

As if Aryal had shot her from bow, Linwe raced for the palace.

Aralorn joined her at the doorway. Unwilling to take any more chances of being seen, she pulled him back until she was sure they both stood in shadow. They stared out. Thus far the Elf had shown a steady demeanor, but as he wiped his mouth with the back of one hand, Aryal saw that it was shaking. He asked, "What are we going to do?"

She told him, "You and the other two are going to leave just like we planned. You'll take this road past the barracks. It doesn't matter where it leads, as long as it gets you out of sight of the piers. As soon as you're out of sight, do whatever you have to do to get to the passageway as fast as you can."

If he had looked shaky before, now he looked downright terrified. "Yes, ma'am."

Moments dragged by. She watched the sailboat get closer. She guessed it was perhaps ten minutes out from docking. Come on Caerreth.

Then Linwe, Caerreth and Quentin exploded out of the kitchen door, racing toward them. She noted with approval that Linwe had had the presence of mind to bring one of the sacks of food.

Quentin searched the area until his gaze locked on her.

Aryal held up her flattened hand. Stop.

His hands shot out in either direction, and he grabbed the two younger Elves, dragging them to a stop. His gaze never left her.

She looked at the boat and at them, calculating angles and line of sight. If they could see the boat, theoretically, someone on the boat could see them. At their current trajectory, they would have about seventy-five feet when they might be visible from the water.

Probably the witch wasn't looking in this direction, but she didn't want to risk it. She gestured to Quentin, pointing to her left, their right. They needed to travel in a wide arc so that they put the bulk of the palace between them. She whispered, "Figure it out. If you can't see the boat on the water, she can't see you."

He seemed to get it. He nodded at her and gestured to Caerreth and Linwe to go to their right. She said to Aralorn, "Come on. We're going out another way."

She helped him gather up their weapons and Caerreth's armor. Then they walked through the long building to the armory section that had its own entrance. This time the angle was better, and she and Aralorn ran to meet the others.

"Her ETA is seven or eight minutes," she said. She threw Quentin's armor at him, dropped the weapons at his feet and joined Aralorn and Linwe as they worked feverishly on buckling Caerreth into his armor. As soon as the last piece was in place, she slapped him on the back and stood back. She ordered, "Go."

Clutching their weapons, healing potion and food, all three of the Elves stared at her and Quentin as they danced backward several steps. Each one's expression was conflicted, with things left unsaid and warring impulses. Furiously Aryal stabbed in the direction of the road with a forefinger. "Go!"

They bolted. Within moments they were out of sight.

She glanced at Quentin. He had almost finished buckling on his own armor.

She turned and made her way back through the armory and the bunkhouse to look out the doorway. Quentin followed. The sailboat had almost reached one of the piers. The witch was almost here.

Aryal had done a good job. She'd thought logically and put the others first, but in that moment, ladies and gentlemen, all sanity left the building.

≡ EIGHTEEN ≡

H er talons came out, and she started forward. She had someplace to be and someone to kill, and she was never late for a commitment.

Quentin grabbed her by the arm and spun her around. "What are you doing?"

"Let go!" She knocked his hand away. "I have to kill her."

Faster than thought, he grabbed her again and shoved her back against the open door. She took a swipe at him, which he dodged. Then he slammed into her, pinning her with his body. "Stop it! You can't go after her right now."

She didn't recognize the sound of her own voice. "She grounded me. She maimed me. Maybe I'll fly again, but MAYBE I WON'T."

She tried to shove him away, but he had braced himself with one foot back, and he pushed against her hard, elbows planted on the door on either side of her face. It left his sides wide open. If he wasn't wearing the armor—if he were the enemy—she could have sliced into his abdomen and gutted him before he had a chance to take another breath.

Except that they had gone beyond committing such destructive acts against each other, gone far beyond it into territory that was unrecognizable to her.

She fisted her hands and pounded at him. It didn't do a thing to shift his position or change the determined expression that hardened his face. "Goddammit, listen to me," he growled. "We will go after her, Aryal. I promise you, we will, but we can't right now. If she finds out that we escaped, she may send some of her pack to hunt the others. They might be able to hold off one shadow wolf in order to cross back over to Earth, but they can't handle several at once. We have to give them as much time as we can."

She stopped struggling as his words sank in. He looked into her eyes, and whatever he saw seemed to satisfy him, because he eased up from pushing against her.

"And here are some hard truths, sunshine," he said, speaking rapidly. "We—you and me—are not ready to confront her. We're partially healed and not fully rested, and there's only two of us. On the other side of the equation, she's not only one of the most dangerous magic users in the world that Dragos knows of, but she also has her pack. We're going to get her, but we have to be in control of how it happens and when, and we have to be at the top of our game. Do you hear me? Right now we have got to get back to the cell block."

Breathing hard, she managed to nod. He gave her a not-quite smile, pulled back, and as she stepped away from the door, he shut it. Then they raced through the barracks, out the door that wasn't visible from the pier, and back through the lower levels of the palace to the cell block. Once they were inside, Quentin picked the lock shut again, and they both leaned back against the wall as they looked at each other.

"She might have had a change of heart," she said. "She might have come back to bring food."

"I really fucking hope so," said Quentin with a hard smile. "But I doubt it. She's already responsible for one death that we know of, and you outed her. We don't know what she's doing, or what she's looking for. She might have just come back to follow a lead."

She said harshly, "Maybe she found what she's looking for, and she's leaving Numenlaur."

He thought about that. "Even if she did, I doubt she can travel as quickly as those three scared Elves can. The others will still make it out first, as long as her pack doesn't go hunting for them." He reached out and squeezed her hand. Her talons had disappeared when he talked her down, and he rubbed the tip of one of her fingers with the ball of his thumb. "And if she leaves Numenlaur, we'll go after her. We're going to get her, Aryal. I swear it."

The tension in her body eased as she soaked in his conviction. She believed him, and it helped to calm the pain that raged inside. She laced her fingers through his.

"Thank you."

He leaned his head back against the wall and gave her a slow smile that was guaranteed to set some kind of internal burner on simmer. "Don't mention it. You can pay me back with sex."

Just like that, from one moment to the next, he brought her from rage to laughter. She admitted, "Sex with you *is* on my to-do list."

His smile deepened. He squeezed her hand. "Yes, but our bargain is a done deal. You'll have to owe me something else. You should know, I charge interest by the hour on debts that are owed to me."

She smiled back at him. Yes, he was always going to be a bastard. It was comforting to know that some things don't change.

They watched out the window and waited. The witch didn't bring food.

A lack of action was also a choice, and it was one that Galya Andreyev kept making. Quentin felt nothing but contempt for her. It would have been better to kill them outright rather than lock them up and let them starve to death. She was the worst kind of murderer.

At one point he walked through the silent cell block, taking time that he hadn't before to note the bodies in some of the cells. What a lonely way to die. If Camthalion had gone as crazy as the story said, these prisoners might have been good, decent people. At any rate, they hadn't deserved this kind of end. Nobody did.

A couple of hours passed. They each ate their fill again and took turns napping. After a while they were going to have to make a decision to leave if nothing happened. At least they would leave better fed, rested and healed. They had gotten the Elves away, and they had weapons, healing potion and magic-resistant armor. This morning's activity might be frustrating, but so far it was tallying in some essential positives.

Then, just after midday, as he paced from the window to the cell block door and back again, he glanced out—and a sailing boat had appeared again on the sea, headed for the island.

Surprise pulsed. He strode to "their" cell where Aryal lay on her stomach, her dark head cradled in folded arms. She had discovered the second bottle of apple brandy, which sat near one elbow.

Something about how she looked in the elegant Elven armor moved him, tall, sleek and deadly strong. Real Elven armor wasn't how the movies portrayed it, at least not the normal kind that regular troops wore. Shiny was eye-catching and stupid, as it made a perfect target. Instead Elven armor was a flat neutral color. All of its beauty lay in the elegance of its creation and shape. The people who loved it most were the warriors who entrusted their lives to wearing it.

Aryal also looked utterly dejected. His chest wanted to start burning again, but he wouldn't let it. He walked over and kicked her foot. "Rise and shine, toots. She's headed back to the island."

She lifted and spun around in one quick movement, and rose lightly to her feet. "Now we know something."

He smiled. "And by now, the others have put in a good couple of hours' run. By tonight they'll be halfway out."

She cast a glance of loathing around her, a sentiment with which he heartily agreed. "Let's get out of here."

He gathered his longbow, quiver of arrows and sword, while she did the same. Then he went to pick the lock one last time. By now he had an intimate familiarity with the internal tumblers, and he had the door open within a few seconds. They went up the stairs cautiously, but none of the shadow wolves were in sight. For the first time since the witch had taken him, he took a deep breath and felt a real sense of freedom.

He turned to Aryal and said, "If we can, we need to use the element of surprise and sneak up on her."

She angled her head, her expression tense, and rotated a hand at him. "Keep going. I'm still not feeling very rational or thinky at the moment."

"Is your cloaking ability strong enough to cover a small sailboat?" he asked as he studied her.

She considered. "I think so. What about your cloaking? You were able to hide the fact that you're Wyr, which is a pretty Powerful ability."

"The problem is that I don't know how far outside of my own body I can cast it," he said. "We're going to have to suppose a lot. She's not a normal human so she might not sleep much, if at all, but the chances are that she will rest at some point at night, and it will be less likely that she would sense any nearby magic."

She narrowed her eyes at him. "Are you willing to make an unknown water crossing in the dark?"

He shrugged. "I can swim. Can you?"

"Yes," she muttered. "I'll bet she uses the wolves as sentries."

"Leave the wolves to me. Again, we don't know enough about her, so this is supposition, but I'm guessing from here to the island is too far for most humans to swim. If she comes from the Russian Steppe, she's probably not one of those rare humans who could make the distance."

"I agree. So we'll sneak up at night and disable her boat." She paused, narrowing one eye at him in a squint. "Along with our own? How are you about swimming that distance back?"

"It'll be uncomfortable but doable. You?"

"Same." Purpose came back into her angular face. "So we leave at sunset."

"I'm down with that." He stretched his stiff back. "In the meantime we've got hours to sunset, and I've a mind to nap in an Elven lord's bed. Come on."

They traveled into the main part of the palace by way of the kitchens, and for a time they wandered in silence, looking at the precious gold and lapis lazuli inlaid in the high, wide walls and marble floors, and gazing out the windows at glimpses of the silent, abandoned city spread out along the shoreline below. Then they came to the throne room and stopped to stare.

A burned body slumped in an ornate chair on a scorched dais. More bodies lay in a semicircle, their throats cut. Scavenger birds had been at them. Other than that, the bodies remained perfect, giving a glimpse of ruined beauty.

After a long look, Aryal turned away. She said simply, "They're dead and it's awful, and I'm done. I'm full up. I can't feel anything for them."

He put an arm around her shoulders and led her away.

They climbed another wide, curving staircase and explored hallways. Quentin opened the large double doors down one hallway and walked into a room that was the size of his apartment at the Tower. A massive bed dominated the room with coverlets and pillows embroidered with gold and scarlet thread.

Wide windows the height of the room looked over the city. The far one faced the white, pillared Temple of the Gods, which stood outlined against the backdrop of the blue-green sea.

There was no doubt in Quentin's mind whose bedroom this was. He walked around the room, looking in doors. One opened to a huge bathroom, with tiled steps that led down to a walk-in tub patterned with an intricate mosaic. The tub was large enough that a troll could bathe in it. Another door opened to a wardrobe filled with sumptuous clothes that were suitable for an Elven male.

Drawn by the dramatic view, he walked back to the far window. The temple was simple and open to the elements. The side facing the palace had steps leading up to the marble-floored interior. The gigantic statues of the gods on either side, interspersed with columns, provided the main support of the plain prop-and-lintel roof. On the farthest side of the temple, a single god faced outward to the sea.

Even though all Quentin could see of that statue was its back, he was certain that it was the god Taliesin, god of all the other gods, the prime mover of the universe.

The bedroom was at the same height as the enormous profiles of the two closest statues, one male and one female, their stern, strong faces looking into infinity. The male statue faced the city, and he held a book tucked under one arm. That would be Hyperion, the god of Law. The female was less easy to identify, but he thought she might be Camael, goddess of the Hearth, age and wisdom.

Aryal joined him at the window.

He said, "Camthalion put himself on the same level as the gods. Can you imagine looking out at this scene year after year for millennia, while possessing Taliesin's Machine? After all that time I wonder if there was anything recognizable of the original man."

He glanced at her. As spectacular as the temple was, she wasn't looking at it. Instead her face tilted up to the wide, cloudless sky, and her expression was filled with so much anguished yearning, it cracked something inside of him.

They were perfect. *Perfect*, which was insanity all on its own. After hating her so vehemently, experiencing this kind of emotional turnaround was enough to give him whiplash. That issue alone should have been more than enough to deal with for, say, five or six years, but on top of that he also knew what was going on in that spiky, passionate head of hers.

She was about to go into war without having enough to live for.

Gods, he didn't want to say the things he was about to say to her. He wanted to shut the hell up, take a bath and go to sleep. Heart-to-hearts gave him indigestion. He would do almost anything to avoid them. Hearing the words "we have to talk about our feelings" was the surest way to get him out the door fast, and he had never looked back before, never up until this point in time, with this woman.

He could walk out of this door too and find another bedroom for himself, except that meant he would leave her alone with that heartbreaking expression on her face. And he would rather die than do that, which meant that somehow he had landed himself squarely in the middle of the Deep Shit Zone for sure.

The thought that he was about to initiate a "we have to talk about our feelings" moment was laughable. But there was his internal whip again, driving him forward. With a sigh, he shut and bolted the double doors, and walked over to sit on the edge of the sumptuous bed. He started to strip off his armor.

"I think I might be getting close to mating with you," he said flatly into the sun-drenched silence. He bent over to work off the leg pieces. "Believe me, I'm very aware of how that sounds. Feel free to laugh if you like."

He sensed when she turned away from the window, but he didn't look up. He started working on the other leg.

Still in that flat, matter-of-fact tone of voice, he said, "You're nothing like anything I would have said I wanted, yet I think you might be everything I need. It's too early to tell for sure. We've spent a week together. One week. Yeah, it's been one week filled with high stress and intense exposure to each other, and I know this kind of thing can happen fast, but sunshine, we haven't even really made love yet. All we've done is fool around a little. I'm sure you can understand the depth of my perplexity at finding myself in this situation."

"Are you somehow going to make today all about you again?"

He tilted his head at her. The sun was behind her, rendering her expression unreadable. He said, "Of course."

He bent back to his task. Elven armor was as light as it possibly could be while still being effective. Still, wearing it over jeans on a scorcher like today was a miserably hot experience, and it was a relief to strip the pieces off. After he took a bath, he was going to raid the wardrobe for something lighter to wear underneath.

She walked over and sat on the bed beside him. He thought he heard her mutter, "So that's what the crowd in my head has been yelling about."

He had been in the middle of pulling the breastplate over his head, so he couldn't have heard her right. "Excuse me?"

"Never mind." After looking undecided for a moment, she began stripping off her own armor. With her head bent to her task, she asked quietly, "If it's too soon, why are you bringing this up now?"

Finally he was back down to his filthy jeans and boots. He took off the boots, then turned to kneel in front of her and began to work at the fastenings of her leg pieces. "You know how it goes. 'Honey, I'm going to war, and I've got something I need to tell you.'" He leaned his elbows on her knees and looked up at her.

She stopped what she was doing and watched him with a wary, vulnerable look. He almost smiled. She handled her own vulnerability like someone else might handle dynamite, her eyes wide as if something were about to explode in her face.

He said quietly, "I want to know that you've got your head on straight when we go to the island tonight. I know you're struggling with a huge amount of fear. You've been doing a good job, but I've watched it swallow you up a couple of times, and I'm concerned."

"I won't do anything that will get you killed," she snapped. She yanked at the fastenings of her own breast-plate and dragged it over her head.

"That's not the point," he said. He reached up to take her face in both hands and insisted that she look at him. "I don't want you to do anything that will get *you* killed. You know as well as I do that a fighter who is struggling with despair is a danger to herself. I don't want you to go into tonight without having considered everything—everything—there is to consider, and yes, that does include me."

Her expression broke, and the anguish came out. She gripped his wrists. "I'm so scared."

"I know you are," he said. "I can't imagine facing the kind of uncertainty you're facing. That's why I'm going to ask you to think outside of the box."

She looked at him with such surprise he had to laugh. He rose up to kiss her. She put her arms around his neck to hug him with such ferocity, he wrapped her up in his arms too. They held each other tightly.

"Some people," she said, "would say that I already think outside the box."

"I don't mean any regular old box," he told her. "I want you to think outside of *your* box."

She pulled back to stare at him. "I don't understand."

"You need to remember all the reasons you have to live, because if someone goes into a life-or-death fight without having those reasons firmly fixed in their mind, often they don't make it out the other side alive. The fact of the matter is, you are not facing an either/or situation, where you either fly or die." He held up a finger. "Here's the first thing to remember. You may be healed."

Her face clouded over. "I don't see how. I—the bone crushed, Quentin. I felt it go."

He flicked her nose, and he wasn't gentle about it, so that she jerked her head back and blinked. "You are not a healer. You can't diagnose yourself, and you don't know what might happen. Say it."

"Fuck you," she said. But she didn't put any heat behind it, and he could tell at least she was listening to him.

"Number two." He held up two fingers in front of her face. "You may not be healed back to what you were before, but you may gain something back. Okay, this one is likely. This might mean you go for shorter flights than you're used to, or it might mean you go parachuting, and you learn how to glide. Maybe we'll need to build a brace for that wing. Don't get me wrong, I know that would be terrible and it would suck, and you would have every reason to rage against it. But you'll be in the air."

"Parachuting?"

He could tell the thought had never crossed her mind, and why would it? She'd never had to consider it before. He lifted a shoulder. "Along with a version of paragliding. You can ride thermals. Eventually you would have to land, but that's true now too. I know it's not the same, and it's not as good. The point is, there are ways that we can make what was done to you survivable. You just have to believe it."

She gripped his wrists so hard he felt his fingers grow numb. "I can ride thermals."

"You can as much as you need," he said gently. Thank gods, she was listening to him. "You can free-fall and do somersaults in the air. Anything you like. I'll go with you. I enjoy parachuting."

"Do you?"

He nodded. "Reason number three. There's your job to consider. You love being a sentinel so much you endured coming on this trip with me instead of throwing the job back in Dragos's face."

"True," she said, very low. "But if I can't really fly—if all I can do is ride thermals and parachute, I won't be the same at my job."

"You'll have to rethink how you approach work and what your strengths are, but that is doable too," he said. "I'm the first sentinel that isn't an avian, but I *am* a sentinel. I won my position, and I deserve it. The same applies to you. Your wings didn't make you a sentinel. You did." He paused to make sure that sank in. Then he said, "Number four. There are people who love you. Niniane and Grym. Hell, maybe Grym is right, and Dragos does too. Graydon's pretty mad at you, but you know he loves you." He took a deep breath. It was time to throw himself on his sword. "Me."

Her eyes dilated until they were mostly black. "You?"

"Yeah, don't dwell on it," he said. Okay, he was done now. He tried to pull back so that he could stand up and walk away.

She lunged forward and grabbed him by the shoulders. "Oh, no you don't!" she said. "You can't just throw a tear gas canister like that into the room and walk away when it goes off."

"I don't see why not," he muttered. He tried to turn away, but her face was ablaze with so much emotion he remained on one knee just so that he could keep gazing at her, and soak up the sight.

"If anybody would have said I was unlovable, I would have thought it would be you," she whispered.

Suddenly he had no desire to go anywhere as his face creased with silent laughter. He told her, "I would have said so too. Then I found out that, even though you are still the most maddening creature I have ever met, you are actually quite lovable."

Her head bent down as she slipped one hand to the back of his neck. She said softly, "And even though you are every bit the dangerous bastard I thought you were, you are really quite trustworthy."

The words hit him between the eyes. They were all the more powerful because he knew how little she cared for returning courtesies, mouthing platitudes or pretty nothings. He said, barely audibly, "I'm glad you think so."

Her long fingers worked at the back of his neck, massaging him. She straightened her back as if steeling herself. "About the mating thing."

His eyebrows rose. "Oh, is that still in the room?"

Laughter flashed in her eyes. Then she sobered. As blunt and direct as always, she said, "I haven't put words to what was going on inside me, but I could be mating with you too. I've never experienced this kind of—total engagement before. You don't need things I'm not interested in giving. You fight me, and you don't back down. You can fight *with* me on the battlefield as an equal partner. You're strong enough to hold your own, and you're willing and able to negotiate."

When she paused as if searching for more words, he held her gaze as one corner of his mouth lifted. "And I sex your ass up."

She burst out laughing. "And that too. The thing is, we have a choice right now. We haven't gone too far, and we can back the hell away from all of this if you want. But before you make any decisions, I want to tell you something. A very long time ago, I made a promise to any mate who might or might not come into my life one day."

Whatever he had been expecting when he initiated this conversation, this wasn't it. He whispered, "What did you promise?"

She stroked his jaw lightly with one hand. "I will never betray my mate and never endanger his life with my carelessness or impetuosity. I will fight for and with him, and always have his back whenever he might need me. I will not leave him, and I will not lie to him, and if he will only be patient and forgiving, I will learn how to forgive too, because he will be the most important thing, ever, in the world to me. I will give everything I have to him, along with everything I can be, if he will only do the same for me."

She couched everything she said so carefully, but those words she spoke were his words. Those promises were to him.

"Why are you telling me this now?" he asked, very low.

"Because as you said, you're going into war too, and you need to know who your fighting partner is," she said without preamble. "You need to know that you can trust me. I heard what you said. I heard everything you said, and while I'm still struggling with all of it, I want you to know that somehow it's going to be okay." Her eyes filled and she struggled for a moment. Then she said, "I might not know the details of how I'm going to survive, but I know that I will, because I could never endanger someone who was even a possible mate by throwing my own life away."

That wild, dangerous part of him. He knew now where it was running, and to whom. The panther sank down and put his head in the harpy's lap. He was an alpha male with too much edge, and he set it all at her feet.

He had never imagined he would find someone strong enough to take everything he was, and willing enough to embrace all of it. He could never have known that the one place where he would find peace was in the heart of the wildest, edgiest creature of all.

As the panther found his peace, the harpy stroked his hair and discovered tenderness. Then everything that lay twisted between them came clear as they reached the heart of the labyrinth they had been traveling together.

≈ NINETEEN ≈

Aryal sat frozen. She didn't know what to do when Quentin put his head in her lap. It was such an extraordinary experience, so surprising and fine. The weight of his upper torso against her legs felt exactly right. The sight of him on his knees was not at all what she had imagined in the heat of her anger and desire, and yet it was perfect.

They were perfect.

She ran her hands along his broad, bare shoulders and along as much of his wide, tanned back as she could reach. Underneath her touch, his powerful muscles shifted below his skin, a mystery cloaked in silk. His body was so well made, she basked in the pleasure of stroking him. She scratched her fingers gently against the grain of his short beard and watched as a shudder rippled through him.

"Talking to you doesn't suck," she said in surprise.

He lifted his head to look up at her, a grin creasing his face. "No it doesn't. How about that." Capturing her wrist, he stood and pulled her to her feet as well. "Come on. There's a tub the size of a small swimming pool in the other room, and I've become obsessed with the thought of getting clean."

She looked down at herself. She had washed her face

and hands with careful handfuls of water from the wineskin, but it had done little more than shift the grime around, and her jeans, along with what remained of her once white T-shirt, were bloodstained and filthy.

With great relief and a lack of ceremony, she stripped. "This outfit needs to be burned."

He went tense. As his stillness caught her attention, she glanced at him. He was staring at her nude body, traveling from her high, small breasts down the length of her narrow torso to her slim hips and long, lean legs. The private tuft of silken hair between her legs was very black against her pale skin. The reddened scars from the recent wolf attack still marked her, but they were rapidly fading.

While her arms and shoulders were in proportion with the rest of her body, they were cut with muscle. She had a natural aptitude for strength in her upper body, which she enhanced with regular workouts using a variety of weapons, constantly building aptitude and stamina. One of the most dangerous aspects of swordfights, or any fight, for that matter, was that they were so grueling.

While she didn't believe that she was beautiful, she didn't have a self-conscious bone in her body, and she liked herself. She had never once wished any of her physical attributes away, and had always believed that all of her flaws were ones that remained unseen. That was why it was a shock for her to encounter an awkward moment, like running into an invisible wall.

Yes, the attraction that coursed between them had been off the charts, but in that moment she couldn't read his expression.

And she wanted him to like her.

His voice turned guttural as he said, "I've never seen you until now."

She looked down at herself with a frown and brushed at one of her breasts with the fingers of one hand. She said wryly, "If you're a boob guy, I guess you're out of luck."

Sexual tension smoldered in the hot afternoon air. She could feel it pouring off him. "You're a knockout," he said. "Your breasts are perfect-sized bites, and your legs could grace a runway. I feel like you've punched me all over again."

He moved toward her, his muscled body tight yet fluid. He was broad across the chest and darker than she, his tanned body a warm brown. He had unbuttoned his jeans and the opening revealed the long, rippled line of his abdomen. The dark blond of his hair was like gold treasure glinting in shadows, and the blue in his eyes looked so much like home, unwanted and unexpected moisture dampened her eyes.

To counteract it, she turned toward mischief and pinched her own nipple, rolling it teasingly between her fingers.

He reached her and knocked her hand away. "Stop that. That's my nipple."

A grin broke across her face. "That's one of the more ridiculous things you've ever said." She plucked at both of her nipples and winked at him.

He grabbed her wrists and yanked them behind her back. "What can I say," he said. "I'm ridiculously possessive."

"And controlling," she said. "And dominant." And playful and sexy, and so damn bad her whole body wanted him. She was empty and aching, and had moistened so that she could feel her own dampness on her inner thighs. She whispered, "I can't believe I haven't taken you inside of me yet."

"Oh, you had me inside of you," he growled. "You had me in your mouth, and I will never forget it. That moment is going to give me wet dreams for decades."

With her wrists held behind her back, her torso arched against him. It was the first time they had come together with so much skin against skin, and the sensation was intoxicating. His body was hot and slightly damp with sweat, and his Power sizzled as it wrapped around her.

And he was so dirty.

"I loved you all spread out on that table like a feast," she said against his lips. "Expect more of that when I get my night. Expect that I'll take a great deal of time over you, and you won't necessarily climax when you want. You'll climax when I want."

He hissed, "Promise?"

"Promise." Her mouth shaped the word slowly, to prolong the glide of her lips along his.

"You're not wet enough," he whispered.

It took a moment for what he said to sink into her hunger-hazed brain. "I'm pretty wet," she managed to articulate.

He lifted his head, and there it was again, the addictive combination of passion and laughter flaring in his face. "I can't tell you how glad I am to know that, sunshine," he purred. He let go of one of her wrists to trail his fingers down the long, curved line of her spine. "But I was actually referring to the pool-sized tub in the other room. I'll scrub your back if you scrub mine."

The thought of sliding against his hard, naked body in the water made her hunger spike, thrumming through her body with agonizing strength. "You offer the best bargains."

He let her go with evident reluctance, and she walked ahead of him into the luxurious bathroom. Soaps, along with jars of salts and lotions, lined the edges of the tub, and stacks of drying cloths filled a decoratively carved oak cabinet against one wall. An ornate screen hid a pull-string lavatory in one corner, and a full-length polished silver mirror stood in a metal stand in one corner. A marble counter with a washbasin and another, smaller silver mirror was set against another wall, along with a long bench with small bottles of oils and fragrances at one end, no doubt used for massages. The Elven lord had liked his luxuries.

She knelt to examine the levers for the massive tub and discovered that it could be filled with either salt or fresh water. She chose fresh and opened the valve wide so that water gushed in. There was some kind of heating system, probably a sun-heated tank, and the water was hot enough for a comfortable soak.

Movement glided at the edge of her vision. As she turned to look, a nude Quentin strode into the room. He was half-erect, that beautiful penis of his in a thick full arc above his tight, drawn-up sac.

His sleek, catlike grace along with those broad shoulders, muscled chest and long bones were a killer mixture.

She remembered all too well what he looked like nude, yet the impact struck her all over again. He gave her a keen, searching glance as she knelt at the side of the tub. Then he walked down the steps. The water had gushed in so fast it was already at his waist. As he came close, his hand snaked out. He grabbed her by the arm and yanked her into the water.

She started laughing even as she fell, rolling so that she hit the water shoulder first. She caught a glimpse of his lean face, creased in a smile, and then the water closed over her head. After the heat and getting so dirty, submerging felt so incredibly good, she didn't rise up right away. Instead she stretched her whole body and turned languorously, wallowing in the sense of weightlessness.

Hard hands grasped her shoulders and lifted her. Water rushed away from her face and as she blinked to clear her eyes, she discovered Quentin looking down at her, his face tight and flushed with intent. His expression was so raw, so naked, she stared, and her heart began a slow, heavy pounding. He exhilarated and terrified her.

For a moment she considered pulling away and leaving. As she'd said, they had a choice now about what happened to them, about whether or not they moved forward to see what joining together as possible mates might bring to them.

But she had never backed away from anything just because it frightened her, and the totality of who he was drew her like a siren's song. He had an extraordinary capacity for both violence and tenderness, and a sensuality so keen it sliced deep into her center.

It couldn't have been balanced of her to tell him that she would live for him, even if she couldn't see how right now. She noted the thought as it passed through her mind, and she gave a mental shrug. Balanced was not who she was. She threw everything she had at life, and this was no exception.

She stood and put her arms around his neck, and he clenched her tightly against him. As they came together, they fit, skin to skin and soul to soul.

Then he loosened his hold to reach for a jar by the side of the tub. Pouring a fragrant liquid into his palm, he rubbed his hands together and began to work the soap through her hair. When his fingers rubbed at her scalp, the sensation ran all through her body. Still tired, stressed and half-healed, she felt as if he had unzipped her. The muscles of her inner thighs started to shake, and she had to force herself to stay upright.

"I don't think I'm going to be able to take much of this," she said unsteadily. Somewhere deep inside, something prideful glared at her. She ignored it, concentrating all of her attention on the exquisite sensation of his large hands moving along her skin.

"That's not true," he murmured. "You can take as much as I can give. You can take anything I dish out. You're the strongest woman I've ever met, and you can take this too."

He coaxed her forward until she rested her head on his shoulder. Then he washed her, his callused hands gentle as he stroked her aching back and shoulders, right at the place where, in her harpy form, her wings joined her body. She went boneless, floating against him as she trusted him to hold her up, and he did.

"It's going to be all right," she whispered. Somehow she would make sure of it.

"I trust you too." He kissed her temple. "If you tell me it's going to be all right, then it will be."

He wasn't any more balanced than she was, because no Wyr in their right mind would mate with someone who was in danger of suicidal behavior or getting themselves killed. Yet here he was, without a single hesitation.

She lifted her head and framed his face in her hands as she told him, "You're crazy."

He shook his head slightly. "No," he told her deeply, conviction in his steady gaze. "I'm just turning sane. Or maybe I'm coming fully into myself, and that feels like it has been a long time in coming."

"Duck down," she said, growing as hungry to touch him as he was touching her.

He obliged her by submerging in the water, then straightening again. The strong bones of his face stood out with his wet hair lying sleek against his head. She took some of the fragrant soap in her hands and began to wash him. Every line of his hard body felt like a revelation, and the intensity of his reaction was blinding.

His body shuddered, and he sucked in air as if he were running hard, running desperately with all of his might to reach some essential destination. Soapsuds slid down his neck and chest, and her fingers followed them, lingering over the bulge and hollow created by his muscles. There was a little oil in the liquid, and it made his skin even more silken. She felt like she was painting him with an invisible message.

Run here. Find me. Love me.

Stay.

He responded as if he had read every word, pushing her forward and coming with her on a wave. As the water closed over their heads, he hugged her against his body as his hardened lips found hers. They turned, floating together as they kissed and kissed, piercing each other ravenously with their tongues, because while they would fight with all their strength for tomorrow, tomorrow might not be there, and now was all they had.

And it felt like flying. It felt like home.

It felt like everything she might have confessed to herself that she wanted, on dark nights when there was no one else around to hear.

She murmured wordlessly, and the water swallowed the sound as she wrapped her legs around his waist and held on to him with all of her strength. Gripping her just as tightly, he rolled to his feet and stood.

Water cascaded off of them as he strode up the steps, carrying her. When she loosened her legs and made as if to stand on her own, he yanked her back up. "Don't you dare let go of me," he muttered. Without the water to buffer them, he felt as if he was burning up, and the full, hard length of his cock pressed against the underside of her ass.

Complying, she tightened her legs and embraced the contradiction that lived inside of her. While she would almost never want a man to carry her, a primitive part in her reveled in the fact that he was so strong that he could, effortlessly.

He strode for the massive bed, never once looking away from her face. How strange, that this man would look at her with such need and desire when once all he could do was look at her with hate. He felt and did everything so passionately, she knew that he would make more mistakes down the road. They both would.

But just like his dark blond hair, he was gold treasure in shadows. He was worth every bit of the effort it would take for her to learn how to forgive him, worth every bit and more.

They reached the bed and he fell on top of her, his big, powerful body arcing over her in need. He ran his shaking mouth down her throat to her breasts, first sucking hard at one then the other quickly, as if he was so ravenous he couldn't wait and had to have them both at once.

The brilliant afternoon sun fell through the windows across her face, blinding her with light. She squinted, gasping, as she felt pierced everywhere, in her eyes, in her body that stabbed her with emptiness, and in her emotions, as every barrier she had constructed against this man fell away.

He lifted his head, a black silhouette against the sun, and paused. Even though she couldn't see his face, she knew he was looking down at her. Then he leaned away as he reached for a pillow, and she could see him again. His expression had turned wicked and tender at once.

"We need to get that sun out of your eyes," he said, his voice raspy as he started to purr—literally purr—again. She watched as he tore a strip of material off the pillow. As he turned back, the look in his eyes was rotten with velvet mischief. "This will give you some shade."

Comprehension dawned, and she sat up. He wanted to blindfold her?

Despite all the uncertainties and danger that lay ahead of them, she smiled, suddenly more happy than she could ever remember being. She said very gently, "I will if you will."

He hesitated, but this time she could sense there wasn't any struggle in him. He merely made an adjustment in his thinking. "Absolutely."

She tore a strip from the shredded pillow, and they blindfolded each other. The last knot was barely in place before he hauled her against his chest, imprisoned her head between his hands and kissed her. He had to quest across the skin of her cheek to find her mouth. The exploration was unbelievably erotic.

Greedily, she ran her hands all over his body as he plunged into her with his tongue. Finally she cupped his stiff penis, and they both made a hoarse, anguished sound. His breathing turning harsh and uneven, he put one hand between her legs and curled his fingers into her slick, hypersensitive flesh.

"I can't wait any longer," he muttered against her lips.

"Good. Come here." She lay back on the bed and he came with her, settling his weight onto her. Together, by feel alone, they brought his cock to her entrance. The tip felt wide, and he paused again to rub himself against her moisture and make sure she was ready for him.

But she had lost all patience. She hissed against his mouth, "Do it!"

He responded as if she had laid a whip across his back, arching his body and plunging into her in one long, hard push. As he impaled her, there it was again, the good kind of pain mixed with pleasure, like brandy and chocolate.

Overcome by impulse, she cheated and pushed her blindfold up, squinting against the sunshine.

He leaned on elbows that were braced on either side of her head, broad shoulders hunched and his head thrown back. What she could see of his half-covered face was etched with some kind of sexual crisis. He shook his head, growled something under his breath that she couldn't understand, and began to move.

Gods, he was the most beautiful thing she had ever seen. She raised her hips each time he thrust into her, and his full, hard length gliding into her tight sheath was everything that she needed, everything. She laid one hand gently against his cheek while she raked her nails down his back, scoring his skin and marking him as hers.

His face twisted. He bared his teeth, reached up to snatch his blindfold away. They both froze a moment, staring at each other, as the thief caught the cheater.

A smile broke over his face, keen and brighter than the sunshine, as he rocked inside her. "I'm tacking that onto your debt."

The mounting pleasure was so great, she could barely manage to pant a few words. "I'm okay with that."

His smile slipped away, and he came down over her, winding one arm around her neck and the other underneath her hips, holding her in such a tight grip he would leave bruises.

She loved it all, she loved him. She brought her mouth up to his and urged him to go harder, deeper, until he pistoned into her, driving her higher and higher toward an unseen peak.

She stretched everything she had toward it, arms over her head and arching her body up to him.

And there it was, that singular moment where she could almost leave the shackles of gravity behind.

Almost.

She reached the peak, and for that one instant in time she existed weightlessly, no longer straining to rise but flawless, floating.

Then the climax took her over completely. Somebody cried out. She didn't know if it was her or him. He bowed over her, shuddering all over, and even as the rhythm of her climax faded away, she felt his cock start to pulse.

It was too good, too beautiful. Need gripped her. She cried out, "I'm not done."

He met her gaze and growled, "I'm not either."

She rolled him over and came up sitting on him, all while keeping him inside. Still gripping her around the hips, he pulled her down and bit her neck. He held on to her, fucking her as she rode him, and overcome by the urgency, she screamed into the bedcovers as she came again.

As did he, bucking up with his hips and swearing.

She clawed at him, beyond words.

He gave her everything she needed, everything she asked from him, and more than she ever expected to receive. In return, she gave him everything she had, every last chaotic, passionate piece.

Matched. Mated.

Perfect.

They did not quite wreck themselves on each other. That would take a few days of the mating heat. Instead, conscious of the passing time, they simply reached a place where they managed to stop.

Need still roared like a race car through his veins, but when Quentin noticed that the angle of the sun had changed, he said against her lips, "We've got to think of tonight."

Breathing unsteadily, she pulled back, and a sliver of rational thought appeared in her stormy eyes. "Rain check," she whispered.

"You know it, sunshine." Because he couldn't help himself, he passed a hand over her breast one more time. "Just as soon as we possibly can."

Foregoing blankets in the late afternoon heat, they sprawled together, limbs entangled. Despite the mating urge that nagged at him, he fell into sleep as quickly and completely as a stone dropped into a dark, quiet pond.

Just as quickly and completely, he woke several hours later.

The sun was close to setting, shadows lengthening throughout the Elven lord's luxurious room.

Aryal lay on her stomach, her black hair falling over her face. Quentin's head rested in the small of her back. He had wrapped one arm around her thigh in his sleep. Her scent filled him with carnal memories. She smelled like fragrant soap and sex.

When he lifted his head and looked along her length, he saw bruises on her hips where he had gripped her. They would be gone entirely in another hour or two. He clenched with the need to lick her everywhere and begin all over again. To avoid starting something he knew he would not be able to stop, he lifted carefully away from her sleeping form.

Out the nearest window, shafts of light lanced the panoramic view of the deserted city like unimaginably long spears thrown by the gods. Soon the city would lay silhouetted against the fiery colors of sunset. Despite his growing obsession with the woman lying next to him, he had to stop and stare. Nature was sending them off to battle in style.

Aryal had bunched bedcovers under her head as a pillow. She muttered into them, "Time to get up?"

"Yeah." Then he couldn't help himself after all, and he bent over to press a kiss to her shoulder, watching covetously as a shiver rippled across her skin. He forced himself to say, "We better move if we're going to pick out a suitable boat before the light goes."

She picked herself up off the bed in one smooth movement, and her expression settled into a harpy's unshakable focus.

They washed quickly. Quentin spared a few minutes to use the Elven lord's flat razor and shave off his new beard, which had begun to annoy him, while Aryal combed through the massive wardrobe. She found sleeveless silk tunics and trousers that were slightly large on her and tight across the shoulders on Quentin, but the lightweight material would breathe while it provided a little buffer against the armor, so it was perfect for their purposes.

Last came the weapons: long swords belted at the waist, short swords strapped to their thighs, and unstrung longbows strapped to their backs along with quivers full of arrows. Aryal used Quentin's blindfold to tie back her hair. When she noticed that he watched her, she muttered, "Souvenir."

He cocked his head, immeasurably charmed by the sight. There she stood, looking as lethal as he'd ever seen her, and . . .

He asked, "Did you just blush?"

She made a face and strode for the door, saying over her shoulder, "I have no idea what you're talking about."

"And now you're running away." He prowled behind her. Inside, delight filled him with airy lightness.

"Don't be stupid. Of course I didn't. And I'm not." She wrestled with the locked door.

"Yes, you did. You blushed and ran away." He reached around her, pulling her hands away from the door. As he unlocked the door, he nuzzled her neck. She smelled clean and wild. The scent went straight to his cock, of course. "It was fantastic."

She shook her head, sounding winded as she said, "Because it's always all about you, isn't it?"

"Damn right it is." He bit her gently, slipping an arm around her waist as she leaned back against him and reached over her shoulder to stroke his hair.

She twisted and kissed him, and he clenched her to him, kissing her back hard and hungrily. How this much emotion had fountained out of nothing was something he couldn't understand, but he would never get enough of her, never.

Adrenaline at what lay ahead had already started to beat a tribal rhythm in his chest. His hunger for her only heightened it. He bent her back over his arm, his kiss turning savage. They were both shaking when they wrenched apart, all lightheartedness and joking lost. She stroked his cheek and looked him deeply in the eye, her angular face serious. He brushed his mouth along her fingers.

Then, having already said everything they needed to say to each other, they left.

He glanced one last time over his shoulder, out the window at the gigantic stone faces of the gods. Hyperion faced the westering sun. The angled light had turned the god's blank eyes golden.

Quentin had never been much for prayer, but this time, he decided to give it a go. *Just see that we find her,* he said silently to the god. *We'll take care of everything else.*

They left the palace by way of the kitchens and stopped briefly to collect more portable food and wineskins filled with water—and another two bottles of brandy, because you never know, they might just be able to hang on to it this time—and they distributed it all evenly into two sacks, along with the vials of healing potion they had gathered from the barracks.

The light was fading fast by that point, so they jogged down to the shoreline and strode along the piers, looking for a small sailboat suitable for one or two people. They found one quickly and Aryal jumped in to hoist the sails while Quentin unfastened the ropes mooring it to the pier. He shoved it off and leaped in. The last of the day's light lay fractured in slivers along the top of the rippling dark waves as they drifted beyond the pier into open water.

Aryal's cloaking settled over the small boat like a shimmering veil. They had to figure out by trial and error how the tide ran, and how to move forward in the right direction using the angle of the wind. Eventually they settled into tacking in a zigzag course. By then the overlarge moon had risen and it shone with so much silvery light, to Quentin's feline gaze the scene turned almost as bright as day.

They took turns eating, while the other remained vigilant at the tiller. Watching the island as it neared, he ate lightly, just enough fuel for whatever came next but not enough to weigh him down. While he swallowed his last bite of wayfarer bread, a flicker of light appeared.

It shone from the building that lay up the steep hill, nestled among the trees.

"We've got her," he said softly. He could sense that Aryal had gone tense and still. He noticed something else too. Two piers at one end of the beach held several moored boats. "There are too many boats. We shouldn't waste time trying to disable them all."

Aryal asked, "What do you suggest?"

He turned to her. "I take point," he said. "The current is running at an angle to the island. When we get close enough, I'll swim the rest of the way to the beach. The witch is smart. She'll have shadow wolves on the beach as sentries. We don't know how, but somehow they're linked to her, so I'll draw her attention. Meanwhile, you sail with the current, land somewhere along the other side of the island and double back so that you come at the witch from behind."

She studied his face. "You'll draw her fire on your own?"

He gestured impatiently with one hand. "Yeah, it's gonna hurt. That just means you'll have to move fast. I'll also try to wait a little while before I engage, to narrow down the lag time."

Did she pause to think about how this might have been her opportunity to get rid of him, as he had once paused to think about her? No sign showed on her tense features. "I don't like it."

"Tough," he said. He turned back to look at the island. "I'm the one who's more equipped to fight the shadow wolves."

"But you'll be facing them both until I get to you. And while Elven armor is magic resistant, it doesn't block everything. Once its resistance has been compromised, it's no better than any other leather armor."

"It's better than a simple frontal assault," he told her. "Her wolves could engage us to cover her retreat, and we'll have expended our energy and given away the element of surprise for nothing. This way—she doesn't know that you survived the first attack, sunshine. She might wonder, but she won't know that you're coming."

She was silent for several moments. "Shit."

"It makes sense," he said gently.

"Okay, already!" she exploded. "But shit!"

He didn't say anything. If their positions were reversed he would hate it just as much as she did, and there wasn't any way to make it better. He studied the fast-approaching shoreline and rotated his shoulders, loosening them up for a swim and a fight. Was that a shadow he saw, pacing the beach?

They reached the point where she was going to have to angle away to avoid landing. He settled his supply sack and a wineskin of water firmly around his neck and one shoulder. Then he wrapped one hand around his arrows, holding them in the quiver, as he braced one foot on the edge of their small sailboat and prepared to jump over.

"Quentin," she said.

She sounded so urgent that he paused to glance at her. The expression on her face was tight, and her eyes burned with determination. Her mouth worked. Then she said, "I'll hurry."

He gave her a bright, hard grin. Then he launched over the side of the boat and hit the water, stopping only for a moment to watch as Aryal and the sailboat turned away. The strong current tugged him in the sailboat's direction, so he couldn't pause for long. He ducked his head and cut across the current, swimming in strong, sure strokes. The armor, weapons and supply sack made swimming awkward, and it was difficult to develop a rhythm.

But he didn't have to go far. After a few minutes, he came up against the furthest boat at the end of the first pier, and he grabbed its anchor chain to tread water. He eased the supply sack, the skin of water, and the longbow and arrows over the rim of the boat as he studied the nearby beach. A path zigzagged up the hill that was so steep it warranted carved steps in places. It led to the top of a bluff. He could just see the edge of the trees at the top.

Down below on the beach, two spots of blackness glided across the sand as shadow wolves paced. They seemed restless. He recovered his breath as he studied them. Now that he knew what to expect, he could sense them quite well. Maybe, as Aryal had said, they weren't the product of a magic spell, but he wasn't convinced. Both wolves carried something of the same magical signature. It seemed too singular, as if stamped with a certain personality.

Did the witch have so much Power that she could cast a spell that acted like thirteen independent entities—and then not only maintain it indefinitely, but across large distances? His credulity balked at the idea.

Did the ones on the beach already know that he was here? Could they attack while he was still in the water, and if so, why did they hold back?

He pulled his own Power up and held it ready. Offensive spells were tricky to cast in battle, because they took time to create and fighting happened so fast. That was why the best and most effective spells were the simplest ones. They were easy to remember in a panic, and quick to spit out and do damage.

And one of the most effective spells of all was one that counteracted other dangerous magics.

One of the shadows stopped moving. It appeared to be facing him. It didn't do anything, but just waited.

He wasn't going to need the bow and arrows for this fight. He pushed away from the boat and glided toward shore, watching both shadows warily. The one shadow wolf never moved. The other didn't stop pacing.

He reached a point that was shallow enough that he could touch bottom with one boot, and that was when a mental voice entered his head, speaking with a strong accent.

Help us.

You speak telepathically? What the hell? He stared at the wolf in front of him, not surprised so much that the wolf could speak to him but that it chose to.

The wolf said, *Beware. If you come to shore, we are bound by orders to attack you.*

Quentin treaded water, thinking hard. It sounded sophisticated, like it really was a thinking individual. *What are you?*

We are Wyr too, the wolf said. *Or we once were. Our alpha mated with Galya. When he was severely injured in battle, she caught his soul and tried to revive him. His body died, but he stayed bound to her. She has become obsessed with finding a way to resurrect him, and us. One by one we have given our lives to prolong hers, in the hopes that she will eventually find a way to bring us back. But she did not tell us that we would be bound to her will, and it has been so long.*

She had prolonged her life through the sacrifice of theirs? Shock and revulsion froze him until he started to sink. He kicked up and treaded water again.

Resurrecting the dead was forbidden in every culture he knew, and he had always believed there was a strong reason for that. It bent an essential event in nature, and the results, or so he had heard, were invariably warped and tragic.

He said, *Help me make sure I understand you properly. She's looking for a way to resurrect you?*

There is a thing mentioned in the very oldest of tales

248

called the Phoenix Cauldron, the wolf whispered. *It was said to have been so Powerful it could bring the dead to life. It was lost long ago when this land was barred from the rest of the world. She searches night and day for it. But I am so tired. Yet she won't let me go.*

She sacrificed Wyr to prolong her life and held their souls against their will. Rage followed closely on the heels of all his other emotions.

Aryal should have landed by now. It was more than past time to make a big noise and end this witch.

He swam closer to land.

As he neared, the wolf whispered, *Some will not fight you with all of their strength, but don't trust Pyotr, the alpha. He is as devoted to her as ever.*

Understood. He stood to walk out of the water, and the other shadow whipped around. It stalked him across the sand.

The wolf that had been talking to him crouched and sprang. Quentin flung out his hand silently to throw the spell he had held ready. He put all the force he could into it.

::Dissipate::

The spell was meant to counteract dangerous magics, and it worked better than he could have hoped. It hit the attacking wolf in midair. The black shadow twisted as if it were in agony. Then with a *snap* and an outcry that rang in Quentin's head, it vanished.

In the distance, out of sight at the top of the bluff, a woman screamed in shock and fury.

So he had gotten the witch's attention.

Quentin ducked his chin down with a dark smile and strode onto the beach, and as the second shadow wolf raced toward him, he pulled his Power together and punched the air with another spell.

Like the other wolf, when the spell hit the shadow twisted and *snapped* into nothingness. He shook his head. Even though they had already been—mostly—dead, he still felt like he had killed them.

Then some sixth sense tickled at him. He looked at the path.

Ten shadows poured over the edge of the bluff. Then the

last one appeared, and that shadow was the biggest and most Powerful of them all.

Yeah, those numbers didn't look so good when Quentin had to throw each dissipation spell one at a time.

A woman appeared at the top of the bluff. Galya. The silver moonlight seemed to hollow out her eye sockets and turn her face to bone.

Come on, Aryal. Move your ass, sunshine.

The shadow pack reached the beach and hurtled toward him.

He gathered up his Power and prepared for battle.

≡ TWENTY ≡

A s the water pulled the sailboat away from Quentin's dark, partly submerged form, Aryal nearly jumped overboard to swim after him.

It didn't matter that everything he had said made sense, or that she had agreed with him. He was going to call all the attention to himself, and that meant he would take some damage. That also meant he was taking a serious risk, and she hated leaving him.

Hated it.

The current ran deep and fast as it swung her around the end of the island. She looked down the length of that side. Holy gods and *fuck*, water broke in white swirls of foam against broken rocks along the coast. There was no place to land the boat.

Then, because she was who she was, she looked up. The broken rocks rose up to a sheer cliff face.

And none of it should matter in the slightest.

She should be able to change into the harpy and fly over every inch of that cursed shore. She screamed out her outrage and pain, silently, hands clapped over her mouth.

Then she pulled her souvenir out of her hair and tied her arrows securely into their quiver. With it slung on her back

251

along with her unstrung longbow, she flung herself out of the boat and tore through the water, swimming hard toward land.

The water helped by picking her up and flinging her against the rocks. She landed against one partially submerged boulder with a force that knocked the breath out of her, and she twisted and shapeshifted all in one desperate move, clawing at the granite to find some kind of hold before the treacherous, foaming maelstrom pulled her back out to sea.

Struggling to kneel on the slippery boulder, she lunged at the cliff face and clung to it, talons digging into the jagged, crumbling rock as she fought to catch her breath. Her entire right side had absorbed the impact. Bones were bruised, and they throbbed with a fiery pain. Tomorrow she would be black all over.

Face tilted up to her goal, she began to climb. If there wasn't a fracture in the rock for her to slip her talons into, she made one, driving her hands and feet at the cliff to gouge out enough of a hollow to hold her weight. Climbing was grueling, exhausting work, and her aching wings hung heavily at her back like a ragged parachute, weighing her down.

She was halfway up the cliff when Power flared, and the witch screamed in the distance. Another time she might have savored the sound, but now fear gripped her. She wasn't far enough up the cliff, wasn't close enough to the battle. She redoubled her efforts, heart pounding when she felt Power flare again. She recognized Quentin's signature.

Then Power flared with a different signature.

The witch had found him, and engaged.

Panic drove her through the rest of the climb, and she didn't pause when she reached the top. Shapeshifting to be rid of her wings, she raced blindly along the edge of a massive, ancient stone building, around a corner and over what must have once been a manicured lawn but was now overgrown with weeds and neglect.

She found a path and took it, even as she reached over her shoulder for the unstrung longbow. A blast of light and Power flared ahead from the direction of the beach. It lit the ground ahead of her as if hell's light poured out from a crack in the earth.

Precious seconds flew away as she stopped to brace the bow on one foot and strained to bend the strong, seasoned wood so that she could attach the bowstring. Then she hurtled along the path to the edge of a bluff and looked over a scene that could have been birthed from her worst nightmares.

Quentin and Galya stood several feet away from each other. The witch appeared unscathed.

The light came from Quentin.

An area along his wide chest, one shoulder, his neck and the side of his face blazed with some kind of spell that shone like a beacon in the night. What she could see of his expression was agonized, and his Power flared spasmodically as he struggled to counteract the attack spell. Dark forms writhed along his legs and arms as the shadow wolves gripped him with black teeth.

Oh gods.

She looked at the witch, who stood with her hands on her hips and watched Quentin burn, and she had never hated anybody as much as she did this woman.

Even though the witch's spell still worked on Quentin, his Power surged. The blast knocked all the shadow wolves away. He flung a hand toward the witch, piercing the air with a deadly missile of Power. The sleek, elegant spell shot toward the witch, who deflected it effortlessly with a twist of her wrist.

Aryal whipped out an arrow from the sodden quiver and notched it, and sighted down the longbow until she was sure she had the perfect shot. Then she loosed it. Despite its speed, her harpy sight could track the arrow's flight.

Magic flared again, and the arrow curved away from the witch. Galya looked over her shoulder, up the cliff and straight at Aryal, her expression filled with surprise, then contempt.

Beyond the witch, blazing in light and blackness, Quentin fell to his knees.

The spongy finger in Aryal's head pointed to a new placard.

Lose-lose.

She went to a place inside of herself where she had never been before, a place that even she recognized was insane.

That's okay.

She nodded. Shook her head. Nodded. She turned and jogged away.

When she reached the tree line, she pulled her short sword, turned around again and ran at the bluff, pushing as hard as she could to hit her maximum speed. As she reached the edge of land, she lunged into the air, shapeshifted and spread out her maimed, half-healed wings.

Searing pain ripped through her.

She couldn't fly, and she couldn't glide, but she could work on directing her descent. So that's what she did.

That's okay, bitch.

Repel this.

Galya had turned back to Quentin for one critical moment. The harpy smiled as she plummeted down, her body listing crookedly. When all was said and done, her life might come down to this: she was just broken enough to fall in exactly the right way.

When the witch caught sight of her, Galya had no time to cast another spell. There was one bittersweet moment when Galya's expression flared with astonishment and the beginning of fear. She opened her mouth to scream.

Aryal slammed into Galya, driving her into the sand. They landed badly in a tangle.

Things snapped inside of her, explosions of more searing pain in the ruins of her internal landscape. Her breath came in on a high thin whine.

Blackness surrounded her as shadow wolves attacked. Even more pain flared as the first one sank its teeth into her shoulder. She shrieked and convulsed into a shapeshift, reverting to her human form that wore the Elven armor just in time before the others arrived. Some hung by their teeth off the Elven armor. A few burrowed in between the plates, looking to chew through the armor's fastenings.

None of it mattered as her attention narrowed to accomplishing one thing. The only way to stop her now would be to kill her.

Galya moaned as she tried weakly to pull herself out from underneath Aryal's body. Clearly the witch was hurt, but she wasn't hurt badly enough, as she gathered her Power to throw another spell.

Aryal punched her in the face. The witch's gathering Power splintered. Bone crunched as the witch's head rocked back, and blood spurted from her mouth and nose. It felt so *necessary*, Aryal punched her again. Vaguely she realized that crazypants had taken charge of the fight.

The two blows alone might have killed the human, but the shadow wolves still swirled around her, and crazypants was determined to be thorough. She saw her short sword lying tilted in the sand a few feet away, along with her abandoned bow. She crawled to the sword and grabbed it. Something was wrong with her hand. It wouldn't close around the hilt properly. It was almost too difficult to crawl back to the witch's sprawled body, but she managed it.

The largest shadow wolf lunged desperately at her arm as she raised the sword, but the Elven armor held against his gnashing teeth.

She plunged her sword into Galya's chest.

Multiple screams echoed in her head. All the shadow wolves *snapped* out of existence.

Crazypants pulled out the sword and stabbed the witch again. She said hoarsely, "That's for what's-her-name who died in prison because you put her there."

And again. "That's for Quentin, who better not be dead."

And again and again and again, driving the sword into the body as her breath sawed raggedly. She raised and angled the sword, and in one wide sweep that set her overstrained back ablaze with agony, she cut off Galya's head. Then she picked the head up by the hair and flung it into the water. "That's for me and each one of my wings, you fucked-up, perforated bitch."

Somewhere nearby, someone coughed, a deep hacking sound.

Quentin said in a hoarse, unrecognizable voice, "Remind me to never piss you off so badly."

He seemed to pause to think about that. Or maybe he was just gathering his strength so that he could utter another word.

"Again."

Quentin lay on his back. He had no idea his body was capable of producing so much pain.

He felt like he was still on fire, all across his chest and shoulder and up one side of his face. Even his lungs felt burned, and he couldn't see out of one eye.

All told, he was pretty happy. He hadn't thought he was going to survive.

Movement drew his attention. He rolled his head to one side and squinted as Aryal crawled lopsidedly toward him. One of her legs dragged uselessly behind her, and she was drenched in blood. She collapsed in a huddle beside him.

He coughed again. Red stars bloomed at the back of his eyes with every excruciating hack. "Any of that blood yours?"

"No," she said. "Not much, anyway. But I'm broken up six ways to Sunday."

"All you still got is bitching and moaning?" he said. "You'll live, sunshine."

And thank all the gods for that. When he had seen her throw herself off the bluff, he felt as if his brain might rupture and leak out his ears. He dragged his hand across the sand toward her. Her fingers closed over his.

"And you?" she asked urgently. "You look really bad, but you're no longer glowing in the dark. That's good, right? Tell me that's good."

Galya had thrown a corrosive spell. At first he had been able to block it, but it had eaten through both the armor and his defenses before he could neutralize it. Dizzy and lightheaded, he tried to cough again and whispered, "There's something wrong with my lungs."

Fear strangled her voice. "I had to jump overboard and

swim too, and I forgot to grab my bag with the food and the healing potion. Where's yours?"

"End boat, first pier."

His pain was receding, along with consciousness. He wondered if he was going to wake up again. Whatever the reality would be, he was glad it had held off so he could party a little bit.

Although he would have preferred something booked at Sardi's, with Aryal on his arm—okay, at his side—and alcohol. Lots and lots of alcohol.

Maybe if he lived, he could talk her into wearing a miniskirt if she paired it with a switchblade and combat boots. One corner of his mouth tried to lift up. Be worth that fight to look at her killer legs and anarchistic smile. Damn, she was a hell of a ride.

He squeezed her fingers and fell into darkness.

Liquid gold trickled down his raw, burned throat. He swallowed reflexively once, twice, then erupted into coughing, and that hurt so bad it brought him back awake.

"Goddammit," somebody said miserably. "It's all about you again, isn't it? Wake up and drink this right now, do you hear me? I hurt so bad, and I'm so tired, and all I want is another hug from you, *AND YOU CAN'T DIE ON ME, QUENTIN, BECAUSE THAT WOULD BE THE FINAL FUCKING STRAW! I SCREWED UP MY WINGS EVEN MORE TO SAVE YOUR LIFE, YOU ROTTEN SON OF A BITCH. PARAGLIDING IS A STUPID IDEA, AND I'M DONE, I'LL BE SO DONE IF YOU DIE! DONE!*"

It was definitely something, to have a harpy throw a screaming shit fit in your face. Just about enough to wake the dead. Her powerful lungs drove each word like a railroad spike into his head. It was like the worst hangover ever times a thousand.

He whispered, "I know I've already bought you, but do you by any chance come with a snooze button?"

"Shut up," she sniveled. "You suck. Drink the rest of this." Her ragged breathing sounded in his ear as she lifted his head with one trembling hand and nudged his lips with the rim of a small bottle.

Half-conscious as he was, he still remembered how

precious that bottle was, and he closed his lips firmly around it so that none of the liquid could escape. She tilted the bottle, and he drank the contents down.

Power glided into his body and started to supernova. She held another bottle to his mouth, and he drank that too, then a third, as quickly as he could just before an upsurge of pain hit.

It ran over him like a steamroller, the Power of the healing potions working through his body to repair extensive damage. It might save his life if it didn't kill him first. His lungs felt like they had been pumped full of napalm, and he arched his back as he struggled to breathe. For years afterward, he would wake up from nightmares of drowning and suffocation.

Aryal bent over him, supporting him as best she could with one arm as she laid her cheek against his good one, whispering, "It's okay, it's okay. Don't fight so hard, it'll pass in a moment. It's going to be okay."

Shuddering, he concentrated on the sound of her voice until finally the pain began to recede, and he sagged against her. His lungs still felt raw and tender, but he no longer felt like he was smothering.

Vision began to return to his healing eye, and as he looked up at her, she came halfway in focus. At some point she had ditched her breastplate, and he rested against her torso. Her gaze was hollowed out again, and she looked beyond exhausted. Her sleeveless tunic was torn, and she was filthy, sandy and still covered in blood. Underneath the blood at her shoulder, her skin looked purple with a gigantic bruise.

"Hey, beautiful," he said.

Her eyebrows rose as she gave him the ultimate in skeptical looks. "You need more healing potion," she told him. She picked up another small bottle and raised it to her mouth to bite out the cork.

He grabbed her wrist. "Wait, how many was that again? We only had five each."

"I drank one. One of the shadow wolves tagged me and I wouldn't stop bleeding," she said. Her voice was beginning to slur. "I had to set my broken leg first. Nothing I could do about the wings. They're so messed up, just, whatever."

The exhausted hopelessness in that made his heart constrict. She had taken so much damage, one potion would have barely taken the edge off of it, just enough to start the healing process again on that bite wound. "You need that one too."

"No." She bit out the cork. "You do, because you're the one-trick pony guy, right? You get better, and then you can help me."

She made sense. As he got stronger, he could help her with at least some basic healing. Reluctantly he let go of her wrist. "Yeah, okay."

She held the bottle up to him, and he drank. Fiery pain started to build again, as the Power in the potion forced injuries to heal. Healing potion could only do so much. The rest was up to the body's resources, but it could sometimes mean the difference between life and death, and it was a strong step forward.

"So you're alive now," Aryal mumbled. "Okay then."

Her arm loosened from around him, and he caught himself on one elbow as he spilled out of her hold. He twisted around to find that she had slumped over in the sand.

His overworked heart thumped. He reached to check her pulse, and while it raced too fast, it beat strongly against his fingers. Relief spun in his head. This trip had aged him something like twenty years.

He looked down her sprawled body and around at the surrounding area. She had maneuvered to the pier and found his longbow too, along with his supply sack, and she had splinted one of her legs with the wood from their longbows, tying them with the bowstrings. The length of wood was much too long for her leg, and she had drawn crazy patterns in the sand as she worked back to his side.

The kind of passion and determination that took made the back of his eyes smart. He had no words for what he saw.

No words, except: "I think you might be both my suicide and my salvation." And he needed her for both. "I love you like a heart attack, woman."

She didn't reply. She was out cold. He turned onto his uninjured side and curled around her, blood, filth, sand and all, and then somebody must have shot out his headlights inside because darkness slammed down on him again.

The sun woke him. He didn't want it to. He covered his head with one arm and drifted for a while, but then it got too fierce. Finally he sat up to look around.

The fucked-up, perforated bitch's body still lay sprawled on the sand where Aryal had left it. Several feet away her head bobbed at the edge of the shoreline. A single bark of laughter burst out of him at the gruesome sight. It hurt so much that he stopped. It wasn't funny anyway.

He bent over Aryal, gently pushing her bloody hair back from her face. Her pulse had slowed to a less alarming pace, and it still beat steadily. The sun had already started to turn her pale skin pink.

It was his turn now to deal with things. He managed to get up on his knees, then to his feet. Part of him was wild to get out of his own armor, but as he looked down at the half-melted mess at his chest, he knew that was going to hurt like a son of a bitch. So first things first.

His supply sack lay beside her, along with all the scattered, empty bottles that had held the healing potion. Okay, there was food in that sack, and hopefully the brandy bottle hadn't broken. Day was looking up. He limped to the last boat on the pier to retrieve the wineskin of water. Now for shelter. He looked in the boats until he found a folded canvas sail. Then he walked back to Aryal, dragging the sail behind him.

Jamming their swords tip first into the sand on either side of her, he took one end of the sail and draped it across the hilts so that the top half of Aryal's body lay in shade.

"I am a goddamn genius," he told her. The cry of seagulls answered him.

After he took two swallows of water, he knelt and lifted her head to moisten her lips with a small trickle. Then he stopped the wineskin and sprawled beside her, half in the shade. He would work off the armor after a little rest. Just needed to close his eyes for a few minutes.

He found one of her hands and laced his fingers through hers.

This time when the darkness sucked him down, it was mingled with peace.

This time he dreamed he was in a sauna. Galya's severed head sat on the bench and sneered at him. She tried to convince him that he wanted to become her shadow panther, and he kicked her into a corner, which was against sauna rules, and somebody started tapping on the door in reprimand, and that pissed him off so much he woke with a start.

Overhead, the edge of the sail flapped rhythmically in a steady breeze that blew off the water. The sun had begun its descent in the sky. They had slept the day away.

Alarmed, he sat quickly, ignoring the twinge of protest in his sore muscles and in the giant scabs at his chest, shoulder, neck and face. He hadn't meant to rest that long.

His injured eye had gummed up, but when he eased it open with a thumb and forefinger, he was profoundly relieved to discover that his sight had almost returned to normal. Hopefully the rest of that damage would heal over the next couple of days.

Turning, he bent over Aryal's still form. Was she sleeping—or unconscious? It was past time that she got more healing herself. Gently he felt down her body. Broken leg, cracked ribs, severely sprained wrist that was now so swollen he couldn't wrap his fingers around it. He lifted up the bottom of her tunic and was horrified to discover that the blackened contusion at her shoulder continued down the entire length of her torso. From the size of it at the edge of her trousers, it probably went down the length of her leg as well.

What the hell happened to her? Was that all from her fall from the bluff? And there were her wings to consider as well. She had taken damage on top of damage.

I'm broken up six ways to Sunday, she had said.

He rubbed the back of his head. The one-trick pony

could only do so much, and he didn't know enough about the healing arts to know if he would hurt her even more by healing whatever had happened to her unseen wings. Caerreth had been right. When an injury was severe enough, as in her crushed carpal joint, sometimes a simple healing spell just fused the damage together.

But he had to start somewhere. He just had to keep it localized. First he worked on her leg, pouring the healing spell over the femur to ensure the break had fused. Then he worked on her wrist. As his Power reduced the swollen flesh, he ripped a length off the edge of the sail so that he could wrap it. That joint was going to need some support as it finished healing.

Next he turned his attention to her cracked ribs, placing a hand along the curve of her torso. He had barely begun when she took his wrist. "Stop," she croaked.

Blood had dried all over her, so that she was almost unrecognizable. He scowled. "No."

"It's too much. You can't spare the strength."

"I can spare it. Just a little more."

"Everything always has to be a fight with you," she grumbled.

He cocked an eyebrow incredulously at her but didn't bother to dignify that with a reply. Instead, sensing how her stressed, injured flesh soaked up the healing like a sponge, he eked out a little more Power before he had to concede that he was tapped, and he had to stop.

She struggled to sit up, and he slipped his good arm underneath her shoulders to help. Her arms slipped around his waist, and they ended up simply leaning against each other. He tucked her head into the crook of his neck and held her carefully.

After a while she reached for the wineskin of water, and when she drank her fill, he did the same. The skin was nearly empty when he had finished. He stoppered and shook it. "Gonna have to deal with that issue soon."

"There'll be fresh water at the top of the bluff." She eyed the path tiredly. "We just have to get up there."

"One step at a time." He dug in the sack and pulled out

wayfarer bread. The apple brandy bottle hadn't broken. Fuck yeah. They ate slowly and took sips of the brandy as they watched the sunset. He said, "If I don't see another wafer of wayfarer bread for a hundred years or so, I'll be okay with that."

She nodded as she looked around, and he did too. The current had washed Galya's head onto the beach beside the nearest pier. A few minutes later, she said as she chewed, "I like to see her rotting."

She sounded so peaceful. He snorted, which didn't hurt quite as badly as it had before. He told her about his dream, and she gave him a dark look that was almost laughter. Of course, that also meant he had to tell her what the shadow wolf had told him, and she paled underneath the coat of her grime.

She whispered, "They were Wyr after all."

"Yeah. Hopefully they're at peace now. Have you ever heard of this Phoenix Cauldron that the wolf mentioned?"

She shook her head and shrugged. "I wonder if it's one of the seven God Machines. Except all the stories say that Numenlaur had only one."

He pushed the mystery aside, finished his wafer and said, "Paragliding is not stupid."

She looked at him blankly.

"The shit fit you threw earlier," he said. "You said—screamed—that paragliding is stupid, and it's not. *It's not*, sunshine."

She ducked her head and muttered so low he almost couldn't hear her, "It is if you're not there to do it with me."

His throat tightened. "That's not ever going to happen."

She turned to look at him, and everything was right there in her eyes. Fear, vulnerability, and a startled, fierce love. Uncertainty.

He stamped on that last bit with the whole force of his personality. "You made me a promise that you were going to make it, no matter what," he growled. "And you will. You will not endanger your mate."

He held her gaze until, blinking rapidly, she nodded, glanced away and then back at him. "You look terrible," she said, her voice unsteady. "Why haven't you gotten out of that armor yet? You must be baking in this heat."

He fingered the scab on his cheek as he told her, "I've been postponing it. I think the tunic underneath has stuck to my chest."

Her eyes widened in horror. "You just *left* it stuck to you? Oh gods, where is a knife?"

"You can't cut it off," he said, baffled. "I think it needs to be soaked."

She waved a hand impatiently at him as she looked around. Eventually she settled on one of the short swords and knelt on her good knee beside him, her other leg awkwardly propped to one side. They used the tip of the sword to cut carefully at the fastenings between the plates, which had swollen from his swim in the salt water. Then they stripped the pieces off of him one at a time. He breathed a deep sigh of relief as the last piece, the damaged breastplate, came away without any trouble.

They looked down at his chest where the tunic was indeed stuck to the giant scab.

Aryal's good hand snaked out. She ripped the tunic off of him.

Fresh fire exploded across his chest.

"GAAAAHHH!" he roared furiously, his fists clenched. *"Why did you do that?!"*

"Isn't that better?" His demonic mate held up both hands in a placating gesture. "See, it's done now, it's all done. We can put it in the past and move on."

"What ever happened to ONE-TWO-THREE!" he shouted.

"That's a vastly overrated system. I never recommend it. The element of surprise is always best." She patted at the air, her expression turning worried as she eyed his raw, bleeding wound. "Er, can you do something about that now? You can cast a healing spell on yourself, right?"

His energy had picked up after eating and drinking, but he didn't feel in the mood to reveal that to her right away. He snarled, "I used up everything I had on healing you, dumb ass, which you would have found out if you had *talked* to me first."

Her eyes widened in dismay. "Oh God, did you really?"

Inside, his dark sardonic sense of humor had started to chuckle. He told her pathetically, "We've got nothing to clean this wound with, and nothing to use as a bandage. I guess we could tear off a corner of the sail and use that if we had to."

Her dismay turned to outrage. "We'll do no such thing! That sail has got to be filthy, and besides, it's thick, rough canvas. We might as well take handfuls of sand and throw it all over you!"

"What am I supposed to do, sit here and bleed?"

She made a face and looked with dread at the steep path that cut up the bluff. "We'll have to get up there somehow. We'll need fresh water soon anyway, and somewhere there'll be something suitable that we can use as a band—"

He cast a light healing spell on himself. The bleeding slowed to a stop as the wound scabbed over.

Her mouth shut with a click and pursed up tight. She accused, "You did that on purpose."

"You *think*?" He looked over the water and his jaw angled out. "I can't stand it any longer. I've got to get clean. Or at least cleaner. And if you think I look bad, you should look in a mirror."

"No need. What I can see of myself is bad enough." She gazed longingly at the water as well. "Are you too mad at me to help me up?"

"Of course not, stupid." He stood, held his hands out to her and pulled her upright. Her leg, still in the too-long longbow splint, canted to one side at a sharp angle.

"I'm sick of this awful splint," she snapped. "I might as well cut it off and be done with it."

"Not yet," he said. "Give it another night to be on the safe side. And even then you should keep your weight off that leg."

He put an arm around her waist and helped her hop to the water. Then they both submerged, clothes and all, and rubbed at themselves and each other to clean off as best they could. Aryal scooped up handfuls of sand to scrub the worst of the dried blood out of her hair and skin.

They didn't take long at the task. He didn't want to risk losing his scabs again if they got too soaked with the salt water, and neither one of them had any business being on their feet for long. If they had been home in New York, they would have been in a hospital.

Afterward they helped each other back to their "tent." Quentin was so exhausted he could barely stay on his feet, and from her pale, set expression, she wasn't any better. Probably, given the state of her injured wings, she was a lot worse.

I hurt so bad, and I'm so tired, and all I want is another hug from you.

He swallowed, stroking her wet hair, and kissed her forehead. She hopped into a turn and leaned on his good shoulder while he held her. He whispered, "I should try to find wood for a fire."

"Don't bother," she mumbled. "It's warm enough and we'll air-dry. I just don't want to lie in the sand again in these wet clothes."

He pulled at the half-unfolded sail so that it lay spread out on the sand. He said sourly, "Behold, a bed."

"It's better than the cell."

"Maybe, but not by much." He helped her ease down onto it and then joined her, making sure that she was on his good side. Groaning, he lay back and held out his uninjured arm. "Come here."

She eased over gingerly and fit herself against him, and he hugged her tight as his world settled into rightness. Her body shook with a deep sigh. She pressed a kiss to his bare shoulder and draped her arm across his waist.

"We should be okay enough by morning to sail back," she muttered. "Maybe avoid the path up the bluff altogether. Don't you think?"

"I do." But they didn't have to face that right now.

The sun had set and the worst of the heat had gone out of the day. A steady breeze still blew off the water, and his trousers felt cool and clammy while his burns felt fiery hot. The sand felt hard and lumpy underneath him, and he had rarely been so uncomfortable.

While he had never been so happy.

Still, despite Aryal's reassurances, he was worried about her. The more time passed, the more likely it was that she would sustain permanent damage to her wings. He was ready to start back home and anxious to see what help they could get for her. But that was another task for tomorrow. For now, as her body grew lax against him and her breathing deepened, he was just thankful they had survived another day. He pulled a corner of the sail over their legs to block off the breeze and fell into another profoundly deep sleep.

Something roused him. A sound, or a great movement in the air. He blinked his eyes open, or tried to anyway, and ended up squinting as his healing eye had gummed up again.

The sky had paled with the beginning of dawn. A large, winged form angled down and landed, along with another. Then another. Wyr gathered around them, shapeshifting into their human forms. Each of them carried backpacks and bristled with weapons.

Quentin poked Aryal gently in the shoulder. She woke and lifted her head to look around.

Almost all the sentinels had come. Alex, Bayne, Constantine. Grym. No Graydon, who must have been the one to draw the short straw to stay on duty in New York.

Dragos had come too, along with Pia and Eva. Pia carried Liam in a baby harness. Linwe was also with the group.

Quentin had never seen Dragos look so flummoxed. Despite the many differences in temperament and personality in the group, every one of them wore an identical expression of blank incredulity as they drew close and stared down at the couple entwined on the beach.

Quentin drew a deep breath. Yeah, well. There was that.

Aryal offered in a helpful tone, "He has issues."

"Shut up," Quentin grumbled.

As some kind of crisis of expression bolted over Pia's face, he pulled a corner of the sail over his and Aryal's heads.

TWENTY-ONE

After taking in the mess strewn all over the beach, everyone leaped into action. Something happened to Galya's body and detached head. Someday Aryal meant to ask what they did with it, although they probably just did the predictable, boring thing and buried her somewhere. All she knew was that the witch's remains disappeared.

Others collected Quentin's supply sack, their borrowed Elven weapons, the empty healing potion vials and the brandy bottle, and folded up the sail they had used for shelter, while Pia and Alex, who was the most accomplished field medic in the sentinels, examined Quentin and tried to examine her.

"Don't touch me," Aryal told them hoarsely. They both hesitated, clearly unwilling to listen when she was so injured.

"Do as she says," Quentin snapped at them. "She needs to see a specialist as quickly as we can get her to one, not another round of blanket healing."

His tone was so harsh that both Pia and Alex recoiled. Pia's expression was tight and closed off with some kind of suppressed emotion as she handed Liam over to Eva. Aryal watched dully as Pia talked with Quentin in a low voice. Then, still talking, they both walked away.

When they returned several minutes later, Quentin was healed. Completely.

During the confrontation two months ago in January, Dragos had been hurt badly—worse than Aryal had ever seen or believed was possible—yet somehow after Pia had reached him, he had risen to his feet, apparently unscathed.

So Pia had done whatever magic hoodoo she knew how to do on Quentin. Aryal was glad for that. It was one less thing to worry about.

Quentin was not unscathed. He carried scars on his chest and shoulder, neck, and along the ridge of his cheekbone and on the brow on one side of his face. She wondered if it was because his wounds were magical in nature, or because he had gone some time and had been partially healed by the time Pia got to him. In the end, the reason didn't matter. He was better, and part of the tight, worried coil inside of her eased.

As soon as Quentin had mentioned a specialist, Dragos strode over quickly to kneel beside Aryal where she huddled and hugged her good knee. She had cut off the longbow splint but didn't want to strain her leg, which she kept straight.

Dragos put a hand on her shoulder and asked his question with a look.

She couldn't say the words out loud. She told him telepathically, *My wings are pretty fucked up.*

Dragos's gold eyes widened in sharp concern. His Power speared through her in a quick, comprehensive scan. Then he shapeshifted into the dragon so abruptly that everybody else had to scramble out of the way.

"We're leaving now," he said to Pia. "We need to get Aryal to a hospital as quickly as possible. Quentin's right, she needs surgery. The broken bones in her wings weren't set properly, and they are already fusing together. Any healing right now might make the damage permanent." He turned to the others. "Stay only long enough to finish cleaning up and do a sweep for more looters, then come home."

Pia, Liam, Eva and Quentin climbed onto the dragon. Aryal couldn't sit astride because of her bad leg, so she sat sideways while Quentin's arms settled around her firmly. Dragos wrapped them in his Power to protect them from the harsh, chill winds in the upper air and he flew with such speed, she watched the route she and Quentin had taken to the shore scroll backward like a movie on rewind.

There was the side street where the shadow wolves had crippled her.

There was the house with the silent, still nursery.

There was the long meadow, rippling like another sea, and the forest, and a quick glimpse of the riverbed that had shrunk to the size of a creek, and last, the Guardian's house set high in the cliff by the crossover passageway.

It was almost like watching the recent events of her life come undone, except that what had happened in Numenlaur, for good or for ill, had marked her indelibly.

Dragos didn't slow as they hit the passageway. Instead he speeded up. Aryal's heart thumped as she remembered how the canyon narrowed at ground level, but thirty feet in the air, the dragon merely banked his wings and used his momentum to shoot through the opening with so little room to spare, she could have reached out with one hand to touch the canyon walls on either side of them.

Immediately past the bottleneck, he snapped his wings out and they completed the crossover passageway without ever having touched earth.

On the other side, the Bohemian Forest looked chill and pale in comparison to the summer heat they had just left. She caught a glimpse of a hastily erected encampment for a much larger group than four inexperienced Elves. The new High Lord Ferion had learned a hard lesson. Unfortunately it was one that had cost the Elves yet another life.

"How much time has passed on this side of the passageway?" Quentin asked.

Pia answered him. "Almost two weeks."

Time had passed more quickly than it had in Numenlaur.

"Plzeň will have the closest hospital," Dragos said. The dragon's deep voice vibrated through his body. "We'll go there."

"No," Aryal said. Everyone riding on Dragos's back turned to look at her. She shook her head at them. She said, "I want to go home to Wyr doctors."

Nobody tried to argue with that. She knew if they were in her shoes, they would want to go home too.

Dragos said, "Then I'll bargain with one of the Djinn for transport to New York."

"Don't bother," she said dully. "While I appreciate the effort, it's not worth any possible danger that might come from a bargain with the Djinn. I've already healed so much from the first time we were attacked, some of the damage has already solidified."

He spread his wings and glided a moment, his body language clearly speaking of his reluctance as he thought about that. Everyone else remained silent, waiting, while Quentin's arms tightened around her to the point of pain.

Then Dragos flew for the airport at Plzeň, where the corporate jet sat on standby. They boarded the plane rapidly with a minimum of fuss. Moments later, the plane taxied onto a runway and took off. When a ruler of one of the largest Elder demesnes on Earth was in the middle of an emergency, he could slash through a lot of red tape.

As soon as the plane reached a high enough altitude, both Dragos and Quentin started making phone calls. Aryal lay on one of the couches, eyes closed against a pounding headache, as she listened to snatches of their conversations.

. . . notify the hospital of our arrival. We'll be there in eight and a half hours, max . . .

. . . call Dr. Shaw, and have her assemble a surgical team . . .

. . . book an operating room and have it on standby . . .

"I don't care if operating rooms are limited," snarled Dragos. "This is one of my sentinels we're talking about. We will get there just as soon as we can, and you will hold that room ready and available for when we arrive, or I will tear through your hospital from the inside out. Got it?"

Coming from Dragos, that was not an idle threat. Apparently the administrator on the other end of the line understood, because that was the end of that exchange.

For the rest of the flight Aryal dozed. When she did wake up, Quentin urged her to drink lots of water, so she did. Occasionally she caught glimpses of Pia, holding Liam and staring at her intently. Weirdly enough, the baby seemed to stare at her too, his soft, miniature Buddha's face scrunched up and pensive.

But that couldn't be right. Pain and tiredness must be making Aryal hallucinate. Liam was only a few weeks old. She doubted that he could even track anything with his gaze yet.

In less than two days, at least according to her internal body clock, Aryal went from a beach in Numenlaur to surgery in Manhattan.

Her arrival at East Manhattan Medical went by in a blur. In her Wyr form, her body and wingspan were much too large and unusual a shape for an MRI scan. Nurses x-rayed images of her wing joints in sections.

Then she met with the surgeon, who was a sharp-eyed Wyr falcon named Kathryn Shaw with thick chestnut hair, honey brown eyes, and a blaze of Power that was as sharp as a scalpel in her nervy, slender body.

Dragos kept Kathryn on retainer to treat high-level staff when needed, and Aryal already knew her. Kathryn had worked on all the sentinels at one time or another over the years, for injuries sustained on the job. That familiarity, along with the fact that the surgeon was both female and avian comforted Aryal immeasurably. Maybe her wings couldn't be repaired, but at least she knew that this surgeon would feel any failure instinctively deep in her gut.

The pre-surgery consult was brief and to the point.

"Hi, Aryal," the surgeon said. "I hear you've had a rough trip."

"You could say that," she said through clenched teeth.

The other female was obviously too intelligent to offer to shake the stressed-out harpy's taloned hand. Kathryn scanned Aryal's wings magically for a long moment, her gaze turning internal while her expression remained professionally neutral.

Quentin never left Aryal's side. While the surgeon examined her, he gripped her wrists and talked to her telepathically while she flexed her hands and suffered the invasion of someone else's Power coursing through her body. The harpy hated it and had to fight to keep from lashing out.

"I won't go under," Aryal said. She stared fixedly at Quentin. "I can't."

"You know that's not a good idea," Kathryn said. "I have to advise against it. It will be safer for you and for everybody else if I put you under a general anesthetic. Otherwise you are going to be fighting your instincts throughout the entire surgery."

"No," growled the harpy. The thought of going blank while someone cut into her body made crazypants want to come out to play again. "You will use a local."

Kathryn and Quentin looked at each other. The surgeon asked, "Can you control her?"

"Of course I can control her," said Quentin nastily. "Every time she lets me."

Kathryn took the reprimand with a steady silence. She looked back at the harpy, her falcon's gaze piercing and calm. "The only way I'll consider it is if you're heavily sedated," she said. "If you endanger either me or my team, I will stop working on you immediately and you won't get me back to the table. You must keep yourself under control. Understood?"

The harpy bared her teeth and hissed. "Understood."

"See you in the theater." Kathryn walked away, muttering under her breath, "God help me, I'm actually going to operate on a harpy while she's still awake. Somebody better give me a medal for this."

"Coward," the harpy snarled after her.

"I think she's probably the opposite of a coward," Quentin told her. "Anyway, I'd go easy on her if I were you. You *are* looking a little like Freddy Krueger at the moment, punkin."

His grip on her wrists was so tight that her hands were

beginning to go numb. Only then did she realize she was struggling against his hold. She forced herself to quit. She couldn't bear to look over her shoulder at her wings spilled lifelessly down the exam table, or she might start struggling again.

Then they waited, and waited. Aryal fisted her hands in the hair at the nape of her neck, held her head and closed her eyes while Quentin paced the examination room. She could hear people talking through the doors. They sounded like they were arguing, although she couldn't hear what they said. She could recognize the voices though. One of them was Dragos. The other was Pia.

So much came back around to Pia.

Then a third voice joined the other two. Kathryn. The harpy's gaze went to the scars on Quentin's face. The muscles in her body were strung tight, but she forced herself to be still and wait.

Finally a nurse came to tell them it was time, and led the way to the surgery room. Aryal limped down the hall, wrestling with panic the whole way.

Quentin stalked beside her. They had both showered at the hospital, and while the harpy refused to don a hospital gown, he wore scrubs. As he had dropped a few pounds in Numenlaur, he looked sharper than ever, the strong elegant bones of his face standing out under the pitiless hospital lights.

They had barely touched down in New York and people were already staring at him in shock and awe. Most of them were women.

The scars on his cheekbone and brow gave a remarkable illusion, as if half his face was masked, and if that wasn't an example of how blind fate could still on occasion strike with immaculate accuracy, Aryal didn't know what was.

To Aryal's eyes, he had always looked dangerous. Now even the thickest, most insensitive of idiots could see it too.

"Are you going to want plastic surgery?" she asked.

He gave her a blank look. "Why?"

"The scars on your face," she said.

He shrugged, patently indifferent to the idea. "If I were

to take the time to do anything, to tell you the truth, I'd rather finally get a rooftop garden over my apartment."

One corner of her mouth lifted, because she loved the scars.

She said, "Good."

Then they arrived. The nurse pushed open the doors for them and they walked into an alien place filled with medical machinery, an operating table and more masked people. Two of them, off to one side, were Pia and Dragos.

The harpy stopped and scowled at them. "What are you doing in here?"

The dragon looked at her, his gold eyes mesmerizing.

Trust us, Dragos whispered in her head. *Leave your panic behind. All will be well, Aryal. There is no need to fight anybody here.*

Ah. It was going to be that kind of sedation. She had wondered, since adrenaline would have helped her to throw off any medication before they could possibly be done with the surgery.

She gave herself over readily to the dragon's enthrallment, and climbed on the table to lie on her stomach, placing her forehead in the headrest as instructed. They wheeled tables in on either side of her to spread out her wings.

Quentin sat cross-legged on the floor so that he could look up at her. He took her hands again in an unbreakable grasp. "Hold on to me," he said. "Don't let go."

"Okay." She struggled not to hyperventilate.

Power filled the room from more than one person, and she lost sensation from the neck down. The harpy cried out as a blind animal panic tried to take her over again, and the dragon whispered. *Trust. No need to fight. All will be well.*

Vaguely she could sense tugging on her body. The smell of her own blood filled the air. They had cut into her. Then came other sounds, like a tapping of either a chisel or a small hammer.

The surgeon said in a cool, calm voice, "I'm going to have to break this again."

Razor teeth. Her carpal joint crushed. Muscles torn.

She was lost in a nightmare, lost . . .

Aryal, the harpy's mate said telepathically. *Look at me. Look. At. Me.*

He had a surfeit of his own Power, and his words penetrated both her panic and the dragon's beguilement. As she looked at him, he stroked her face, and she knew that he would do anything he had to so that they survived.

Tell me again the promises you told me in Numenlaur, he said.

Her lips shook. *You need reassurance now? You really are high maintenance, aren't you?*

You know everything's always all about me, he told her, the steady, concerned look in his eyes belying their attempt at banter. *Please. Tell me again.*

There were so many words to that promise, and people were making noise and doing things to her, and she almost screamed at him to fuck off, all of it swirling in her head like a tornado looking to break out of her body.

Then something clicked inside, and she could focus on him.

She said, *I made a promise to you before you came into my life.*

I know you did, he said. There was so much love in his eyes. So much. *And I'm so grateful for it.*

I will never betray you, she said to him. *I will never endanger your life with my carelessness or impetuosity. I will fight for and with you. I will—I will—*

Out of her sight, someone started a tiny saw, and her expression twisted.

Quentin rose up on his knees. The intensity in his blue gaze burned into hers, pushing everything else away. He said to her strongly, *I will always have your back whenever you might need me.*

Realization hit. He had memorized every word of what she had said.

That was when she found her center.

She whispered, *I will not leave you, and I will not lie to you, and if you will be patient and forgiving, I will learn how to forgive too. Because you've become the most important thing in the world to me. I'll give everything I have to you, along with everything I can be, if only you will do the same.*

And remember, there's more, Quentin said. *Because somehow it's going to be okay.*

She rested in the adamancy in his gaze. Then she said, *Because I could never endanger my mate by throwing my own life away.*

He smiled at her. She didn't understand why he looked so proud, because she still felt whacked-out and slashy.

And paragliding is not stupid, he said. He tilted his head and kissed the harpy's lips. *As long as we do it together.*

That's a bargain, she whispered.

The best bargain of all. He was a magician, all right. By using only smoke and mirrors, he had somehow managed to banish the last of her panic.

That was when something really odd happened. Speaking with brisk authority, Kathryn ordered the rest of the surgical team out of the room. Murmuring in puzzlement, they filed out. As the last of them left, the scent of someone else's blood—Pia's blood—filled the air.

Aryal said out loud, "What the fuck are you guys doing back there?"

"Hold on a few moments longer, Aryal," said Kathryn somewhat breathlessly. "You're doing an awesome job. We're almost finished."

A new Power began to fill Aryal's body, and it was simply ravishing, cool like moonlight and exquisitely clear, like the finest crystal. It filled her entirely and took all the pain away, all of it, and bathed her spirit tenderly with the finest hope.

"My God," Kathryn said. "Will you look at that."

While Aryal heard the words, they didn't hold any meaning for her. She was lost in rightness and a floating sensation like freedom. Through it all she watched Quentin as he swallowed hard.

Vaguely she grew aware that Dragos was speaking again. This time, quite unlike his beguilement, his tone was harsh and commanding. "Nobody speaks about what just happened in this room. Not to anyone, do you understand?"

Quentin's gaze shifted from Aryal's face to the people who stood behind her. She watched as his expression turned careful. He nodded.

"I'm bound by doctor-patient confidentiality, and I've already given you my promise," Kathryn told him. "I won't say a word."

"See that you keep it," Dragos said. He never had to say "or else."

Aryal turned her head as Dragos and Pia walked out.

Then Kathryn laid a hand at the back of Aryal's neck and squatted to look her in the eyes. The surgeon pulled down her mask. Her honey brown gaze was teary, and she was beaming. "We're done," Kathryn said. "Everything looks so much better than I could have hoped."

She shivered spasmodically. "It looks good?"

"It looks more than good. It looks amazing." Kathryn kept a steady, firm pressure on the back of her neck. "But I'm going to tell you something before I let you up, and you need to listen. Okay?"

"Okay."

"What happened just now is a miracle, and I do not use that word lightly. From the hopeless mess that I first saw to what I sense right now—there's no comparison." The surgeon's expression sobered. "So pay attention when I say this to you. Do not take any chances with this opportunity. Your wings were so bad I was convinced you would never fly again. Now you have a real shot, but you must stay out of the air for two weeks."

"Two weeks?" she whispered. Her mind went blank. She had never been out of the air for two weeks in her very long life.

Kathryn's eyes were sharp and stern. "You're a big girl. You can make your own choices, and I don't order my patients around. It's up to you whether or not you decide to take my advice. But you have injured and then reinjured your wings. If you don't give your body a real chance to recover, you might rip away everything of the very great gift that has just been given to you. You are not cleared for work. No crises, no excuses, no exceptions." The doctor paused to let her words sink in. "Do you understand what I have just said?"

"Yes," she whispered.

"Good." Kathryn patted her. "Now I'm going to release the numbing spell and let you sit up. I want you to shape-shift back into your human form and stay that way for fourteen days."

Aryal and Quentin looked at each other. Quentin said, "She will."

It would be fourteen days before she knew for sure whether or not the miracle had taken hold.

Before she knew if she could fly again.

Fourteen days.

The wait was going to kill her.

═ TWENTY-TWO ═

W hen Aryal shapeshifted back into her human form and sat at the edge of the operating table, Quentin was ready with a clean set of folded scrubs. He helped her into them. Then he stroked her hair as she leaned against his chest.

Dragos and Pia had already disappeared, and so had the surgeon. The door opened, and a nurse approached with a wheelchair. "I'm here to take you to your room now."

Aryal's head snapped up. She stared at the wheelchair with wide-eyed repugnance.

Quentin told the nurse, "Hospitals are for sick people, and we're going home."

The nurse's face froze. "Okay," she said uncertainly. "Just wait a few minutes while I get some release forms for you to sign. I'll be right back."

They didn't wait. Instead they walked slowly down the hall, arms around each other's waists. He asked, "Your place or mine?"

"There's awesome delivery in the Tower," she said, enunciating each word with the carefulness of the extremely tired. "No need to cook."

"There's pretty awesome delivery over the bar too," he told her.

"Then I don't care."

"We'll go to my place."

While he had waited for Aryal as she had gotten x-rayed, Quentin called Dragos's assistant Kris, who had shown up shortly afterward with a new iPhone for each of them, each one already downloaded with all of their contacts, along with two slim wallets with expense cards and cash.

He pulled his phone out of his back pocket. The time on the screen read 8:32 P.M. He thumbed the lock off and dialed Rupert at the bar. "Hey boss," the half troll rumbled. "Glad you're back in town. Aren't you a little early?"

It took a few moments for Quentin to connect. Rupert was referring to their original two-week ban from New York. He said, "Never mind that, things have changed. I'm on my way home now. Stock my fridge with food from the corner grocery, would you?"

"Sure thing," said Rupert.

"Thanks."

"Since we're talking, can you answer some bar questions?"

"No." He disconnected.

A hospital representative caught them before they could slip out one of the exits, and Aryal had to sign release forms after all.

By the time their taxi pulled up to Elfie's, it was past ten o'clock. After the summer heat in Numenlaur, the early April evening was pleasantly sharp and chilly. The bar was going strong, which was a good thing because he just remembered he didn't have his keys. They could slip upstairs through the interior entrance, except . . .

He looked at Aryal's pale, angular features as she watched the crowd in the bar. No way was he up for that kind of explanation. Not until tomorrow. Or maybe next week. "Are you all right with waiting on the stoop while I go inside and let us through?"

"Yep," Aryal said. She looked kind of dreamy, like she was stoned.

"Are you okay?" he asked suspiciously.

"Yep," she said again. "I feel pretty good, considering."

He left her and went through the bar. People hailed him, and everybody hitched to a stop, staring at his face and at the scrubs. He waved to them all, ignored the chorus of comments and shocked questions, strode through to the stockroom, let himself into his private stairwell and found Aryal sitting on the stoop outside, leaning against the corner of one wall.

He opened the door and bent over her—and found her sound asleep.

He gathered her up gently, carried her upstairs and put her, and himself, in bed.

His exhausted, overstimulated mind ran compulsively through the survival list.

Food, water, shelter, clothing.

Love.

He pulled Aryal's sleeping form against him, tucked her head into his shoulder, put his face in her soft, clean hair and slept.

Sometime in the middle of the night, they both woke. Their body clocks were all screwed up. They made love with silent urgency and fell asleep afterward while Quentin was still inside of her.

That dictated the pattern of the next few days.

Waking, making love. Eating, making love. Sleep. There was a disjointed rhythm to all of it, like tacking in a zigzag pattern in a sailboat against a crosswind.

He lost himself in the sensual evidence of her, her scent, her skin, her deadly, sleek muscles, the startling softness of her breasts and the incredibly lush prison of her inner flesh as she gripped his penis. And he moved, and moved, and moved inside of her until they both sobbed for breath and shuddered helplessly from the ecstasy of it. That wild, dangerous part of him that had been running so hard knew that it had found what it was looking for, and had finally come home.

When they talked, there was no beginning or end to the conversation. It was as if it had gone on forever. He began to wonder if that was a little bit like what Aryal had referred to the night of the sentinel party, when she had talked of immortality.

His father had always sworn that while Quentin could change into a Wyr form, his energy felt Elven. He had a feeling he was going to find out with Aryal what immortality was like.

"What could Pia be?" Aryal asked. "Did she bleed when she healed you too?"

"Yes," he said. They lay with their limbs tangled, and she cradled his head on her breast. He mouthed her nipple without urgency. They had already spent each other. "I can only think of one creature." He said it slowly, because the idea was so outlandish. "But I thought they were a myth."

"A myth like dragons, or harpies?" she asked, her mouth tilted, and he had to concede her point. "If she is one, then I understand now why she hasn't revealed her Wyr form to the public. She'll be hunted for the rest of her life if she does, and what about the baby? No, that's not right. We know his Wyr form is a dragon. That's why they thought her gestation period was going to be so long, until he managed to flip into a human baby before she went into labor."

"If she is one," he said grimly, "it doesn't matter what the baby's Wyr form is. He'll be hunted too."

"I guess I can understand why Pia came with Dragos to Numenlaur," Aryal said sleepily. "But I don't know why they brought Liam with them."

Quentin shook his head. "Actually, you've got that backward. This time Dragos came with Pia. She told me when she healed me. Originally he had only intended on sending the rest of the sentinels, but Pia insisted on coming because she was worried we might be hurt. Then Dragos wouldn't stay behind, of course. Since Dragos wasn't going to go into battle, Pia felt safe to bring Liam too. She wanted to keep the baby with her, because they were concerned that the time slippage might be significant."

Aryal coughed out a chuckle. "Did she really insist? Good on her. I wondered when they all showed up. I mean,

Galya was a handful, but come on. It only took two of us to take her down."

Quentin grinned. "That it did."

After that they fell into a thoughtful silence.

They began to recover their strength and stamina. Not that the mating urgency let up, not by any means—it was far too soon for that—but they began to have room to consider other things.

Quentin checked his voicemail and text messages, and he discovered that Pia had returned the phone call he had made before he left New York, and she had left a message for him too.

"Hi, Quentin," she said. "I appreciate you calling, and I know that you're sorry for what happened. We've both made some pretty big mistakes, and it's okay to forget about it. Just don't do it again, and we can let it fall into the past where it belongs. Okay?"

As he listened, at first he didn't remember his apology for his fight with Aryal in the hallway. For a moment he thought she referred to what he had done last year, and he felt shocked into newness, washed clean. Then the context of her message came clear, and he had to smile at himself, albeit a bit crookedly.

Still, a touch of that newness remained, and he took her message to heart, setting it all behind him to concentrate on now, and the future.

Ferion had also left a message, one filled with deep, heartfelt thanks to both of them. Quentin told Aryal about it as he texted Ferion in reply. You're welcome. Ever heard of something called the Phoenix Cauldron?

Ferion replied almost immediately. No. What is it?

What the witch was looking for in Numenlaur.

Then, because the question remained on his mind, he shrugged and texted Dragos. Galya was hunting for an item called the Phoenix Cauldron. Do you know what that is?

The silence lasted just long enough to make him wonder. He had already heard from the older sentinels that Dragos didn't like to put sensitive information into writing of any kind.

His phone rang. He answered.

Dragos said without preamble, "If Galya was looking for a physical item, it's no wonder she didn't find anything. The name is misleading—that's a resurrection spell, not an item. The results are monstrous. Any records of how to cast it were supposed to have been destroyed a very long time ago. But you know how that goes. What people are supposed to do, and what they really do, are often two different things." He paused. "How are you two doing?"

"Good," said Quentin. "We're good."

"You did well in Numenlaur," Dragos told him.

Quentin remembered all too well Dragos's expression as he had stared at the witch's body on the beach. He had looked astonished, then approving. Clearly he hadn't thought that Aryal and Quentin could take down Galya by themselves.

Not that Dragos's opinion mattered to him, but still.

"Thanks," he said, smiling. Both men disconnected without good-byes.

Aryal recovered too, but she didn't thrive. Her appetite was fitful, and she lost weight. At odd times he caught her looking out the window, up at the sky. Once he woke in the middle of the night. He rolled over to find her already awake, staring bleakly at nothing. She grew jittery, distracted.

He wasn't having it.

He started to bark at her like a drill sergeant, driving her through the days and nights. Telling her to eat. Snapping when she didn't pay attention.

On the fourth day, he nagged her into going with him to the gym at the Tower. People stared in wonder, especially at him. Either they were looking at his scars, or they were wondering at his sanity.

Bless them, they were probably doing both. He ignored them.

"Come on, let's fight," he said to Aryal. "What will it be—sword, nunchakus or hand to hand?"

She glanced at the training mats and shook her head. "I'm not interested."

Inside, his heart pounded. Could she really pine away despite all of her promises to the contrary?

"Oh, no you don't." He advanced on her. "You will pick something, or I will pick for you."

She shrugged and a touch of sullenness entered her expression. "So, pick."

He snagged his ankle behind her foot and elbowed her hard, knocking her flat.

She took her time rolling over to her hands and knees. When he looked in her eyes, a faint anger had begun to spark.

He slammed her down again, hard as he could.

She came up faster.

Doctor said Aryal couldn't use her wings. Didn't say a word about anything else. And he discovered he was mad at her for scaring him when she jumped off that cursed bluff, and for not hitting him back. For not eating or sleeping well. For not trying hard enough.

He lunged forward again.

This time she blocked him.

They stood face-to-face, straining against each other.

She glared. "You suck!"

He smiled. "There you are, sunshine," he purred. "I missed you."

They fought each other single-mindedly until they were both on the mat. Then she scooted over to put her arms around his neck and hug him fiercely. "Sorry," she whispered. "I'll do better."

He put his face in her neck and held her tight.

When he finally loosened his hold and they went to stand, Graydon and Grym were there to offer them a hand up. The other sentinels wore sober expressions. Behind them, a wide-eyed crowd had gathered to watch the fight. Now that the fireworks were over, people began to drift away.

Graydon pulled Aryal upright and into a tight bear hug. "Good to see you surface," Graydon said to her. "I almost came over to bang down Quentin's door."

"I almost did too," said Grym, as he gave Quentin a

smile as sharp as if he had pulled a sword. Telepathically he said, *I have just one thing to say about you and Aryal.*

Hit me with it, said Quentin with an equally sharp smile. He shook out his arm muscles and readied himself in case Grym's message became physical.

If you betray her in any way, said Grym, *I may not be able to kill you, because that would kill her. But I will hurt you very, very badly. And repeatedly. That's a promise.*

Quentin relaxed, and his smile turned real. "I wouldn't have expected anything else," he said aloud.

Grym ran his fingers through his black hair, blew out a breath then gradually relaxed.

Whatever Aryal and Graydon said to each other was private too. Afterward, Graydon turned to him and clapped him on the shoulder. "Good to see you. I'm glad you guys are home."

Quentin studied the First's craggy, good-humored face. Graydon had said it in all sincerity. "It's good to be home."

The days continued to trickle by. Alex gave them each a hug and a gift of the top fifty Oscar-winning movies on DVD. Bayne and Constantine brought stacks of pizza and beer one night, and stayed overlong.

Aryal showed Quentin her apartment in the Tower. He took one long look around at the chaotic mess. Then he said, "I think it's a good thing if we each have our own place for a while, yes?"

She grinned. "Yes."

After their fight in the gym, she ate better but still had trouble sleeping. When her face started to grow tight and stressed, he made love to her with single minded passion until they both fell into oblivion.

To work off nerves, they went running, sometimes for hours on end until their bodies poured with sweat, setting two treadmills in the gym on their highest setting. They burned out the motors in two pairs of treadmills. Nobody complained.

One evening, wearing a pair of her jeans and one of his old sweatshirts, she disappeared for a short time. He said nothing when she left his apartment. He'd had a key cut for her, and really, he couldn't watch her 24/7. He was with the surgeon on that one. She was a big girl. In the end, it was up to her to decide to do the right thing.

He regretted that thought almost immediately and paced furiously, because he had developed all the obsession in the world needed to watch her 24/7, if only she would show up again so that he could get to it.

A key turned in the lock forty minutes later. He spun away from the living room window where he had been staring out blankly.

Aryal walked in. She carried a longish bag and looked settled on some kind of decision.

"Hey, sunshine," he said. His tone was mild. He was such a goddamn liar.

"Hi." She shut and bolted the door behind her.

He picked up a novel he was trying to read and thumbed through the pages. "Where'd you go?"

"To a store I know." She took a deep breath that shuddered a bit, and then it was her turn to pace through the wide-open area. The jitters were back. Her gaze bounced to him and away again. "I haven't said it yet, and it's past time. I love you. And I am really grateful for what you've been doing over the last several days." She craned her neck from side to side. He saw, grimly, that her hands were shaking. "I have one more favor to ask."

"For God's sake, just spit it out."

She reached into the bag, drew out a crop and threw it at him. He stared without catching it. It struck his chest and fell with a clatter to the floor. Whatever he had braced himself for, he hadn't expected this.

He said, "Aryal."

She had never asked such a thing of him before. This was a game changer.

This was not what they were together. They played at games of dominance and bargained for time with each other, and that was one of the very best things they did together, the strain of the give and the sweetness of the take, all leavened with the spice of uncertainty.

288

She tore off the sweatshirt. She didn't wear anything underneath, her racy, streamlined torso bare. "I need you to do this. I feel like I'm going to explode if I don't do something. I'm like an addict. It's—" She looked outside at the sky, her face stark. "It's my food, water and air. It's all of that, and we aren't even paragliding."

They had talked about trying to paraglide, and had decided against it for the two-week wait. She didn't trust herself not to shapeshift if she got into the air.

"I get it," he said, and he did. Her pain crawled in his marrow. The waiting and the uncertainty were a cruel combination. If they only knew one thing or the other, they could take steps to deal with it.

Her face clenched. She kicked off her shoes, tore off her jeans and came to stand in front of him.

"I have to get this feeling out," she said through her teeth. "Help me get it outside of my body."

Slowly he picked up the crop and he turned away as he looked down at it. That whip she had inside of her that was so like his—it wouldn't stop driving at her until she got some relief.

"I love you too," he said. He turned back around and struck at her, a fast, controlled blow across one thigh.

She jerked and bit back a strangled sound. She said, "Again."

He walked around her, struck at her buttocks and watched as a reddened welt raised against her pale skin. While he was no stranger to whipping scenes, his experiences had always before had a sense of playfulness to the game.

This wasn't playful. This was raw. He felt so strange, heavy and aching and his chest started to burn again, and all he wanted was her inner pain to ease so that she could get some peace for a little while.

"Come on," she said. Her nose sounded clogged. "Do it."

The crop rose and fell across her back, that beautiful back with the etched muscles that was so strong and feminine at once. He said from the back of his throat, "Please tell me if this is helping."

Her head nodded jerkily. "I—I think so."

His arm rose and fell.

Rose and fell.

Every time he watched her jerk under a blow, he seemed to step outside his own body. He struck her again, and the crop almost fell out of his nerveless fingers. He honestly didn't know how much more he could take.

Then he walked around to face her. Her eyes were closed and her face had turned peaceful. All strain had eased from her features. As soon as he saw that, his own crisis of strain eased until he felt light-headed.

He asked her softly, "Do you need more?"

She fingered the welt on her thigh. "No," she whispered. "The pain's all on the outside now." She looked up quickly and searched his gaze. "Did we go too far?"

He shook his head. "There isn't anywhere I wouldn't go with you."

The truth, laid out between them.

Wrapped in a double negative.

Perfect. Kinked.

Her mouth pulled into a wry smile. She walked over to him and kissed him gently, her lips caressing his. "There isn't anywhere I wouldn't go with you either."

"You owe me now," he said. As he licked her lips and caressed her breasts, his cock hardened.

She didn't even try to quibble. "I do, don't I? What do I owe you?"

"A collar around your neck, and your wrists handcuffed," he whispered.

She drew back her head and looked at him askance. "We've had that conversation already."

"Yes, and we're not finished with it. Remember—I said, what would it take? *You* said my soul for all eternity." His sense of humor surfaced. Brimming with sensual mischief, he cocked his head and held out both hands. "I've lived up to *my* side of the bargain. I thought that might mean something to someone like you, since you revel in legalistic thinking."

She started to laugh, her face creased with genuine humor. "You got me. You rotten son of a—"

He put a hand over her mouth. "Stop talking. There are much, much better uses for your mouth than that."

I agree, she told him telepathically.

She ran her hands down his body as she knelt and unzipped his jeans. He stroked her hair, staring without blinking as she pulled out his penis and kissed the tip. Then she took him in her mouth and suckled at him until his breath sawed in his throat and he pumped into her.

She reached up with one hand. He laced his fingers through hers and held on until his own climax ripped through him. A harsh, shaken groan broke out of him as he spurted into her mouth.

Afterward, he whispered, "My turn." And he nudged her onto the couch so that he could spread her legs wide. Her fluted sex was so beautiful, so drenched, he bent his head and feasted on her until her body jerked underneath his hold. She gave her own climax to him, crying out sharply as she shuddered.

He pushed her to climax again, and again, until finally she lay lax, eyes half-closed and drifting. Then he couldn't stay outside of her a moment longer. He eased his cock inside of her, rocking gently into the warm, tight home she made for him. She wrapped her legs around his hips, nuzzling at him as he moved.

He thought their joining this time was about tenderness, but then something happened, some switch flipped between them. She growled or he did. His rhythm picked up urgency. Gods, he could not get deep enough inside of her. When they both climaxed that time, it felt wrung out of them, all wildness, all passion turned inside out in the blaze that consumed them both.

Afterward, as she stroked the back of his neck and he looked down the length of their entwined bodies, he knew one of the deepest reasons why they fit together was that they drove each other until they finally achieved peace.

• • •

Quentin wasn't about to leave anything to chance.

He talked with her late into the night and made plans for when the fourteen days were up. He knew that having something concrete in her mind would help, and it did.

She would try a short flight at dawn. If she couldn't manage it, they would head out immediately for the nearest regional airport and he would give her the first paragliding lesson. One way or another, she would be in the air that day. All day, if she needed.

And that did help. Her volatile emotional spinning stopped, and she was able to calm down and focus.

They asked Dragos and Pia to join them on the rooftop of the Tower.

"I don't think I can stand a lot of spectators," Aryal said. "But I want them there. Dragos can be my spotter in case— well, in case. And I wouldn't even be trying without Pia."

"I agree," Quentin said. "It's a perfect plan."

Both Dragos and Pia responded readily and said they would be happy to be present.

Quentin and Aryal spent a sleepless night on the rooftop, wrapped in blankets and watching a fabulously clear swathe of stars. As a bright dawn broke over the water, the rooftop door opened and Dragos and Pia walked out. Dragos wore black camouflage pants and a T-shirt, and Pia wore something fleecy that looked soft and comfortable. They had left Liam with a nurse.

"There you are," Aryal blurted out. She shot to her feet, a hectic flush staining her cheekbones.

Quentin rose almost as quickly. By the time he had straightened to his full height, she had already shape-shifted into the harpy. She held her wings closed and tight along her back, her feral face miserable and fists clenched.

"Good morning," Pia said. She smiled at Aryal.

Quentin couldn't stand it. Waiting the last two weeks had been such an agony for Aryal, and pleasantries were like rubbing salt into the wound. He nodded to Dragos and said to Aryal, "Let's go. Do it."

She jerked her head in a nod. They walked together to the edge of the building, and she hopped up on the ledge. Then she turned back to face him. The tension came off her in palpable waves, and she still had not unclenched her wings.

The harpy looked at Dragos, who walked over to stand by the ledge as well. He regarded her calmly. "If you need it, I will catch you," Dragos said. His gold eyes were as steady as the earth.

Quentin might never like the dragon much, but in that moment, because of Dragos's steady promise to his unnerved mate, Quentin loved him.

Aryal glanced at Quentin. She appeared to be frozen.

So she preferred the element of surprise, did she?

He shook his head as a fitful wind blasted his face, and he struck her in the middle of her breastbone with the flat of his hand. The blow was so strong it knocked her off the ledge.

As she went backward, he said, "Time to rip off the Band-Aid."

Something about that wind must have irritated his recently healed eye, because his vision blurred with wetness as he watched her tumble in the air.

Then her wings snapped out.

She reached for the sky with both hands.

The harpy surged into the air with a joyous scream so primal it raised the hairs on the back of his neck and damn near pulled his heart out of his chest. She soared, wings hammering down, and he roared back at his mate as he soared with her in spirit.

Distantly, he heard shouts and cheers. Word must have gotten around, because a crowd had gathered on the sidewalk. A quick glance down revealed that all the other sentinels were present, their faces tilted up to watch the harpy's flight.

Dragos's expression was alight. Pia wiped her eyes with one sleeve.

Aryal rose, dove and looped up again. Eventually she drifted down to land on one knee in front of Pia, where she stayed, and Quentin realized she was offering full obeisance.

Pia's face worked. She looked profoundly moved and immensely uncomfortable, and she started to shake her head.

"I finally figured you out," said the harpy. She angled her head to look up at Pia with a sly sidelong smile. "You really do poop sparkly rainbows."

Pia's eyebrows shot up. She blinked.

Dragos folded his arms. He looked exasperated, as he did so often with Aryal. "What the hell does that mean?"

Aryal stretched out her wings that were all the more beautiful for the scars they bore. She met Quentin's smiling gaze.

She asked him in an innocent tone, "Was it something I said?"

Do you love fiction with a supernatural twist?

Want the chance to hear news about your favourite
authors (and the chance to win free books)?

Keri Arthur
S. G. Browne
P.C. Cast
Christine Feehan
Jacquelyn Frank
Thea Harrison
Larissa Ione
Darynda Jones
Sherrilyn Kenyon
Jackie Kessler
Jayne Ann Krentz and Jayne Castle
Martin Millar
Kat Richardson
J.R. Ward
David Wellington
Laura Wright

Then visit the Piatkus website and blog
www.piatkus.co.uk | www.piatkusbooks.net

And follow us on Facebook and Twitter
www.facebook.com/piatkusfiction | www.twitter.com/piatkusbooks

piatkus